"I am not a wanton woman, sir knight."

At Tarian's words, Wulf's arms tightened around her waist. "Nay, you are not."

"And I am not evil."

He traced his nose along her cheek. "Nay, you are not."

"I have feeling as any other woman."

His fingers swept her breasts, molding them into his hands. She squeezed her eyes shut, reveling in his touch. For so long she had merely existed, never knowing the true meaning of living, not until he touched her.

His eyes blazed in passion; his body was tense. "I have feeling as any other man, Tarian. I want you, here and now. Give yourself to me."

She hissed in a breath and looked at him. He waited only for her signal to proceed. She felt as if she stood on the edge of a great cliff, and that if she jumped there would be nothing below to catch her but either the craggy rocks or the deep swirling water.

"If you've been waiting for the perfect medieval series, this is it. Karin Tabke does for Norman knights what J. R. Ward has done for vampires, with hot alpha heroes and the fiery heroines who tame them."
—Monica McCarty, *New York Times* **bestselling author of** *Highlander Unchained*

KARIN TABKE

MASTER
of
TORMENT

Pocket Star Books
New York   London   Toronto   Sydney

Pocket Star Books
A Division of Simon & Schuster, Inc.
1230 Avenue of the Americas
New York, NY 10020

This book is a work of fiction. Names, characters, places, and incidents either are products of the author's imagination or are used fictitiously. Any resemblance to actual events or locales or persons, living or dead, is entirely coincidental.

First Pocket Star Books paperback edition December 2008

POCKET STAR BOOKS and colophon are registered trademarks of Simon & Schuster, Inc.

For information about special discounts for bulk purchases, please contact Simon & Schuster Special Sales at 1-800-456-6798 or business@simonandschuster.com.

Cover design by Lisa Litwack. Illustration by Franco Acornero.

Manufactured in the United States of America

10 9 8 7 6 5 4 3 2 1

ISBN-13: 978-1-4165-5503-2
ISBN-10:   1-4165-5503-X

To Liz Kreger, a real-life warrior princess

Acknowledgments

Again to my family for leaving me alone so that I can do what I love to do so much. To my dear friends Edie Ramer, Josie Brown, Tawny Weber, Poppy Reiffin, Sylvia Day and Sharon Long, you ladies are the wind beneath my wings. Thanks for tolerating me!

I also want to acknowledge my friend Monica McCarty for this story. As many of you know, Monica writes Scottish Highlander stories, which she bases on factual characters. Taking her lead, I dug through the many written pages of historical lady warriors and much to my surprise and delight, I unearthed a story of a Viking lady who was left at the altar. Not one to be humiliated, she mustered an army and forced her bridegroom to the altar, where she subsequently slew him. A woman scorned, indeed!

And I could not have written this wonderful story without the expert guidance of my editor, Lauren McKenna, who holds nothing back in her ever-wise suggestions and demands when it comes to my stories. Thank you for always being honest.

And hubby? You are always my reason for getting up each day. I love you.

The Blood Sword Legacy

Eight mercenary knights, each of them base born, each of them bound by unspeakable torturer in a Saracen prison, each of them branded with the mark of the sword for life. Each of their destinies marked by a woman.

'Twas whispered along the Marches that the demon knights who rode upon black horses donned in black mail wielding black swords would slay any man, woman, or child who dared look upon them. 'Twas whispered that their loyalty was only to the other and no man could split them asunder, nor was there enough gold or silver in the kingdom to buy their oath. 'Twas well known that each of them was touched not by the hand of God but by Lucifer himself.

'Twas also whispered, but only by the bravest of souls, that each Blood Sword was destined to find only one woman in all of Christendom who would bear him and only him sons, and until that one woman was found, he would battle and ravage the land . . .

Prologue

May 1st, 1067
Draceadon, Mercia

Ornate sconces burned brightly along the stone walls of the opulent chamber, illuminating it and all of its vivid colors like a gem-encrusted crown. Velvet-appointed furniture a king would envy graced the thick wool rugs, but what caught one's eye when they walked into the chamber was the enormous bed. Though the heavy curtains of the elaborately carved four-poster were drawn, deep snores from the occupant permeated the lavish chamber, alerting anyone near to a presence.

'Twas her runaway bridegroom, Earl Malcor of Dunloc.

The bile in Lady Tarian's belly rose. She breathed in slowly and exhaled slower, listening intently, being sure his breaths were of a man in the deep throes of slumber. Her fingers fondled the leather hilt of her broadsword, anxious to see the deed done.

Once her circumspect inventory of the room showed there to be no other escape route but the thick oak portal she had just come through, and that her men were in place, Tarian glanced over to Gareth, her captain of the guard, who held the earl's squeamish manservant. His honed sword blade leveled snugly against the servant's throat. She nodded to her captain before turning back to the shrouded bed.

Despite the encumbrance of her mail, Tarian glided a step closer to the bed. She pressed the tip of her sword into the slitted fabric and slowly pushed it aside. Only the orange blush of a tallow candle and the pale skin of a man's back glowed within the darkened space.

A knot formed in her belly, not of fear but of revulsion. 'Twas whispered her betrothed preferred to spend his time with squires, not maids. 'Twas also rumored he had commissioned a dungeon in the bowels of the fortress where he "entertained."

"Malcor, did you think I would not come for you?" Tarian demanded, her husky voice ringing clear in the room.

Most men would have risen in stark surprise and fear. Not so her intended. Without the barest hint of surprise or concern for his well-being, Malcor rolled over and speared her with a malicious glare. The linen sheet rode low on his thighs; and for all that he was a well-muscled man, knowing what she knew of him, the view repulsed her. Tarian set her jaw and stood fast, her motives for her appearance unwavering despite the lewdness of the man who had run like the coward he was.

He stretched and answered lazily, "Did you think, Lady Tarian, that I would care?"

Tarian forced a blithe smile. She did not feel so carefree as her gesture might have indicated, but this man would only see her for the true warrior she was. To show him weakness on any front would find her a victim of the earl's sadistic nature. Carefully, her gaze held the glittering angry one of her betrothed. She felt no anger with her guardian for his choice. It was either marriage to Malcor, the perverted Earl of Dunloc, or, more reluctantly, the convent. For no other mortal man would have her to wife.

The cloister did not want her, nor she them. Her Godwinson blood, while a curse, was also her salvation. She was bred to fight, bred to lead, and, despite the sins of her father, bred to breed with the finest blood of Europe, not spend endless days and nights on her knees praying for forgiveness she seriously doubted any god, even one so forgiving as hers, would grant.

So, marriage to the earl it would be. And with God's blessing a child would be born of their union. Her smile tightened. She required only one thing from this man, and, despite his preference for squires, she would extract it from him at swordpoint if necessary.

"How remiss of me, Malcor, to think a noble such as yourself would hold sacred a betrothal contract. 'Tis well I know up front the character of the man I will marry."

"There will be no marriage," he ground out.

Barely perceptibly, she inclined her head toward her betrothed. From behind her a score of armed soldiers fanned out, their swords at the ready. Tarian pressed the honed tip of her own sword, Thyra, to Malcor's chest. Pale lips pulled back from long yellow teeth.

She could not honestly begrudge him his anger. She was in effect forcing a marriage he did not desire, and she would, at swordpoint, if necessary, force him to perform his husbandly duty. How ironic would it be, then, that she conceive a child of a man who despised women? And she, the daughter of a royal rapist. Was she not following in her illicit sire's footsteps? "The sins of the father will repeat in the sins of the daughter." She had heard the words all her life; now she would breathe truth into the curse.

"We will wed this night, milord, or you will not wake to see the morn." She looked up to her right, just past her shoulder, and smiled at Gareth, who had handed off the servant to another of her guard. "See that Earl Malcor is a properly dressed groom."

She turned back to her intended. He might not fear her, which was foolish, for she was well schooled in the art of war, but her guard was a force all of his own to be reckoned with. He would not stand back should Malcor decide to get heavy-handed with her. Tarian grinned up at the enormous man and shrugged, suddenly not caring a whit for what Malcor desired. "Or not, if he doth protest too much."

"You will regret your action, Lady Tarian. Your guard cannot always be within reach," Malcor threatened softly.

The edge of steel in his words alerted her. A small ripple of apprehension skittered down her rigid spine as her gaze dropped to his. Stark contempt filled Malcor's pale blue eyes, and his pallid skin blanched whiter beneath his flame-colored hair. She would find no succor from this man soon to become her husband. She would find only hardship. But with a child and the title of Lady of Dunloc, much could be forgiven. For life in a convent that cringed at the mere mention of her name would drive her mad. She nodded ever so slightly to her intended. "Your own priest awaits us, milord; pray do not dally."

As she swept regally from the chamber, she said to Gareth, over her shoulder, "And, Sir Captain? Be sure he washes all traces of squires from him. I would see my husband clean in my wedding bed this night."

"Thou art the devil's spawn! I will not wed with thee," screamed Malcor.

"Aye, you will," Gareth said as he pressed his point with his sword.

"Nay! 'Tis said she is cursed!"

Tarian turned at the door, her sword raised. "Are we not both cursed?"

He stared at her in mute horror.

Stepping back into the chamber, she leveled the blade at her reluctant groom. "Make no mistake, Malcor. This eve will find us both in that bed as man and wife. And should you continue to resist me?" She glanced at Gareth and smiled. "I am not above forcing myself upon you." She stepped closer. She could see the wild dilation of his pale eyes. "Try now for once to be a man of your word. Honor your vow to me."

Malcor moved back into the furs. "Nay! *Never*. I will not have the mark of a witch upon me!"

Tarian smiled tolerantly and nodded. "So be it, then. You will not be the first reluctant bridegroom in England."

A fortnight later, Tarian knelt beside the sapphire- and gold-embroidered pall that covered her dearly departed husband. The priest's low voice droned one prayer after another. The dull ache in her back throbbed. But 'twas not from the endless hours of kneeling, then standing, only to kneel again. It was from the force of her dead husband's foot on her back when he'd kicked her from their bed three days past. For him, it had been the last time for all things earthly. Where his soul traveled at this moment she could only guess. And she did not care. There would be no alms to the churls of Dunloc, and there would be no alms to

Hailfox Abbey just down the way for the priests to pray. Nay, Earl Malcor deserved where he was going, and she held no guilt in watching his speedy descent to hell.

Finally Father Dudley's voice came to an abrupt end. Silently he signaled to the gathered few that prayers were at an end. The body would be taken to a prepared place just outside the chapel doors: as was the custom, neither Tarian nor any others would witness the interment.

She was helped to her knees by her stalwart guard, Gareth. "Milady?" he said softly, awaiting her direction. She smiled up into his concerned eyes. His unwavering devotion to her was her only salvation in these dark days. Had he not been the mouse under the bed since her arrival at Draceadon, *she* would be the one being buried, not Malcor. Her gaze darted across the pew to Lord Rangor, Malcor's ambitious uncle. His arrival the day before Malcor's death had been a blessing in disguise. When questioned on the state of their marriage, Malcor had unbelievably confirmed not only that they were wed, but that the relationship was *in facto consume*.

Only she, her dead husband, Gareth, and her nurse knew the truth.

Rangor, dressed in rich scarlet- and saffron-colored velvet, with the requisite black armband, gesticulated toward the altar and the dearly departed, then presented his arm to his niece-in-law. "Lady Tarian, do me the honor of accompanying me back to the hall." It was not a request but a command. And since she was curious as to what he was about, Tarian nodded her head to Gareth and took Rangor's proffered arm.

As he swept her down the long aisle, then out into the warm spring breeze, her black hair whipped around her head. She had not bound it as a wedded woman, nor as a widow should. Indeed, she left it down and beribboned. Nor did she wear a widow's black. She could never be accused of false emotions: the relationship she had with Malcor was not veiled for the sake of propriety. They despised each other. That he was dead was of his own making.

Wordlessly, they approached the stone and wooden fortress known far and wide as Draceadon. Dragon Hill. It was a worthy structure, and one she would call home for many years to come. She chewed her bottom lip and wondered just how she would orchestrate such a maneuver. Whilst she had no chance to produce an heir, the law, as it was, was on her side. But England was a swirling cesspool of intrigue and anarchy: the old ways might not hold sway.

At the threshold of the great hall, Rangor stopped and took her hand into both of his. "My lady, I would have a most private word with you, if I may," he entreated.

Once again Tarian acquiesced to him. Not because he demanded it, but because she did. He looked past her to where Gareth, along with half of his garrison, stood. A most formidable sight to any man or woman. Always, she was grateful for their presence. "Completely private," Rangor insisted.

"My man will stand back."

Rangor's manservant appeared from inside the hall, as did Ruin, Malcor's sniveling manservant. Her bile rose. The two were a matched pair: she'd see Ruin gone from Draceadon immediately. Easily, Rangor led her across the wide threshold of Draceadon. No sooner had she stepped into the coolness of the great hall than the heavy doors clanged shut behind her and the bolts were thrown. She whirled around to find a half score of Rangor's men blocking her retreat. She turned to Rangor, who stood, too full of himself, beside her.

Gareth's loud voice called to her from the other side. He was pounding on the door, demanding entrance.

"What is the meaning of this!" she demanded.

Rangor smiled. It held no warmth. "I have a proposition for you, Lady Tarian, one I wish you to think about with no counsel from your man Gareth—or anyone else, for that matter. And I would have your answer now."

Dread churned in her belly like the crashing waves of the ocean on the jagged rocks of the Welsh coast. She cast a subtle glance around her: Rangor's men surrounded her on all sides. "Ask me what you will."

Rangor bowed, then stood erect and faced her. "I propose we visit the priest after my nephew is secured in the ground."

Tarian frowned. "For what purpose?"

"To wed."

Tarian gasped. The continued pounding on the door coupled with his shocking proposal rattled her every nerve. Marry Rangor? Never! Inconspicuously her eyes darted around her for the closest weapon. While her jeweled dagger hung from her woven girdle, a sword would better suit what she had in mind. She could wield the weapon as well as any man, yet none was in her reach, and Rangor's men were many and fully armed.

Her best defense, then, was her shrewd mind. Her initial reaction was to tell the man under no circumstance would she wed him, and she would not. But the game they played must be played with a level head. She was well aware she trod on very thin ice. "I am honored, milord, but I am a widow of only three days. 'Tis not decent to wed so soon."

Rangor's smile widened. He bore the same long yellow

teeth as his nephew. Involuntarily, Tarian shivered as she relived the pain of Malcor's teeth in her back. And though the family resemblance was strong, where Malcor's skin had been smooth with the barest hint of a beard for a man of four-and-twenty, Rangor, twice his nephew's age, had the rough freckled skin of one afflicted with the pox. Nor did he have the tall, muscular shape of his nephew. Nay, Rangor reminded her of a spineless eel, and any contact with him on any level was out of the question.

"I promise you, milady, I do not covet boys in my bed. I am a man on every level and would prove a lusty groom."

Tarian kept her composure, and quickly formed a lie to buy her more time. "Be that as it may, sir, your nephew had no problems in the marriage bed. Indeed, as virile as he was, I should be heavy with child by the New Year."

Rangor's smile faded, but he pressed further. "I do not believe you. I know my nephew, and I know he could not stand the sight of a woman."

"The bloodied linens were produced."

"Sheep's blood."

"Nay!" she denied, shaking her head. "My virgin blood!"

He waved her off. " 'Tis of no consequence. I would have us wed by sunset on the morrow."

"Nay, I cannot."

"You will," Rangor pressed.

She stiffened with resolve. "Nay, I *will* not. You cannot force me."

"You forced Malcor."

Tarian forced a smile. "I but reminded him of his public and private oath to wed with me."

"Would you give up title here?" Rangor asked, sweeping his arm out toward the vast hall.

Tarian stood her ground. "My title here is not contingent upon my wedding with you, Rangor."

"It will be when I inform the king you murdered my nephew."

Tarian's defiance cooled. There was that. "Malcor's death was of his own making."

Rangor inclined his head toward Ruin. "He says different."

Tarian narrowed her eyes at the simpering fop. "He lies." She turned back to the noble, and despite the continued pounding on the door, she spoke calmly and played her hand. "But it matters not. I anticipated your intervention here. I have sent word to Normandy. I would have William decree me Lady here over you. The messenger left the day of Malcor's death."

Rangor's pale face flushed crimson, his cheeks puffed, and his fists opened and closed at his sides. "You will rue the day, Lady Tarian! Draceadon and all that belong to it are mine by right of blood. I will not have a murderess sit upon the dais while my nephew molders in the earth by her hand!" He turned to his guard. "Take her to the dungeon!"

Tarian drew the jeweled dagger from her girdle. Whirling around, she stabbed the closest man to her, then backpedaled to the door that quaked under Gareth's wrath. The guards pressed close upon her, but she would not go down without a fight. She had whirled around again to attack the next nearest man when her hand was caught from behind. A fist squeezed her fingers until the dagger dropped clattering to the stone floor. Unceremoniously she was hoisted onto a set of wide shoulders. "I will kill you for this, Rangor!" she screamed.

The ignoble stalked toward her. It took three men to subdue her sufficiently. He pressed close to her face but was smart enough to keep away from her teeth. "You have time to change your mind. A fortnight I will give you. Either we wed by the time William's messenger arrives, or I will inform him you are dead, executed for the murder of my nephew and earl!"

"Be prepared to present my body, Rangor, for I have Malcor's will. He leaves all to his lawful wife!" She laughed at his stunned face. "And I leave it all to the Abbey at Leominster!"

Rangor blanched. "Where is it?" he whispered.

She spat at him. "You will never find it!"

In a slow swipe, he wiped the spittle from his face. "Enjoy your stay with the rats, milady. I hear they have a taste for human flesh."

One

May 27th, 1067
Rouen, Normandy

It seems, my good knight, I require your services once again in that troublesome land of mine across the channel," William said none too happily to Wulfson de Trevelyn, the captain of his elite guard *les morts*.

Wulfson bowed deeply to his king, who waved him up with an impatient gesture. The Duke of Normandy and recently crowned King of England paced the thick wool carpet of his antechamber. William was dressed in the regal garb of one of his station. Yet his mail was nearby, a constant reminder that nothing had come easy to him, and at heart, he was a true warrior. Wulfson's king had fought since he was a lad to hold onto one legacy left to him by his father, and had brought an entire country to her knees to claim another promised to him by a dead king.

"I am, as always, my liege, at your service," Wulfson said.

"It seems conquering an entire nation is not enough to bring down that insufferable Godwinson dynasty."

Wulfson's interest had been piqued when he was privately summoned to his sovereign's antechamber. Now his complete interest was engaged. "Sire?"

William, nearing forty, but still a hearty man, had the strength and agility of a man half his age. His cagey eyes smiled despite his rancor. "Aye, lad, it seems the grand-daughter of that blackguard Godwine by his eldest son, the outlaw Sweyn, has managed to not only wed with Malcor the Earl of Dunloc, a most strategic ally to the west, but the bloodthirsty bitch has proceeded to slit the poor fool's throat whilst in their marriage bed!"

Wulfson whistled in surprise and, he had to admit, awe. He'd heard tales of the Wessex women. Saxon and Viking blood ran hot and deep in their veins. Some, he'd heard, had fought beside their men at Stamford Bridge. They were a lusty, warlike bunch. And he could well relate. His own lust for battle was his life's blood.

William poured a hearty draught of wine into a golden goblet. He handed it to Wulfson, then poured himself one.

Wulfson accepted the offering and quietly contem-plated why he had been called to his liege. William eyed him sharply. Wulfson considered his king's position in the matter, and mused out loud. "Should the House of Wessex raise its greedy head, who is to say a blood niece to the Usurper with ties to several thrones could not rally an army to claim for her son what is rightly yours?"

William drained his cup and slammed it down on the side table. "She *has* an army! 'Tis how she brought the earl first to his knees and then to marriage."

Wulfson chortled. "Hah! Now that is a twist, a lady forc-ing a man to marriage!"

William began to pace anew and mumbled, "Would that

I had a few more such as she here to guard my borders, I would have no reason to toss and turn at night."

Wulfson bowed to his troubled king. "What would you have me do, sire?"

William turned and faced his captain. "You are among the few in whom I place my complete trust. You and your Blood Swords are also the best at what you do." William scowled again. "I have received three missives in a week's time regarding what brews in Mercia. One from the lady herself asking that her claim to Dunloc be validated. The second is from the captain of her guard alerting me to her capture by her uncle by marriage, Rangor of Lerwick. And the third from Lerwick himself, informing me the lady is a witch who cast a spell upon his nephew and then slit his throat, only to lay claim to Dunloc's holdings. Rangor, of course, now claims the holdings by right of blood, and begs me punish her for murdering his nephew."

"The lady is a murderess, and a widow without issue. What claim does she have?"

"There is no valid claim by her if what Lerwick says is true, but she claims to have a valid will." William stopped his agitated pacing and speared Wulfson with a steely glare. "The lady is a thorn in my side that will fester if left untended. Her dastardly deeds aside, *any* living Godwinson is a threat to England, and so a threat to me. In your capable hands, sir knight, I put her life. See to it she no longer poses a threat to any man."

Wulfson was about to take another draught of his wine, his arm halted, poised in the air at his king's words. "But, sire, she is a royal."

"A royal who murdered an earl!"

Wulfson stood silent, giving his king time to think his request through.

William slammed his fist into his hand. "I know of no other way."

Wulfson scowled. He had no issue with seeing to his king's order—but he was not convinced the means would justify the end. Their eyes met, and Wulfson saw only determination in the king's gray eyes. William rarely changed his mind once it was set. Wulfson clicked his heels together; his spurs jangled.

"Consider the deed done, sire."

William's lips drew into a tight line before he spoke. "The fewer who know of your reason for returning to that insufferable isle the better. I will not have it said King William murders noblewomen, even though the law would support her execution."

Wulfson nodded. "I will send word ahead, then, to Rohan, for more men."

William turned, poured himself another cup, and took a long draught. "'Tis a wise move. But there is one more thing. A small hindrance, to be sure."

Wulfson waited, already anxious to turn his horse's hooves back onto solid English soil.

"Rangor has arrogantly laid claim to the holding despite his request for my intervention, and he refuses to release the Lady Tarian. Understandably, the lady's army has laid siege to the manor, refusing any person near it."

"I shall see them both removed."

"I do not doubt it, Sir Wulfson. But tread lightly," William cautioned. "While I care naught what happens to the lady's army, I want no enemy of Rangor. He has long-standing alliances with the Welsh, who are already causing problems along the border. See the deed done, discreetly, and in proper time, so that I may find a suitable Norman bride for the new master of Dunloc."

Wulfson bowed to his king, then quickly exited the chamber, his blood quickening in anticipation.

England awaited.

Two

June 6th, 1067
Draceadon, Mercia

L ord Rangor!" Wulfson called out in clear English, to the huge stone and wooden edifice that was known far and wide as Dragon Hill. While it was well situated upon a sweeping hill, there was no moat, either wet or dry as was popular in France, nor was there a drawbridge. Only a high wall surrounded the structure, with two impressive metal-studded wooden doors shut tightly against any and all predators. The fortress's tall stone and timber walls and sweeping ramparts were, in Wulfson's experienced eyes, not unscalable. But damn nigh so. During his many years of warring, he had never found a fortress impenetrable. So long as he was patient, he was always able to find the crack and then exploit it. He had every reason to believe the same strategy would apply here. Time was his ally this day.

For should the errant lord behind the foreboding walls refuse his entreaty, he would then find himself crushed beneath the severe wrath of not only the Blood Swords but the mighty fist of William. "I come in the name of King William. Allow us entry!"

When no answer came forth, and in no mood to dally with the arrogant Saxons, Wulfson raised his right arm. Turold, his mighty black destrier, shifted his weight on his mighty hooves. "Easy, lad," Wulfson soothed the savage beast.

"Light the arrows!" Wulfson called. He did not need to turn to either his right or his left and see the chore met. His brothers-in-arms, *les morts*, William's elite death squad, would notch not one or two, but three arrows in their longbows. In no time the wooden part of the fortress along with the interior buildings would fall; and with that, their entry would be guaranteed. 'Twas no more difficult than his morning visit to the privy.

Seasoned warriors, all of them. The task was complete in less time than it took to blink twice. Wulfson lowered his arm, and the sweet whooshing sound of two dozen flaming arrows arched high over his head, sweet music to his ears. He raised his chin, and from beneath his black conical helmet he watched the arrows arch, come together, then dip as one, and rain unmercifully down upon the resisting people of Draceadon.

Save for the few shrieks and screams from above, he did not expect an immediate return on his assault. He turned slightly in his saddle and looked to his right, where dark knights dressed as he in black mail, their black horses tacked as his in black leather and metal spikes, notched three more arrows. Ioan, Warner, and Stefan; to his left, Rorick, Thorin, and Rhys. The seven of them, minus his comrade Rohan du Luc, had for the last seven years operated as one unit. It seemed strange and oddly discomfiting not to have Rohan at his side. It was like missing a hand or an arm. But the man awaited the birth of his first child, and though he had made a good argument to accompany them,

Wulfson had shrugged this endeavor off as something they could do in their sleep.

He was here to dispose of Lady Tarian, an enemy of the state. And a mere woman at that. 'Twould not cause him much effort. Indeed, he expected to be back in Normandy within the fortnight.

He nodded his head, and the arrows took flight a second time, the same high arch lighting up the damp gray sky like a mass of fiery shooting stars.

Once those arrows found home, Wulfson turned to his men. "Notch the skins, aim for the cookhouse chimneys." 'Twas an old ruse that worked every time it was deployed. Though deadly swordsmen, his men were such expert bowmen as well that they could shoot a thick hide from a quarter-league away and hit their target in the eye. This time, they had simply to shoot up the fortress walls to the crest of the billowing chimney tops. Once the structure caught fire, the flames would spread, and soon, like rats in a flood, the inhabitants would flee for air and meet on the highest ground. By then, Wulfson and his men would have scaled the burned-out walls and be done with it.

Wulfson nearly yawned. 'Twas a squire's chore.

But before they let the hides fly, a voice called out from atop the forward rampart. "Cease your attack and identify yourselves!"

Wulfson raised his shield. "Show yourself if we are to *parle*!" he called to the man, being very careful not to come close enough to the edge of the walls that they could be doused by burning pitch or a hailstorm of stones and nails. Thanks to the Lady Tarian's garrison that he had encountered in the wood just past Dunloc village, Wulfson knew that the fortress, while in looks foreboding, held not the necessary fighting implements. Barely a bow resided within the walls. With most of the men lost, first at Stamford Bridge and then Hastings, there was naught but women and children for the most part to protect the manor and lands. Save for the full stores to hold out in a prolonged siege should there be one, Draceadon was sorely unprepared for any invasion.

Acting as if he had important news for Lady Tarian, Wulfson was able to beguile the captain of her guard into assisting, and the man Gareth was a fount of information.

"You say you are here in the name of William, but who are *you*?" an articulate voice challenged. Most likely Rangor, the lady's dearly departed husband's uncle, certainly not a villein.

"I am Wulfson of Trevelyn, captain of *les morts*, King William's private guard. I have a private matter to discuss on his behalf with Lady Tarian."

A long pause ensued. Wulfson nodded his head, and the hides flew. More time passed, then suddenly billows of dark, churning smoke erupted overhead.

Moments later, the same voice called down to Wulfson. "Inform your king the Lady Tarian is dead."

"How convenient for Rangor," Ioan said from beside Wulfson.

"Aye, how convenient indeed." Wulfson looked up. "Your words will require proof. Open the gates and present her body!" Wulfson called to the rampart. Then he turned to Ioan at his immediate right and said for the ears of the Blood Swords only, "Let us hope he speaks the truth. 'Twould save me the chore."

Ioan chuckled, the sound ominous. "Should you be unable to perform, Wulf, I have no such problems."

Wulfson scowled beneath his helmet, his eyes wary. "Nor do I. An enemy of the Crown is an enemy of the Crown, no matter the sex. 'Tis all the same to me."

As the two men continued their conversation, a body was tossed over the rampart wall. Wulfson was urging his mount to back up when the body of a richly dressed woman landed at Turold's feet. Ever the veteran of such distractions, the great black stood perfectly still, awaiting only his master's command.

"'Tis she, now begone!" the voice from above commanded.

Wulfson glanced up at the rampart to see a flash of dark green fabric disappear behind the stone.

"God's blood!" Ioan said. "The man has no honor!"

"Aye, 'twould appear I may have underestimated the man's ambition."

"This body has decayed. 'Tis not a recent death," Rorick pointed out. "The belly is corrupted."

Wulfson nodded, his gaze resting on the twisted, broken body before him. Cautiously he dismounted, and bade his Blood Swords be wary. The woman's neck was at an unnatural angle, but that was not what he suspected had killed her. Dark brown hair covered most of her face. He bent beside her. Though a murderess, the Lady Tarian was a renowned beauty, with raven-colored hair, and eyes, they said, the color of the North Sea. She was also known for her small stature, and this woman, though dark of hair, was long of limb. He brushed the tangled hair from her face. Dark molted skin was pulled tight across thick cheekbones. Her mouth gaped open, dark rotted teeth clenching onto a black swollen tongue. He pushed open an eyelid. Though the pale film of death clouded it, he could plainly see that the natural color of the eye was dark, mayhap brown or black. Certainly not the eye color that the warrior princess was said to possess. He looked further down her broken body to her rough hands. The hands of a villein, not a royal.

Wulfson looked up toward the tower rampart. What kind of fool did Rangor take him for? He stood to his full height, and turned to Gareth, the captain of the lady's guard. He would be sure.

"Is this your lady?"

The tall Dane walked slowly forward, as though he could not bear to see for himself, and though he wore a helmet, Wulfson could see his face blanch, and fear stood in his eyes. Fool! It was obvious he held more than a sense of duty for the lady. Gareth took one look at the body and let out a long sigh of relief.

"Nay, sir, 'tis not my lady."

"Step back then, man, and have your men bring forth the rams. I tire of Rangor's games."

Once the rams were brought up, it did not take very long for the thick English-oak doors to give way under the combined forces of Wulfson's men and those of Gareth. Wulfson watched the Dane's determination to get to his lady, and he gladly allowed him to expend his and his men's energy. 'Twould serve Wulfson well once inside, for when the man learned his lady would be jumping from one form of prison to permanent exile, there would be yet another battle to stand and deliver.

She would pay with her life, not because the rumors called her witch, or because she was an accused murderess. Nay, her most dastardly deed was her relationship to the late King Harold. His blood niece could not be allowed to keep her powerful position among her fellow Saxons.

All Godwinsons were a threat to William, and this one most especially. Her blood was too blue and too royal. It was blood that her countrymen and women would take up arms to protect, should she give birth to a son of Dunloc.

Gareth had been a fount of information. After the good lady had lovingly slit the throat of her groom and Rangor got wind of the deed, her men had all been expelled from the castle. Tricked, as it were. All but his lady. Gareth had waited, laying siege, trying in vain to rescue her from the demented uncle. To no avail. So the captain of her guard was most helpful when Wulfson came upon him just that morn.

The deep droning cadence of the kettle drum keeping the pace, not only for the double battering rams but to intimidate and instigate, rang ominously clear in the morning air. Just as the door gave way, thick waves of fiery pitch were hurled from above. Ever wary, Wulfson had kept his men to the back of the rams. The horrific screams of several of Gareth's men as they succumbed to the bubbling black ooze were lost on Wulfson's ears. He'd heard the cry of death and torture too many times for it to bother him. He and his Blood Swords had survived hell to tell about it. The inhuman things man did to man were but part of what drove Wulfson to watch his back, work his muscles every day to their capacity, and continually hone his skills. He had no illusions that he would live to see a gray beard and grandchildren. If he lived to forty, he would die a contented man, but he would never go down without the fight of his life.

He reined Turold away from the fiery globs of humanity and watched unnerved as Gareth tried in vain to rescue the three men. There was naught anyone could do for them.

"Pull them away and continue!" Wulfson commanded.

"Sir!" Gareth protested. "They are my men!"

Wulfson pointed his sword toward the charred black mass. "Time flies on swift wings. They are doomed. Slit their throats if you must, but get on with it!

Gareth stepped forward, sword drawn and raised. Wulfson snarled and drew the second of his short swords from the double scabbard at his back, as each of the Blood Swords drew down on the balance of Gareth's men who came to aid their captain. Wulfson squeezed Turold's sides and drove the massive horse into the fray, pressing one sword tip into Gareth's chest. "You dally with men who live over those who will die. Move aside or drop where you stand!"

Gareth stood his ground, a big hulking Viking of a man, much like Thorin who now sat astride his great destrier behind Wulfson, ever watchful. A warrior, no doubt, but Gareth's fatal flaw was that he possessed a heart. Wulfson shook his head. Fool. Heart was what got a man killed.

He pushed past the reluctant warrior with his men behind him. They would not waste another moment on another's weak stomach. No wonder Gareth's lady was at the mercy of Rangor. He probably hadn't had the stomach to stand up to the Saxon noble.

Wulfson glanced up at the rampart, then back to the thick door that hung from the hinges. While not wide open, there was enough of a gap that if he and his men pushed as a unit on horseback, they would plow through to what he knew from Gareth's detailed description was a sizable bailey, then a small courtyard farther up. And there they would need the rams once more. No doubt they would be pressed upon with more pitch, for the interior fortress walls were tall—they could be seen from the village road, towering high like the wings of a great dragon.

"Prepare to enter the bailey," Wulfson called to his men, then motioned for them to draw close. When they were all in a tight semicircle around him, he gave his instructions. Once they understood, he called over to Gareth. "Have your archers cover my men as we go through. I want a barrage of arrows to preceed us. Continue with the assault until I give word to cease!"

And so it played out. Wulfson and his men took up the huge battering rams, and astride their great black warhorses they slammed through the oak portals into the bailey, where they were indeed met with a deluge of arrows. But they were prepared. With shields raised and in the manner of the old Roman tactic of the turtle, they moved as one unit toward the door leading directly into the fortress. A hail of arrows flew past them toward the inner ramparts, and the curses of men as they were struck made Wulfson smile. As they neared the wide doors, Gareth and his men brought up the rear with the two rams, and once again the drums took up the cadence as the action was repeated. There was no pitch this time, and no other form of attack came. Indeed, the inhabitants of the bailey worked fervently to save their dwellings from the fires. But it appeared all had gone quiet in the fortress. Had they used up their meager stores of ammunition?

In no time at all, the thick doors were breached. But instead of bursting through, Wulfson held up his hand for his men and those of Gareth to halt.

During the long moments that hung heavy before the final breach on the edifice proper, the haze of the late morning sun, coupled with the weighty silence, hung around them like a sodden woolen mantle. The ominous quiet disturbed Wulfson more than a full-out attack. Rangor, no doubt, had something up his sleeve for their entry into the fortress hall.

Still astride, with shield raised, Wulfson moved off at an angle, so that he could not be seen from inside except by someone close by. "I give you a last chance, Rangor," he called into the great hall. "Surrender yourself and the Lady Tarian or I will be forced to destroy you."

"She is dead!" The voice rang shrill . . . and near. Just inside the great doorway.

"She may be, but I have no proof. Allow me entry so that we may *parle*. William wishes no quarrel with you, sir. He values your allegiance, as well as that of your allies to the west. I have only come to speak to the lady. Once I have, I shall return to my lord and master in Normandy."

"Give me your oath you will not harm me."

"I give you my oath I will not harm you, unless I or one of my men should be provoked."

Long minutes sweated by. Wulfson was becoming increasingly irritated.

"I give you my oath you and your men will not be harassed."

"Then come forward and present yourself."

A slight sound not too far off from the great hall caught Wulfson's attention. From astride Turold, he watched a man, mayhap a few years older than William but not nearly so fit, emerge from the darkened abyss. He wore rich clothing, and his aristocratic lines were well defined. But what set him off more than his garments and bearing was his flaming red hair and his pale blue eyes. He reminded Wulfson of a wily Icelandic fox. And at that moment he knew that under no circumstance was this man to be trusted.

The noble's eyes darted to Wulfson, his men, then behind to Gareth, who had come to stand almost even with Wulfson. "I am Rangor, Lord of Dunloc. How may I be of service to my king?"

"You are not lord here!" Gareth said, stepping past Wulfson, whose left arm, sword in hand, shot out to prevent the Dane from moving forward. Under his breath, Wulfson cautioned the guard. "My good man, I respect your anger. But I am in charge here. Stand back."

Expecting Gareth to immediately comply, which he did, Wulfson turned his attention back to Rangor. In a slow slide, he dismounted, and with both swords in hand he strode toward the haughty noble. Aye, Rangor stood tall and erect. Arrogant. His pale eyes showed barely a hint of fear, but Wulfson did not need to see it in a man's eyes—he could smell it. Like the great furry beasts who wandered the island using their senses to field their prey, their enemies, and their mates, Wulfson's instincts were highly honed. Rangor was a man with secrets. And he was afraid.

"Where is Lady Tarian?"

"As I have already told you, she is dead."

"The body you tossed over the rampart is not that of the lady. Do you have another for me to peruse?"

"Nay. There is no body," Rangor admitted.

"She lives! I swear it, I would know of her death!" Gareth cried out unable to contain himself. Rangor smiled a slow sadistic smile and coolly regarded the captain of her guard.

"Aye, you would. 'Tis immoral, your lust for her. Had she lived, in nine months' time we would no doubt see proof she was not worthy of the title she bore. For I would wager every hide of land I own the wench would spill a blond giant of a child," Rangor sneered.

"How did the lady perish?" Wulfson demanded.

Rangor focused those inhuman pale eyes back on Wulfson. "She succumbed to a wound she sustained when she killed my nephew. Her body was returned to her guardian Lord Alewith in Turnsly."

" 'Tis a lie," Gareth hissed.

"*Why* did you lie?" Wulfson softly questioned, not wavering from the knowledge he knew in his gut—as did Gareth—that the lady lived.

Pale blue eyes lifted to the ceiling, then darted left, then right, before returning to Wulfson. "I—I feared my liege would not believe the truth."

" 'Tis not he you should fear, my lord, but me. I come in his name. He gives me the right to not only speak on his behalf but to act." He stepped a foot closer and pressed both sword tips to Rangor's chest. "And I deplore a lie. 'Tis akin to treason. Do you know how William deals with traitors?"

Slowly Rangor shook his head. Wulfson noticed the sheen of sweat that glossed his brow. Whilst it was a warm day, moisture hanging over them like a wet blanket, it was cool inside the great fortress.

If looks could have sliced Wulfson in twain, he would have fallen in two even sections to the stone floor, so sharp was Rangor's gaze. "I do not wish to cause my king or his man undue distress, but before we continue this dance, Sir Wulfson, let me remind you, as you are the king's guard: my cousin Rhiwallon and his half brother Bleddyn are

Welsh kings in their own right. Both are very protective of their kin."

Wulfson smiled and moved closer, the sword tips digging deeper still into Rangor's rich clothing. "Tell your Welsh kings I welcome them in the name of King William to pledge their loyalty. The sooner the better."

Rangor gasped. "Do you beg for a fight?"

"Nay, I speak only the truth. You will find, milord, that I am a man of few words but quick action. I do not play the coy word games you nobles seem to be so fond of. I call a sheep a sheep: whether black or white, it is still a sheep. Now, tell me where I may find Lady Tarian."

Rangor set his jaw, but Wulfson read reluctant resignation there. Rangor would find it in his best interest not to make an enemy of the king's guard. Wulfson nodded, lowered his swords, and inclined his head toward Rangor. "I would have the keys on your belt, sir."

Ioan, Rorick, and Rhys stepped forward. Instinctively the noble grabbed the keys in his fists, but sense quickly reigned over his impulse. He maneuvered the large circle from the leather-and-chain belt and handed them to Wulfson. "She is below in the dungeon, by now no doubt only a carcass for the rats to feed upon."

"Pray she is still alive, Lord Rangor. William does not take kindly to his royal subjects being executed without his approval." And Wulfson wondered why he uttered the words. For if the wench was not dead when he found her, she would be shortly thereafter.

"Gareth, show me the way."

Leaving three of his men and most of Gareth's to keep order in the hall, Wulfson and several of his men followed the hulking Dane, each grabbing a torch from the sconces along the walls. Once past the great hall and the larders, they progressed down a narrow passageway, then made a sharp right turn, and were met with a thick, metal-strapped door. " 'Tis down there," Gareth said, pointing to the door.

Wulfson inserted one key, then another, until the lock ground free. The door opened, and Wulfson preceded them down the slick, narrow steps. The stench that hit him as they descended into the bowels of the fortress would have had a lesser man emptying his guts then and there. He heard several men retch behind him, and knew with a certainty they were Gareth's. Despite the stench, he and his brother Blood Swords had smelled worse. The stink of death still permeated their dreams, and the mark of the devil branded each and every one of them. Compared to the Saracen prison in which they had spent nearly a year of their lives, this was minor.

Wulfson still had a marked limp, and scars above and below his skin—no thanks to his captors. He held the torch higher, and focused on finding the lady so that he could quickly dispose of her. He had decided he would do the deed swiftly and without witness, once she was discovered. Here within the bowels of the fortress, under cover of darkness, it would be easy enough. Even with Gareth behind him, Wulfson had no compunction. If he had to slay the Dane as well, so be it.

As they assembled in the well of the chamber, Wulfson scanned the stone walls, noting the many sets of manacles that hung from them.

"Malcor found amusement at the expense of pages and squires here," Gareth said, contempt heavy on every word.

Wulfson snorted in disgust. He knew of men who preferred men, but boys? He could not fathom the notion. Death was too good for the likes of the earl. The lady had done the entire country a service by slicing him ear to ear.

Except for the scurrying rats, the chamber appeared to be empty. Ducking low, torches raised, they spread out and searched each cell, each corner, each crevice, ultimately coming up with no being living or dead. Yet the fresh scent of feces, mingled with the acrid stench of urine, was prevalent.

Filtering back into the center of the chamber, surrounded by the men, Wulfson stood for a long moment, his hand held up for complete silence. And listened.

Heavy silence ensued, broken only by the heavy breathing of the mail-clad knights. Wulfson raised his arm higher. They held their breath, not one of them breathing. A rat squeaked and scurried across Wulfson's boot. He stood still and listened.

There, from ahead, a small muffled sound. He strode back into the cell directly in front of him and held the torch high. As it was a moment ago, it remained empty now. His eyes scanned the floor, closer this time, and there he saw it. The swath of something heavy and wide had been recently marked across the dirt floor, darker in color than the rest of the dirt. He squatted before a large hewn block of stone, while Ioan peered over his shoulder.

" 'Twill take two of us," Ioan said, then took Wulfson's torch and handed it to Rhys, along with his own. Rhys moved in, with Gareth pressing closer and holding his torch high. Eerie light flickered in a give-and-take dance along the damp stone. Wulfson grasped the right corner, and Ioan the left. With a mighty heave, they pulled back on the stone. In a slow ragged scrape, it came toward them. As Wulfson turned it away from him and the torches rose, he stopped all movement.

He grabbed the torch above his head and pressed it toward the hole in the wall, peering closer at the creature inside.

Three

Wulfson's heart seemed to stop for one inexorable beat. From behind some type of metal device, a helmet with cross bars and what appeared to be a bridle of sorts, glittering eyes the color of the ocean stared at him. From what he could see of her face, it was a muted mass of bruises. His hands reached out to her, and she hissed and spat like a cat being dunked in water.

"My lady . . ." Gareth whispered from behind him. Wulfson moved closer to her, his gaze catching every detail: a bloody chemise twisted around her waist, the sharp rise and fall of her breasts hardly discernible beneath the combined caked blood and dirt of the floor. Deep purple bruises, along with the crisscross markings of the lash, etched her arms and thighs. His gaze moved back to hers. In quiet amazement and a grudging respect for the woman who had not only survived such torture but still had fight left in her, he could not look away. He raised his right hand to touch her, to see if she were indeed human. The movement elicited another hiss, followed by a clawed hand digging into his gauntlet, halting his movement. He nodded, and withdrew, but not to ease her comfort. His hand slid to the leather-wrapped hilt of his short sword. As his fingers closed around the well-worn grip, he could not tear his eyes from her defiant glare. What kind of woman *was* this?

Slowly he pulled the weapon from the leather sheath, intending to ease her suffering for all time. As the blade slid from the sheath, his eyes dipped, unable to meet hers when he plunged the sword deep into her heart. The fullness of her breasts trembled beneath the dirt and blood that covered her. A fleeting stab of regret pricked at his belly. He ignored it and pressed the tip of the blade to what he knew would be a silky-smooth spot between the full globes. As he moved to press the steel into her heart, he made the mistake of looking into her eyes.

Time halted for the briefest of moments. Transfixed, as if drugged by some potion, Wulfson watched a lone tear track slowly down her cheek, leaving a bloody stream in its wake. And at that precise moment, something deep inside him shifted.

It was also at that same instant that Gareth came undone. "She belongs with me!" he called hoarsely, lunging forward. Wulfson flung his hand back, staying the Dane. From the commotion and scuffle behind him, Wulfson knew the man was contained.

Never breaking eye contact with the specter crouched before him, Wulfson said, "Her fate is not in your hands." Her eyes narrowed at his words, and her back stiffened. In silent defiance, she dared him to harm her.

"Whatever lies Rangor has spilled to your king I can disprove them!" cried Gareth. "She is not a witch. She is not a murderess, nor is she an enemy to the Crown! I will stake my life on it!"

"She is what she is, sir captain. I cannot change the facts," Wulfson answered.

"She is with child! Wouldst you murder a babe as well?" Gareth pleaded.

"I doubt even had she been with child it would have survived the torture."

"Be not so sure of that, Sir Wulfson," Rangor said from behind him. At Wulfson's notice, the noble moved to the doorway, filling the space. "The wench has a penchant for survival. With her herbs and spells, she no doubt extracted Malcor's seed from his unholy body and nurtures not one heir of Dunloc but a spare as well."

Grabbing the lady's hands, Wulfson drew her from the dark hole, hoisting her up to her feet. She cried out, collapsing against him. Not wanting to but having no other choice, Wulfson lifted her up into his arms. She weighed no more than a mite. He turned with her in his arms and faced Rangor, Gareth, and his men.

"It matters not." The small body in his arms tightened at his words.

"You are wrong, my stubborn Norman," said Rangor. "Princess Gwladus of Powys is not only my goddaughter, but first cousin of Malcor, and should her cousin's heir be murdered in cold blood, her father, the mighty warlord King Rhiwallon, will be most unhappy. William will lose more than he can calculate. Add to that the lady's mother is a Welsh abbess, and very much alive and in the care of Powys. You would tempt the devils for a fight. Should I school you with regard to her royal blood of the North?"

Wulfson scowled. It seemed the lady's pedigree extended well beyond Godwinson. Which only made her all the more dangerous.

Rangor continued. "Aye, you are wise to listen to reason. The lady is great-grandniece of Canute, which makes her kin to most kings of Scandinavian descent. Like the Vikings, the Welsh are not weak, as are the Saxons. The Marches are thick with fortresses and warriors who will stoop to any measure, including witchcraft, to see their homes and their blood kin protected. With the lady's death by a Norman hand, and even the suspicion she died carrying the heir of Dunloc, there will be more than the wrath of hell to pay. Does William court more loss so soon?"

"Should the lady spill Malcor's brat, where does that leave you?" Wulfson demanded.

Rangor smiled. "I intend to have the lady as my wife."

Tarian struggled in his arms, her strength pitiful. Wulfson tightened his hold, and she grunted in anger, but settled.

"You would wed with the woman who slew your nephew and raise another's issue?" Wulfson shook his head and sneered. "I think not."

"You underestimate my affection for the lady."

Wulfson made the mistake again of looking down at the bloody, dirt-encrusted creature in his arms, and she turned her head to look up at him once again. He found himself speechless. Her eyes sparked in furious rage. She turned her head back toward Rangor, the metal of the head device grinding against Wulfson's vambraces. "Indeed, is this how a Saxon lord courts his lady love?"

Rangor shook his head. He took a step closer. "She is insolent and thinks herself a man's equal. She has her own army! No wife of mine will dress in mail and sit like a man astride a warhorse. Her—punishment, though a bit harsh, is but a way to show her who is lord here. She would have come around, if not to save herself, then the child she may carry. Marriage to me would be the justice I exact for the murder she committed."

Wulfson contemplated the dilemma. If the loss of life was forgiven by the family, and if the lady carried the heir to Dunloc, blood kin to the Welsh kings, and word got out that William had ordered her slain in cold blood—things would not settle well for his liege, to be sure. For the Welsh had allied with Harold, and were now rumored to be allied with Edric, the wild and unpredictable Saxon Earl of Mercia.

But, he thought, should her womb prove empty, then there would be less cause for alarm. Rangor might think he would wed with her, but William would choose a Norman bride for the new earl and be done with the Lady Tarian. Wulfson nodded. Prudence over haste ruled this day. By an unforeseen twist of fate, the Lady Tarian had managed to buy a few more days on this earth.

He would immediately send word to William, of course. In the meantime? He handed her off to Gareth, who gladly claimed her. Time will tell us if her womb bears fruit." And as he said those words, Wulfson had the most uneasy feeling that, despite the outcome, his orders would remain the same, for the child, whilst it might be kin to the Welsh kings, would also be kin to a dead king, and that bloodline could not be resurrected under any circumstance.

"Captain, see the lady to her chamber, and her maid secured," Wulfson directed, then turned to Rangor. "You, milord, are forbidden to see the lady under any circumstance. Should you do so and be found out, you may consider yourself a prisoner of the realm."

Not giving the noble a chance to argue the point, Wulfson swept past him, shoving the slighter man aside with a well-placed shoulder. His anger tangled with his frustration over the sudden change of events. He was a knight of William, a warrior, a killer, and here he was to languish, waiting for proof positive that an enemy of the Crown show signs of pregnancy!

"Sir Wulfson!" Gareth called. "The key for the helmet and bridle, please."

Wulfson growled low, and though wanting no further dalliance with the lady, he would not release the keys to the captain. Wulfson jammed one of the smaller keys on the leather ring he had taken from Rangor into the device, and turned it. The metal scraped, but the lock turned and the split face of the mask popped open. The lady gasped, as if a huge pressure on her skull had been relieved. Deep indentations near her temples and forehead looked angry and red. Wulfson swore under his breath, then took the same key to the wide metal bit strapped around the bottom portion of her head.

As the metal piece clanked against her teeth and then rolled from her mouth, her small sigh of relief tested his resolve. Her lips were swollen, but when she licked them he saw straight white teeth behind them. His gaze met hers, and for the third time since he had laid eyes on her, something deep inside him twisted. Her eyes did not spark fire, but now they had warmed and glittered unnaturally.

"*Merci*," she said, her voice nothing but a husky rasp. Wulfson clicked his spurs together and nodded, then turned on his heel and nearly ran from the chamber.

*   *   *

Tarian closed her eyes and for the first time since Rangor had thrown her in the dark, dank bowels of Draceadon, she felt a small measure of peace. Gareth's strong arms supported her frame. Never remotely plump, she was even less now. She could not remember the last time she had eaten. Clean air filled her nostrils as they left the hellhole. Her lids fluttered as the light of day assaulted her. She rolled her head closer into Gareth's shoulder, but groaned as her temple hit upon the clasp of his mail. Her mouth was numb, her fingers cold, and the rest of her body one massive ache.

Despite her great discomfort, she tried to smile as she remembered Rangor's frustration with her. The device had been constructed to keep her from raining belittling barbs upon Rangor's head each time he visited her and failed in his repeated attempts to penetrate her. She had scoffed at his poor endeavors. Like his nephew, he could not muster what was required to keep his rod stiff enough to make her a woman full-blown.

A hard shiver shattered her thoughts. The Norman knight who came to her rescue, only, it seemed to take her life, would have no such problems, she was sure. Aye, even in her condition she recognized a virile man when she saw one.

Despite his virility, he had no honor. Had not Gareth interrupted, the Norman would have sliced her heart wide open and that would have been the end of her. But spared she was, for the moment. And with the reprieve, she would find a way to survive both Rangor and the Norman.

She loosened her body, and settled more securely in Gareth's strong arms, as her thoughts crashed violently together like warriors on the battlefield.

* * *

Wulfson stormed from the dungeon, followed by his men, and Rangor, who nipped at his heels like a terrier, asserting his right to the lady and all that came with her. If the Saxon did not shut his mouth and leave him in peace, Wulfson might yet slay a Saxon noble this day. *Jesu*! He was a knight, a warrior, captain of a great man's guard—not a nursemaid to mollycoddle these bickering Saxons. As he strode back into the hall, he called for a scribe, and immediately sent word to William of this most annoying hitch in his step.

Against his better judgment, not wanting to be another man down, he had only one option: to hand the message over to Warner's care. The knight would place it in William's own hands.

As Warner and his squire took horse and rode south toward the sea, Wulfson called his men, Rangor, and Gareth to him. When the lady's guard did not appear, Wulfson cursed. "Where is the Dane?"

"No doubt mothering his lady," Rangor spat contemptuously.

Wulfson glared at the noble. "From the looks of her she will need more than mothering. 'Tis a miracle she survived." Had he but come the next day, nature would have taken its course, and, like Warner, he would be on the road home to Normandy.

"My intent was never to see her dead, sir, but as I said, to convince her marriage to me would be the better choice. Her only other option would be rightful execution."

Wulfson cast a disparaging glance at Rangor. He could not blame the lady for holding out. The Saxon was a most unsavory specimen of a man.

A servant brought out several pitchers of mead and

poured for the men. Several more hauled in platters of meats and breads, and set them down on the lord's table, which had not been cleared from the morning meal. Continuing to stand, Wulfson and his men drank and ate. Once his thirst and hunger were eased, Wulfson cast a wary eye on the Saxon noble. "Where do you call home, Saxon?"

"Lerwick, to the northwest. I have several smaller holdings further up. I am therefore a most worthy bridegroom."

Wulfson scathed him with a glare, assessing the validity of his words. "What became of your nephew Malcor?"

Rangor's face paled. "She slit his throat whilst he slept."

" 'Tis a lie!" Gareth boomed, making his way down the narrow passage to the upper floor. "He was fully awake when the deed was done. 'Twas he or she, for he was bent on taking her life! He did not deserve to live after what he did to my lady."

" 'Twas murder!" Rangor shrieked. "She can pay with her life or pay by marriage to me. Either way, she will pay!"

Wulfson held his hand up for silence, and cast his gaze to the Dane. "How fares the lady?"

A storm cloud of emotion gathered upon the hulking Dane's fair face. "She is alive. Barely."

Wulfson turned his attention back to Rangor. "A man who mistreats a woman is no man at all."

Rangor cocked a brow and said arrogantly, "But not one who will slay her outright?"

Wulfson refilled his cup. "There is no honor in cowardly abuse." When Rangor made to speak again, Wulfson bellowed, "Enough! I will not be nettled by your womanish complaints! Until such time as the lady is well enough to make an appearance and a midwife has the opportunity to examine her for the signs of pregnancy, there will be no more discussion about her!"

Rangor stood, properly cowed. Wulfson lowered his voice and strode to the head of the lord's table. He turned and faced the many who had gathered. Though England was overrun with Normans, the invasion and the shire had suffered a great loss of men to battle, and the Norman hammer had not yet infiltrated much to the west. Until now.

"To every man, woman, and child who call themselves Saxon and cleave to this shire, until you are informed otherwise, consider me lord and master here. I come in the name of King William to settle a dispute that does not involve any of you. I will tolerate no interference, and should I suspect any nefarious actions, I and my men will strike first and ask questions afterward."

He watched anger cloud most of the faces, Rangor's especially, and continued. "We are not Barbarians, and unless provoked, you will be safe under our guard so long as we reside here. Only you can make life unpleasant for yourselves."

Wulfson faced Rangor. "I will tolerate no interference from you especially. Consider that my last warning." He turned to Gareth and repeated the words. The Dane scowled, and his men closed ranks around him. They were a well-appointed group, but Wulfson had no doubt as to the victor should he and his men clash with this able-bodied guard. There were more camped out in the meadow down the hill, and while the sheer numbers concerned Wulfson, he doubted an attack was forthcoming. But he never underestimated his enemy. Along with word of the lady, Wulfson had asked William for more men. He would be prepared, for he had a feeling deep in his bones that William would be more adamant than ever to see to the lady's demise. Her Welsh connections coupled with her Godwinson blood made her too attractive to those who would use her to seek the throne.

A clash was inevitable. And, as always, he would be prepared.

Darkness. It was the only thing that frightened her. Now it surrounded her, pressing into her with the relentless intensity of a hot iron. Tarian moaned when she tried to open her eyes, the pain of the effort too much to bear. Yet she must! For days her dreams had haunted her. The nights with Malcor and his deviant actions. Like a wagon wheel rolling endlessly down a mountain, the endless days and nights spent in his dungeon of horrors repeated in her mind's eye. He had lured her down there one day, only to shackle her to the wall and . . . she squeezed her eyes tighter. Rangor had done the same. The sadistic nature ran true through the line. She moved her body, and cried out as jagged lashes of pain spread like quicksilver down her back and legs. Her limbs felt weighted down and every part of her throbbed.

"Easy, lass," a soft voice said from beside her.

"Edie?" she hoarsely called to her nurse, and even that effort caused her great exertion.

"Aye, I am here."

The heavy heat of the room clogged her throat. Her skin was on fire. A cool damp linen was pressed to her forehead, then her cheeks. The sheet was lifted, and she knew from the soft concussion of the air that she was naked. The cool moistness moved across her body.

Where was she? "You are safe, milady. Safe from Malcor and safe from Rangor. Gareth sleeps on the floor before your door. Sleep, sweeting, sleep."

Tarian gave way to the heat and pain of her body, her muscles relaxing as she let out a long breath. Safe. She was safe.

More dreams. A devil on a fire-breathing black beast. Black mail, black helm, black heart. She could not escape his brilliant eyes. He had come for her, not to save but to slay!

Voices whispered close by, but they were not clear. Her name spoken with urgency. Had the black knight come back for her?

She thrashed in the bed, her body sweating, the room stifling. Her chest expanded for air, she was suffocating. Hands grasping the sheets, her body strained against an imaginary hand pressed into her chest, forcing her down. *"The sins of the father will repeat in the sins of the daughter!"* Malcor shrieked as he bit her back, his long yellow teeth sinking into her flesh. Tarian screamed, the pain too intense.

"My lady," a deep voice soothed. Gareth?

"Stand back, Viking," Edith's old wheezing voice commanded. " 'Tis not decent for you to see her thusly."

"I have seen more than you could imagine, old woman. I will tend her now. You have been without sleep for three days; go to your pallet. She is safe with me."

The voices had drifted away, and with them the nightmares. Tarian lay awake, coherent, unmoving in the bed, and listened. Deep breaths from close by, and soft snores farther off. She still ached, but the heat was gone from her body. Slowly she opened her eyes. The room was dark; only a single candle illuminated it from the side table behind Gareth, who sat hunched chin to chest, softly snoring beside her in Malcor's great chair.

She moaned as she tried to brush the hair from her face. He was instantly alert, as was Edith, who for an old woman was quick, and beside her in an instant. Two sets of concerned eyes peered at her. In a most vulnerable moment, hot tears stung Tarian's eyes. Both Edith and Gareth cracked wide smiles.

Edith pressed her lips to Tarian's cheek. "The fever has broken," she said, relief heavy in her words.

Tarian closed her eyes and hoarsely whispered, "I am hungry."

A deep rumbling sound erupted from Gareth's chest. Slowly she opened her eyes again. Their gazes caught, and she could not be sure but it appeared her captain's blue eyes glistened with moisture. She tried to smile, and when she could not, she whispered, " 'Twill take more than Malcor and that fop of an uncle of his to break *me*, Gareth."

He nodded and stepped back. "I will get you food." He turned and hurried from the room.

Turning her head slowly on the pillow, Tarian watched her nurse pour wine from a skin on the sideboard. "Edie, tell me what happened."

The ancient woman, older than anyone Tarian had ever encountered, smiled softly at her over her hunched shoulder. Tarian could never remember Edith without the thick white hair, deep wrinkles, and cheery brown eyes that rarely snapped in anger. Never had she seen Edith lose her composure. She was all things to Tarian: mother, sister, friend, nurse, maid, and confidant. Tarian knew little of Edith's past, only that she was somehow connected to Tarian's mother, also called Edith, the former abbess of Leominster. "Let me tend to you, and once you are more comfortable and your belly is full, I will explain all."

Some time later, though able to move with only the speed of a turtle, Tarian sank into a cool bath and allowed Edith to gently tend her. Her long hair was washed and patted dry with a thick linen towel. As Tarian slipped on a soft linen chemise, Edith changed the soiled linens of her bed. Gareth entered with a tray laden with what seemed like the contents of the entire kitchen. Close on his heels was a servant with another tray, and behind him yet another, his tray heavy with wineskins and goblets.

"Gareth," she said, clearing her throat. She winced at the pain. "You should not do a servant's chores," Tarian lightly chided.

He set the heavy tray on a nearby table, turned to her, and bowed. "Save your voice. You will need it." He poured her a draught of wine. "Now, do as your faithful servant commands, and drink."

She smiled, and her heart swelled for this man who had, ever since she could remember, been her mentor and protector—but more than that, her friend. Edith disapproved of their closeness, but then most people disapproved of Tarian in general, so she never gave the unorthodox relationship with her captain much thought. He was the sole connection to the father she had met on only two occasions, and of whom she had only a vague memory. Sweyn Godwinson, eldest son of the great Godwine, had bidden the Viking who had fostered with her grandfather to swear his oath to always watch over her—since she, like her sire, was an outcast.

Gareth was a man of his word. And though coin had

been exchanged, Gareth's loyalty had long ago transcended both the oath and the coin. He loved his lady, and would lay his life down for her on any given day if she but asked. And, Tarian thought, recently she had not even to ask.

Only because she was so weak and hurt so badly did she allow Edith to cluck around her like a one-winged hen and Gareth to pace like a man just about to become a father for the first time.

She sipped the wine, wincing as it burned her throat. But she must drink, and eat, too, to regain her strength. Even in her weakened state, she could smell a battle brewing around her, and to be the victor she must be strong in heart, mind, and body.

With a gusto she did not particularly feel, Tarian ate. Once her hunger was sated, she demanded, "Tell me all."

When Edith and Gareth looked at each other and the color drained from her maid's face, Tarian knew it was bad. "*All* and *now*."

Gareth pulled Malcor's chair up close to face her on the bed where she had returned. Though her fever was gone and she had fortified her body with food and drink, she was still as weak as a spring lamb.

"The Normans are here," he said grimly.

Memory sparked. Aye! The black knight! Her nightmare was real! "He came to slay me," she whispered.

Gareth nodded. Edith slapped his back, and Tarian shook her head. "Edie, did you expect Gareth to tell me anything less than the truth?"

"Nay, but 'tis too much too soon."

Tarian shook her head and stopped immediately. Her neck was stiff, and the gesture cost her. "Nay, I must know all now, so that I may plan my strategy."

Gareth frowned. "The Normans are fierce."

"How fierce?"

He wiped his hand down his short blond beard, smoothing it. A sure sign he was irritated. "In all honesty, I have never come across such worthy warriors. I have watched them from your window. They practice from dawn to dusk. They work as one unit, then as individuals. Every one of them is three times the warrior of one of our men. I cannot even begin to explain to you the intricate moves they put their destriers through. Moves I have never seen. 'Tis amazing to watch."

Tarian scowled. "You sound smitten."

Gareth had the decency to color. "Nay, impressed. So much so that I fear we will have to fly from here under the cover of night through the back passageway as soon as you are able, or else face certain death if we stay."

Tarian stiffened and she winced. "I will not leave Draceadon."

His blue eyes locked with hers. "His king sent him here to destroy the Godwinson line. You are the surviving child of the eldest son, a slain king's brother. You pose a great threat, milady. We cannot beat the Normans. I fear he has sent for more of his kind."

Tarian refused to believe a handful of knights could best her garrison of men. "What are a few more Norman knights?"

"Not any Norman knights. These call themselves Blood Swords. Thorin the Viking tells me there are more."

"Who is their leader?"

"The one they call Wulfson of Trevelyn."

Tarian crumpled her brow in thought and ignored the pain. "'Tis a Saxon and a Welsh name—how can he be Norman?"

"I know not. 'Tis not my place to ask."

"Was he the one who took me from the dungeon?"

"Aye."

Her entire body tightened, just a little, as she remembered his bold green eyes, and the way she had reacted to him even when she was at death's door. When he had touched her she had felt his life force spear into her skin, as if lightning had struck, and when in that briefest moment of a heartbeat he had hesitated, the dagger poised but not moving forward, she had seen doubt in his eyes. And something else. Something she had no clue to. "What manner of man is he?" she whispered hoarsely.

"Hard," Edith answered. "But Gareth would know better than I. I have been here these four days past."

Tarian looked to her captain. He nodded. "Hard, steadfast to his king. He sees all. Nothing escapes his notice. He does not make hasty judgment."

Tarian plucked her bottom lip, and winced. It seemed there was not a part of her that did not hurt. So, her home was overrun with demon Normans, and the captain of her guard was ready to throw all they had worked for to those hungry wolves. Her anger rose. "What of Rangor?"

Gareth smiled. "He has managed to nettle the Norman to the point of being relegated to the old armory."

Tarian smirked. 'Twas too good for him.

"He presses for your hand," Edith interjected.

"That will never be. I would give up Draceadon before I would lie with him."

Gareth's eyes softened. "A babe would solve many of your problems, milady."

She raised her eyes to him and then looked to Edith. "You both know there is no chance of that."

"Wed with Rangor and give yourself the advantage over the Norman and his king. He will not harm you if you are wed to the man; his Welsh connections are too strong," Gareth encouraged her.

"My blood is still Godwinson blood, Gareth. My choice of husband will not change that." She fought back a yawn, for it pained her. "My strength wanes, and I must think. Let us speak more on the morrow."

Four

For the first time since she awoke from her fever and learned her home had been overrun with Normans, Tarian was alone. Gareth had much that needed his attention, and he trusted the Norman when he had given his word that his lady would not be disturbed. Edith also had chores to tend to, and when she sent a girl to sit with her, Tarian shooed her from the chamber. She wanted time alone. It was what she preferred, it was what she was accustomed to. It had been so all her life. There had been no children of like nobles to play with as a child; even her foster sister, Brighid, who was younger, was kept from Tarian. Lady Gwen, Brighid's mother, had made it plain to Tarian that her influence was not welcome on her golden-haired daughter. Tarian smiled.

That did not stop Brighid from seeking her out. And Tarian admitted she cared deeply for the girl several years her junior. She was feisty, and had a mind of her own. But even with the stolen moments with the girl she considered her sister, more oft than not, Tarian spent her time alone. And she felt very alone now. For so long, she'd had to rely on her wits and agility to keep her from harm's way, and in so relying on those traits she had served to drive the wedge deeper between her and most nobles. She was cursed, marked as she was by a small red birthmark just inside her thigh that resembled a shield. Hence her name. Shield maiden.

She lay quiet, listening to the sounds from the bailey. Life went on at Draceadon, with or without her. That stung. She had great hopes of restoring the fortress to its former glory. It was one of the few stone structures in the area, and though it was the lesser of Malcor's holdings, it had the most history, and was most strategically positioned high on a hill near the Welsh border. She had immediately fallen for it when she and Gareth came out of the forest below in search of the earl who, it was rumored, hid behind Dragon Hill's massive stone walls.

Breaching the fortress had been easy. Malcor had underestimated her refusal to live out her days in a convent. Once married, and for the sake of the children she'd hoped she would bear, she had tolerated his perverse attention. A woman of conviction and determination, one who had slain men on battlefields from York to Hastings, even she, in the short time she had been his wife, had not been able to withstand his violent nature. And so, to survive, she had done what she had to do.

She pressed her hands to her chest and felt the strong beat of her heart, then closed her eyes. A dark, unsettled feeling moved through her, an uncertainty that perhaps she was in a bog from which she might never be free. Her country still licked deep wounds of defeat. It occurred to her that the rules of engagement had drastically changed since her marriage to Malcor, and to get back into the challenge she too would have to improvise to overcome this new threat. And to do so would require not might, but shrewd and subtle maneuvering.

Her eyes flashed open. She would not have what she had worked so hard to gain taken from her merely because Malcor's repugnant uncle fancied her for his bride. Her days of being under a man's thumb were over! She had lived with the stigma as the cursed spawn of the devil all her life, and she had shrugged off the sneers and the narrowed glares, along with the hushed conversations of which she was the topic. Mayhap now she would use the curse to her advantage. Let it fly as her standard. And let any who tried to take what was rightfully hers feel the wrath of the devil's spawn!

Tarian expelled a long breath, wincing as her chest loosened. In her current state of weakness, she could barely fathom the supreme effort it would require to stay a widow, and at the same time keep what she had won.

Once again the feeling of being completely alone overcame her. The thought of spending the rest of her life in the cloister terrified her more than any battle. God terrified her. The nuns terrified her, and of the three abbesses she had met in her travels, the moment she spoke her name the look of shock, horror, then disgust had been enough to turn her away.

So she had found her way with a sword and her guard. It was not a bad life. Her enemies she met face to face. And that was more than she could say of life at court. Her uncle King Harold had been most gracious in his invitation to her to come to Winchester shortly after his coronation. He was a great man, of a great family, a most worthy king. He had allowed her and her men to participate in the rigorous drills in anticipation of William. When word came of Norway's King Hardrada's pending invasion, she had joined her liege without hesitation.

Harold proved to be a mighty warrior, and she felt a deep abiding respect for him. Their victory celebration had been short-lived. Less than a month later, her beloved uncle fell at Hastings, and a part of her fell with him.

The Normans were vicious and arrogant. She despised them as much as any Saxon, probably more. They had taken her golden uncle from her, from England, as well as from his brothers, her uncles. In her eyes no man could replace him.

The clear sound of steel clashing against steel roused her from her musings. Hoarse shouts and the neighing of destriers alerted her to activity below. Her blood quickened: 'twas the sound of soldiers. Carefully, she moved so that her legs hung from the side of the bed. Pain pricked her every inch. The wounds from the lash were just beginning to heal, and her muscles that had been pulled taut, then twisted and bound, had begun to loosen up. Her head, though, caused her most discomfort. She could still feel the clasp of metal at her temples and the hard bite of the bit in her mouth.

With shaky legs and the help of several chairs along the way, Tarian made it to the slitted window of her chamber. There was a stone seat she could sit upon, and with only a small effort she could peer clearly down into the side of the bailey, where warriors of old had prepared for battle and where the Norman knights of her present went about their daily training regime.

She watched for nearly a candle notch as they moved through rudimentary maneuvers, suppling their horses as well as themselves. Several of the formations were familiar to her, but most were not. But regardless of what they did, horses and knights alike performed in perfect precision.

Once the warm-ups were complete, the knights settled in for more intricate maneuvers. They paired off facing each other, and one dark-haired knight with a double scabbard strapped to his back, *à la florentine*, who had caught her eye from the very beginning, called most of the maneuvers and set the pace.

At his sharp command, his horse's great haunches lowered to the ground, and she watched in amazement as each destrier, bearing the weight of not only the heavy studded tack but of a mailed knight, leaped up and slightly forward, kicking out with its hind legs, only to repeat the maneuver several more times. She had seen similar maneuvers at Hastings, but nothing so expert as this. No wonder these men were William's elite guard, known as *les morts*.

The lead knight called for them to halt, and when he turned to face the high walls of Draceadon he looked up. Even though she was sure he could see but her shadowed form from where he sat upon his mount, she could feel the heat of his gaze bore into her.

'Twas he, the one they called Wulfson. Tarian caught her breath and moved back from the window, not realizing she nearly hung out of it. She'd been found out!

Would he demand she present herself? She could not, not yet. She was still too weak, and the visible wounds she suffered at Rangor's hands had just begun to heal. Her pale skin was a mass of bruises, and her face, an asset, was naught but a mass of cuts and swelling. Nay, when she made her appearance, she would be at her best both on the surface and within. She would need every weapon in her arsenal to deal with the likes of Wulfson of Trevelyn.

His sharp command to resume brought her back to the stone sill. She peeked down and, in womanly appreciation, watched his manly form and the way he maneuvered his horse as easily as if he were but plucking a lyre.

Slowly she backed away from the window. Her legs shook, but not from her injuries.

Wulfson felt her presence long before he spied her watching from above. Her brilliant sea-colored eyes haunted his dreams. She had burrowed under his skin like a flea on a hound, and the irritation was most unpleasant. When he halted in the middle of the maneuvers and looked up, his fellow knights followed his gaze. "She watches and plots against you, Wulf," Thorin said from beside him.

Wulfson's blood warmed. "Aye, and she will lose all as her uncle did."

Thorin laughed and slapped him on the back. "Why do we wait?"

Wulfson scowled. "A precaution only. William will want to consider the Welsh alliance she could bring. Rhiwallon and Bleddyn chomp at the bit to spill more Norman blood."

"Methinks, my friend, it is just a matter of time before we push the Welsh border west."

"Aye," Ioan agreed as he maneuvered his mount around to face the two men. "'Tis a language I should learn, as I wager I will find myself in the arms of a Welsh lass sooner rather than later."

The men laughed and Wulfson said, "I speak it with great authority. I spent many years in Gwent."

Rhys, Rorick, and Stefan gathered round, allowing their mounts to blow. Since their arrival, the air hung heavy with unshed raindrops. Today the heat was most oppressive. Black clouds gathered overhead, and a low rumble of far-off thunder rolled toward them. Wulfson cast a wary eye skyward. "This cursed weather will turn us into rusted statues!"

And as the men sat upon their mounts and conversed, by some compulsion all six of them looked up to the vacant window of the lord's chamber.

"I fear should William give the order to proceed," Rhys said, "we will be met with more than a slight resistance. We should do the deed stealthily, and whilst the dragon sleeps."

Wulfson nodded, not feeling particularly good about having to slay a woman. And a noble one still less. He was a man of high conviction, would follow his king through hell, but the idea of being the one responsible for snuffing the fire from those brilliant eyes left him feeling cold and unclean.

Thunder rumbled closer, followed by a shift in the air. It became heavier, an ominous omen of what was to come. Wulfson cursed. "Let us wait out the storm in the hall. I have no desire to rust."

And so the next days passed. Wulfson and his men were up long before the crow of the cock getting in what exercise they could in the few bright spots between the sultry storms that seemed to plague the area. The skies would be clear and blue in the morn, and by the midday meal become dark and ominous. Just as ominous were the blue eyes from above, Wulfson knew, that watched him and his men with keen interest. Her presence unnerved him on a most primal level. It was something he could not exactly put a name to, but he knew she was more dangerous then the jagged flashes of lightning that preceded the harsh thunderclaps. For that reason alone, he had not pressed for her to make her appearance.

Tarian spent the days of her recuperating watching and learning, and despite her hatred for all things Norman, she found herself admiring the prowess of the black knight called Wulfson. His commanding presence on the field was undeniable, and to her chagrin she watched Gareth and her own men watch the Normans and then go about their own maneuvers, in an attempt to reenact what they had just observed.

On the tenth day of her convalescence, as Edith prepared her bath, the old woman said, "The Norman is deadly, milady."

"Of that I am fully aware, Edie." Tarian moved to the window seat, and was glad to notice, when she tucked her knees beneath her, that the pain was nearly gone. So were most of the bruises. Pink scars still crisscrossed her back and legs, but with the daily balm rubs Edie insisted on—and which in truth were pure heaven—they too were fading. Her heart, though, remained hard and closed. Her determination to hold on to at least Draceadon grew each day as her body healed. Her hatred for Rangor grew in insidious leaps and bounds. At the first opportunity, should he give it, she would see him planted beside his nephew.

"Has the Norman's man returned with word from William?" Edie asked.

"Nay."

Tarian smiled. And he would not. Gareth had positioned a handful of men to snag the knight on his return, and hold him until such time Tarian had full control; and with the backing of the Welsh kings, to whom she had sent word for help, she would see the Normans either gone from Draceadon or become a permanent part of the landscape.

And though she had planned well, too much of her future rested on her Welsh in-laws. She sneered and boldly stood on the window seat, peering down to the bailey. She smiled. She was not surprised to see the Norman on the ground, a broadsword in each hand, going through intricate maneuvers. He thrust and parried and cut down the wooden soldiers they had erected. He was bare-headed and bare-chested, with only the scabbards to his back, the leather straps crossing his chest, his legs clad in his mail chauses. Sweat gleamed on his skin under the hot rays of the sun.

He turned, and as he cut the head off the effigy, then swept his other sword downward, slicing the wooden arms off the mannequin, he looked up. Tarian gasped, and instead of retreating she held his hard gaze. His great chest rose and fell from his exertion, his long dark bay-colored hair clinging to his shoulders. His hands rose, the blades in his hands pointing heavenward, and sunlight glinted off the steel. His power moved her beyond simple admiration. Something else stirred in her, something she had never experienced before. Something . . . dangerous.

He brought down the blades and swept them across his waist, made a short bow, then turned and destroyed what was left of the effigy.

Her mind raced with images of such a man lying beside her in bed and the pain or pleasure he could evoke, and with that thought another chased it. There was no question of his virility. He no doubt had bastards littering every camp he had stayed in.

Edith came up behind her, and said softly, "A Norman babe would not be a bad thing, milady."

Tarian hissed and whirled around. Edith spoke her brazen thoughts! Heat flushed her cheeks. And yet, even as she rejected the idea, she knew it might be the only way. Wide-eyed, she stared at her maid. The old woman smiled. "Do not deny you are attracted to him."

"He is a Norman!" Tarian tried to refute.

"Aye, and you are too bright to ignore the fact that they are here to stay. Use him to your advantage. He will not slay a woman who carries his child, not even for his king."

"But! What guarantee do I have that I am fertile?"

"In less than two days' time you will be ripe to conceive. Take his seed, and a month's time will tell us if it strikes fertile ground or not. Then keep what is yours."

Nervously, Tarian gasped. "How do you know my time is ripe?"

Edith took her hand and pulled her toward the tub. "Your time comes every twenty-eight days. Your courses struck the day the Norman dragged you from that hellhole. No one noticed the blood amidst your torn and dirty rags. 'Tis widely known among midwives that most fertile women conceive a fortnight after the first appearance of flow. 'Twill be a fortnight in two nights' time."

Tarian stood silent, stunned by the turn of events. Was it the only way? "How—how will I get him to lie with me? He is not dense. He will know what I am about."

Edith lifted the chemise from Tarian and helped her into the bath. "You forget, sweeting, I am well versed in herbs and potions. My mother was a renowned midwife to noble ladies. A simple balm of rose musk and violet and a few other herbs will put the Norman into a deep sleep, and when you awaken him he will be ravenous for a woman. He will have seed enough to sire a new nation. When he wakes the next morn, you will be gone, and but a fleeting dream."

As she sank into the warm water and it softly sloshed against her skin, Tarian dared to think of what his hand would feel like upon her. She shivered hard and wrapped her arms around her knees, bringing them close to her chest. "I dare to hope he is not nearly as violent as Malcor."

Edith smoothed her hair back from her cheeks and made low soothing sounds. "Malcor is dead, my sweet child. You have nothing to fear from him. He was the devil's spawn."

Aye, and the Norman? Heat flared in her veins. He was the devil himself.

Five

It has been nearly a fsortnight!" Wulfson bellowed as he paced the long length of the great hall. Pent-up energy, frustration, and lust for an enigma erupted in an ugly display of temper. "I demand the lady be presented at once!"

He stopped his pacing and faced the great assemblage of men. They were as restless as he. They hungered for battle. They hungered for a woman. The endless days of monotonous exercise and patrols had only served to whet their appetite for real swordplay.

"Sir Wulfson," Gareth said, coming down from the winding stairway. Wulfson's eyes traveled past the Dane's head to the hallway above, to where the witch lay, no doubt concocting spells. "My lady is not yet well enough to make an appearance."

"*Jesu!* What does it take?"

Gareth stopped several paces from the raging Norman. He shuffled his feet and looked to the matted rushes. "I know not, milord knight."

Wulfson would know. "Is she with child?"

Gareth's head shot back, but he answered quickly. "The midwife says it can take months for some women to show the signs of a child."

"It has been over a month since she lay with Malcor. Surely that is enough time!"

He was itching to put the place behind him.

"I would see for myself as well, Sir Wulfson," Rangor said, sweeping into the hall with several of his men behind him.

Wulfson narrowed his gaze at the older man. His initial perception had proved to be correct. Rangor of Lerwick skulked about the manor as if he had secrets to hide. His constant righteous diatribes had long since worn Wulfson's temper thin. On more than one occasion, he had had to be held in check by one of his men, as his fist was on its way into the noble's mouth. His men taunted him, but they too had had enough of the baron.

"I am sure you *would* like to see for yourself, Rangor, but you will not have the chance. The lady is not a cow to be examined by would-be buyers."

Ioan scoffed, as did Thorin who stood close by. Wulfson shot them both a glare. His fists opened and closed, and as he looked around the great hall he felt as if it mocked him. They were down to six knights, surrounded by the lady's well-armed and seasoned garrison and a contingent of Rangor's men. 'Twas turning into a suicide mission.

His eyes swept the hall and landed on Gareth, who if truth be told did not overly concern him. The man was besotted with his lady. 'Twas unnatural the way he flitted between his garrison and the chamber above. Wulfson scowled. Mayhap there was truth to Rangor's accusations. The Dane, while past the prime of his life, had plenty left to sire a child or two. Aye, it was whispered he had never

married because he only had eyes for the witch he protected. What spells had she cast on the men about her?

Malcor, a deviant known for his preference for squires,
had succumbed to her, as had his uncle who, though a fop
in Wulfson's mind, could be construed by the ladies a virile
man, *and* the captain of her guard? No wonder the cloister
did not want her. His scowl deepened. Nor did he.

And as of yet Wulfson had not heard back from William
on the matter. But he did not expect to hear so soon. In
the missive, he had requested more men. He had also sent
word to his brother-in-arms, Rohan du Luc, who resided in
Alethorp two days' hard ride to the east.

Once again he paced the hall, debating on forcing the
issue: the lady presenting herself or waiting for reinforcements. The warrior in him drew on prudence. No purpose
would be served to have the lady dragged from her sickbed.
But his cock throbbed with his imagined image of her. In
his mind he had created an exotic creature that would only
be tamed by his hand.

"God's blood!" he swore, and turned on his heel, bent
on seeing for himself this woman who plagued his every
waking moment.

The lookout called that riders approached. Thank the
saints! Any interruption would be better than this endless
waiting.

He swept out of the hall and called to his Blood Swords
to follow. A bedraggled group of men, bearing a standard he
did not recognize, made their way up the road and into the
bailey. As they approached, Wulfson noted that they were
foot soldiers, bearing fresh wounds. Slung over a horse was
the body of a servant who bore the yellow and blue colors
of the hawk standard.

"'Tis Alewith's men," Gareth said, stepping past Wulfson and his men. They followed.

"Who, pray tell, is Alewith?" Wulfson demanded.

"Lady Tarian's former guardian."

The soldiers quickly told the tale of how they were ambushed just past Hailfox Abbey, and the attacking thugs had spoken of plundering the monks. "Methinks they were Normans," one soldier said before he collapsed in the dirt. His comrades were too wounded to assist him.

Wulfson balked at the accusation. Welsh, Saxon, Scot, or even Irish, but not his countrymen. William was adamant in his edict: *There will be no illicit plundering of the Saxons!* 'Twould only force them to dig in deeper, and that was the last thing the king wished. He wanted to smooth the transition as much as possible, and harassing the Saxons for no reason was simply not acceptable.

Wulfson turned to the other soldiers. "Were they knights or afoot?"

"Afoot, a score or more," the one who had collapsed croaked.

"To horse, men!" Wulfson called, his voice high with excitement.

"I will show you the way," Gareth said, making his way toward the stable.

Vigorously Wulfson shook his head. "And leave your lady prey to Rangor?"

Gareth halted, his skin paling. "Aye, how could I have thought to leave her? I'll send the smith's son Barton with you. He can show you the way to the abbey. He grew up not far from here and is familiar with the area."

*   *   *

The abbey was intact, as were the monks. Wulfson questioned them, and was assured there had been no mishaps that day. Convinced that all was as it should be, he and his men rode through the surrounding countryside, and while they found evidence of a skirmish not far from the abbey, there were no clear tracks.

He wondered at the Saxon's claims, but the evidence was proof enough they had been attacked. In these times random assaults were not uncommon. And he had first-hand experience of Saxons disguising themselves as Normans or Vikings to plunder their neighbors. 'Twas acts of desperation. Wulfson snorted in disgust. Desperate or not, he would never see the honor in pillaging one's neighbor.

And so they spent the balance of the day familiarizing themselves with more of the countryside and keeping a sharp eye out for the cowards.

Later that day, when the knights thundered up the hill to Draceadon, Wulfson immediately became suspicious when the lookout did not herald their arrival. All seemed too quiet for such a bustling place. Dread infiltrated him, and he spurred his horse faster.

As they entered the courtyard, Wulfson barely came to a stop before dismounting and hurrying to the great doors. He flung them open, and the sight that greeted him stopped him in his tracks.

The hall was completely empty. Eerie silence rested on Wulfson's shoulders with the weight of his mail. As the Blood Swords followed him in, they too abruptly halted at the emptiness. Wulfson drew both swords and ran to the stairway, his men following, sure he would find the chamber door to the lady's room flung wide and her gone.

Instead, he was met with Gareth's sword. "What goes on here?" Wulfson demanded.

"Stand back, sir, the lady is not to be disturbed," Gareth warned, standing his ground.

In a great swipe, using both swords as one, Wulfson flung Gareth's sword from his hands, and a brace of the Dane's men stepped forward from behind him in battle positions. Wulfson pressed a sword tip to each of their chests, and pinned them to the wall. Rorick maneuvered Gareth in the same fashion, but against the opposite wall. "Do not engage me; you will die for the effort," Wulfson warned.

Slowly, angrily, the men raised their arms in acquiescence. Wulfson stepped back but held his swords. "Where are the servants, and that yap Rangor and his entourage? The hall is empty."

Gareth's face flushed crimson in his anger. Or, Wulfson decided, his sagging pride.

"Nothing is amiss. The servants tend Alewith's messenger and men. I sent Rangor from the hall under the threat of violence. He is no doubt plotting both our demises amongst the ruins of the tower."

Wulfson scowled and backed farther away from the chamber door. He pointed to the door with his sword. "The lady?"

"Continues to gain her strength within."

"What message does Alewith send?"

"That my lord should arrive in time to break the fast on the morrow. He comes to see to the health of his charge, and, my guess is, to take her back to Trent."

"Trent?"

Gareth nodded. "Aye, of all the places milady has lived, Trent gave her the most hospitality."

"You make it sound as if she lived a gypsy life."

Gareth's lips drew into a tight line. "A gypsy had it easier."

Wulfson visualized a dark-haired, blue-eyed waif of a girl reaching out for acceptance only to find dirt kicked in her face. His jaw set. 'Twas a scene to which he could well relate. He had spent much of his own youth being tossed back and forth between a blood family that did not want the blight of him on their doorstep and a foster family that had grudgingly, but for a considerable sum, taken him in.

Wulfson sheathed his swords to his back. "Give the lady notice. She is to present herself when her guardian arrives in the morn. Should she fail to do so in a timely manner, I will personally see her brought down." Gareth opened his mouth to argue. Wulfson stayed him with a raised sword. "Her time is up, captain. We would know her condition."

Wulfson turned on his heel and strode down the stairway followed by his men, feeling, despite the day's adventure, more restless than before.

Tarian moved back from the doorway and looked to Edith. "My time is up."

The old nurse smiled, her wrinkles crinkling deeply around her eyes and mouth. "Nay, sweeting, your time is ripe. Tonight you will visit the Norman, and in the morn, when asked if you are with child, you can give the honest answer of ignorance."

"But—"

Edith shushed her. "It can take months for some women to show the signs. Many women are not even aware. For others it is immediate. We have time, my love, be patient and trust me."

This was not an area Tarian was remotely schooled in. Horses, swords, and how to fashion an arrow she knew; of things domestic she did not. "How will I know?"

"You will miss your courses, your breasts will become tender and plumped, and as slight as you are, your belly will swell within two months' time as your body prepares to grow the babe. You may get the morning sickness, though it can last throughout the day. Your mother, poor thing, spent many a day hovered over a chamber pot."

Tarian stiffened at the mention of the woman who bore her. No mother was she. She had given birth to her, yes, but then abandoned her in shame. Had Edith not taken Tarian to her sire, who handed her off to one of several successive foster families, she would not be alive. Tarian owed Edie her life. And now, once again, Edie came to her rescue.

"I fear him, Edie, as I have never feared a man or a woman in my life," she confessed.

"What? The shield maiden fears a simple man?"

Tarian tried to muster a smile, but felt the tremble of her chin. A virgin warrior was she, and though she could meet a man in battle with no fear, the thought of meeting one in bed terrified her. Combined with her fear, her conscience nettled her; she was not one to gain the upper hand by nefarious actions, but she could see no other way out of her dilemma.

Edith caught her trepidation, and took her hands into her own. "The Norman is virile, he is strong, and I suspect he has not had a woman for some time. And he will be anxious, but you must set the pace, as you would with your stallion." She pulled Tarian away from the window and deeper into the chamber. "Come, I'll prepare a rosewater bath, then rub you down with oil."

"Rose, 'tis not my scent, Edie."

"Aye, that I well know. You do not want him to smell you out at your first public meeting, do you?"

Tarian smiled slyly, her nervousness fading. "You are a devious woman, Edie."

The old woman cackled and nodded. "'Tis kept me alive these seventy years."

After her bath, Tarian admitted, "I would have some of your experience this night, Edie. I know not what to do."

Edith set about laying out oils and linens. "Nature will guide you."

Tarian slipped from the bed where she sat. "It did not guide Malcor."

Edith scoffed. "A man who cannot rise to a woman such as yourself is no man at all."

"What kind of woman am I?" Tarian asked as she came around and poured a cup of wine from the side table. It did not quell the nervousness in her belly.

"A beauty with no equal, a woman with the brain of a man and the will of a queen. You are a prize among all prizes, Tarian. Never forget it."

"I am the daughter of a man called *nithing* by his king and his brothers, an outcast of the lowest form. I am no prize."

Edith caught her breath and turned angry eyes upon her. "*Never* say that word in my presence!"

Tarian stood straight and proud. "The term does not offend me as it once did, Edie. I know my strengths and I know my flaws; I am but a woman trying to make her way in a man's world where they make all the rules. What more can I do?"

"Play the game better."

Tarian smiled. "Aye, and am I not a chessmaster?"

Tired and still frustrated despite the day's excitement, Wulfson climbed the steps to the well-appointed chamber he'd claimed during his time there. It was the only consolation he would grudgingly concede. He had grown accustomed to the thick mattress on the sturdy bed. Despite his frustration, he had found sleep the moment his head hit the soft downy pillow each night. Though he had offered to share the rich accommodations with them, his men spread out on pallets in the hall. 'Twas best for their safety that way. The old fortress, while simple in construction, had fortifications that few other large dwellings in this land could boast. Unlike most English manor houses, Draceadon resembled more a castle. The place had been a refuge over the last two centuries not only from the warring Welsh, but also from the Norse, and from the bloodthirsty Irish pirates when they skulked inland.

Aye, with the Welsh border not too far off to the west, Draceadon had seen many battles, and had been a worthy protector for the peoples. But Dunloc had not seen to its maintenance. Wulfson suspected the fortress would have been a sight to behold in its glory days. As it was, William would order it torn down and a castle stronghold to replace it. 'Twas his goal to outfit the island with castles to repel all invaders.

Wulfson scowled. On the morn, they would no doubt see more Saxon soldiers, as in these times Alewith would not travel light, though he doubted they would have much fight in them. William's hammer of a fist was well known among the westerners and the southerners. Those north of the Umber had yet to be brought to heel, but Wulfson had no doubt they would be, as would these people of the West.

Slowly he undressed, and was about to put to good use the warmed water left out when a soft knock on the chamber door jerked him from his thoughts. Standing only in his braies, he bade the person enter.

Instead of his squire, Rolf, an old woman he knew to be the Lady Tarian's servant, bobbed her head and hurried into the chamber, bearing a tray of food, a skin of wine, and a sturdy silver chalice. She made haste to place them on the small table by the cold hearth. "Sir knight, your evening repast."

"Where is my squire?" Wulfson demanded.

"He lingers with the others in the hall."

The plucky lad was no doubt in search of a wench for the night. With so many men lost in the last year, the manor teemed with the fairer sex. The boy would pay for his dalliances. Wulfson's scowl deepened as a sharp jab of desire struck his loins. It had been months since his last woman. He would do well to find himself some solace for the night. It would soothe the irritated edges of his temper. His rancor rose. 'Twas no simple wench he craved, but the witch who resided down the hall.

He would wager his horse she was a mass of thorns and thistles in bed. He cursed, and looked up to see the old woman staring at him with wide eyes. He cursed again, so lost in his thoughts had he been that he'd forgotten her presence. This place, this Dragon Hill and its enigma of a lady, was addling his brain.

"Begone," Wulfson tiredly said. She scurried out of the room pulling the heavy door shut behind her. His men had ribbed him hard when he left the lord's table at the late meal, his trencher untouched. He knew they understood his frustration and unwillingness to languish idly by while the Welsh were rattling their swords just across the border. Since the time he had arrived, it seemed his presence and reason for being in Dunloc were known by all. His sour mood carried into the evening, and, in no mood to be further ribbed by his men, he had retired, forgoing the evening repast with them.

Wulfson poured a hearty draught of wine and nearly drained the cup. The mulled spices were soothing, and soon he found himself finishing off a second cup. The roasted venison and simmered vegetables smelled appetizing, and, as with the wine, he found himself eating the meal with a newfound gusto. Clean and sated, he rubbed his hand across the deep scar along his chest. The uneven scars were as familiar to him now as his hands and feet. Even the ache in his right thigh he had grown accustomed to. He would never live a day without pain. 'Twas well, for it reminded him of how close he had come to glimpsing his maker in hell. When his time came, he would burn, but not a minute before.

"The bait has been set," Edith said softly, as she closed the door to her mistress's chamber.

"What of his squire?"

Edith cackled and rubbed her hands. "A-wenching, to be sure."

Tarian turned from where she stared at the low fire in the brazier. She let out a long nervous sigh. "How long will the herbs take to prepare him?"

Edith cackled again, the laugh turning into a fit of coughs from which she quickly recovered. "Not long, not long. The knight I beheld had a fierce restlessness born of hunger." Edith motioned to the bed. "Come, my dear, let me rub you with the rose musk. It will tempt him beyond mortal control."

Tarian swallowed hard, and for the tenth time in the space of minutes she questioned her action. Would it prove disastrous? Would he harm her in his herb-induced ardor? Would he know her when they came face to face? As Edith's strong hands worked into her tense muscles, Tarian relaxed. The soft intoxicating scent of rose musk soothed, but it also made her aware of the woman she was.

"The oil will relax you. Just give in to it, allow yourself to go limp for him when he enters you, or 'twill be uncomfortable," Edith instructed.

"There is pain?" Tarian asked, pushing up on her hands to look at her nurse.

Edith pressed her back into the linens and worked the oil into her back and buttocks, then her legs. "Only for a moment. But if you relax it will take the sting out."

Tarian contemplated the information. It could not hurt *that* much, since so many women seemed to enjoy the sport. She settled into the linens and allowed Edith's hands to massage her into a soft pile of mush. Once she was wrapped into warm linen, Edith helped her from the bed and guided her onto the low stool before a smoky mirror. Picking up a brush, she stroked the long thick tresses. "Your hair shines more brilliantly than the finest onyx, and your skin looks as milky fresh as it did when you were a blushing bride. You have healed remarkably well. The Norman will not recognize you."

"Let us hope the herbs are strong enough that he does not remember this eve at all." For if he did? All would be lost.

"He will think it all but a dream."

"Pray he rises to the occasion." Another hard shiver rent her, this time spearing her in the loins. She prayed she was fertile, and she prayed the knight would not use her overmuch.

Edith cackled again, this time louder. "I made sure that would not be your problem this eve."

Tarian stood, letting the linen drop to the floor. Edith smiled as she gazed upon her charge. "He is not worthy of you, my love."

A warmth sloshed lazily across Tarian's body, which the oil rub had warmed in a most pleasurable way. Edith helped her into a fine silk and linen chemise, part of her wedding trousseau. In a sudden wave of panic, Tarian grabbed Edith's arm. "Stay close, Edie, lest I need you."

The old nurse patted her lady's cheek. "There will be naught for me to do, my pet. Nature will guide you, and this night the Norman's seed will strike fertile ground. Just remember to relax." She patted Tarian's cheek again. "You are a warrior princess. 'Tis the Norman who will need aid this night."

With those final words of wisdom, Edith pushed aside the tapestry near the bed and pushed open the secret door.

Six

As quietly as a breeze, Tarian pushed the heavy tapestry from the doorway and slipped into the knight's chamber. Her back pressed against the sturdy wood of the wall, she stopped and held her breath. Low moans of agony startled her into a rigid standstill. A curse followed the injured sounds, the noises of a man caught in a trap unable to free himself. Her gaze quickly assured her there were no other persons in the room save the flailing form on the huge bed. She swallowed hard and cautiously stepped into the room.

In the low glow of the candlelight she could see the Norman knight, Sir Wulfson, spread-eagled and naked on the bed fighting off an imaginary demon. His body glistened with a low sheen of sweat, his words a jumbled mess of French and some other language she did not understand. His anguish, mixed with a feral fury, terrified her. Yet she moved closer. Her eyes raked his large form. While Malcor had been well muscled, this man was even more impressive. The long lines of his arms and legs rippled in perfect symmetry as his body thrashed against an unknown assailant.

She moved closer and gasped. Seared into his wide chest, the imprint of a broadsword so clear it could be an actual one marked him from the bottom column of his throat well into his groin. She swallowed harder this time as her eyes traveled lower. He was quite—large. Panic began to nibble at her resolve. How could she receive his seed if she could not take him into her? Her thighs clenched in rebellion. She closed her eyes at the imagined pain of him breaching her.

His body tensed as his hips rose, his arms outstretched but pressed to the mattress as if some unholy force pinned him to the bed. He let out a loud curse, then screamed in agonizing pain.

Moved beyond any normal comprehension, Tarian hurried to the bedside. "You are not in harm's way, sir," she said softly in Welsh. "There are no enemies here."

His skin flinched beneath her fingertips, but his body quieted. She continued to speak softly to him in her mother's native tongue. Bent over him, her long hair swirling about them in a dark shroud, Tarian felt, more than saw, his eyes open. In a quick movement, his long arm snaked around her waist, and in the next instant she was flat on her back with a raging man looming above her and a dagger pressed to her throat.

"Please, sir, I mean you no harm," she croaked in French.

His wild eyes peered at her but did not see her. His mighty muscles quivered around her, but he made no further movement. 'Twas the potion, no doubt. Carefully she ran her fingers along the long length of his right arm, the one that held the dagger to her throat. "I have come to pleasure you, milord knight." As if experienced and made solely for the pleasure of a man, she did not hesitate in her seduction. Her life depended on her success. Slowly she undulated beneath him, and was rewarded with the instant swell of him against her hip. She caught her breath, not expecting such a sudden reaction to her. In deliberate exploration, she trailed her fingertips down the hard ridges of his forearm to his hand. Slowly she wrapped her fingers around his fist and moved it away from her throat.

His eyes, still dazed, lost some of their rage, and though his muscles still quaked with tension she felt the shift of his body. Turning her head, she pressed her lips to the inside of his forearm and worked his fingers loose from the hilt of the dagger. When his fingers relaxed, she slid the weapon from his hand and dropped it to the floor.

In the low light, she smiled what she hoped was a convincingly seductive smile and arched toward him. A low rumble formed deep in his chest, but still he watched her warily. She rose higher, this time pressing her lips to the scarred skin at the base of his throat. Heat radiated from his body to hers, and a surge of energy jolted her. He cursed and thrust her from him, rolling over to sit on the edge of the bed.

Time stood still for Tarian at that moment. Shame swamped her, and she dropped her gaze to her lap. Twice in a month's time she had been rejected by a man she was attempting to seduce. Was she truly cursed? Uncertainty, inexperience, and embarrassment dismantled her resolve. Her eyes rose and held his. Her heart thudded like a hammer against her chest, tightening it. A swarm of angry wasps buzzed wildly in her belly. She could not breathe.

He rubbed the heels of his hands into his eyes and shook his head before peering back at her over his shoulder. As if an imaginary hand pushed her forward, Tarian rose up on her knees and slowly untied the silk laces of her chemise.

His dark-green eyes widened, then narrowed. She smiled a tremulous smile, hoping he would see it as a sign she offered nothing but herself. Carefully, like a wary wolf, he watched her as she pulled the chemise from her body. Though she still bore scars from her time in the dungeon, they had faded enough that in the low glow of the candle they would be but smoky shadows. When her breasts were bared, Wulfson hissed in a long sweep of air. And for the first time in her life Tarian's body responded in kind to a man. Her nipples tightened and a quicksilver stream of warmth flooded her body. A thrill of excitement blazoned through her. Her breaths became shorter, shallower, and though it was not warm in the room, a radiance infused her skin. In that moment she understood the power a woman could wield over a man. But she gave herself no delusions. A man such as the one she was at this moment seducing was only allowing her to do so because she had drugged him. In the clear light of the day, with a clear head, she doubted even the most wily seductress could turn his head if he were set on another course.

And 'twas a shame, for this was a most striking man. Long dark hair that was not cut in the shaved fashion of the Normans but more the fashion of the northern men framed a face that was like a tortured angel's. Deep emerald-colored eyes, framed by dark slashed brows that at that moment crowded together in consternation. A fine aquiline nose with nostrils that flared ever so slightly, like those of a wolf who knew his enemy was near but did not want to give himself away. His lips were full and held more promise of destruction then pleasure. Tarian swallowed hard and dropped her gaze lower. The vision of those lips ravaging her body sent a hard hot thrill down her spine. The only blight to his troubled features was a small crescent-shaped scar on his square chin. A shadow of dark stubble marked his face where a beard would grow if he allowed it. But she knew that though he did not shave the nape of his neck, he did shave his face, and she found she liked the look. Many Saxons had been stripped of their glory, their heads and faces shaved. Mostly to humiliate. But it did not matter, for whether they cared for them or not, the Normans were here to stay; and a warrior at heart, Tarian would use every weapon in her armory to see victory at the end of the day.

Testing her confidence, she subtly thrust her breasts toward him. Immediately he responded. She smiled, her confidence growing. He reached a scarred hand to her and pressed it to her right breast. Her heart leapt toward it. Tarian closed her eyes and bit the inside of her cheek to quell her sudden modesty. The sensation of his hand upon her was not unpleasant. Indeed, he warmed her body. Malcor's hands had been cold, soft, and cruel, but this man's were warm, hard, and, for the moment, gentle.

She pressed her body full into his hand, and he turned to fully face her.

"Who are you?" he demanded hoarsely, moving across the bed to her.

"I am the woman of your dreams come to seek mortal play." She moved into him and pressed her lips once more to the base of his throat. She stroked his arms and pressed herself more fully against him. While he did not resist, he did not engage, either. But the burgeoning length of his manhood gave testament that while his brain might not want her, his body did.

Tarian moved closer, so that now the heat of his shaft molded into her belly. Wulfson hissed again, and this time he left no question to his desire. His long arms caught her up to him, and held her with the strength of a steel band. He yanked her hair back so that her chin jutted up and her eyes met the challenge of his. "Then play we shall, my fairy princess." He pushed her back into the thick coverlet and in a sudden rush of fury his hands and his lips ravaged her.

Unprepared for his ardor, Tarian cried out in alarm. "Do not play coy now, princess. I will have what you have so wantonly flaunted," he whispered against her breast.

His knee pressed between her thighs, spreading them. Sudden panic filled her. He was big and heavy, and he would crush her beneath his body. The thick length of him pressed boldly against her thigh. 'Twas not to be this way! She was to be the seductress, not the ravaged.

But when his lips captured a nipple, and he suckled her, she gasped in surprised pleasure. Heat flooded her limbs, crashing together at the juncture of her thighs. His right hand ran the length of her waist to her hips, then to her thigh.

His muffled words of passion were lost in his enthusiasm for her body. In a torrent of heated ardor, he consumed her inch by inch. And try as she might to remain in control, she was at his mercy.

His hand moved between her thighs. Her instinctive reaction was to close them. Pressing her palms against his warm chest, she whispered, "Gently, my lord, gently."

His eyes blazed, his body tightened, and she knew he exercised great control. "Break me gently," she whispered again, and she watched his features loosen. She slid her fin-

gers into his thick hair and rolled slightly to her side, pushing him over. To her amazement, he allowed her. Now their
positions where reversed. Her long hair shrouded them.
Slowly, deliberately, she lowered her lips to his, and was
shocked to find them warm and soft. His arms tightened
around her waist, and she pulled back, and slowly shook
her head. Her hair swept across his cheeks and chest, and
he hissed in a long breath. When he loosened his hold she
bent back to his lips, and this time hers lingered. A wash of
desire swept across her body. When he opened his lips and
his tongue swept across hers, she moaned. She felt the rise
of him press against her, but he did not tighten his hold on
her. Slowly she explored his mouth, tasting, then nibbling
at him. He tasted of all things male, the sweet vestige of
wine on his tongue. She swept her tongue across his bottom lip. He groaned, and this time his hands slid from her
lower back to her bottom, his fingers digging into her flesh,
and though it hurt, it also sparked a primal desire in her.
Her hips pressed hotly against his, and, as a woman was
meant to, she undulated into him.

It was too much for him. He swept her into his arms
and reversed their positions. "I haven't the strength to play
the swain," he said huskily, as his lips dropped to hers in a
voracious kiss.

Tarian was swept away by his passion, and by her own
longing to be coveted. His hands swept across her breasts,
the thick fingers toying with her hardened nipples. The sensation was new and luxurious. She moaned and arched more
fully into him. His lips scorched her there, and she gasped
out loud. The moment was taken away from her by his desire
and his experience, and she didn't care. Like a puppetmas-
ter, he pulled the strings to her body, and she allowed it.

In a slow glide, he slid his right hand lower to her belly and rested it there. His hand was so big that when he splayed it across her he covered her. She looked down at the shocking sight and her entire body shuddered. Lower still his hand went and when his fingers moved lightly across her downy mound she caught her breath and held it. She did not expect to feel so alive, so aware of her body, so raw. Had Edie given her the same potion in her wine? He pressed his palm to her mound; her thighs quivered, and, her body strung as tight as a bowstring, she waited in breathless anticipation for what was to come next.

With feather lightness, he swept his blunt fingertips across her nether lips, and Tarian thought she would die of shame. But the emotion was hurried along with an unbridled desire for more. He gave her more. He rubbed the tip of his thumb against her hardened nub; the action caused her body to jerk against him, as a hot stab of desire shot to her womb. She hissed in a long breath, and slowly exhaled.

Deliberately he moved his fingers slowly back and forth across her puckered flesh, and in the wake of his salacious caress, she felt herself moisten. She closed her eyes, forcing herself to relax more. A soft moan escaped her lips when he pressed his fingertip more firmly against that wanton piece of her, and she gave up all control. Wulfson's lips made a hot wet trail from each of her breasts to settle into the deep cleavage there. "You have bewitched me," he murmured hoarsely against her skin, and once again Tarian felt something move inside of her. He craved her. Who she was, what she was, did not matter any longer. This man touched her as no other had.

As the words left his mouth, his finger slid into her wet

opening, and she knew a sublime sensation she had never imagined existed. The slick hot folds of her body clenched around him and she thought she would die of pleasure. She grabbed his shoulders, arching into him, her nails digging into his skin. He hissed in a breath just before his lips latched onto a nipple as he moved his finger in and out of her in a slow, delicious slide. Helplessly, she clung to him, and with a will of their own, her thighs opened wider wanting more of him, all of him, to fill her. But he made her wait. He made her body sizzle and burn as his fingers and lips tortured her flesh. He pushed her to a place she had never imagined, and though she felt as if she stood on the edge of precipice and wanted to jump off and fly with the eagles, she hung there suspended by wild intense longing.

He whispered words she did not understand in hoarse encouragement. His hips ground against her thighs.

"Take me now," she gasped, trying to gulp air.

He rose from her, his eyes locked with hers. "Now," she whispered between forced breaths. His finger slid from her body and she cried out. He gathered her close to him and with no help from her, the thick hot length of him slid into her. She arched into him and gasped. More in shock at the alien feeling of him penetrating her body. Then she cried out in pain. Quickly she bit her lip and did all that she could to muster her body to relax. She would give her inexperience away. But it could not be helped. He was too big for her. Her virgin body was unprepared for him. He stopped his penetration, his hips and arms quivering as he held himself off her yet still inside her.

She opened her eyes to find him staring at her in some confusion. Dread swirled around her. He would know she was virgin if she continued to act as one, and then all would be lost. Taking a deep breath, she sank her fingers into his hair and pulled his lips down to hers, and opened herself wider for him. "Come to me, sir knight, fill me with your glory."

His lips crushed into hers and her cry as he pushed through her maidenhead was lost in his kiss. "*Jesu*," he moaned against her lips. And once the barrier was broken he thrust deeper into her. Her body stretched to accommodate his width, and despite the pain and her shock, her body moistened more to help his penetration.

She held back the sudden onslaught of tears, not understanding her emotion. She would not allow herself to question what she had just done. Instead, she wrapped her arms around the man who took more than her breath away, and allowed him to carry her off to uncharted territory.

She relaxed as much as she could, closed her eyes, and let her body respond as nature intended it to. And when her body finally moved in time with his, giving what he took and taking it back from him, she could not say it was unpleasant. Indeed, the fire that he had sparked earlier burned hot inside her again.

The power of him, as his hips undulated and swirled against her, took any vestige of resistance away. He was the incarnation of every maid's dream. And for this night he was hers. She did not want to think of what the morrow might bring.

His lips swept hers, picking her up and setting her to flight. Her body moved to a new level of sensation; a storm built inside her, and try as she might to push it to rain down on her she could not. She felt the quickening in his body: his thrusts became shorter, more intense, more focused. She clamped her inner muscles around him and arched. He cried out, his voice thick and full of passion as he came in a wild ravenous burst, the force of it so powerful she felt his seed warm inside her. He hung suspended above her, the tight planes of his face taut, his jaw tight, his great body jerking as hers milked every bit of his fluid from him.

The deed done, he collapsed against her, their slick bodies heaving as they each tried to recapture a normal breath.

Tarian lay still as her body cooled, and felt oddly un-fulfilled. Wulfson rolled from her and lay on his back, his thigh touching hers. Slow moments dragged by. Time now was her enemy. The longer she stayed, the more time his body had to dilute the potion. She needed to leave him, and take all traces of her person from the room. Yet beneath his great body was her chemise. The warm stickiness of his seed mingled with her blood, dried between her thighs, and still he did not move. Finally, his deep, even breaths gave way to slumber. And for some unknown reason, she wanted to pound his chest and demand to know how he could for-get her after such a traumatic experience.

She shook her head. He did not understand, and even if he did she doubted he would care. Men rarely did. 'Twas best this way. No emotional entanglement that they would regret.

As Tarian pulled away from him, she was stopped short by a sharp tug of her hair. She turned to fend him off but saw that 'twas her hair caught beneath his shoulder, not his hand that stayed her. Carefully she pulled the dark tresses from beneath him, but scowled when she saw the blood-stained fabric of her chemise crumpled beneath his thighs. 'Twould not be as easy to extract.

*　　*　　*

He dreamt again of soft thrusts of flared hips moving against him. The full breasts of a goddess pressed against his lips, demanding his attention. Soft cries of pleasure tickled his ear. His cock filled instantly, the heat and weight of it full against his hip. He smiled and reached for the warm body so close to him. He came up with only air. In an instant, Wulfson sat up in the bed to see the nymph slipping from his side. "Nay," he softly said, and pulled her back amidst her distressed cries. He wanted his dream to continue.

Spurned on by something more than his ardor, Wulfson swept her up into his arms and tossed her back onto the bed. His eyes searched hers. They were oddly familiar. . . . He blinked back the sudden cloudiness in his vision.

"Please, sir knight, I beg you, let me go."

He pressed her back into the pillows, his body by no means sated from one tumble.

His eyes raked her slender form, resting on curves that were meant for a man's pleasure. His rod filled to hurting. He slid an arm around her waist and brought her to his lips. Her back arched and those sweet creamy globes quivered. The rose-colored tips were wide and round, the nipples puckered in reaction not to the chill in the room but to his assault.

"Nay."

"Please," she begged.

He caught the urgency in her husky voice, but the urgency between his thighs took precedence. He pressed her back into the pillows. "One more time, my sweet dream princess." He sank his teeth into her creamy neck. She arched into him, her soft rose scent sending his senses reeling.

Her arms slid around his neck and Wulfson smiled

against her. He raised his head to look into her odd crystalline-colored eyes. They glittered with tears, making them sparkle like precious gems cast against the white beaches of Dover in the afternoon sunlight. Her breasts heaved in her disheveled state, but he knew there was more to it than that. She did not completely find his rutting distasteful. Nay, she fought some other demon; he was not the culprit.

"Do you fear me?" he softly questioned.

Vigorously she shook her head, no.

He pressed his lips to her bare shoulder and nibbled her soft skin. "Then why do you cry?"

"I—I know not."

He closed his eyes and pressed his nose to the soft place where her neck met her shoulder, and laved his teeth down the thick vein of her neck. "Stay here with me. I would not hurt you." His fingers trailed along her arms up to her shoulder, down her throat to the high swell of her breasts. He watched in silent wonder as her skin pebbled and her nipples hardened. He reached down to a nipple and suckled it. She moaned and moved beneath him.

In a slow movement, he rolled her over to her belly, even though she protested. "I will not harm you, princess. You will weep with pleasure." His hands swept down the delicate curve of her back. He scowled as he traced a fingertip down what appeared to be the scar of a lash. His finger traced it down to the ripe swell of her bottom. Several more faded scars crisscrossed the soft skin there. He pressed his lips to one full cheek.

Her hips pressed into the mattress and her muffled moan of pleasure encouraged him. In long sweeping caresses, his hands smoothed the scars. His lips trailed along her back.

He slid his arm under her belly and brought her up on her knees. He felt her body tremble. "Easy, princess," he whispered against her bottom. Her musky essence as he parted her thighs wafted up to him and he inhaled her deeply. 'Twas not a scent he would likely forget.

He pressed his lips there and she gasped, pulling away from him, turning over wide-eyed. " 'Tis not decent!" she cried.

He smiled and pressed her back into the pillows. "There is nothing indecent about a man loving all of a woman's body." He looked down at his burgeoning shaft, then speared her with his gaze. "Touch me as I have touched you."

She moved back deeper into the pillows until the headboard stopped her. Wulfson chuckled, finding her innocence a breath of sweet fresh air. He took her hand and pressed it to him. He sucked in a harsh breath at the sight of her delicate fingers wrapped around him. His eyes caught her surprised ones.

"You are warm." She squeezed, and had he not been on his knees her gesture would have brought him to them. "And soft."

He scoffed. She smiled. "Like velvet." He closed his eyes and pressed into her hand. Slowly she maneuvered her hand up and down, his hips following her movement. Soon he was on the verge of eruption when she stopped.

He opened his eyes, searching her face, and found only silent awe. "Do you still want me to leave you be?" he asked.

She rose up on her knees facing him. "Nay," she breathed, her soft breath tickling his lips. His blood quickened, and if it was possible he swelled even more in her hand. At that moment he could not remember ever having to exercise such rigid self-control. If she did not yield to him soon, he would not be able to keep himself from her. "There is time yet." She slid her lithe arms around his neck and pressed her body full against his. "I will not deny you what you seek. Take me."

Sliding his arm around her waist, he slung her around and into the pillows, where he followed, and sank his throbbing cock into her warm moist folds and nearly came that instant. Never had he had such an urge to mate as he did at that moment. She cried out, but he felt the quickening in her blood as he moved inside her. "Come with me this time," he murmured against her breast. He could not get enough of her sweetness. She was all things carnal. Her skin was as soft as silk, her fragrance that of roses in a spring shower, but her essence drove him mad. And the treasure between her thighs was tight, and hot, and pulled him incessantly down into the deep dark abyss that was pure paradise.

Seven

Wulfson woke to the thundering sound of Rolf filling the brazier with coal. "Cease that racket!" Wulfson hissed between clenched teeth. His head felt as if Turold stampeded through it, his mouth was as dry as the deserts in Africa, and his cock was swollen to painful. He grasped the throbbing member and flinched. He was full, but he was also tender.

He squeezed his eyes shut and remembered a vague dream of a princess coming to him in the night, offering herself to him not once but twice. He rubbed his aching head and swung his legs over the side of the bed, thinking the headache was worth the dream.

"Sir Wulfson?" Rolf asked quietly. "How may I attend you?"

Wulfson shook his head and waved the boy away. "Begone from me. I will see to myself as I did last eve."

The boy, nay, young man, reddened and shuffled his feet. "Milord, I—"

"Silence! Begone."

Never one to question his master's command, the squire was gone in a twinkling. Wulfson lay back on the bed and pressed his right hand over his eyes. The soft scent of a woman filtered beneath his nose. He opened his eyes, and despite the pounding of a thousand hammers in his head, he grinned. While he could not remember the details, he was no fool. The essence of a woman clung to his hand, and he grasped his cock again. Yes, definitely used. His other hand reached across the bed, smoothing across the rumpled linens to the pillow and grabbing it. He pressed it to his nose: a rose scent clung to it. His dream woman wasn't as immortal as she would lead him to believe.

"Milord?" Rolf called from the doorway. "Lord Alewith and his train have arrived."

Wulfson scowled and tossed the pillow to the bed. "Did you send a woman here last eve?"

Rolf's face crinkled in confusion. "Sir?"

"A woman, the opposite of a man, *did you send one to me last eve?*"

"Nay, sir."

"Did my brothers?"

"Not that I am aware, sir. They saw to their pallets directly after the meal."

Confusion reigned in his head. This place was casting spells on him. He dismissed the notion. "Fetch me hot water, and send Rorick to entertain them until I descend."

Rolf bobbed his head and hurried to his chores.

Used to mustering under the direst of conditions, Wulfson took his time. He had given Lady Tarian enough time to recover. He'd waited a fortnight for this day. Now, she could await him, for he would not appear anxious. But as he tried, he continually found himself biting at the bit to go below, and with an anticipation that likened to the thrill of battle he felt the same sensation in his eagerness to come face to face with the enigma that had haunted him these last fourteen days. Strapping his sword belt around his waist, and his double scabbard across his back, then securing it at his chest, he strode from the room, wanting to get the meeting over and done with. The English were a sullen lot who would just as soon cut him where he stood as wait until he found slumber to stab him and his men in the back. He would welcome the sunny shores of Normandy over this moldy wet blanket of an island any day.

As he strode down the narrow passageway between the few chambers above the hall, Wulfson caught Gareth's tall form hovering outside the lady's chamber. Thorin stood stoically across from the guard, and nodded his head, his hand resting comfortably on the hilt of his great sword. His huge Viking ax rested snugly against his other hip. Wulf snorted in admiration. He'd seen heads fly off shoulders after meeting the great ax Thorin called Beowulf. 'Twas a fitting name.

"Heed my call, Captain. See your lady downstairs with no delay."

Gareth stared unmoving at Wulfson. "Do I have your word no harm will come to her?"

"Nay," Wulfson said, continuing down the hall and the circular stairway that led to the great hall. "You do not."

A great group of people milled about there. His Blood Swords, along with Rangor, the lord's cronies, several villagers, and the constant ebb and flow of servants. Through it all Wulfson could see not only a tall, noble Saxon who carried on a rather heated conversation with Rangor, but a young noblewoman of no more than ten and six, her long golden hair barely concealed beneath her snood. His blood warmed. For she did not wear her clothing in the bulky unflattering fashion of the women of this place but cut a more fashionable figure, like the noblewomen in Normandy, with her formfitting kirtle.

A roar from his men went up as he descended the last step, and Wulfson grinned. He had a sudden hunger for sustenance. He grinned wider and rubbed his hand across his chest, feeling the odd sensation from the scar, vestige of so many years ago when that Saracen devil seared his sword into his chest. The burn he would never forget, and the scar was a constant reminder to him to always be prepared. All eyes turned to him as he strode arrogantly into the hall. His men, as he himself, were always dressed for battle. Leisure time in courtly garb was not part of their hard life. He and his brothers, they were always ready to mount and seek out the enemy, and he was not blind to the fact that there was far more treachery afoot within the ancient halls of Draceadon this day than on any battlefield. So be it. He was prepared.

Rangor stepped forward, a snide smile twisting his lips. "Sir Wulfson, I see the accommodations serve you well."

"Well enough." He turned to the tall, elegantly dressed Saxon. He nodded to the man, who, while dressed in finery and holding himself in a most regal way, also bore the wary eye of a soldier.

He bowed to Wulfson as Rangor made the introduction. "May I present Lord Alewith of Turnsly, Marlow, and Sharpsbury, and recent guardian of the widowed Lady Tarian, and his daughter the Lady Brighid."

Wulfson nodded. "My lord, why have you come this day?"

The older man's face reddened, but he did not stumble on his words. "I have come to take my ward home."

Wulfson smiled, a gesture not meant to endear. The

golden-haired girl, Brighid, caught her breath and brought her hand to her mouth as their gazes clashed. "The lady will not be leaving Draceadon."

The girl gasped. "But you *must* allow Tarian to come home!"

"Shush, girl," Alewith admonished. He raised pleading gray eyes to Wulfson. "My pardon, my daughter forgets herself."

Wulfson shrugged, and realized the girl was younger than he first suspected. And while some men might have no qualms about sharing a pallet with a child, he was not among them.

Once he set the girl aside, the noble faced him fully. Wulfson watched him muster his nerve. "I am afraid I cannot accept your response. Tarian belongs with her family. I insist you allow her to return with me."

Wulfson swept past him to sit at the lord's table. "I have a great hunger this morn, Lord Alewith." Wulfson swept his hand to encompass his men, who sat with him at the high lord's table. "Please, sit and sup, so that we can discuss the matter of your former ward."

Alewith turned a jaundiced eye upon Wulfson, then upon Rangor, who nodded. Brighid was seated alongside Rhys, her father and uncle flanking her other side.

As the meal was laid out with haste, Wulfson nodded, and speared a chunk of coddled egg from a bowl with his table knife. As he was about to take a bite, a loud cough from the table below the lord's table halted him. He lowered a stare to Father Dudley, a most annoying man who reminded him of a terrier, constantly yapping at his heels. He had made repeated pleas for the release of Lady Tarian; Wulfson turned a deaf ear to the man each time.

Wulfson lowered his knife and his head, though he was still able to watch all that transpired before him in the room. He smiled to himself and saw that the Blood Swords did the same. Once the prayer was said, the men dug in with gusto. As he slowly chewed, Wulfson watched his guests from beneath lowered lids. He washed the egg down with a goblet of milk and asked, "How is it, my lord, that you and Rangor appear to be the epitome of health, when most of England's nobility fell at Hastings, and its survivors still show the ravaged signs of war?"

Alewith choked on the piece of meat he had just swallowed. He sputtered as his daughter pounded him on the back. He raised a hand to stay her assault while he collected his breath. Wulfson noted once again the richness of his garments and the rings he wore. While he was not overdressed in the way Rangor seemed to enjoy, the noble wore just enough not to be called a popinjay. The man's dark gray eyes held shrewd experience behind them, and he was, Wulfson decided, more dangerous than Lerwick, who wore his emotions on his tunic sleeve like a woman.

The latter scowled but did not reply, waiting instead for Alewith to take the bait. Which he promptly did. Sitting up straight, the Saxon smiled sourly. "Sir Wulfson, I can assure you that I fought as hard and as long as my fallen countrymen. That I escaped death is a testament not only to my own skill with an ax and sword but to the loyalty of the men surrounding me; but if you must know the absolute truth, the young lady who I have come to take home had my back throughout the day. A more fearsome warrior I could not ask for."

Wulfson scoffed and was glad he had not taken a bite of the braised meat on his knife tip. His men chortled. "Do you mean to say, Saxon, that that scrap of a woman we found on her deathbed in the bowels of this hovel held a sword against William at Hastings?" Rorick incredulously asked.

"And before that, Stamford Bridge!" Brighid sparked, coming to her feet. Alewith tossed an indulgent smile at the girl, but quickly pulled her back to her sitting position before shooting her a warning glare.

Wulfson grinned and rubbed his chest. "She no doubt met up with those cowardly Bretons! An old woman with a raised broom could have shooed them off." The men from Brittany had returned home in disgrace for their cowardice on the battlefield.

Alewith smiled and nodded. He looked like the fox that had just raided the henhouse. "Since I know not if we are to become friend or foe, I will refrain from extolling my ward's prowess with not only a longbow but her own good sword."

Wulfson snorted and bit off another hunk of meat and chewed. He glanced across the table to his men, who all sported the same mocking gloat he felt. " 'Twould explain why Harold ultimately fell."

Alewith stiffened and leaned across his daughter to speak directly at Wulfson. "He was a mighty warrior and the favorite of the people. He was a man all of England respected."

Wulfson stood, drawing one of the swords from his double back scabbard with both hands. He raised it high amongst the screams of the women and the cold stares of the men, then hurled it across the room, where it landed with a sharp thunk in the wood support beam behind the sapphire-and-gold dragon standard hanging above the great hearth. The velocity of the impact tore the fabric in half. "Harold is dead, and William is king!" Wulfson stormed. "I will hear no more mewling about what a noble man your usurper was. I was there when he swore to my king he would uphold Edward's oath to William for the throne of England. He broke his oath, and any man, great earl or not, who breaks his oath is no man in my eyes!"

"Wouldst you not make an oath if a sword were pressed firmly to *your* throat as well as those of your brother and nephew?" a husky female voice said from behind him. The hall went tomb silent, and the hair on the back of Wulfson's neck rose. So did his cock.

"Tarian!" Brighid cried, but her father grabbed her arm before the girl could run to the woman who, Wulfson knew at that moment, was going to test his mettle as it had never been tested before.

Slowly he turned, as did all the Blood Swords. When he faced her, the sharp intake of breath from his men whisked past him, and even that of her guardian, but loudest was the strangled cry that came from Rangor. The sound was a mixture of admiration, dread, and unrequited lust.

Wulfson's glare caught hers across the room, and for one brief space of time, his heart did not beat.

She was, in a single word—enchanting. Like no other woman he had ever laid eyes upon. And, he noted with a dry smile, not dressed as a young widow should be. Her long ebony hair hung in thick, rippled waves around her shoulders and down to her softly flared hips. Blue, crimson, and yellow ribbons were braided into two long strands that ran down the side of her face. And *Jesu*, what a visage. Finely arched brows framed brilliant sapphire-colored eyes that at the moment snapped with irritation, and, he realized, with a passion few men could match. His cock flexed. Her nose was smallish and pert. Her wine-colored lips were full, the top one reminiscent of a cupid's bow, the bottom, even tight as it was now, pouty.

His eyes dropped. She wore a rich embroidered blue woolen and linen kirtle over a soft sea-green undertunic. The bodice was laced tight, the fabric taut across full round breasts. Around her slender waist hung a thick embroidered leather belt, from which hung a sheathed broadsword. Thick gold and silver bracelets encircled her arms, from her wrists to just below the elbow. While they were ornate, they were also thick, and, he suspected, a worthy shield to the delicate skin beneath. Her left hand fondled the leather-wrapped hilt of her weapon, which he could tell even at the distance between them was a prime piece of weaponry. The Saxons were renowned armorers.

Wulfson smiled leisurely, his blood coursing wildly through his veins. The familiar excitement swirled in his belly, much as it did when he faced the enemy. He longed to see just how expert a swordswoman she was before he spread her on the nearest pallet. But he checked the urge. Not only was she a noblewoman, but she was a marked one.

His eyes moved past her to Gareth and Thorin, who stood behind her, both watching him closely. Wulfson's smile widened. The fortnight-long wait had been worth this magnificent sight.

He bowed, and said softly, "An oath is an oath, Lady Tarian."

She smiled and curtsyed. "I will remember that well, my lord knight." She looked past him; to Rangor, he was sure. "Would you give your oath to see my home rid of the scourge that would have me rest so soon beside my dearly departed husband?"

Wulfson stepped forward, and as he came closer to her, his eyes traversed her face and form. His body warmed more the closer he came to her, and a sudden sense of familiarity stung him. He halted next to her and cocked his head, his eyes taking in every aspect of her. Even her voice sounded familiar. He smiled slowly, and watched a soft flush of pink tinge her cheeks.

Making a short bow, Wulfson huskily introduced himself. "I am Wulfson of Trevelyn."

She made a shallow curtsy. Wry amusement twisted her full lips. "I am Lady Tarian of Dunloc."

"So I have heard." He stood staring down at her, unable to comprehend her beauty and the air of sensuality that was as much a part of her as those remarkable eyes. "My lady?" He extended his arm as a noble would to his lady. Tarian's eyes narrowed, but she reached out and placed a firm hand on his arm. He drew her around and as they walked to the lord's table, Wulfson asked, "Now, tell me, of which scourge do you speak?"

As he set her down in the space beside him, Tarian forced back a shiver. The potion had been potent, but he suspected. She saw the spark of recognition in his deep green eyes. Panic sprang up out of nowhere, seizing her belly and twisting it. But she calmed herself and played it out. What panicked her more was her unexpected reaction to him, so strong in the light of day. Her body warmed the instant he turned those brilliant eyes of his upon her, and the way he raked her with those eyes made her feel as if she stood naked before him. She knew well what crossed his mind. Her cheeks warmed again. The same thought crossed hers. She'd held her breath, watching him closely for the slightest sign of recognition of her, and when she heard his question she held her breath again. He seemed, though, to second-guess himself. Which was well. She could not afford for him to rethink.

"Why, sir knight, you of all people should know of whom I speak," Tarian said sweetly.

Wulfson grinned; his teeth were white and straight. "Let us see how the day plays out before I give my oath."

The knight took the seat beside her, and as he reached for his table knife he paused and looked at her through surprised eyes. His nostrils flared, and for a moment she thought he had caught her perfume. But she had prepared well. Last night's rose scent was not her usual, the honey-violet scent she wore now. She prayed he would not recognize her.

She raised a brow. "Sir? Do you sniff your prey like a wolf before you slay it?" The low noise at the table quieted at her words. Tarian stared up at him, her look fierce. "I would know now your plans for me."

Wulfson grabbed his knife from the table where it stuck in the wood. He brought it close to his chest and turned the sharpened tip toward her. Her breath caught in her throat but she did not dare move. In a light caress, he placed the flat side of the tip to the bend of her jaw; then slowly he drew the blade down to her throat and lower still to the full swell of her breasts. Tarian sat rigid, yet oddly warm. Did he mean to do the deed here? Now? Gareth might die trying to save her, but her captain and her men, who had all turned at her entrance, were seasoned warriors and well weaponed. More than her head alone would roll if she were murdered. Would the Norman sacrifice a few of his men to do the deed now, in public, when he could bide his time and spare the lives of many?

She breathed in a deep breath; the blade pinched her soft skin. Her gaze caught his, and she was not sure what she read in those emerald depths. Fire, to be sure, but was it the fire of the chase, the anticipation of total domination over one's prey? Or was there more to it then that? For he was a hunter of the most violent kind, and she knew all too well that his passion was as fierce as his fighting skills—for which he and his men were renowned.

Long seconds dragged out; she did not so much as flinch. Instead, she pressed herself into the blade. "If you have come to see me planted beside my husband, do it now and save us all the anxiety of the hunt."

His lips quirked. "You do me grave injustice, Lady Tarian."

She cocked a brow in question.

"You have given up the chase before it has really begun. I would think a warrior of your ilk would be champing at the bit to prove herself."

Tarian smiled, and pressed her hand to his thigh. He hissed in a breath. "Oh, but sir knight, that is where you are most incorrect. I have been engaged since the day I was born."

His eyes narrowed as if mayhap he realized he was not the one in control. She took advantage, and pressed more firmly against the blade tip.

Though his hand held steady, moving neither forward nor away from her, when the tip broke the sensitive skin on the swell of her breast from the pressure she exerted, Lord Alewith slammed his fists down on the trestle top. "Enough! Do not harm her! She is my ward and I would see her safely back to Turnsly."

Wulfson looked past Tarian to the man who had raised her. She slid her hand down his forearm to rest upon his fist that held the knife. It was the same knife he had pressed to her throat last night. Wulfson's nostrils flared, and the entire hall watched with bated breath his next move. She felt more than saw Gareth off to her right, and she knew that unless she gave him the signal he would not impede her strategy. He had learned many years ago that what might look like a foolish deed was often well planned, and the wiles of a woman could do more damage to an unsuspecting foe than any blade.

But Sir Wulfson of Trevelyn was not any such man. His eyes caught hers, and he cocked a dark brow. In her gut, she knew he was there to dispose of her; why, exactly, she was not sure, but if she gave him the lead he would take full advantage of it. "I am lady here, and as such I have the right to know what business your king has with Dunloc."

"I am here to see to your welfare—among other things."

She moved away from him and turned back to the trencher she was to share with him. "I am well, as you can see. Please leave, and take that scourge Rangor with you."

Wulfson shook his head and stabbed a chunk of meat from the bowl of pottage. As he chewed, he looked at her, his eyes ravishing every inch of her. He was beyond bold. His arrogance was unsurpassed, and when she looked up and down the trestle top she recognized he was but the twin image of his men. She nearly snorted in contempt, and felt disgraced that she had sought a Norman's bed. Despite her impression of him in the light of day, she had relished him last eve. When she had slipped from the bed, she felt a sense of loss she could not put a name to. When she made it back to her room, Edith sat in her chair with her distaff in her hands, a pile of wool in her lap and a knowing smile lighting up her face.

Tarian awakened several times in the night to the illusion of hot lips and strong hands stroking her body. Frustrated by her passion for the Norman, she admitted she wanted to experience it again. For it had been nothing like any encounter in her life. Yet she felt that there was more to it. Her body ached and she knew not how to ease it. Instinctively, she knew the answer to lie with the knight down the hall. Each time she flung the covers from her and sat up in the bed, her pulse racing and her breaths heavy, Edith looked on, that smug smile still plastered across her face. Tarian threw her pillows at the old woman and commanded her to cease looking and see to her pallet.

This morn, she could not look her nurse in the eye, and dressed with amazing speed, nearly bolting from the room into Gareth's chest.

Her body warmed. And despite her frustration, she cast the dark knight a sideways glare from beneath her lashes, and could not deny that he was a most remarkable specimen of a man.

Eight

Her earlier hunger was overrun with anxiety and excitement, and Tarian only picked at her meal. The Normans devoured every morsel in sight. Whilst they dined, Tarian decided to leave the argument that was to come, to after the breaking of the fast. She wanted to be mobile, not seated between two hulking Normans with her men out of reach. She would plead her case and see to it that Rangor and Alewith returned to their respective manors.

She was not a woman who needed a man's protection, not even from these Normans.

"How came you to learn our tongue?" Tarian casually asked Wulfson.

"My mother was Saxon. I spent time in Dover with her brother as a young lad."

"Why not with your dam?"

Wulfson scowled a warning. Tarian immediately understood and retreated. Byblow that she was herself, she could well understand a mother's scorn for an unholy child.

"Are you with child?" Rangor blurted out from down the table. Tarian stiffened, as did the knights flanking her.

Heat rose in Tarian's cheeks. Heat not of embarrassment, but of indignation. He had no right to ask her such a question. But when she looked to Alewith for support, she saw only quiet questioning in his eyes. She swallowed the lump of bread she had just chewed and straightened.

"Time will tell."

Rangor stood and turned to peer down the trestle top to her. "If there is no heir, then you have no claim here."

More than irritated at his relentless demands, Tarian stood as well. She would put his incessant claims to rest once and for all. "I have claim here because Malcor gave me all in his will."

"A fraudulent document, no doubt! He would never leave his estates to a woman!"

"Where is the document, Lady Tarian?" Wulfson asked as he too stood.

She looked up at him and glared. "In a safe place where no devious hands can touch it."

Wulfson nodded, but pressed. "I would see it."

Tarian cocked a brow. "You can read?"

Wulfson nodded. "Well enough." He returned a cocked brow. "And you?"

"Better than well. 'Twas the only way the monks at Turns Abbey could keep me from causing more disturbances."

Satisfied with her answer, Wulfson looked past her to Rangor. "The document will be produced and examined for its validity. My decision will be final."

Rangor came around from the men and approached, a long sniveling sneer twisting his thin lips. "Even if the document proves authentic, if there is no heir, by our law she must relinquish the earldom, and the lands and title that go with it, to the next living male in the line. I am that male. The *only* one."

Alewith stood as well, and moved around to stand beside Tarian. He took her cold hands into his. Before he could utter a word, Rangor strode closer demanding, "It has been a month since Malcor's death. Have you missed your courses?"

Tarian's cheeks flamed. Every man, woman, and child in the hall waited for her answer.

"Rangor!" Alewith hissed. "Mind your manners!"

Sword drawn, Wulfson extended his arm, the razor-sharp tip of the blade pointed at Rangor's heart. The Saxon slowed to a halt several steps from Tarian. Wulfson's men slowly stood, surrounding the belligerent Saxon and drawing their swords as well. Tarian's heart beat high in her throat at the deadly display. Her gaze rose to catch Gareth's, and she read his respect and awe for these knights of William.

"Since the conquest, there is no room here for courtly manners, Alewith," Rangor sneered. "We hang onto our land by our fingernails." He turned back to Tarian. "Answer me!"

Tarian remained silent, her face set.

"Tell us, child," Alewith urged softly.

For him, a man who had been more generous than he needed to be, despite the small fortune that was entrusted to him for the royal byblow, Tarian could never deny Alewith anything. Slowly she shook her head, and lied. "Nay, sir, I have not."

Rangor threw his hands up and spun halfway away from them. His narrow shoulders hunched over, he seemed to be deep in thought. Then he straightened and whirled around. "It matters not. The midwife explained how inconsistent a woman can be, especially with strife swirling about. There is still time."

"I see no significance either way, Rangor," Alewith said, "I have no reason to doubt Tarian and the validity of the will." He looked up at Wulfson, who still held his sword extended toward Rangor. "Does William uphold our laws and customs, or is he bent on destroying those as well?"

"William is a fair man. He is also loyal to those who are loyal to him."

Alewith, Rangor, and Tarian stood slack-jawed at the absurd statement. Tarian turned on him. "How can you say such a thing? He killed our king and most of the nobility and untold freemen of this nation. Harold's brothers, my uncles, along with many of my cousins, fell that day. Your duke had no right to come here: the Witan voted unanimous that Harold should be king!"

Wulfson sheathed his sword—an insult in light of the heated conversation. "William was promised the throne by Edward. That is as binding as a will." Wulfson's eyes narrowed. "How would you feel, my lady, should we all at this moment vote to give Rangor this place? Does it make it his? Or does the last will and testament of the former lord hold sway?"

" 'Tis not the same," Tarian defended.

"It is the same, and if you will not do what is best for you"—he looked up and sneered at Rangor—"nor what is best for your illustrious uncle, I am here to see to William's interests, and so to that end, it will be those that will be best served."

"I will not be a pawn in any man's game, not even a king's!"

Wulfson leaned toward her and warned, "The game has

just begun, my lady, and do not for one moment think I crossed that miserable Channel and wore down the hooves of my horse for naught."

"I will not be forced from my home!"

"That is yet to be determined, but—" His eyes narrowed and a small smile twisted his cruel lips. "If you are with child, your chances of surviving here may improve. If you are not, then seek a husband immediately, for you will need one."

"I have made a bid for her hand," Rangor said, stepping forward. Tarian could barely swallow. It had taken every shred of willpower and guts she had to bed with the Norman, but Rangor of Lerwick? His wet lips, pale eyes, pockmarked face, and clammy white skin made him as undesirable to bed as a slippery eel. She would go to the convent before she would lie with him.

"I have told you, I am not interested in marriage with you." Her eyes narrowed and she fondled the hilt of her sword. "Will you trick me again, Rangor, and throw me down the steps to the dungeon now?"

His face paled to the shade of curdled cream. "Coward," Alewith hissed. "I did not believe the messenger when he told me such a tale."

"I meant her no harm. 'Twas only a way to turn her to my wishes," Rangor defended.

"I would have died before bedding with the likes of you, Rangor," Tarian spat.

Rangor's pale eyes iced. "You are *nithing*, as was your sire. No man will have you!"

Tarian gasped and slapped the Saxon lord. Rangor grabbed her hand and yanked her hard away from the Norman. He turned her around and moved to draw his sword.

But Wulfson anticipated the move. With lightning speed, he reached past Tarian and clasped the lord around his throat with both hands. Shaking him loose from Tarian, he lifted Rangor clear off the floor. Rangor's men came together but the Normans held them back.

"You sorely try my patience, Saxon," Wulfson gritted.

Gareth strode angrily toward them, his hand on his sword, his face red and blustery. "*You* are *nithing*, Rangor," Gareth seethed, "Say that word again to my lady and I will slit your throat from ear to ear."

Rangor's pale eyes bulged out of his head, his feet kicked, his hands frantically grasped at Wulfson's locked around his neck. He made pitiful noises as Wulfson continued to hold him in the air. Wulfson's knuckles whitened as they closed tighter around the noble's neck, and sharp wheezing sounds erupted from the closed throat.

Tarian, along with every other person in the hall, stood in silent awe. The Norman's great strength and his indifference to the life he was snuffing out was as terrifying as it was shocking.

As a warrior, Tarian recognized a mortal enemy when she saw one, and she knew in her gut that Rangor would go to the ends of the earth to posses Dunloc and her. In that, she should keep silent and let nature take its course; or, as in this case, let the Norman do what Normans do best: kill. But she was also a woman who saw the consequences that would follow in the wake of Rangor's murder. His Welsh relatives would not only hold the Norman accountable, but word would spread that she'd done nothing to stop it, and therefore she would be an accomplice. And that she could not have. She needed her allies to the west if she were to have any leverage against Norman usurpation.

The choice to save Rangor's life was not made because she was a woman and a nurturer; it was made because she was a woman and a warrior who had no qualms about playing both sides against the middle to hold what was hers by marriage.

When Rangor's body went limp in the Norman's hands, Tarian stepped forward and pressed her hand to Wulfson's. "Please, sir knight, spare him."

Wulfson's piercing gaze speared her. "I will give you my oath that should I allow him to live this day, he will be a constant source of irritation to us both."

Tarian nodded, and pushed against his hand to lower Rangor. "I can handle him." She smiled at the fearsome knight. "Can you?"

Wulfson's hands opened and Rangor fell to the floor with a dull thud. Tarian calmly regarded the Norman. His cool gaze and deadly energy sent a chill of fear along the back of her neck and down her spine. When the time came for this man to snuff out her life, he would do it as easily and as indifferently as if he were flicking a flea off his hand.

Ignoring Rangor's gasping form on the floor, she looked over the gathered throng for Rangor's manservant, but did not see him. Instead, the whiny Ruin, her late husband's revolting manservant, hung back like the coward he was behind several other servants. "Ruin, get your carcass over here and see to Lord Rangor." Tarian looked up at Wulfson and curtsyed. "I have been abed too long, and seek fresh air. If it is permissible, I would see to my horse and exercise him."

Wulfson stared down at her for a long moment before he extended his arm. "Allow me to escort you."

Tarian cocked a brow. "Do you not really mean, allow you to walk with me as my jailer?"

He shrugged his great shoulders and smiled a twisted half-smile. "It matters not how you interpret my offer. It stands as it is. Should you refuse, you will while away the hours this day in this smoky hall. The choice is yours."

She nodded her head ever so slightly, and said, "'Tis obvious your mother did not raise you. You have the manners of a boar."

The color blanched from his face and his lips pulled tight into a harsh line. "'Tis more than I can say for your sire, Lady Tarian."

She curbed the impulse to slap him as she had slapped Rangor. She did not doubt she would suffer brutally at his hand, and while her mettle was strong, she could not bear the humiliation he would cause her in front of her people. She trod on a winter pond where the ice was parchment-thin, and if she made one false move she might find herself drowning in its icy depths.

"Touché, my lord knight. Never was there a more loving pair than your dam and my sire. May they rest in peace."

Wulfson cocked a brow. "I never said my dam lived or died."

Placing her hand back upon his brawny forearm, she softly said, "I could see she was dead to you in your eyes. Whether she is actually in the ground or buried in your heart, she will glean no love from her son."

Her response did not require an answer, and he offered none. She turned then to face the still stunned crowd. Her eyes touched on Alewith, then on the silent but ever alert Brighid, and finally on her guard, whom she warned off with her gaze. She would test the Norman waters on her terms, and with no intrusion.

"Should I not return in a reasonable amount of time,

Gareth, alert the Welsh—and Rangor, should he come to." While her voice held a serious note, her lips quirked into a small smile when she looked up at the arrogant knight. He stared down at her, a spark of amusement in his dark eyes. If she could not overpower him with sheer force, she would wheedle her way in with guile. She cocked her head toward the great double doors. "Shall we?"

He moved her through the throng that parted like the Red Sea.

Nine

"Hlow is it, Lady Tarian, you came to wield a sword?" Wulfson asked as they came upon the vast stables. They were, Wulfson had noted admiringly from the first day, in better condition than the hall. It was obvious the former lord had a solid eye for horseflesh. The few fleet mares were of fine desert bloodlines. Wulfson thought in passing how well the blood would blend with that of Turold, a great warhorse of Spanish heritage.

He noted the way Tarian's body went from the slow fluid stride they enjoyed as they left the hall to her abrupt rigidity when he posed the question.

"When one is born the daughter of a great earl by way of the rape of an abbess, one not only does not have God on her side, but she does not have the support of the royal line either. There are three recourses for a woman such as myself. Find a husband, which in my case took all of my twoscore years to locate, because despite my pedigree, the curse comes with me, and even with a king's ransom I could snare only the most undesirable of spouses. My next option was the convent, when in this case looks at me as the devil's own spawn and has made it very clear my unholy presence is not welcome within its holy walls; so lastly, I have done what I have done—armed myself with knowledge and a sword. Used what I have to stay alive." She glanced up at him and said, "It is all about surviving, no?"

He nodded, impressed. "Aye."

As they entered the long structure they were met with the low nickers of the horses. The odd little man, Abner, who was the stablemaster, scurried forward and bobbed to Tarian and Wulfson. "My lord, my lady?"

"Saddle my black and the lady's gray."

Tarian glanced up at Wulfson curiously; he returned the look. "I have admired your stallion's depth of muscle and Spanish bloodlines. His only vice is his fondness to bite any hand that reaches in to scratch him."

Tarian grinned. "He is not mean, only discriminating."

Wulfson grunted. "He has been ridden by a woman too long." Tarian's head snapped back, but he flashed her a mesmerizing smile and moved closer to her. "He needs to be ridden by a man to break that ugly streak."

He checked himself, fighting the urge to take her into his arms. She was as lethal as any plague and a noblewoman to boot. But—he caught a whiff of her violet scent—she made it incredibly difficult to resist. . . .

Heat swirled between them, and as much as Tarian wanted to ignore the man's pull, she could not. He was as hot-blooded as her stallion, and the image of her riding the man, not the horse, warmed her. "A hand that breaks is a hand that will never earn trust."

He raised his hand and trailed his knuckles along her

cheek, and softly said, "I would never be such a fool as to break a high-strung creature. The ride would lose its appeal."

Tarian could feel the hard thump of her heart against her chest. It was the same feeling she had had when she stepped onto the battlefield in York against the Vikings, the same exhilarating feeling she had had fighting so close to Harold at Hastings. She rose to the challenge of her enemy, for that was what this man was.

She raised her hand to his cheek, mimicking his gesture, smiling when he flinched. "The stallion shies from the mare?"

He grabbed her hand and opened her palm. He pressed the sensitive skin there to his lips, and, as a stallion would when he mounted a mare, he bit her. She gasped, but instead of shying from him she pressed her palm more firmly into his teeth. Heat sprang up from her thighs to her breasts, and that tingling sensation he had evoked from her body the night past returned. She felt the flicker of her nostrils. Parting her lips, she tilted her head back, exposing the soft skin of her neck, and Wulfson took the bait. He growled low, yanked her hard against him, and sank his teeth into the flesh there. The shock of his touch and the ferocity of it stunned her. Her knees trembled and she felt as if they had turned to soggy willows. He pulled her harder against him to keep her from crumpling at his feet.

His other hand dug into her hair and he pulled her head back, forcing her to expose more of her throat. His lips were searing, his tongue laved her jugular, and she quite honestly thought she would go up in a puff of smoke, her body was so hot. "You, my lady, are a most shameless widow."

She laughed at his words. Tarian had never cleaved to

the rules of society. Why should she, when that same society cast her out as if she were marked with the pox? Breathless, she hung in his arms, not wanting to be the one to retreat. She would match this warrior of William's step for step, gesture for gesture, and if the time came for her to defend her life against him, she would have no hesitation to draw her sword and fight to the death of one of them.

He raised his head from her, his lips swollen from his assault. Her breasts felt heavy and the churning feeling in her belly would not subside. His eyes had darkened, and he caught her with their intensity. "An oath you want and an oath I'll give. Use your wiles as you will, Lady Tarian, and I will gladly take what you so boldly offer. But my loyalty is to my king first, my men of the Blood Sword second, my horse and own sword third."

She laughed again, hoping the sound hid her trepidation. He would see to her death as sure as they were both standing there, regardless of his lust for her. "What is it you think I offer?"

His hand slid from her hair to her neck, then lower, to rest on her left breast. Her heart leapt at the intimate touch. He smiled and rubbed his thumb across the puckered fabric beneath. "This."

She slowly shook her head and stepped back from him. "Never that."

"You lie."

"Nay, I do not. I am a Saxon noblewoman. My uncle was king of this great land, my ancestors kings and queens. I would never lie with a common soldier, and a Norman one least of all."

Wulfson's eyes narrowed, but he nodded. "I think mayhap 'tis *you* who may be in denial."

"My lord and my lady!" Abner called as he led both destriers into the open area where they stood. "Your mounts are ready."

Wulfson threw his head back, and his laughter rang to the rafters. Abner stood unsure and looked to his lady for guidance. " 'Tis not of concern, Abner, the Norman is addled."

The groom assisted her to mount, and it bothered Tarian that he should. But she had no choice. She was not of tall-enough stature that she could reach the high stirrup of Silversmith's saddle. When she was mail-clad, an assist was even more necessary. She scowled at Wulfson, who despite the greater size of his stallion over hers, and his great height and mail-clad weight, effortlessly mounted the black. His green eyes danced in glee. "We will not go far without a guard, and I without my helm."

When Tarian mounted, the pale skin of her thighs was exposed above the linen chauses she tied just below her knees. Wulfson's brows shot up. "Would you repeat what Godiva, the former lady of Mercia, was so fondly remembered for?"

Tarian bristled. "This is not Coventry, and whilst I protest your presence, I will do it clad. If you have such a problem with my attire and exposure of skin, do not look."

He urged his mount forward. "I have no such aversion, but you may find yourself the recipient of unwanted attention."

She grasped the reins with one hand and fondled the hilt of her sword with the other. "I have no aversion to using this trusted blade to quell a knave's insult."

Wulfson laughed again, and his parting shot ranked her beyond her boundary. "Methinks you are but a hissing kitten with only sharp claws to do her bidding. You will find we Norman dogs digest kittens to break the fast."

She laughed at the image. "If a king had faith in my ability, so should you."

Wulfson shook his head. "Harold must have been desperate."

She frowned. "You continue to insult me."

He turned and looked at her with a cocked brow and an expression that belied her words.

"I will admit, at first my uncle was greatly amused by my claim. But he soon came around when one of his huscarls took liberties with my person, and I set him straight with my sword." Wulfson's expression did not change. He did not believe her. "Do not underestimate me, sir knight. It will be your undoing."

He smiled and nodded. "Consider your dire warning heeded."

Wulfson scanned the quiet countryside. He was not comfortable riding without his men, but he would not show his concern to the woman who rode like a man beside him. The movement of the saddle against his groin was becoming a hindrance. He grumbled, and the sound was not lost on the lady.

"Does some injury pain you?" she glibly asked. Her eyes danced with glee, and he knew at that moment she was on to him. He grinned. She intrigued him more than any one person had in his lifetime. She was a lady, true; her manners, speech, schooling, and bloodline screamed it. But she was as exotic and saucy as the spiced meats he had grown to relish during his time in Iberia, before his capture and torture. After their narrow escape, he and his fellow Blood Swords had made haste from that ungodly land to Normandy, where they had serendipitously met up with William.

"Tell, me, sir knight," Tarian chirped, "are all men guided by the sword between their legs over the sword in their hands?"

Wulfson coughed at her audacious question, but he answered truthfully. "For some, the demon between a man's legs makes all of his decisions. But for others, such as myself, and my fellow Blood Swords, while we pay heed to it, it does not govern our actions or our decisions."

"Why do you go by the name of Blood Sword?"

Wulfson stiffened at the question. He was not a man who made much conversation, yet he found himself enjoying his parlance with the widow. But he had never shared his horrific experience with another living soul except with the eight men who survived it with him. " 'Tis a name given to a knight who earns his living by the sword."

She peered at him and seemed to be satisfied with the answer. As they descended along the well-worn road from Draceadon to the rest of the world, the thick copse of trees outlining the forest, the clouds seemed to have darkened threefold. Wulfson cast an eye skyward. "Does it always rain in this place?"

She nodded, and as the road forked Tarian gave the gray his head. They sprinted past Wulfson, who cursed. She shook her head, her long dark hair following her like a dark shield. Wulfson spurred the destrier and the chase was on.

Much to his frustration, he could not catch up. The gray, though a destrier, was lighter and fleeter of foot than his great black. The beast was also not bogged down with mail, and the lady's weight was that of a mite. When he thundered around a sharp bend in the road, he swore out loud. For the next half-league he could see down it, and Tarian was nowhere in sight. He had been duped! He had fallen for her guile! Rage infiltrated every inch of him. He would not fail his king!

He pulled up Turold, his mind quickly assessing the situation. If she were ahead, she would be in sight. Since she was not, she must have turned off the road soon after she made its sharp bend. He backed up to where the road turned out and cast his gaze to the ground. The turf was still moist with the last rain and though well traveled, the fresh churn of four large shod hooves darkened it. He looked into the thick copse of trees where the tracks led, and decided that if she could make it through the forest, so could he. And when he got his hands on her he would throttle her and end this futile charade. He smiled grimly. But not before he did what he had wanted to do to her from the moment he laid eyes on her that morn.

Turold burst through the low bramble and maneuvered through the English oak and ash trees. While the forest was thick, it was not as nonnegotiable as he had first thought. Her trail was clear, and so long as he had light and determination he would find her. As he drew deeper into the wood, he reined up Turold and listened. First only the twittering of the birds overhead disturbed the heaviness of the air, then rustles amongst the thickets as small inhabitants scurried to escape some intruder. Then voices. Welsh. Dead ahead, and coming closer. As he sat silent and bent his ear toward them trying to decipher what was said, the sharp hiss of an arrow passed so near to his right ear it nicked the outer tip before finding a home in the oak behind him. He drew his sword, deftly turning toward the direction of the assault, cursing himself again for riding out with no helm or accompaniment.

Soft laughter filtered from the direction of the arrow.

"How is that for a kitten? Sir knight?" the soft husky voice that gave him gooseflesh called to him. His eyes narrowed, and Tarian materialized from the forest, bow in hand, maybe thirty steps ahead of him. Directly across from the voices that continued to come closer.

He put his finger to his lips, drawing her caution. She cocked her head and heard them as well. Instead of the look of stricken panic he would expect from a woman, Tarian smiled and drew another arrow. The soft breeze blew her long hair from her face, exposing the high noble cheekbones, and while she had the honed look of a predator, her femininity was undeniable. And the way she sat half barelegged astride her destrier made a man's mind wander with thoughts of her straddling him thusly. Wulfson snorted in contempt. 'Twas no wonder she had survived Hastings. The warriors she encountered were no doubt mesmerized by her beauty, giving her the opportunity to strike first, and as deadly accurate as she was with that bow, she must have slain numerous Normans. His blood simmered. She was a banshee disguised as a goddess. But he was not swayed by her wiles.

The voices grew in volume, and just as Wulfson reined Turold to back up into a more discreet spot between two huge oaks, Tarian did the same. Her horse silently reversed, blending into the copse. Wulfson sheathed his long broadsword at his waist, then drew the deadly twin angels of death, Azrael and Sariel.

His fingers grasped the leather-bound hilts, the grips molding perfectly to every contour of his hands. Wulfson could feel the quickening in the stallion's flanks. As did his master, the warhorse found his true passion in the heat of battle.

The Welsh voices broke the small clearing just ahead. Just as a red hound trotting ahead of them stopped in his tracks and lifted his nose in Wulfson's direction, alerting the Welsh to his presence, Wulfson struck. He grasped the black's sides with his thighs, and the great horse broke through the bramble and thickets, shielding them into the clearing and into a half score of armed men.

Sword in each hand, Wulfson urged the destrier forward, his mighty battle cry shaking the birds from the trees, the great horse's large razor-sharp hooves clearing the way. Though surprised, the men quickly rallied and formed a loose circle around the lone knight. Unperturbed, Wulfson pressed upon the man nearest to him, and in one wide arc of his right arm, he separated the man's head from his shoulders, his silent scream of terror lost forever. A sharp prick of pain in his shoulder did not deter Wulfson, and he pressed through the gauntlet, both swords meeting flesh and bone in a sickening cadence. He broke clear of the mangled circle and spun back around to reenter it. Using his legs to direct Turold, he gave the destrier the command to rear up on his hindquarters, and when he came down Wulfson sliced the air, then the flesh on either side of him. Agonized screams filled the heavy air; it only served to spur Wulfson on. He was in that place where everything around him narrowed down to survival, his vision focused completely on his enemy. The horse rose up again, and this time did a half pirouette, keeping the foot soldiers from his master. But the great horse had to come down sooner or later, and laden with weight of his mailed master, he came down sooner, and into the thick of the fight. The men swarmed Wulfson, despite his hacking off their body parts. As they pressed, Wulfson shifted his weight in the saddle, and in a low voice commanded his mount, "*Capriole*." Turold rose on his haunches and leapt forward and kicked out with his hind legs. The man behind him screamed in pain. "*À nouveau*." The great horse repeated the movement; it was enough to push them back, but they swarmed again. Turold fought to keep the men at bay, but they were too numerous and well weaponed.

Twice Wulfson found his body breached. But the thrill of the fight overrode any pain associated with the wounds. He would tend to them later. Tunnel-visioned, he not only maneuvered himself around their attackers but one by one he slowly divested them of their limbs. As Wulfson swung around in his saddle to finish off the last of them, he noticed several bodies he had not touched lying on their backs, eyes staring skyward, with arrows piercing their chests.

In just that heartbeat of time, the last of the Welsh rushed him. Wulfson turned and brought both swords together as one to slice the man in half, but he never came close enough. His attacker's body jerked forward then backward; his dark eyes widened in surprise. He folded to his knees, then fell face-first in the damp soil at the destrier's hooves, a broadsword buried deep in his back.

Wulfson looked up to see Lady Tarian coming toward him still astride and barely winded. A deep pall of clouds settled over the thick wood. A jagged flash of lightning ripped across the gray sky, followed by a sharp crash of thunder just above them. Neither Tarian nor Wulfson acknowledged it. Both sat on their horses, each staring at the other.

Breathing heavily, blood soaking his blades, his arms and legs, Wulfson scanned the carnage. Half of the men were dead by his sword, the other half by arrows. He looked up, and caught the heated gaze of the warrior princess. She did not seem to have even broken a sweat. Calmly she sat upon her stallion, her quiver empty, her bow snugly put away in the leather sheath just behind the high pommel of her saddle.

She pointed to the dead men. " 'Tis well, milord, that I came to your rescue, or your blood would soak the ground, not that of these errant Welsh."

"Why did you flee in the first place?" he demanded.

She threw him a smile over her shoulder. "To prove that I could."

"I will take better care next time."

Tarian dismounted, and made her way to her sword. She pulled it from the dead man and bent to wipe his blood on his undertunic. Once the blade shone again, she sheathed it. Without looking up at Wulfson, she moved around the dead, stepping over them and lifting their cloaks and tunics. " 'Tis ignoble for a knight of the realm to scavenge," Wulfson said scornfully.

Tarian cocked her head back and gazed at him through narrowed eyes. "I am not a knight of the realm, sir, and while it may appear I am looking for trinkets, I assure you I am not." She bent down to one man and lifted his tunic to reveal a blue wren on a sable field. " 'Tis what I seek. My godfather's blazon. He will not be pleased with me."

Wulfson intently watched her from his saddle. "And who, pray tell, is your godfather?"

"Lord Orwain, Queen Hear's half brother."

"Queen Hear?"

"King Rhiwallon's wife."

Wulfson scowled. The Welsh were getting bold. Lightning blazed across the blackening sky, the following thunder closer than before. Wulfson looked skyward. "We will be soaked if we do not find shelter soon, and I have no desire to see rust upon my mail. Do you know a place close by where we can wait out this storm?"

Tarian grinned and nodded. She walked back to the gray, and Wulfson watched in amusement as she made one attempt to mount the big horse. He urged Turold toward the pair, and had he been a lesser man her arrow-sharp glare would have stopped him. But Wulfson of Trevelyn was unlike any other man. He dismounted, and when he did, he felt the first pang of pain from the fresh wound to his leg. Jagged shards shot up his groin. He didn't look down; the wound didn't matter now, though it would have to be ministered to. He grabbed Tarian up into his arms, and nearly tossed her atop the high back of the gray.

He grinned as he caught a quick view of the dark down that shielded her pink nether lips. His cock swelled at the vision, and though his bloodlust for battle had subsided, the sight he had just been gifted churned up another passion altogether.

Tarian drew as much of her skirts down her legs as she could, all the while holding him with a furious glare. Wulfson stared her down and grinned. "I was not sure there for a moment if you were but a pretty squire. I am assured now you are nothing of the sort."

Tarian kicked the gray, startling him, and she moved past Wulfson and deeper into the wood. Wulfson hurried to mount the black, but felt the strength ebbing from his right leg. 'Twas the same leg that Ocba the devil of a Saracen had put in a wooden vise for amusement one day. Wulfson had passed out from the unbearable pain of it. When he awoke, he had been chained back up against the wall; the only way he could keep his arms from dislocating was to stand on his good left leg. Any pressure on his right sent him into fits of agony. He still walked with a decided limp, but the pain was bearable. It only ached, it seemed, when the winters were overly cold and wet.

Lightning lit up the darkened sky with the intensity of the fiery star he had witnessed with his own eyes the year before. It was followed by an ear-shattering clap of thunder, and then the heavens opened and rain poured from the sky.

Wulfson cursed, and urged the black to follow the gray.

Ten

While he lost sight of Tarian more than once in the onslaught of rain, Wulfson was able to follow the well-marked tracks of the gray. They had turned back in the direction of Draceadon, but he was not overly concerned. They were close enough that if he wanted to make a run for it they could be within the fortress by the high sun of the day. But he was meticulous when it came to his equipment, and his mail was a most prized possession, given to him by his king just before they departed last year for Hastings. William's own armorer, Gilbert fitz Hugh, had created the unique black mail. Only *les morts*, William's elite guard, had the honor of wearing the masterpieces. And Wulfson, along with his Blood Swords, took great pains to preserve the gift. It was not only elaborate but constructed with such expert craftsmanship; the tightly welded piece had repelled many an arrow and sword when other mail would have allowed passage.

He was glad to see Tarian's gray tied up under a lean-to attached to an old stone dwelling. Wulfson scowled. From where he stood, he could detect no roof. Indeed, the architecture looked unfamiliar. The small cross-shaped holes that served as windows in the crumbling ruin gave the structure away. While his liege was a devout Catholic, Wulfson, having lived through hell, was not sure any god would treat his people suchly. He had no great faith, nor any great fear.

He tied the black next to the gray, and as he entered the dim confines of the crumbling edifice he stiffened, his hand wrapping around the hilt of his sword. Always wary when he entered a room, he scrutinized the woman across the hewn stone floor who had managed to start a small fire in the hearth. He didn't cast an eye northward, but surmised there was a roof since where she stood was dry, though thick green moss grew along the north wall of the room, and branches from the outer foliage grew through breaks in the crumbling mortar. The space, though open, was stifling. But his eyes came back to rest on the nymph standing in only a damp green garment by the flickering flames. His blood warmed at the sight, and once again he cursed his weakness.

"Is it your aim to drive us out of here with more heat?"

Tarian looked up at him and smiled, and he immediately went on the defensive. It was not any smile. Nay, her smile was that of a woman who thought herself very much in control of herself and the man she was bent on destroying.

"I am soaked to the bone, and if you are as worried about your mail as you say, then you will strip and come close and dry it as quickly as you can with the aid of the fire."

Wulfson nodded, and noted her kirtle and chauses hanging over a chair back to dry near the fire. He also noted the way her damp garment clung to her womanly curves. "'Twas my intention."

"Of course it was."

He unhooked his scabbards and set them to the side, but kept them close. He eyed Tarian warily as she approached him. Her damp clothing clung to her curves so strictly that though the room fairly steamed, the very noticeable outline of her nipples was undeniable. His rod filled more. "I am not incapable of undressing myself."

Tarian snickered and stepped closer. "Do you fear my touch, sir?"

Wulfson grinned and pulled his hauberk off, and then his mail leggings.

Tarian fought to keep her breathing at its normal pace, but when he removed his gambeson and stood only in his undertunic, braies, and linen chauses, she could not help but admire his form. When he pulled off his undertunic, she caught her breath. The sight of the sword burned into his chest in the light of day was more gruesome than it had been by candlelight. The pain he must have endured, and survived it—commendable. She resisted the urge to reach out and smooth her fingertips across the red scar, as if somehow that would relieve him of pain long endured. Her eyes traveled past his muscled chest and lower to his flat belly, then, out of womanly curiosity, to his groin. She blushed. The full rise in his braies could not be ignored. Yet her gaze traveled lower to the ragged slash in his chauses. The crimson stain on his thigh alerted her. Her gaze rose to his and she caught her breath. His nostrils flared and his deep green eyes burned like molten emeralds. His jaw was set and his lips thinned in tension.

"If you do not wish to be ravaged by me at this time, madame, I suggest you stand back."

Tarian swallowed and nodded, but moved back toward the fire.

She watched in quiet fascination as he sat down on a short bench next to the hearth and painstakingly rubbed the water from his mail with his undertunic. The crimson spot on his lower thigh deepened in color and volume.

"How came you by the scar on your chest?" she asked.

He stopped the rubbing motion and cast a hard glare. "A reminder of who I am."

"Who are you?" she breathlessly asked.

"A bastard knight of the bastard king, who kills on command."

"You make it sound so noble."

Wulfson eyed her cryptically, but kept at his chore. "It is."

Tarian stood, and slowly began to pace the small area. "You came to kill me, did you not?"

When he did not answer her, she spun around and came closer to him. "'Tis because I am a Godwinson?" Wulfson looked up, his eyes clear, hiding nothing. "What does your king fear? That I will raise up an army in the name of my uncle and seize the throne of England?"

Wulfson nodded, then softly said, "History has a way of repeating."

"If William is so concerned the Godwinson line will rear its head to rule, then why not chase after my cousins Magnus and Godwine, Harold's own sons?"

"They hide in Dublin. But mark my word, the day they set foot in England they will be hunted down."

Tarian threw up her hands, and in a quick movement she unsheathed her broadsword from where she had hung the scabbard on a peg on the wall. She had meant to hand it over hilt first to the Norman, but he was up and weaponed so swiftly she could not believe a mortal could move so fast. He pushed her hard against the wall, one sword to her throat, the other to her belly. "If you were a man, you would be lying in halves on the floor."

He stuck one sword into the timber behind her and grasped hers from her hand. " 'Tis lighter of weight than a man's."

She scowled. "Of course it is. I could not wield the weight of yours more than a minute."

He grinned and pressed his body full against hers. "I would wager you could not handle the full weight of me for more than a minute."

Her body steamed, and with only her undertunic separating her from him, Tarian was acutely aware of his maleness. He rose harder against her hip, and though she had walked that dangerous road with him just the night before, fear of his intentions gripped her.

His nostrils flared and she knew he caught her scent. His eyes narrowed. "Would you play me for a fool, madame?"

Vigorously she shook her head, denying what she knew to be true. He tossed her sword to the floor, and keeping her pinned with his short sword, his right hand moved down her belly to her hips. "Nay, do not trespass!" she cried.

Wulfson's piercing green eyes held hers. A soft sheen of sweat covered his chest and throat. She felt as if she were about to be swallowed up in a wild whirlpool.

He pressed the palm of his hand to her mound, and Tarian hissed in a breath. She had no control of the hot shards of desire shooting through her. Her breathing increased in volume and her breasts swelled with more weight. She could no more ignore the primal cords that bound her to this warrior than she could change the color of her eyes. He had awoken something in her body the night before, a craving, a hunger such as she had never known, and did not understand. Whatever it was, she could not deny it. But she would do her mightiest to control it. He pulled up her tunic in slow fistfuls, his eyes never leaving hers. As the fabric cleared her thighs, her soft musky scent wafted up between them. He closed his eyes and softly inhaled. When he opened them, she knew he knew. Her body quaked in fear. Would he end her life now?

What he did next shocked her. His fingers slid beneath the fabric of her tunic and in a slow easy slide he dipped into her wetness.

"*Jesu!*" She gasped and fought the urge to open wider for him and press more intimately against him. Instead, she clamped her thighs around his hand and grasped his shoulders. "Pray, stop your trespass."

His finger pushed deeper into her, and Tarian could not suppress the deep moan of pleasure that escaped her chest. "Pray, Tarian," he said as his lips pressed to her ear. His tongue licked her and shivers rent her entire body. "Who trespassed first?"

With every muscle she possessed, combined with the will of a mighty warrior, Tarian pushed him away from her. When she moved across the room to the hearth, she glanced back at him. He stood, sword in his left hand, bare-chested, his other sword poking his braies for release. He had let her go, and they both knew it. He brought his right hand to his nose and inhaled her scent, his gaze never leaving hers. She shivered, and now, despite the applied honey and violet scent she had prepared and applied to her body, her natural scent overrode it.

"Honey musk. A scent that, once experienced, I would never forget." He stepped closer to her, his eyes blazing, not, she realized, in lust or passion, but in fury. "What game are you about, Tarian Godwinson, that you should drug me, then see yourself spread upon my bed in the middle of the night?"

She shook her head in denial. "I know not of what you speak. I only met you this morn."

"Nay," he softly said. He sheathed his sword and turned back to her. "Remove your garment."

"What?" she indignantly demanded.

"You heard me."

"Why?"

"Why do you think?"

"Is this a barbaric attempt to exert your power over me?"

"I am master here. Do it now, or I promise, you will not like how I will remove it."

Tarian swallowed hard, resentment at his humiliation riding her. "Give me your oath you will not touch me once it's removed."

He shook his head and stopped halfway toward her. "I swear no oath to you. Remove it."

Tarian looked past the hulking knight to where Thyra, her sword, still protruded from the wooden wall, then to Wulfson's twin blades near his broadsword. She would have to get past the nimble knight to get her hands on any weapon, and from what she had witnessed she was no match for him. She straightened. So be it. It would not be the first time he would see her naked. But it would, she decided, be the last. For all that there had been a momentary reprieve, she was intelligent enough to know that it was only a matter of time before William reconfirmed his kill order. And to that end, so long as this knight lived and breathed, she would not. There was only one alternative. But in the meantime, she would demonstrate just who had power over whom.

She smiled a slow seductive smile, and as Salome had danced for Herod, Tarian slowly and seductively raised the damp tunic. As it passed up to her thighs Wulfson's eyes blazed brighter. At her waist she heard a slow hiss emerge from his chest, and as she raised it past her breasts he cursed. When she pulled it over her head, then pulled it away from her long hair and shook the damp tendrils from her shoulders, she watched his body twitch and stiffen.

From beneath lowered lids she smiled up at the knight. He stood ramrod stiff now, as an oak in a brutal storm; he did not so much as flinch. Tarian arched her back and her full breasts jutted toward the Norman, her nipples hard and distended. Her flat belly fluttered under his heated scrutiny. Her smile deepened and she ran her hands up her sides to her breasts, grazing the tips with her fingertips. They both hissed in air, she at the hot shot of desire the caress evoked and Wulfson, she could only surmise, from the sight of her touching herself.

"Do you like to see my hands upon myself, sir knight?" Tarian boldly asked. When their gazes caught and clashed, she realized his great chest rose and fell in a quick staccato. "Would you touch yourself for me?"

Wulfson groaned. "You are wanton," he said softly, his voice even lower than its normal deep timbre.

Tarian relished the control she had over this man sent to destroy her. She dug her fingers into her long hair and pushed the mass up on top of her head. Thus she proudly stood, every angle, every curve of her viewable. Slowly she turned and came back around to fully face the warrior who, she noted, had stepped closer.

"Do I please you, milord knight?"

"You would please any man."

"'Tis not any man I wish to please."

His eyes narrowed. "Do not set your sights on me, madam. I will be gone from this damp clime before too long."

"With my head upon a platter?"

He stepped closer to her and reached out a hand to her breast. "Mayhap," he said, barely audibly. He slipped his long arm around her waist and pulled her toward him. "Mayhap not."

"Mayhap, milord knight, you will wake to find my sword buried in your chest one morn."

He yanked her hard against his chest and lowered his lips to hers. "Never fear. There are more Blood Swords where I come from. You cannot defeat us all." Before she could utter a word, his lips descended upon hers.

Wulfson told himself he would resist what she so shamelessly taunted him with, but then he decided that would serve no purpose. His body burned too hot to be denied. And though she might want to deny it, she burned as hotly for him. He smiled against her lips when her body went limp in his arms. He gathered her closer and wished there were at least a pallet in the small area. But there was not, and though he had taken many a maid on the floor or the grass, he did not want to with Tarian. The wench had pride. She was a noble lady of royal blood; she deserved better then a quick tryst on the dirt and stone floor of an abandoned

Celtic ruin. And as he realized what he'd just thought, Wulfson knew he had waded too deep into her waters.

He growled, and as he was about to set her from him, she kneed him hard in the groin. He grunted in pain, his arms loosening, and she was gone. When he looked up through the haze of his pain, he found her sword tip pressed to his heart. His blood, already quickening, thrummed through him like a runaway stallion. He stood to his full height, and though he read murder in her eyes she had not done the deed. She looked magnificent in her fury, her petite body, so perfectly shaped, flushed pink in her excitement.

A storm more ferocious raged in her eyes and face. But he would not be swayed by it. Nay, now he would show her once and for all that if her destiny was to die at his hands then it would be so.

"I saved your life. Does that not count for something?" she demanded.

Wulfson shook his head. "Nay, you nearly cost it."

She pressed the tip into the thick scar tissue on his chest. "You are a most arrogant man, Wulfson of Trevelyn. Had I not filled those men with my arrows, I would be safely back at Draceadon enjoying an afternoon respite with Brighid."

"Had I not pulled you from the bowels of that place, you would be dead as we speak."

She threw her head back and laughed, and it was just the distraction Wulfson needed. He slapped the blade away from his chest, grabbing Tarian's hand that held it, and squeezed. She cried out in pain but did not release the hilt. She twisted and turned in against him, knocking them both off balance. Wulfson was not used to such a small, slippery foe. He guarded what made him a man as the length of the blade struck downward in their battle over it. He pushed

Tarian back against the wall, and when she hit the timber with a hard thump, Wulfson grabbed the sword from her. He pressed it horizontally across her chest, then shoved her back into the wall, keeping her completely immobile. One wrong turn and the honed blade would slice her open. As it was, the upper edge dug into the tender flesh at the top swell of her right breast. A small drop of blood beaded above the steel where it hovered, then dripped slowly down the side.

"Lady Tarian, you sorely try my patience."

Her ocean-colored eyes glittered in fury, and he felt a different pain rise up between them. Her eyes widened, and he grinned, despite the most precarious position they found themselves in. "It seems I am a man who not only enjoys watching a woman touch herself but one who likes rough play." He tossed the sword behind him, where it clattered against the far wall. Before she could move, he dug his fingers into her thick hair and pulled it back so that she could do naught but look him in the eye. "Do you want to continue this charade of cat and mouse, or do you want to lie with me here and now?"

"I would never lie with a Norman!"

Her words did not hurt. Her refusal to lie with him did. "You lay with me last eve. What has changed?"

"You are mad to think I would come to you in the night! I would never do such a thing! I am a widow of just a month."

His hands moved through her hair, drawing out her long tresses. "Is this the way a widow wears her hair?" He nodded toward her clothing on the floor. "Is that how one who is in mourning dresses?"

Tarian remained mute. Wulfson studied her for a long

time. "Why, after he had agreed, did your husband refuse to marry you?"

If it were possible for her to look more furious than she had moments before, she did. " 'Tis no concern of yours."

His hand slid down her belly and rested just above her mons. He felt her flinch, and resisted the urge to sample her honey. "Are you with child?"

Taking a deep breath, she answered him honestly. "I do not know." He stood still, watching her for any clue she lied. "Does it matter? If your king decides to see his original order met, the child will die with me."

Wulfson drew her close, his head dipped; his lips hovered just above hers. "If you are such a resourceful warrior, why do you act as if when the final order comes you will hand me your sword to do the deed?"

She rose up on her toes and pressed her breasts against his bare chest. His muscles tightened. "I would never do such a thing, because I do not think you have it in you to kill an innocent woman and babe." She nipped his bottom lip and hung onto to it. He jerked his head away, blood beaded on his bottom lip. Tarian laughed. "My husband called me Lilit."

Wulfson swiped his thumb across his lower lip and saw the blood there. He licked it. "Who is Lilit?"

Tarian laughed again, her voice this time verging close to hysteria. He shook her and she sobered, then looked him hard in the eye. "Lilit was a succubus of the highest order." His eyes narrowed, and she explained. "Lilit came to warriors in the night, and as she made love to them she sucked their vigor from them, so the next morn they were useless on the battlefield, where they succumbed to their enemy only to be reunited with her in their death."

"Did Malcor fear you?"

"Indeed, and he had much to fear."

"Did you slay him?"

" 'Twas either he or me. I chose to live."

Wulfson stepped back from her. "Get dressed. The rain has waned, and I would see us back for the midday meal. I have a great hunger."

Tarian nodded, and as they dressed she noticed again the growing bloodstain on his leggings. "Your wound will fester if it is not tended."

"I will see to it."

As they mounted and turned their horses toward Draceadon, the distant thunder of hooves from the west road leading toward the town of Dunloc met them. Wulfson inclined his head to her to ride behind the ruin, and they hurried to see and not be seen.

Eleven

A handful of armed soldiers on horseback thundered past the chapel, followed long moments later by at least twoscore foot soldiers. If they could be considered soldiers. They reminded Wulfson more of churls playing at war. The argent lion emblazoned on the sable standard was familiar; he had seen it at Hastings amongst the Saxon army.

"'Tis Rhiwallon," Tarian said after the train passed.

Wulfson scowled. Between Rangor's men, Tarian's guard, and now the Welsh king's detail, the Blood Swords, though worth five men apiece, had become sorely outnumbered.

"Does the mighty knight fear the Welsh?" Tarian snidely asked.

Wulfson scoffed, turning to her. "Did I fear them earlier in the wood?"

She smiled and shook her head, her long hair swirling around her waist. For the hundredth time that day his blood quickened at the sight of her. Her pluck and exotic beauty gave him pause nearly every time he set his gaze on her. "Nay, but you must admit, knowing I had your back, there was little to fear."

Wulfson scoffed again and urged Turold forward. "I will admit for a woman you have a talent with the bow."

"Hah! I can shoot the eye from a boar at seventy-five paces."

Wulfson shook his head.

"I can!"

"You would have to prove such prowess to me. But for now let us return to Draceadon and hear what Rhiwallon desires of you."

"He desires that I go to Powys for his protection."

Wulfson waited for her to catch up to his pace, then said, "I will not allow it."

She shrugged. "I have no desire to leave my home."

Wulfson eyed her sharply. "You are as mysterious to me as any woman I have come across, Lady Tarian."

"I am many things to many people, sir knight, but there is no mystery to me. I want what every woman wants. A safe home to raise her children."

"Safety is difficult to guarantee."

"Especially when there is a price on one's head."

"There are no rules on the battlefield."

She flashed him a smile that stirred his cock. "Aye, of that I am clearly aware."

"You make light of a serious situation."

She flashed him another disarming smile and leaned toward him, and said softly, "I will not die by your hand, Sir Wulfson."

He leaned toward her, catching her deep blue eyes with his. "Never underestimate the enemy. 'Tis the most fatal of flaws."

He watched the color rise in her cheeks. "Aye, and so I say the same to you. Do not forget it."

Wulfson sat back in his saddle and contemplated the erect back and proud set of her shoulders. A niggling trepidation clawed at his gut. Here was a foe he had never come face to face with. Nor one he had been trained to defeat. He thought he understood the workings of the fairer sex, but this Saxon witch mystified him. His cock burned with a heat he fought to quell. Lilit, Malcor had called her. Mayhap the earl knew more than most. The warrior princess was a demon, and either he had dreamt of her coming to him or she truly had, and in her demoness form no less. He scowled deeply. He found not only his strength to be tested this day, and had the wounds to prove she had sucked his usual vigor from him. But he had not used his brain to its fullest capacity when he rode off with no helm, gauntlet or company, and was Turold not so expertly trained in the art of war he would not have won the day. He gave the horse an affectionate pat on the neck, and was rewarded with a snort and shaking of his great black head. Aye, Turold, like all the Blood Sword mounts, was of the finest Spanish blood.

His lips twitched in a half-smile. They had left Iberia with more than their lives that fateful day. His mood was quickly soured with the realization that had Tarian not come to him in the night, he would have had more sense about him and been most capable of quelling the Welsh single-handedly, and in shorter order.

His eyes narrowed, and he made the decision right then and there to stay as far from her as humanly possible. She was deadly in her treacherous female form, and, being but a lowly male, he found himself battling his inhuman desire for her.

*   *   *

As they approached Draceadon, Tarian's excitement grew. Her message to her Welsh kinsman King Rhiwallon had been received. And with the arrival of his messenger and guard, the charade would now commence in full. She held back a gloating smile. The Norman knight had been all too correct in his statement that there were no rules on the battlefield. She of all people understood how the wiles of a woman could confuse a man and make him think more than twice, and not with the head on his shoulders. Even Malcor in his depravity had not been immune to her. He had named her sole heir to all he held. That document alone, should she outwit William and his Blood Swords, would be her salvation.

Aye, she was counting on Rhiwallon's demand that she come to him in Powys, so that she could refuse. Rangor would plead his case and the Norman would deny them both. But Tarian thought that if she could convince the Norman to give his oath to Rhiwallon, Rangor, and Alewith that no harm would come to her person, and to return to Normandy in return for Rhiwallon's pledge of alliance, along with that of Rangor and Alewith, surely William would consider such an offer. 'Twas no secret the Welsh held no love for William. But mayhap she could barter an alliance. Because with Rhiwallon would come the kingdom of Powys, and his brother King Bleddyn of Gwynedd, and that combination William would not be able to resist.

Aye, she would tread very carefully. Tarian's insides churned when she thought of the consequences she would pay should the Norman discover William's messenger would not be returning anytime soon. Several of her guard awaited his entering Wycliffe Pass just over the hill. He would not be harmed, but neither would he deliver the king's answer to Wulfson's question, unless of course William changed his mind.

"What treachery brews in that head of yours, Lady Tarian?" Wulfson asked, sidling closer to her. So lost in thought was she, she paid him no heed. His leg brushed against hers and she caught his hard stare.

"I but wonder what intrigue awaits us ahead."

Wulfson's lips drew into a tight line. "I pray all parties involved understand William's affection for his Blood Swords, and also his wrath should he find himself without them."

"Do you fear for your safety, milord knight?"

"Nay, I fear for yours."

Tarian shook her head. "I do not understand you. One moment you are bent on seeing me planted in the ground, and the next you fear for my safety? Which is it?"

Wulfson ignored her question, and it was as well, for when they turned the bend the fortress Draceadon rose up like its namesake, a giant dark dragon, and spilling out from the bailey more horses and soldiers. Gareth, followed by several Normans, had just broken free and galloped toward them.

"My lady!" Gareth called as he came near, his voice full of relief.

She looked past him to see the tall Viking called Thorin and another knight, Rorick. She could not see their faces behind their black helms, but the tight jaws gave away their ire.

"Wulfson!" Thorin said, reining up to them, "We had given you up for"—his one eye speared Tarian—"lost."

Wulfson scoffed. "Hardly, my friend. We but waited out the rain under cover. Tell me the mood of the Welsh."

Rorick snorted, and looked from Tarian to Gareth, then back to the clogged bailey. " 'Tis the captain of Rhiwallon's guard. He would speak only to you. But my guess is he has come for the lady."

" 'Tis best, milady, you go with them," Gareth said to Tarian.

She stiffened in the saddle. "I will not leave here."

Gareth eyed the Normans and softly pleaded, "Milady, blood is at stake. For your welfare 'tis best to be gone from here."

She nudged Silversmith forward. "I will not leave Draceadon to Rangor. 'Tis mine. *He* can go to his cousin!" The big gray sprinted past the knights. Wulfson's curses behind her, along with those of his men and Gareth, brought a grim smile to Tarian's lips. She would not be a pawn in this man's game. She was lady here, and heir or not, lady she would stay!

As they entered the crowded bailey, Wulfson noted that the Welsh were smart enough to know with whom they dealt. They parted as if he were their own king. His men stood outside the great hall, a most fearsome gauntlet. He noted that Tarian's men, while not standing with the Blood Swords, were yet close enough to them to debate whether they stood together or not. However, Rangor and Alewith stood firmly with the Welsh. Wulfson was not fooled by Gareth's indecision. Better for Gareth to look as if he stood with the Normans than to look completely at odds with them. Rangor and Alewith were not nearly as clever.

Wulfson scowled and dismounted, handing off the reins to Rolf.

"Sir Morgan, King Rhiwallon's captain of his guard,

wishes a word with you, Sir Wulfson," Rangor said, stepping forward, his eyes riveted on Tarian. Wulfson made to step toward her to assist her in her dismount, but was warned off with a sharp glare. Instead, Gareth assisted her. Wulfson stood back and turned to the tall, dark Welshman Morgan.

He approached Wulfson and gave him a curt nod, and said in Welsh, "I am Morgan ap Rhys, and have come with word of my liege, Rhiwallon of Powys. I beg we have a private moment to speak."

Wulfson nodded and strode away from the throng, keeping close to his men but not close enough for any to overhear.

When he stopped, Morgan stopped beside him. Withdrawing a sealed document from a leather pouch that hung from his waist, he handed it to Wulfson. "Shall I call my scribe?"

Wulfson shook his head. "Nay, I have knowledge of letters." He broke the wax seal with his thumb and unrolled the parchment and read:

> *"Greetings, Sir, I pray this missive finds your master, William King of England and Duke of Normandy, well. I trust also my cousin by marriage to my late blood cousin Malcor, Lady Tarian of Dunloc, is well, for her good health is of the utmost importance to not only myself, Rhiwallon King of Powys, but also to my brother Bleddyn King of Gwynedd. We have such affection for the lady that we beseech you to entrust her to the care of Sir Morgan and his guard to return forthwith to Powys. In return for your obedience, I pledge my assistance to William against my enemies should he find himself in need of it along the*

Welsh borders. We will also give you escort as far south as Colford, and sufficient gold to see you return to Normandy a wealthy man. I also ask that you instruct my cousin Rangor of Lerwick to secure Draceadon for the lady's eventual return to her home.

    By my command, Rhiwallon."

As Wulfson read the command that the Welsh king had no authority to make of William's vassals, he worked hard to maintain his self-control. The ruler's audacity astounded him. He wanted the lady in his lair for the same reasons William wanted her dead. And Rhiwallon was wily in his words. While he alluded to an alliance with William should he need it, he would do so only on the condition that Rhiwallon's enemies were the instigators. What if his own brother should decide to attack? The alliance would bear no water. Aye, it was time to tread very carefully through this bog.

Without giving the Welsh captain even a glance, Wulfson turned to face the gathered throngs comprised of Norman, Saxon, and Welsh. His men stood alert, ready to defend or attack. His eyes caught those of Rorick, who stood closest. The big Scot understood, and moved to stand beside Tarian, while Thorin moved up behind Gareth. Sensing what was about, Rhys, Ioan, and Stefan tightened their stances and soon they were a solid mass of knights, soldiers, and nobles, with a lone woman in the middle. Wulfson cursed under his breath and turned to Morgan. "Let us discuss this matter over the afternoon meal." It was not a request.

Wulfson swept toward Tarian, and as he passed her he grabbed her arm and pulled her along with him. Gareth made a move. Wulfson dropped her arm and turned. "Give way, Viking."

Wulfson's men formed a diamond-shaped barrier around them, and as one they moved into the great hall.

In a mad rush to see the tables set, the servants swarmed like ants, and Wulfson had to admit they were well schooled in their duties. Within a very short time all were seated: Wulfson with Tarian beside him, the Welsh captain to his left, Alewith to Tarian's right and Rangor relegated further down the table between Thorin and Gareth. Wulfson indicated that the other Blood Swords should sit amongst the Welsh and Saxon soldiers, and keep a sharp eye on them.

The numbers were stacked against them should either faction decide to press the issue with might. Tarian remained quiet and calm, but Wulfson did not expect anything less from her. She was not only beautiful and able to wield a sword and bow like a man, but she was cagey, not one to rush to conclusions or to press an issue before it was ripe. He was sure she was as intrigued as he, and would do her best to maneuver the current climate to her favor.

It occurred to him as he gazed down at her dark head and listened to her husky voice that she would make a most prized wife. Malcor was a fool.

Once the blessing was said, Tarian did not hesitate to ask, "So, Morgan, how fare my uncles Rhiwallon and Bleddyn?"

Wulfson stiffened as he stabbed a piece of roast mutton with his table knife.

The man glanced at Wulfson, who ignored him, and said, "Both are well. My liege Rhiwallon is most anxious for your visit."

Wulfson waited silently for her response. Mayhap he would not have to be the villain here. "I too look forward to a visit, but I cannot travel at this time."

Morgan scowled and set his cup aside. "I should despair to bear such news to my liege. It would please him greatly if you returned with me."

Daintily Tarian plucked a piece of choice meat from the trencher she shared with Wulfson. As she chewed the morsel, she shook her head. "I shall write to my uncle and explain my situation here."

Morgan scowled, and his body stiffened. "I have been instructed not to return without you, my lady."

Tarian laughed, the light and melodic sound shooting straight to Wulfson's groin. "Then by all means make yourself at home here, Sir Morgan." She looked steadily at him and said in a very low, firm voice, "I will not leave my home. I may be with child and do not wish to travel. The visit will have to wait."

"My lady," Rangor interrupted from down the table. Tarian and Wulfson both scowled. "For your continued health, it is best you go to Powys."

Tarian shook her head. "Nay."

"Rangor is right," Alewith added.

Tarian pushed away from the table and stood. "This is my home, and I will not be driven from it." She looked down at Wulfson and said, "Go back to your king and tell him he has no enemy in Tarian of Dunloc. I would give him homage and soldiers should he need them. I pledge my oath."

Rangor hissed in a long breath. "What if the Marches should be breached by the Normans?"

She cast a weary glance down the table. "I am Saxon and Welsh, uncle, but my king is Norman. What would you have me do?"

"Ally yourself with your blood kin!"

She smiled wryly. "My blood kin are mulch in York and Hastings. My dam cannot bear to hear my name spoken in her presence." She looked over to Alewith and Brighid. "My guardian and sister of my heart, while they have treated me as one of them, cannot claim blood ties to me." She looked back at Rangor. "I have no blood kin. I have Draceadon. Do not speak to me again of leaving. I have the will and I have my men. It is all I need to plead my cause."

She gave Wulfson a sharp glare. "No man, not even your king, will take it from me."

"There is always the convent," Thorin interjected, and as the words tumbled from his man's lips Wulfson felt a chill whip through his bones. It would be a catastrophe for that body and that brain to be sequestered from the world behind the heavy black robes of a nun.

Tarian hissed in a long breath. "Bite your tongue, Viking! God wants nothing to do with me, nor I with him!"

"'Tis blasphemy!" Rangor screeched, his words echoed by Father Dudley.

Tarian clenched her fists and pounded the trestle top. Anger swirled like a storm within her. She felt her skin warm and her eyes start from her head. "*Blasphemy?* My father captured my mother, *an abbess*, then repeatedly raped her for a year. Not even a king's decree could force him to release her! I am marked as the devil's spawn! I would find nothing but bone-weary toil to repent for the sins of my father. 'Tis no life for any woman. I will not stand for it!"

She looked at them all, their jaws slack; even Wulfson, it seemed, was shocked. She smiled grimly. "Think what you will. But I will not abide by any of you deciding how I will spend the rest of my life." She looked down at Wulfson and said, "And should your sword find a resting place in my heart, be warned: my uncles, though I defy them their invitation now, will not be pleased."

"You will remain here until I hear from William. His word will be final." Wulfson stood and spoke to the entire hall. "I am lord here until further notice, and I decree"—he looked pointedly at Morgan, then Rangor—"that the lady will stay under my care until such time I deem it otherwise."

"Send her to Normandy and allow William to hold her hostage," Rangor said coming around.

Tarian gasped in shock. "Never!"

"Aye, 'twould solve the problem, Wulf," Thorin agreed.

"Let William have a tangle with her. He will see to her future," Rorick agreed.

Panic tore through her. It was the ultimate solution, making the most sense. Everyone would get what they wanted. Everyone but she. Tarian glanced up to Wulfson and found his contemplative stare. "Nay! I will not go to Normandy!"

"Then wed with me now, Tarian. 'Tis not unusual," Rangor cajoled.

Moving with the speed of a cat, Tarian spun around, drawing her sword, and stood at the ready. "I have told you, repeatedly. I will *never* wed with you!"

When Wulfson said no word, Rangor grew bolder. "I have wealth, Tarian. Combined with Dunloc, we would have more than most kings!"

Defiant to the end, Tarian vigorously shook her head and pressed her sword toward him. "Let us settle this here and now, Rangor." She gestured toward his sword. "Should you defeat me, I will wed with you. But should I win?"

She smiled grimly. "You will leave here today and never return."

Rangor grinned from ear to ear and bowed. "'Twould be my pleasure." He glanced up at Wulfson. "I will not harm her."

Much to her fury, the Norman nodded and stood back. "Clear the hall," he commanded.

Twelve

arian! *No!*" Brighid cried, as she came around the trestle. Her hip slammed into it and she cried out in pain.
Tarian made to move toward her, but stopped when to her
utter amazement the one Wulfson called Rhys hurried to
her side and with the chivalry of a king helped her to her
feet. Forgetting her foster sister, the girl blushed deeply and
allowed the handsome knight to assist her. Rhys appeared
to be the youngest of the Normans, and the quietest.

Tarian looked up to Wulfson, who scowled. 'Twas his
favorite expression, she decided.

"Set her aside and forget her," Wulfson said in French
to the knight. His reward was a stiff glare, but Rhys moved
away just the same.

"You, sir knight, have the manners of a boar," Tarian
said.

"And you have the temperament of a wasp," he replied,
then stood back and extended his arm to the now cleared
area. "My lady warrior, the floor is yours."

Sword in hand, Tarian did not wait for Rangor to gather

his poise. She struck without warning, slamming him on his shoulder with the flat of her blade. A collective gasp rippled through the hall, and soon bets were being made.

Rangor was not daunted. He drew his sword and crouched, swinging the blade low to catch her off her feet, but Tarian was more seasoned than that. As the sword edged near her, she jumped, scaling it. As she landed, she whirled and returned the parry, catching Rangor off balance, and in the process she sliced through a leather garter.

He snarled and stood to his full height, and with both hands on the hilt in a hacking motion, he came at her.

Wulfson stood in quiet amazement as he watched the nymph dance and twirl around the Saxon, drawing him close only to have him take a swipe and miss, and herself come around and connect. She was small and nimble and wily as a fox.

Sweat beaded Rangor's forehead, and though the lady warrior was a bit winded, she was the one who maintained composure.

Rangor was getting sloppy in his zealous frenzy to possess her. And Wulfson could not blame him. As he watched her thrust, strike, and parry with such deadly precision, his blood quickened. He imagined her doing the same thing with him, only with no clothing and no sword.

Rangor's frustration and now his humiliation took control over his lust for the woman. Wulfson stepped closer to the circle. Rangor rushed Tarian and her leg banged the corner of a trestle. She lost her balance, and Rangor pounced. Wulfson moved to pull her out of harm's way but was stayed by Thorin's brawny arm.

Tarian rolled under the trestle and popped up on the other side, kicking Rangor in the backside before he realized what she had done. He hit the rushes with a loud thud, and when he rolled over, her foot was on his chest and her blade pressed to the vital vein in his throat.

The hall erupted in cheers and Wulfson felt a sense of relief he had not known he held. He caught Thorin's sage gaze, and the Viking lowered his arm, and mumbled, " 'Tis a shame. Rangor could have spared us more time here."

Tarian kept her sword pressed to Rangor's throat. "You have lost, uncle. I expect you to keep your oath to me." She stepped back, removing the blade from his person. "Begone from here and do not darken my doorstep again. You are no longer welcome." She sheathed her sword and turned her back on him and looked up at Wulfson. "How was that, milord, for a kitten?"

Wulfson grinned and lightly rubbed his chest where the scar tingled. "Not bad, but then, you fought a puppy."

Tarian's eyes sparked in brilliant fury. Heat flared to every point in his body and he could not remember ever having seen such a magnificent sight in his life. She reminded him of the coal-black Barbary mares in Iberia, imported from the deserts in the Holy Lands. Full of fire and majesty. Aye, she would not tame down for just any master. She would require a patient and gentle but firm hand, but before that she would have to trust. He scowled. Trust was one thing he could not give her.

Brighid broke the spell, rushing into her foster sister's arms, crying as any woman would. As the girl seemed to disintegrate into a puddle of tears, Tarian pulled her along, shushing her, and soon they were gone from the hall.

Rangor stood amongst his men and those of Rhiwallon. "My oath is my oath," he began to Wulfson. "But by blood right, I have claim to this holding."

"Take it up with William."

Rangor made a short bow and said, "I will plead my case in person, and be sure I will inform him of your own lust for the lady."

Rangor's words struck Wulfson to the quick, and though it should not have bothered him, for he knew his king had the utmost confidence in him, it nettled him that his lust for the lady warrior was obvious to others. He smiled stiffly and looked around to those who waited for his response. "I am a man, Rangor, and she is a beautiful woman." He looked to his men and asked, "Is there one among you who would not take a tumble if she but offered?"

Rorick grinned and Thorin chuckled, shaking his head. Stefan stood beside Ioan. They both shook their heads. When Wulfson's gaze touched on Rhys, the youngest of the knights, whose grin was wide as the fortress doors, he turned back to the irritating lord. "Dogs, all of us! By all means, inform William of this unheard-of affliction."

Giving Rangor his back, Wulfson spoke to Alewith, who stood silent, his face reddening. Wulfson nodded. "My pardon, sir, but the taunt required an honest explanation."

Alewith nodded and remained silent.

Wulfson turned his attention to the Welsh captain. "As the lady extended an invitation to you to stay until such time she changes her mind, you may, but your men must go. Seek the hospitality of the hall this night, but to do so you will hand over your weapons." Before Morgan could respond, he turned to Alewith. "Your men as well."

Both stepped up, sputtering their anger over such a request.

Wulfson held his hand up for silence. "Should there be any aggression from without *or* within and your services be required, your men will have their weapons returned. Should we require assistance."

"'Tis preposterous!" Alewith groused.

"Then feel free to take your men and your daughter and return to Turnsly forthwith. I see no need for your presence here."

Alewith did not back down. "You have nothing to fear from me, Norman." He nodded to Wulfson. "If you would indulge an old man who cares for his charge, 'tis why I am here."

Wulfson chuckled. "You are correct on all accounts." He sobered and speared the lord with a glare. "Hand over your arms or leave Draceadon."

Alewith set his jaw, but bowed and withdrew his sword, handing it hilt first to Wulfson, who accepted it. His men followed their lord, the Blood Swords collecting a vast assortment of swords, daggers, and axes. When Wulfson turned to Morgan, the Welshman bowed, clicked his spurs, and stepped back. "I will return to Powys with my men." He turned then, and strode from the hall, calling to his men to follow.

Wulfson looked across Alewith's head to Thorin and Rorick, who were close. "We will see the Welsh again, I have no doubt," Rorick said.

Wulfson nodded. And they would take every precaution.

Alewith excused himself and stalked from the hall, Gareth retreating as well. With the hall cleared of those he could not trust, Wulfson called to the nearest servant, "Bring ale for my men," then inclined his head toward the table before the cold hearth. "Come, Blood Swords, let us discuss the happenings of this most interesting day."

Once his men were gathered around, Wulfson told them of the day's events, being sure not to leave out the very important fact that the marauders he and the lady had disposed of bore Welsh colors, Welsh who were related to the infamous lady warrior.

"You say the lady winged your ear from fifty paces?" Ioan asked, incredulous.

Wulfson fingered the wound, and turned to show them all. "Aye, see for yourself. 'Tis but a nick, as she intended."

"And she killed the last one standing with her own sword in his back?" Stefan skeptically asked.

"Aye, she hurled it from her horse. 'Twas a perfect throw. It hit the knave right between the shoulders. He went down like a sack of turnips."

"And you say she took out five with her bow? One arrow to the heart of each of them?" Rorick demanded.

"Aye, I was too busy with my own defense, but when all was done, I counted five with arrows in their chests, and one with a broadsword in his back."

"I do not believe it!" Rhys shouted. "No woman could perform such a feat!"

Stefan nudged his friend. "Even Thorin with one eye can see she has the skill of a seasoned warrior. Look how she toyed with Rangor."

At the mention of his name, all eyes turned to the Viking.

Thorin scratched his chin, fingering the crescent-shaped scar they all bore. Wulfson knew the Viking had the mind of a steel trap, and though he sported an eye patch, it did not curb his ferociousness as a warrior. If anything, it made him more aware. "What are you thinking, Thorin?" Rorick asked.

"That this exploit has turned into a quagmire of intrigue. 'Tis unfortunate we could not have arrived one week later. Our troubles would be dead and buried."

Wulfson fought back a scowl at his words. While his friend spoke the truth, the thought of finding the lady he saw today, the woman who had haunted his dreams the night past, dead was unsettling. She had the vitality of ten men. She was an amazing creature that should be set free, not caged or killed.

"*Jesu!*" he cursed out loud at his thoughts. Five sets of eyes stared at him.

Thorin's eyes narrowed. "What afflicts you, Wulf? Has the wench gotten under your skin in such short order?"

"Nay," Wulfson denied, shaking his head. He moved to a safer subject. "I cannot argue the obvious. I find that the longer we stay here, the closer we come to disaster. The Norman Earl of Hereford, William fitz Osborn, has his hands full farther north, and that mad Saxon Earl Edric, though he has pledged his fealty to William, I know he sleeps with the Welsh. There will be more blood shed. Soon."

"I say we send her packing to William," Ioan chimed in. All but Wulfson nodded in agreement.

"The Welsh circle like vultures. Keeping the lady here is like dangling fresh meat in front of a hound. It seems she could well be the spark to a terrible clash of Welsh, Saxon, and Norman," Rhys said.

"William wants no quarrel with them, but should they press the issue they will be set back, and lose much of what they had for the effort. William will seize every hide of land that he can," Rorick said, then added, "And do not think for one moment Rangor is not running to his Welsh kin before he goes to William."

Wulfson could not disagree with any word. He looked over to the silent Stefan. "What think you, Stefan?"

"I think we should leave this place, with the lady in tow, and hand her over to William."

Wulfson shook his head. "He does not want the responsibility. He already has her only surviving uncle as hostage these many years past. The move would make him appear afraid of all things Godwinson. That aside, it would look to the Welsh as if he blinked first. William would rather cut off his sword arm than show any hint of weakness. Nay, Normandy is not the answer." He paused for effect. "At least—not yet."

"If we are to stay here, Wulf," Thorin said, "then we need more men. We have not the numbers. And this crumbling place could not withstand a full-out assault."

Wulfson stepped back from the hearth and contemplated the situation. "With no delays, Warner should return within the next handful of days. And with him, men." He looked to his men. "I have sent word to Rohan that he and Manhku should answer the call. And along with them more men."

Thorin grinned. "The last time I saw du Luc he was more nervous than a lad with his first woman. His lady should give birth by summer's end."

Stefan laughed. "I would have wagered my horse and sword when we began this journey together, he of all of us would be the last to be led around like a lamb by a woman."

They were interrupted when a servant set a tray of full goblets of ale down on the table. Each man grabbed one. Wulfson hoisted his cup and said, "A toast to Rohan and Isabel—may their first child be a strong son!"

A second cup followed, and a third and fourth cup.

Tarian fairly stewed in her chamber. After promising never again to challenge a man to a swordfight, She'd been able to calm Brighid down sufficiently to get her into bed, and now, after rocking her as Edith had done when she was a babe, she watched as Brighid slept fitfully, tangled up in the mass of sheets.

Sensing Tarian's short-tempered mood, Edith stayed clear of her pacing lady. As did Brighid's timid maid.

Tarian gave her foster sister a final glance, then stopped suddenly. Emotions she was not aware she possessed clashed in her head and her heart, and those emotions she refused to acknowledge were what caused her such anger.

How dare that Norman step back and allow her to challenge Rangor! What if by some ill chance the baron had bested her? Was she truly *nithing* to the bore? After today? *Jesu*! She had saved his life! And the way he had touched her in the ruins. Heat flushed her cheeks at his remembered touch. He shocked her, to be sure. But would he just hand her over like a used garment? She flung herself into the hard stone window seat and peered out, half expecting to see him standing in the dusky twilight, his hands fisted, staring up at her.

Nay, that would mean she occupied his mind, and it was apparent she did not!

She slammed her fists on the sill. "Argh!"

"Tarian?" Brighid cried out from the great bed. She hurried to the girl, waving off the girl's maid, who popped out of the corner, and shushed her back to sleep. Once Brighid's breaths evened, Tarian moved back to the window, and, more controlled, now she peered out. The great forest of

Dunloc spread out before her, straight ahead. To her right, where she could not see from her vantage point, were hides and hides of cultivated land. The soil was rich, and Dunloc had once been a thriving farming community. Some three leagues past the hill, in days past, the town there had teemed with an eclectic array of artisans. Glaziers, copper- and goldsmiths, some of the finest weavers in the land: all had called Dunloc home. The multitude of colors extracted from the soils in nearby hills was in high demand. Aye, the place had potential to become one of the great contributors to the Crown, but Malcor had neglected not only the magnificent fortress Draceadon, but the town and people as well. He preferred his time at the English court, before William, and, after the conquest, the smaller Welsh courts. His largest estate, Briarhurst, farther north and the place where they were to wed, was magnificent. But Malcor had gone to ground here at Draceadon. And here she had been imprisoned, and here she stayed.

As her gaze swept back to the darkening bailey she noted among the torches not only many of Rangor's men milling about but those of Morgan. She looked further and squinted, and saw Gareth and his men in full gear, and they too appeared as if they were about something.

She hesitated to go below and learn for herself what was about. Though she would enjoy nettling Rangor more than she had, she knew it would not be prudent to do so. He appeared then from the stable, a groom leading his horse, and beside the baron strode Morgan. They appeared to be in deep conversation. In unison they both looked up and caught her staring at them. She scowled but would not back away.

So the two plotted, did they?

"I will be in the hall, Edie, if you should have need of me."

Before the nurse could utter a word, Tarian strode from the room and down the hall to the sound of Normans making merry. Silently she hurled several ugly epithets toward them and continued down the stairway.

When she breached the last step, every Norman eye in the hall settled on her, their voices trailing off to mute. As one they grinned, and she scowled. What had the chivalrous knight imparted to them? Heat rose in her cheeks.

"Do you gossip like a girl and tell secrets that are not yours to tell?" she demanded of Wulfson as she strode into the hall.

The men grinned wider. So, he had told them of their little tryst, had he? "Do your men make sport of the fact I nearly cut your heart out with nary a stitch on my back?"

When all eyes widened, Tarian flushed hard. " 'Tis what you told them, is it not?"

Wulfson grinned and slowly shook his head. "I but extolled your prowess with bow and sword. Would you have me tell them of your other virtues I discovered this day?"

Her jaw dropped. But what she did not expect was to see his men turn scowls upon him. Wulfson raised his hands in mock surrender to them. "She was the one who insisted we disrobe and dry our clothes by the fire. I could do naught but obey."

She strode toward him and punched him in the chest. He looked at her, stunned that she would accost him thusly. She did not care. "You knave! 'Twas not like that."

Her hand smarted from the assault, but she would not have these men think her a wanton.

"How was it, then?" he asked boldly.

Her eyes narrowed and she stood her ground. "We were soaked to the skin, and your mail rusted. 'Twas the best way to preserve it. 'Tis not my fault you could not keep your eyes in your head or your hands to yourself!"

Wulfson chuckled and nodded. "I give you that." He turned to his men. "I assure you, the lady made sure there was no other dalliance."

Tarian held her breath and wondered why he skirted the entire truth. He turned back to her. "Does that confession please you?"

Hesitantly she nodded. " 'Tis enough." And for some ungodly reason, his preservation of her honor greatly pleased her.

"I saw Rangor and Morgan putting their heads together outside of the stable and their men assembled. What is about?"

"Rangor, as you know, prepares to leave here. Morgan refused to give up his weapons for the duration of his stay, and with no other option open to him and his men, he also is leaving."

So, 'twas the Normans, her guard, and her guardian's handful of men. She nodded her head toward the Norman leader. "Nicely done, Sir Wulfson. Nicely done."

"Would you have them remain armed and take a chance they could spring at any time?"

"Nay, 'twas a compliment, not a mock. I do not overly trust the Welsh." She looked up into his bright eyes. "Nor do I trust you. Would that I had more men, then you would have been given the same option."

He threw his head back and laughed, his men joining in. "And thwart William?"

Setting her hands on her hips, she nodded. "Aye, your king cannot at his whim take what is not his."

"England *is* his, milady. To ignore that fact is to set yourself up for a hard fall. As you would steer your horse to a specific place, steer your mind to William. He is strong, he is determined, and he will not be denied!"

She moved closer to him, their toes nearly touching. "Neither will I."

"For a woman who has everything to lose and no way to keep it, Lady Tarian, you boast much," Thorin said from behind her.

Tarian whirled around. "I do not boast! I but speak the truth. There is no reason for your king to interfere here! I have pledged my oath to him. What more does he want from any Saxon?"

"Guarantees," Thorin said.

"My oath is not my guarantee?"

Thorin shook his head. "Your uncle gave his oath; he swore it on a relic, and look what followed."

Tarian laughed at his comparison. "My uncle had no choice but to swear. Had he not, he'd be rotting in the bowels of a castle in Rouen. Do not compare me. The situations are not the same."

"He would be alive, as would thousands of Norman and English," Thorin defended.

"I can assure you, sir knight, as one who has spent time in a torturous dungeon, it is no life at all. I would rather die on the battlefield for what I believe than die a slow miserable death at the hand of a barbaric bastard!"

As she spoke, Tarian noticed the faces of each of the men around her close off and harden to hewn edges. Wulfson grabbed her arm and turned her to face him. "William is a bastard, of that there is no challenge, but he is not a Barbarian."

She yanked her arm from his grasp. "Do you call what he is doing to me now not a form of torture? We await your man for word as to whether I am to die! And if I am with child? He would take that life too?"

Wulfson's jaw tightened, but Tarian pleaded her case, "Your king, *my* king, is not a man of compassion. I offer him all and he throws it in my face. I cannot win with him." She moved away from the men and turned to face them all. "I will not hand over my sword for you to do the deed." Her eyes touched on every knight in the room. "You too will suffer loss, I guarantee it!"

They stood, the Norman knights facing the lone Saxon woman, and she read in their eyes that they knew she spoke the truth. An impasse. She would lose her life, for they would not defy their king. She smiled then, and laughed when all of them reacted in surprise and stepped back. "Though Rangor swears it, I am not a witch. But I am a warrior, and determined to see my child grow to manhood."

The knights remained silent. To break the tension, she cast an eye to Wulfson's leg. "Do you have designs on a particular tree stump?"

"A tree stump?"

"You have not tended your leg."

Wulfson shook his head, not overly concerned. "Nay, there has been no time with the day's excitement."

"Do you have the skill to sew yourself up?" Tarian asked, doubting that, even if he did, he would relish the chore. 'Twas painful no natter who held the needle.

"I will do it," Rhys said, stepping forward. "I but need a sturdy thread and a needle."

"Hah!" Wulfson said stepping back from the young knight. "I saw the botched job you did on poor Ioan last month. I will do it myself before I allow that ham fist of yours near me. Rest easy. Rolf will see to it when he finishes with the horses."

"Come to my chamber and I will see it done," Tarian said, exasperated, and wheeled from the men and proceeded back to her room. 'Twas not out of concern for the knight she offered to sew him up; nay, she would press her case more. In private. Nervous tension set her temper on edge, and her demeanor, usually amicable, was sorely tested. She felt as if she walked a narrow gap high above a churning sea.

She swung the door open with a clatter, forgetting Brighid. Edith started in her chair, dropping her distaff. Her sister's maid dropped her own embroidery, and Brighid murmured something unintelligible.

Softly Tarian called to her nurse, "Where is the needle and thread?" Edith's brow furrowed in question. "A man needs his leg sewn. Where is it?" Tarian asked.

Edith rose and walked to the great chest of drawers, and pulled the bottom one out. She reached in and extracted a flat basket. "Would you have me do it?" Edie asked.

"Nay, I will see to it." Tarian moved into the room and took the basket from her. As she walked back to the chamber door she had left open, the knight appeared.

"Back to the hall if you please, my sister sleeps. I do not wish to disturb her."

Wulfson stood silent for a moment not moving. "My chamber, if you have no objection, Lady Tarian. While I have no great modesty, I don't wish to be seated amongst the populace in the hall in just my braies."

Tarian heisted for a moment. She glanced back over her shoulder to Edith, who had that same knowing smile on her lips as she'd had last night and this morn. Tarian whirled around. "Very well, but your door remains open."

Wulfson stepped back and swept his arm for her to pass. "Of course."

Tarian swept past him down the hall and stopped outside his chamber.

"How did you know 'tis where I sleep?" he mocked.

"'Tis the only other solar with a bed large enough to bear your weight," she snapped back.

He smiled and pushed open the door and allowed her to stride through, and when she did, the night she spent there came flooding back as if she were reliving it. His scent filled the room. Spicy, with a hint of sandalwood and leather.

Good to his word, Wulfson did not shut the door, but his squire Rolf did as he entered. "Sir, I was told you were in need of me?"

The boy stopped short when Tarian turned to him. Perplexed, he looked to his master. "Sir?"

"Who told you I needed your assist?"

"Thorin, he said you—" Rolf looked to Tarian, who cocked her head and raised a quizzical brow. He had the intelligence to pinken under her sharp eye. He turned back to his master and swallowed hard. "He implied you might find a sword to your throat and that I should watch your back."

Wulfson threw his head back and laughed with carefree glee. He slapped the boy on the back, nearly sending him across the room. "See to the Viking! I can fend for myself."

Rolf hurried from the room, slamming the door solidly behind him. Wulfson turned to Tarian, who stood rigid near the cold hearth. "The Viking was right to send the squire. One wrong move from you, Norman, and you will find your throat slit."

"As you did to Malcor?" His eyes glittered.

"Aye, as I did to Malcor." She pointed to a short bench. "Strip down to your braies so that I may take a look."

He nodded, and as he undressed, Tarian unpacked the basket. But she needed fresh water. She called for a maid in the hall, who set about bringing a pail each of warm water and cool water, and clean linens. When Tarian returned to the room, she noted the knight had indeed stripped to just his braies. He stood with his back to her, and she noted a weeping cut just below his right shoulder. She also noticed the deep scars of a lash. Without thinking what she did, she pressed a fingertip to one that crossed his shoulder blade. His body stiffened.

"How came you by these?"

"The same as you. A barbaric bastard."

She traced her finger down to the small of his back where another deeper scar marred him. "This one?"

"Iberia, fighting the Saracens."

She touched the raw wound of earlier that day, and he flinched. "You will have two more to herald your battle with the unruly Welsh."

He turned, and his eyes swept hers. She reached up and pressed the palm of her hand to his chest, resting it on the scarred tissue. "Tell me true, how came you by this?"

"I told you. A reminder of who I am."

"Who made sure you never forgot?"

"The man I was paid to destroy."

"Did you?" He cocked a brow. "Destroy him?"

"Aye, with the help of my brothers. We all bear the mark."

She reached up and touched the crescent-shaped scar on his chin. "And this?"

He grabbed her hand and slowly brought it to his lips. Instead of kissing her, he sank his teeth into her palm. She cried out and pulled away from him.

"My mind is weary and my body fatigued. No more questions from you."

A servant knocked on the door, and, given permission, strode through the open door and set the bucket of steaming water on the floor next to the bench, along with a pitcher of cool water on the side table. Tarian dismissed her and pointed to the bench. "Sit. I will tend your shoulder first."

From the moment she cleaned the wound to when she bit off the last thread after the last stitch, he did not move even a muscle. And her hand did not waver or shake. 'Twas easy, his back was to her. But when she steeled her body between his hewn thighs to get the proper angle to sew up the larger of the two wounds, she immediately felt his body stiffen and his manhood rise against her side. She steadied his thigh and looked up at him, the needle poised, to caution him against any movement, but the words stuck in her throat. His green eyes blazed and his nostrils flared, and she felt like a hare in the sights of a wolf.

"Sir, please, I cannot concentrate when you look at me thusly."

"*I* cannot concentrate with you between my thighs thusly."

"But—'tis the best angle."

"So you are to say Rolf would have had to sit between my legs to adequately tend me?"

Heat rose in her cheeks. "I—he—no, 'twould have been awkward for you, I am sure." She repositioned herself more toward his knees. "Let me sew the wound."

He nodded, but his eyes did not waver from hers. Hastily she broke his gaze and set about the chore. As when she tended his shoulder, he sat perfectly still. But she felt the tension in him, and his erection had not subsided. Indeed, it had grown. When she bent down and bit through the last thread, his body flinched. But it was not from the pain of the wound. Slowly she sat up and did not dare move. Her heart thudded hard against her chest, and her breaths came out in short shallow bursts. Wide-eyed, she looked up at him. His intense gaze sent warm shivering waves of desire across her skin. When she pressed her hand on his thigh to steady herself, he hissed in a sharp breath.

He brought her chin up higher with two fingers. "Lady Tarian," he said hoarsely, "you try my patience and my desire more than any woman I have encountered. I beg you, if you do not want to keep me at constant swordpoint, do not touch me as you do. I am a mere mortal and find you most difficult to resist."

"Really?" she breathed, and moved more fully against him. He hissed in a breath, and she could feel the thick length of him against her breast. She closed her eyes, parting her lips for the briefest of seconds, remembering the delicious feel of him inside her. Her eyes flew open and she cried out when his hands yanked her up and she found herself straddling his good leg in a most unladylike manner, his lips hovering above her. Their breaths were warm, the air was warm, and their skin was warm.

"Do not toy with me, madame. Continue with your play and you will find yourself on your back with your skirts pushed up and me buried to the hilt in you."

Her pulse quickened. 'Twas what she wanted! She gasped at her wanton thought. Her eyes locked with his. She licked her dry lips. He growled, pulling her closer to him. His manhood pressed against her belly and his bare thigh pushed against her wet opening. She bit back a moan, and steeled herself, fighting the overwhelming desire this man instilled in her. His fingers dug into her arms. " 'Tis actions such as that, Tarian, that will see you on your back," he gritted.

Breathless, she hung in his arms, using every measure of restraint she possessed not to move against him. Only the linen of his braies separated what made them man and woman. "How could you take me with such abandon when your king wants my head?"

"My king is not a fool," he softly said, his lips lowering to hers. "Nor am I." Then he kissed her.

Thirteen

Tarian stiffened in his arms, wanting desperately to melt into him and allow him to take her to that place again in one passionate thrust. But, she told herself, if she allowed him this time, then there would be another and another, and . . .

She stilled, and when she did, his lips rose from hers, his deep green eyes intensely searching her face.

"How can you, Tarian, sit so hot and creamy on my bare thigh when you know why I am here?"

She gasped, his question shocking her. But her answer shocked her more. "I too am no fool, my lord knight."

His eyes widened and she felt him surge against her. "What are you saying?"

She pressed her hand upon his chest and felt the hard thud of his heart. "I am not a wanton woman, sir knight."

His arms tightened around her waist. "Nay, you are not."

"Despite the sins of my father and my forcing Malcor to wed with me, I am not evil."

He traced his nose along her cheek to the bend in her neck, inhaling her. "Nay, you are not."

"I have feelings as any other woman."

His fingers swept her breasts, molding them into his hands. She arched into them and moaned. His lips sank into her neck and his hips moved up against her. She squeezed her eyes shut, reveling in his ardent touch. For so long she had merely existed, never knowing the true meaning of living, of lust, of passion, not until he touched her. She craved it as much as she craved life.

"I have feelings as any other man, Tarian. I want you, here and now. Give yourself to me."

"I—I—" She could not say the words. She shivered, and pressed her hands to his chest. "I—"

He shook his head and untied his braies. Standing with her in his arms, he pushed them down his thighs and sat back down on the bench, bringing her down with him, where she straddled him. His hard smooth heat slid against the soft inner flesh of her thighs. She hissed in a breath and looked at him. His eyes blazed in passion, his body was tense; he waited only for her signal to proceed. God's blood, she wanted him. She wanted him to fill her as he had the night past, as he did in her dreams, as she had envisioned earlier in the rain.

She felt as if she stood on the edge of a great cliff, and that if she jumped there would be nothing below to catch her but the craggy rocks or the deep swirling water. But the fall would be freeing, exhilarating, unlike any other experience; and should she survive it, she would be stronger for it.

Tarian closed her eyes and arched into him, her hips thrusting forward slightly. "Look at me, Tarian," he softly commanded. She kept her eyes closed, afraid of what she would see. He lifted her slightly, and said again, "Look at me when I enter you."

Her eyes fluttered open, and it was as if last night never happened. She was as nervous as a virgin; but unlike a virgin, excitement and anticipation buzzed through her, mayhap so much so because she knew the sublime pleasure his body could give hers.

His dark eyes full of passion and promise, he lowered her gently onto him, and when he slid his fullness into her Tarian realized she would crave him always.

He groaned in primal satisfaction as he slowly filled her. His eyes never wavered from her face. Hers widened at the sublime sensation of him filling her. She fought the urge to close her eyes and just allow him to take her to flight, but she could not let herself become so vulnerable.

"Tarian," he whispered. "When you are ready."

Perspiration moistened his brow, and she knew he exercised great control not to gallop away with her astride. At the thought, she smiled. "I had a vision today of us riding together thusly." The instant she made the confession she regretted it. He smiled and moved into her. He caught her off guard, and she did close her eyes and soaked up every sensation as if it would be the last time. A sharp tug of regret needled her. 'Twould be the last time: if she allowed herself to give into her cravings, then they would control her. And she could not afford to be manipulated by desire . . . or any other force.

"You are shameless, Tarian Godwinson."

"Aye, and you are dangerous."

His cock flexed inside her and she felt her muscles embrace it. He hissed in another breath.

"I am ready, milord. Let us ride."

He galloped away with her. It took her only a few tries to synchronize with him, and when she did, she felt as if her body would come apart. She hung onto his wide shoulders; his hands gripped her hips, moving her up and down, back and forth, and he filled her so much, touching her in a place so deep inside her, that every time he did she bit back a cry.

His lips pressed to her throat, and his teeth nipped at her skin. His body pushed in and out of her with the force of a battering ram, and in the midst of it all, she lost her breath, lost control, and experienced a sensation so sublime she nearly fainted from the intensity of it. Her eyes flew open and she stared at him in surprise. He smiled tightly and increased his pace as she melted around him in one desirous wave after another.

She felt the shift in him. His fingers dug into her bottom, his breath came sharper and shallower. His eyes narrowed. Tarian dug her nails into his shoulders as she desperately hung onto him, and tightened her muscles around him. "*Jesu!*" he harshly cried. Thrusting hard and high into her, he filled her with his seed. She clasped her thighs tightly around him, wanting every bit of it.

Raggedly they clung to each other. She licked her dry lips and he pulled her face down to his and kissed her deeply, his tongue moistening hers. She swelled and pressed into his embrace, molding herself to him, wanting to hold onto his strength forever.

He flexed inside her, and she spasmed against him, catching her breath.

His kiss deepened, and he pressed his forehead against hers. "What just happened to me?" she gasped, still trying to come back to earth.

"A complete release. 'Tis similar to what happens to a man."

She stilled and looked at him, her eyes questioning. "Does it feel the same for you?"

He grinned wider. "Aye, 'tis the best feeling in the world."

She frowned, suddenly feeling as if she had made a colossal mistake. Not the deed, but experiencing it and wanting more.

He traced his knuckles across her bottom lip. "What bothers you?"

She nipped at his hand, catching a finger between her teeth. His body surged in hers, and she wondered how soon he would be ready to go again. She laved her tongue across his skin, feeling quite the vixen. Sex, she decided, was not something to be whispered about behind closed doors, but something to be shouted about from the rooftops. She opened his scarred and calloused hand and pressed her lips to his palm. He hissed in a sharp breath. She looked up at him and smiled like a coquette. "I have heard from many women that they find the act distasteful. That most certainly was not."

His intense eyes did not waver from hers. "Was it distasteful with Malcor?"

Tarian stiffened, and her flirtatious mood instantly dissolved. She used the break in mood to disengage from him. She slowly stood, and when he slid from her she cried out. He reached for her, but she spun away from him, suddenly feeling extremely vulnerable. "Please do not ask me about my dead husband. He caused me great pain and humiliation. I would put that time behind me."

Wulfson stood and grabbed a linen and wiped himself clean, then hitched up his braies. "My pardon."

Tarian stood for a long time and watched him dress. She wrestled with the conflicting emotions and feelings swirling so crazily about inside her heart and her head. She did not regret her tryst with the knight, despite everything. If he slew her at that moment, he alone had given her a pleasure she had never dreamed existed and that in itself justified the deed. Nay, she had no regrets. But it could not continue.

"Sir, it seems you have caught me at a weak moment."

He tied his chauses to his braies and looked over at her. "Do you regret it?"

She answered honestly, "Nay. I do not, but please do not press me again. I have no desire to become your leman." He scowled but nodded. "And I would ask that you do not share what just occurred with your men."

"I am not a knave, madame."

"I did not imply that you were—it's just that—well, men have a penchant for crowing their conquests."

Wulfson bowed, then slipped his undertunic over his head. "Your secret is safe with me."

"Thank you." Tarian grabbed up the sewing basket and strode from the room.

When Wulfson returned to the hall his men stared at him as if they could see the thoughts in his head. He scowled. Angry with himself, angry over the situation, but mostly angry at the Welsh witch. He was a seasoned warrior whose self-control, though tested regularly, had never fallen, but at every turn he found his will tested and breached by the lady. He cursed himself for his weakness for her. She had gotten under his skin the moment he set eyes on her dirty, bloody body in the bowels of this place, and she continued to haunt him, so much so that he would have staked his life on her having come to his chamber in the night and seduced his will from him. And what was that to what had just transpired? He felt the blood heat in his veins and his cock rise. *Jesu!* He could not have resisted her for the lives of his men!

"Say what is on your minds," he blustered as he poured himself a full cup of ale. The hall had begun to fill for the evening repast.

"Pray tell, Wulf, tell us what plagues *you*," Rorick said, filling his own empty cup. Wulfson cast a glance to Gareth, who with his men approached.

"'Tis nothing time away from here will not cure." He wondered if he spoke the truth.

The meal awaited only the lady of the manor. Wulfson scowled when long moments later he was informed she had retired for the evening.

His scowl deepened the next morn when she did not make an appearance, and after three more days of her refusal to preside over her manor, losing his temper at last Wulfson strode up the stairs and burst through her door. The girl Brighid cried out, as did the maid Edith and the other maid. He stepped into the chamber. "Where is she?" he demanded.

Edith stood, and for a servant she met his eye unwaveringly. "Of whom do you speak, milord?"

"Lady Tarian! Where is she?"

Edith smiled. "She is not in the hall?"

Wulfson's temples throbbed with the infusion of blood. He stepped closer. "She has not stepped foot in the hall these four days past." He lowered his voice to menacing. "Where is she?"

Edith's brows rose in mock surprise. "I suspect she is out for a ride then, milord."

"Unchaperoned?" he demanded, incredulous.

Edith laughed. "You of all men know she requires no man's protection."

Wulfson spun on his heels and stomped out of the room, down the stairway, out the hall, and to the stable. Her gray was in his stall. His fury mounted. Had she flown? Could he blame her? Would he in her position wait for the death sentence? Though Warner had still not returned, he was not overly worried, since he could be awaiting a suitable tide to cross the channel. Yet Wulfson felt an unease bite and scratch at his belly.

The unease intensified when Gareth, followed by several of his own men, encountered Wulfson standing furious in the stable. "Where is she?" Wulfson demanded.

"She is not here?" the guard asked, surprised.

Wulfson's eyes narrowed. "Do not play me for a fool as the nurse already has. The lady is not in the manor nor is she here. Her horse eats his morning oats."

Color drained from Gareth's face, and Wulfson knew he did not lie. "She—I have slept at her door each night. I have another man posted during the day. She did not slip past."

"And she did not climb from the window either!" Wulfson railed.

Angrily he strode back to the lady's chamber. If he had to whip the information from her nurse, he would. But when he arrived, she too had disappeared. Frustration so complete he thought his head would split in half engulfed him. He threw his hands up in frustration and turned on Brighid. "Tell me where she is or I will nail you to the manor doors until you do!"

The girl screamed, which brought not only Gareth running into the room but her father and several of his men. Wulfson's jaw was clenched so tightly he thought it would crack into pieces.

"Leave her be," Alewith commanded, gathering his daughter into his arms. His eyes blazed in indignation. "She has no hand in what Tarian does."

Thorin spoke softly to the girl. "Tell us where she is. Her life is at stake."

"Nay, I will not tell you! Her life is more at stake here!" She turned murderous blue eyes on Wulfson.

Frustration, fury and fear tangled in an ugly battle in his belly. "At the risk of your own life, tell me where she is," Wulfson menacingly said.

Alewith pushed her behind him and stood his ground. "Touch her, and there will be hell to pay. She will not give Tarian up."

"I have no wish to harm the girl, my lord, but either she tells me the whereabouts of the lady or she will spend time in the dungeon until she does."

"Who is the barbaric bastard now, Sir Wulfson?" Tarian asked, striding into the room, her bow and quiver slung over her shoulder.

Every person in the chamber turned, as a collective sigh of relief escaped them all. But none so much as Wulfson. He would deny to his death that he felt a sense of elation at the sight of her, and it had nothing to do with failing his king. Joy sang in his hard heart. She was a sight to behold, as always. Her cheeks were flushed red and her hair a wild mass around her, festooned with festive ribbons entwined throughout. Her casual dress for the hunt only accentuated everything female about her.

"You play a dangerous game, milady, not only with your own life but those of others," Wulfson said, taking a step closer to her. Her violet scent wafted around his nostrils, teasing him and torturing him at the same time. His cock filled, and had he not had an audience he would have given in to the craving he had for her.

"I do not play at love and war, sir."

He forced back a tight smile. "You are no longer permitted to leave this manor unless you are given permission by myself or one of my men."

"And should I not?"

"Then you will revisit the place we first met."

Tarian nodded, and turned to the crowd in her chamber. "Would you leave me to a private word with Sir Wulfson?"

They stood, all of them, including his knights, as if she had just asked them to cut off their right hands. "I would have it done sooner rather than later." She moved to the door and swept her arm toward the hallway. "Now, please."

"My lady—" Gareth started. She raised her hand in a halt position. "The terrible knight has no reason to fear me. I give my word I will not harm a hair on his head."

Thorin and Rorick snorted as they strode from the room, and Gareth's brows shot up. "Go, Gareth."

Wulfson's heart beat in his chest with the velocity of a smith's hammer. As soon as the door was closed, he was upon her, pressing her into it. "Do not play with me, Tarian," he ground out. He could not help dipping his head to her hair and breathing in her scent. His blood coursed hotly through him, and he felt his control losing ground against his ravenous hunger for her.

He knew she felt a similar sensation. Her body warmed beneath his hands. He dug his fingers into her hair, mussing the ribbons, and forced her to look at him. "I am not a lad to be led around by my cock."

She pushed him off and strode into the middle of the room. "Nor am I a girl to be toyed with."

"Why have you hidden from me these four days past?" He stood stone still, afraid that if he went near her again he would not be able to control his body's yearning.

"I have not *hidden*, I have been unwell."

"You lie."

"Nay, I do not." She turned and set her bow and quiver on the chest near the hearth, then whirled around to face him. "What is it you expect of me? To sit here in my chamber and while away the hours as we all await word from your king? Tell me now, did you come here for the sole purpose of taking my life?"

He could not answer her. By his not answering, she knew.

"You are not man enough to tell me? But you are man enough to have your way with me? And then have no compunction in slaying me should your master command it?"

He remained silent.

She began to pace the floor. "What manner of man are you to do such a terrible thing? Have you no pride? No conviction?"

He stood silent and took it. He could not answer in his defense. She spoke the truth. And he felt as if he belonged in a cesspit.

She strode up to him and grabbed his right hand and pressed it her belly. "What if a child grows there? Will you kill an innocent babe?"

Wulfson pulled his hand from her grasp but she held it tight. "Tell me now, would you, if your king commands you?"

A sudden rage arose in him, a rage at the situation and a rage that his king would ask such a thing of him, an honorable man. He pushed her back against the wall, his fingers digging into her belly. "I cannot go against my king!"

She pressed her hands over his. Tears glittered in her eyes. "'Tis murder, Wulfson. Murder."

He extracted his hand and pushed away from her, and as if every demon in hell chased him he ran from the chamber. He called his men to arms and gave Gareth the order not allow the slippery lady from his sight.

Troubled as he had never been in all his life, Wulfson took his anger, lust, and confusion out on his men. Though they only practiced, he went after each one as if he was his sworn enemy.

When he drove Rhys to his knees, Thorin and Rorick grabbed Wulfson by his shoulders and drew him away. Wulfson shouted out in fury, shaking them off. Turning on them he stood spent. His fight was gone. He threw his swords to the dirt. "I cannot murder a woman with child."

His men shook their heads. He looked at each of them through narrowed eyes. "Tell me you could do it. Tell me and I shall hand over this cursed place to your sole command."

He clashed gazes with Thorin, who remained silent, then Rorick, Stefan, Rhys, and finally Ioan.

"Send her to Normandy," Thorin said.

Wulfson bent to pick up his weapons; as he sheathed them he shook his head. "So that some other can do the deed? There must be another way."

"I know not what can be done, Wulf," Stefan said. "Most especially if she carries the earl's child. The blood of Welsh kings and a Saxon king? Nay, she would be even more of a threat."

No option was suitable to keep the lady alive. And with a foreboding dread, Wulfson knew that the minute he laid eyes on Warner he would know what William's word would be. "Come, let us patrol this miserable place."

Tarian watched the knights thunder from the bailey toward Dunloc. Her hand slid to her belly, and she wondered if she were at that moment growing a babe inside her. " 'Twill take more than a few days to see if the seed bears fruit, milady," Edith said from behind her.

Tarian turned to the nurse and smiled tiredly. "I don't know what to do, Edie."

"I say we fly from here. To Powys, where you will be safe."

"And give up Draceadon?"

"Aye, is your life and that of the child worth this rubble heap?"

Tarian looked out the window at the stretch of forest and the surrounding land. "What life would I have in Wales? As a hostage?"

Edith came and stood behind her. She pressed her hands to Tarian's hair and smoothed the long tresses. "I know it is the last thing that you wish, Tarian, but you should give Rangor more thought." Tarian stiffened. "Hear me, girl. He is noble, he has strong allies in Edric, he would become earl, he will protect you, and he has the ear of two Welsh kings. He has several bastards to his name and is virile. He would not leave you wanting for children."

When Tarian did not answer, Edith continued. "Malcor was evil, and if you could bed with him, then why not with Rangor, who in his twisted way desires you above all women, and who would not harm you?"

"If I bear the Norman's child there will be no question to my right here."

"Aye, among the Saxons, yes, but the Norman king? All the more reason to see you removed."

"I will use my coin to buy more men."

Edith let out a long breath. "Let my words simmer in your mind. You will see I am right."

Tarian shook her head and continued to stare across her vast estate. But she knew in her gut that Edith, who never spoke a word in haste, spoke the truth.

She peered at her nurse's hunched form. Aye, Edith spoke true, but Tarian still had in her hand dice to throw. Her men awaited the interception of Warner, who was no doubt on his return to England from Normandy. Regardless of the king's decree, time was her ally, and she would hold the knight until such time as Wulfson became unmanageable; then she would trade her life for his man's. So sure was she that Wulfson would not sacrifice one of his men for her life that she was able to form a different strategy with a clear head, on the slim chance she was wrong.

The evening meal passed in relative quiet. A heavy hush hung above them, and as much as Alewith and Brighid tried to start conversation, the Normans, as Tarian and her men, were quiet. The servants sensed the mood, and the people from the village who sat at the other end of the hall did as well.

Greatly troubled, Tarian excused herself and found her

bed early. Wulfson followed, retiring to his own chamber shortly after. He felt as if the weight of the nation settled squarely on his shoulders, and he did not have the first thought of how to remedy the ills of this place, and, if he were to admit it, the bruises to his heart. He shucked his clothes, and when Rolf came in with steaming buckets of water, he dismissed the squire and saw to his own bath. He wanted no interaction. Mayhap alone with no chatter he could devise a solution that would satisfy all parties involved. Once clean, he dropped to the bed and stared at the ceiling with his hands locked behind his head. He was no closer to resolution then he had been when he climbed the stairway to his chamber.

Not since his time in Jubb, the Saracen prison where he and his fellow Blood Swords had forged a life pact and nearly lost their lives, had he been so contemplative.

He was a man of few words and all action. He had learned early in life not to expect anything from anyone; it only served to disappoint, and disappointment hurt. His men and his horse were his family, and he had never felt the urge for a companion other than them.

Tarian's ocean-blue eyes floated in his mind's eye, her soft laughter and her tenacity. She fascinated him on all levels. His physical reaction to her each time he saw her was as strong and undeniable as the rising sun every morn. He could no more control it than he could the moon and the stars, and in all of his six-and-twenty years of life, nothing had scared him more.

He slammed his fists into the covers and rolled over to his side. He closed his eyes and wondered, if he prayed to God, would she materialize?

In a way, she did. In the heavy air of the room, he caught

a whiff of rose scent. He grabbed the pillow next to his head, and closing his eyes he brought it to his nose and inhaled deeply. His rod filled, and he groaned as that familiar ache she instilled in him began to grow painful. He was not fooled. The rose perfume did a poor job shielding her natural honey scent. But why? Why had she come to him, a stranger sent to destroy her? Did she think to wheedle her way into his heart? He cursed. She had wheedled her way into his every thought! He cursed again, this time in self-loathing. She had used him well, and had succeeded in her ploys. He was but a way for her to gain control! And he, blind fool of a man, had not seen it coming!

He threw the pillow from him and sat up in the bed. His eyes traveled the room and stopped at the large tapestry to the right of the bed. He rose and went to it, unhooking the bottom corner, and lifted it.

Only a stone and wooden wall met his stare. He pressed his hands to a block, and then worked his fingers back and forth, searching for any telltale sign of a latch. His frustration grew when he could not locate a way to what he was sure was a hidden passageway. He grabbed the candle from the table next to the bed and held it down near the floor, and smiled. The imprint of a small foot in the dust gave her away. Now, more determined than ever, he worked the perimeter until finally he heard a small creak. He pushed with both hands as cool air swirled around his feet. He donned his braies and slipped through the opening, following the footprints down a dark passageway to what he knew to be the lord's chamber.

For long moments he stood on the other side of the secret door that led to her chamber. He knew she was not alone, that the two maids and her foster sister slept in the room with her. But he could see for sure if the passage was accessible from her chamber. He set the candle down on the floor and found the indentation to spring the door just above a timber. Silently the door opened. He stood still and listened for voices. Only soft snores met him. He pushed wider, then slipped behind the tapestry and into the dimly lit room. The heavy drapes of the bed were pulled back to allow air flow, and Tarian lay on her side facing him in slumber.

Brighid was all the way over on the other side of the bed. From where he stood, he could see she slumbered. The maids were on pallets at the end of the bed, both older and both snoring with their mouths open. He stepped closer to Tarian. He could see her face in the low light of the candlelight. Her brow puckered as if something unpleasant plagued her dreams. Her lips moved as if she murmured a secret. He stepped closer. He ached to touch her. But he did not.

Long minutes passed. He stood rooted to the floor, his eyes never leaving her. She moaned, and when she slid her hand up to her breast he held his breath. She arched, as if a man's hand caressed her, soft moans escaping her lips. His blood warmed and the ache to touch her became unbearable.

"Wulfson," she breathed his name in her dreams.

He stepped closer, on the verge of losing all control but he held back; the torment of her being so close yet unable to touch would break him. He stepped back, and as he turned to duck back into the secret passage, he gave the bed one last glance, and froze. Brilliant eyes peered at him through the candlelight. Before he lost all, he ducked into the passageway and closed the door behind him.

He did not find sleep until the crow of the cock, and it seemed as if only moments had passed when Rolf awoke him.

"Do you ail, sir?" the squire asked.

Wulfson grumbled. "Nay, why do you ask?"

"You are never abed this late."

Wulfson rolled to the edge of the bed; his bare feet touched the carpet. He glanced toward the tapestry and his heart stopped. There, embedded in the wall, was an arrow with sapphire and gold feathers. He started to laugh, and Rolf looked at him as if he had gone daft.

"I could eat the black! See that the servants prepare a feast to break the fast; then we shall wear the shoes down on our horses this day."

"Sir?"

"I want to know this place as if I were born to it. There is strife in our future, and I wish to be prepared."

When Wulfson descended into the hall, he was surprised to see Tarian, but he did not show it. He gave her a curt bow. "My lady, you seem rested."

"Aye, more so than others."

He grinned, then seated himself beside her. "Touché."

After the meal was blessed, Tarian announced, "I should like to accompany you and your men on your daily patrol today, and when such time as you practice your drills, I would also like to partake. Most especially, I wish to train Silversmith to move as your horse does on the battlefield. I have much to learn."

The men snorted, and Tarian ignored them. Wulfson looked as if he were choking on the coddled egg he had just bitten into. "I do not jest," she said.

He took a long swig of mead and swallowed, then

looked at her, incredulous. "I will not have a woman ride with us."

"Are you insecure in your manhood?" He scowled heavily, and she knew she had an opening. "I will be in full mail and helm as you. No one will notice."

"*I* will notice."

"Not if you look the other way."

"Nay, 'tis not safe. Morgan and your uncle no doubt lurk."

She shook her head. "Nay, they do not. Morgan has returned to Powys, and Rangor is on his way to Winchester."

Wulfson's jaw dropped. "How do you know this?"

"I pay my spies well." When he did not speak, she continued, "Do not underestimate me, sir. My life and estates are at stake. Do you think I have sat idly by allowing the fates to determine the course of my life?"

"Lady Tarian," Rhys said from down the table, "I for one would have no aversion to your riding with us. Indeed, I am eager to see you in action. I find Wulfson's tall tales of your prowess a bit too much to swallow."

"Did you not witness her handling of Rangor?" Brighid asked, incredulous, from across the table. Tarian smiled at the girl, who she knew held a soft spot for the handsome young knight.

"Mayhap I could teach you how to wield a sword," Rhys said smiling, and without breaking his gaze with Brighid, he speared a piece of meat with his knife and chewed meaningfully. Brighid pinkened, and Alewith cleared his throat.

Tarian smiled up at Wulfson, who glared daggers at his man. Tarian pressed her hand to his, and he flinched. " 'Tis just a hand, sir, no need to fluster."

He pressed his thigh to hers and turned heated eyes toward her. "You play with fire, Tarian, do not push me. I am at my limit."

She threw her head back and laughed. "Then a vigorous day in the saddle is what is in order!"

"More like a cold swim in yonder pond," he grumbled under his breath.

Tarian refused to give way to his morose mood. "It can be arranged. The water is clear and clean, and most refreshing after a day in this insufferable heat."

Wulfson's dark eyes burned into her. He lowered his lips to her ear. "Is that an invitation?"

His warm breath caressed her cheeks, and Tarian felt her weakness for him encompass her like a warm blanket on a cold winter's eve. "The pond is there for anyone's pleasure."

"Do you swim?"

"Well enough. I suppose you are an expert."

He grinned, his humor restored. "Normandy has vast white beaches, where we train the horses in the salt water. 'Tis good for their legs. The sand builds muscle and stamina. After a long day, the water is a welcome respite. With the deadly tides, if one is not a strong swimmer one may drown."

"Is your country beautiful?

"Aye. And the weather is more welcoming."

"'Tis an unnaturally hot spring, with more rain than normal. Do you find the area so loathsome?"

He stared at her for a long moment. "Nay. Quite the contrary. I find the landscape and the local sights pleasing." His gaze held hers, and she felt a fluttering in her belly.

"Do you have a lady love awaiting your return?"

Color drained from Wulfson's face and he recoiled. "Nay! I am a bachelor for life."

"Do you not want children and a spouse to assist you with your estate?"

"To have either, a wife is required."

"What is so wrong with a wife?"

Wulfson turned to his meal. "I do not want a mewling nag nettling me at my every turn. I am a knight of William. My place is where he sends me."

Tarian stiffened. "Your perception of a wife is muddied by those who take no pride in their wifely place."

"What of you, Tarian? Do you wish to marry again?"

She smiled. "Nay, I do not want a mewling nagging husband nettling me at my every turn."

He laughed, but his face settled into a more serious mode. "I know not how this will end, but if I were you, I would seek a high-ranking husband, preferably a Norman noble, and give him sons as soon as possible."

"Why a Norman?"

"Because Saxons are losing their estates at an alarming rate. As you are aware, William has no great trust for them. 'Twould be wisest to blend your blood."

Tarian considered his words, and realized he spoke true. Rangor was not the answer.

"Do you have a worthy Norman noble in mind?"

Wulfson scowled heavily, and turned away from her. "Nay."

The meal concluded with light chatter and banter, but Wulfson's words had struck a chord with her. A Norman noble? 'Twas so obvious, why had she not thought of it? She did not know if she could stomach marriage to a Norman. Her eyes cast a sideways glance to the Norman knight she had been more intimate with than most wedded couples. If she could respond to him, mayhap there was hope. She sighed heavily.

Events were spinning out of her control, and she was beginning to feel she might not succeed. She pushed away from the table and stood. The knights, along with every other man seated, rose. Tarian bowed her head toward Wulfson. "I will meet you and your men shortly in the courtyard." She turned away from him before he could argue. "Gareth, see that my horse is battle-dressed."

Fourteen

Wulfson was not about to wait for the lady. His men ribbed him for giving in; he blamed Rhys. As they mounted, he paused in mid-movement and watched amazed the small form fully mailed and helmed striding toward them with the obvious gait of a woman. His men too stopped all action, and watched in stunned shock as she made her way toward them. Her long black hair swirled down her back and around her waist, giving away to any doubters the sex of the person under the mail. Her mail was shiny silver, as was her helm, from which a jaunty yellow plume bounced with each step. Her broadsword, strapped to a leather belt, hung from her narrow waist; her bow was slung across her back, and her quiverful of arrows hung from her right hand. She looked every bit a warrior and carried herself with the smooth grace of one.

"In all my years I have never seen a woman in mail," Thorin said, slowly whistling.

"William should use her as his standard bearer; the enemy would be too stunned to engage," Ioan said, a chuckle in his voice.

"God's blood!" Wulfson cursed. "She *is* a distraction. How can you men condone this? She will get us killed!"

His men grinned, and for the sheer sake of the novelty, and to also bait Wulfson, they did not discourage her. Gareth tossed her up into the saddle as he had no doubt done one hundred times before. His familiarity with the lady warrior stung Wulfson. He swiped it away as he would a buzzing bee.

She reined the gray up and spurred him forward. When she was several strides past them she pulled back on the reins and looked to the six knights, who sat unmoving upon their destriers in open shock.

"Come, lads, let us stir up trouble this day. I have a yearning for a fight!" Tarian called to them, then spurred her horse.

"*Jesu*! She is mad!" Wulfson grumbled. He turned to his men and threatened, "And I am daft to allow this! If she gets herself in trouble do not look to me to extract her. She is your worry!" He reined the black around and thundered after her vanishing form, his men close on his heels.

They settled into a short two-abreast phalanx, with Tarian breaking formation in the middle. 'Twas not what Wulfson had intended but it just naturally fell that way. He and Thorin, who bore the king's standard, rode point, Tarian behind them. Rhys paired with Rorick, and Stefan and Ioan brought up the rear. In that formation she could easily be surrounded by them in a quick square.

"The village of Dunloc is three leagues past the left fork in the road," Tarian called to Wulfson. He nodded, already knowing the exact location of the town. They continued in silence, the normal conversation and camaraderie of his men absent. He knew their silence stemmed not only from Tarian's presence but because they were acutely aware of how close to the Welsh border they were. Remaining silent but alert would keep them alive.

They made the bend in the road and continued at a brisk pace, the horses and the men feeling their morning oats. And Wulfson had to admit, the combination of the powerful thrusts of the formidable steed beneath him, Williams's standard flying arrogantly in the air beside him, and knowing the most beautiful woman in the kingdom rode behind him stroked his ego to considerable girth. Aye, he felt as if he were the conquering hero of the land.

As the small town rose up to the left ahead of them, Wulfson reined his horse in that direction, and slowed. They had deliberately avoided the village since the first patrol more than a fortnight ago, finding no warmth from the sullen villagers. Not that Wulfson had an aversion to sullen Saxons, but he was not wont to engage in battle with women and old men who had only brooms and scythes as weapons. 'Twas no contest, and he considered it needless slaughter. So they avoided the place. But today the sun shone bright in the blue skies and he had a curiosity about the town, so he had allowed the venture. He also admitted he wanted to test the waters as to the inhabitants' mood toward the lady who had slain their earl.

From the minute the first villagers set eyes on them, Wulfson had a bad feeling. Hatred sparked like fire from their eyes and they were not bashful in their contempt. And though the place bustled with activity, it had the downtrodden edge of squalor. Several structures were burned out and others had no roofs; the few that did were in a sorry state of repair.

"Malcor's neglect is obvious," Tarian said to Wulfson. Several villeins overheard and stared at her, their jaws agape. "He gave these people no consideration. He thought them backward."

"We are not backward churls! We are artisans!" a woman shrieked from behind them. Wulfson stiffened.

"Silence, Lady Tarian," Wulfson warned. He watched the eyes of several bystanders widen. He silently cursed. Word would spread like wildfire.

Once they came upon the small town square along the main merchant street, Wulfson slowed his pace, bunching up his men to a tighter formation.

"Why do you slow?" Tarian asked.

"Silence," Wulfson said, his tone hard and low.

" 'Tis the witch of Draceadon!" someone shouted from the gathering crowd.

"The one upon the gray!"

"Murderess!" A hailstorm of shouts erupted.

Wulfson swore again, and immediately shields went up, his men forming a protective square around Tarian. As one unit, in the same direction as she had watched from her window, they moved forward and to the side out of harm's way. Confused by the close proximity of the horses and the manner in which they moved, Silversmith pranced and worried at the bit. "Steady, lad," Tarian soothed, "Steady."

A missile of rotten fruit hit Tarian in the back of her helm. Before she could react, it was followed by rocks and chunks of wood and anything else the villagers could hurl.

The crude weapons bounced off the men's shields but several struck Tarian.

Her heart raced, not with excitement but in anger and frustration, and also in sadness. These were her people and they did not want her! Would she ever fit in anywhere?

"Bastard of a rapist! Begone. Take your Norman pigs with you!"

Within, Tarian cringed, but on the outside she kept her poise, her back straight, her eyes forward, her hand steady. She'd heard the insults all her life; she had learned to deal with them. Most of the time they did not hurt, but today they struck deep. Here she was, in a place she'd thought would welcome her, only to find once again she was not wanted. The sins of the father. Would her life ever run smooth?

As the missiles continued to make their way not only to her but to the knights, Tarian glanced to Rhys on her left. He, as the others, did not appear overly worried. He did not look her way but kept focused on the growing mob. "Steady, my lady," he softly cautioned, "Keep the pace and do not break from the formation."

She nodded, and felt a sense of power amongst these men she had never experienced. They were so well trained, their skills honed to lethal; she knew that no matter what the villagers did, she would come to no harm under the protection of these men. And with that knowledge she threw her shoulders back more, lifted her chin, her gaze sweeping those around her, meeting their eyes, and defying any one of them to challenge her right to be there.

The sharp hiss of an arrow narrowly missed her head but with a solid thunk found a home in Silversmith's neck. The horse shrieked in pain and reared, his front hooves digging into the back of Wulfson's black. The destrier did not flinch, but Silversmith came awkwardly down, and she could feel the stallion's panic. Expertly she maneuvered him, calling to him to calm. He reared again. Tarian kept a steady hand on the reins but when another arrow whizzed past, this time sinking into the thick leather of Wulfson's saddle, the gray threw his head and took the bit. Panicked, he bolted, forcing his way between Wulfson's horse and Rhys's steed, nearly climbing over the great horses to be gone from the attack. Wulfson grabbed her right rein as Silversmith slammed against him, but the gray would have none of it. He whipped his head around, then threw it again, and the reins yanked free from Tarian's hands. Tarian grabbed the high pommel for balance, for once the stallion had broken free of the formation, at a full-out crazed gallop the gray stumbled his way through the square, and as the mobs drew closer around him raising their brooms and forks, he reared again. Though Tarian held on, she battled for control, and finding the reins she pulled him up. But he took the bit again, and under a sudden barrage of rotten fruit, vegetables, and stones the horse screamed in fear, bucking and rearing in his panic to be rid of the attackers. The crazed mob pushed closer, until bodies pressed against her legs and her horse stood quivering in stark terror.

A brawny arm reached up from the motley group and dragged her from the saddle. Silversmith bolted from the crowd. But Tarian was prepared to fight and as she went down she drew her sword. And though she landed on her back in the dirt, she had wits enough to plunge upward in short shallow jabs, and find flesh. A man screamed in pain, and as more hands reached for her, tearing off her plumed helm and a gauntlet, she thrust up and hacked until most backed off and made way for her.

She could barely see from her vantage point that Wulfson and his men circled the mob, forcing them closer and closer together into an immobile bunch, at the same time herding them away from her. Swinging around the flank, Wulfson came around, and as he passed her, she reached up and he grabbed her by the arm, hoisting her up behind him. She landed with a loud whoosh behind him on the black's hindquarters, but she would take it over being the center of the mob's angry attention. Quickly the villagers were sufficiently quelled and Wulfson, with both swords drawn, pointed them at the red-haired giant who appeared to be the ringleader.

"Cease your attack at once or prepare to meet your maker!" he shouted. Turold stood perfectly still, the angry swell of churls having no effect on him. Yet Tarian could feel the tight bunch of his haunches beneath her ready to attack should his master but give him the signal. "I hold authority here under the proclamation of King William. Defy me, you defy him! He deals harshly with traitors, as do I. Further action against me or my knights will constitute an act of treason!"

"The bastard is not the king of our choosing!" a woman shouted. A turnip flew from the crowd, hitting Thorin in the chest. He did not flinch.

"Give us the witch so that we may burn her!"

"*Murderess!*"

Anger swirled savagely and quickly rose to a height she had never experienced, and with it Tarian could no longer hold her tongue. "Silence, all of you!" she shouted from where she sat. "You know not of what you speak! You call

me a witch when your lord Malcor was a deviate!" She
looked past Wulfson's shoulder to the crowd. "How many
of your sons did he drag up the hill? How many of them
never returned?"

Stunned silence answered her. "You call *me* a witch?
What then was *he*?"

She slid off Turold's back. She heard Wulfson's sharp
curse for her to return but she ignored it, and strode into
the crowd. He moved to grab her arm, but she flung him
off. Angrily she faced the people she hoped to serve and
in return be served by. "I am not your enemy. I am your
emancipator. I did not slay the earl in cold blood; I fought
for my life against him in that dungeon of horrors. 'Twas
him or me, and I chose to live!"

She moved toward the big red-haired man. "What manner of man are you to attack a Saxon noblewoman?"

His hauntingly familiar pale eyes narrowed, and he
looked past Tarian to the knights behind her. "What kind
of men are *those*?" he defied, pointing his crude club at the
knights. " 'Tis whispered they have come to finish off Dunloc and take it for themselves."

"That, my good fellow, remains to be seen."

She moved further into the crowd. "Earl Malcor neglected Dunloc; I know, I see it. This place is a shambles.
And while I find your loyalty to him admirable, it will be
different now. Despite his deviance, he knew the value of
giving me, his widow, title here." She stepped up onto an
overturned cart, and now could look over the sea of faces.
Anger, frustration, and fear met her head-on. "I am your
lady now, not the Normans, or Rangor." She extended her
arms and hands palms up, and pleaded, "I but ask that you
give me a chance to bring prosperity back to Dunloc."

Blank stares answered her plea. "Who is reeve here?"

"Dead at Stamford Bridge!"

"No one has replaced him?"

The redheaded man raised his club. "I am Ednoth, bastard half brother of Malcor. I am leader here."

Tarian nodded. "I pray the family resemblance is only skin-deep, Ednoth."

His eyes widened before narrowing. "Do not insult me with your accusations."

"Then return the favor."

He subtly nodded his head. "There are deep wounds here. They will not heal overnight." He looked past her to the knights, who kept swords pointed and at the ready.

"Aye, sir, England still bleeds." She turned back to Wulfson, who watched only the crowd. "Let us part now, and when there is a more temperate climate, we will speak of building our future here." She looked up to Wulfson, who sheathed his left-handed sword and extended the hand to her. He hoisted her up again and she settled behind him.

She looked over the crowd. While their mood had subsided, there was still much open hatred in their eyes for her and the men she rode with. She could not blame them. She would feel the same too, and a few promises from a woman of her background would do little to settle their restlessness.

With nothing more to be said, in amazing precision, without a word spoken, the six destriers backed up as one at an angle, completely extricating themselves from the villagers, who wisely parted for the great horses to pass. It was not until they were clearly out of missile range that they turned their steeds on their hind legs in unison and galloped toward Draceadon. As they set upon the road, not one word was spoken. But she could feel the anger tense in Wulfson's body.

She wanted to deny that the incident was her fault, but she could not, for the truth was obvious. Silversmith, as seasoned as he was, was not accustomed to the other horses and the tight formations. The arrow in his neck had been the catalyst. He had much to learn, as did she, in the art of war. Tarian feared for the horse's welfare, but knew he would return to the place where he was fed. Resigned to her part in the melée, Tarian did not engage any of the men in conversation. Indeed, so focused were they on their surroundings they probably forgot her existence. She let out a long breath and tried to relax, but could not. The ride back to Draceadon was long, uncomfortable, and silent.

As they broke into the small valley lying before the great fortress, Gareth with a handful of her men came thundering out from the bailey. When they saw the contingent of knights, they slowed.

Tarian saw the worry in Gareth's eyes before she heard it in his voice. "Your horse, milady, he took an arrow? Are you injured?" he asked as he saw her mounted behind Wulfson, his eyes looking up and down her body for any injury.

Wulfson snorted. "The lady's only injury is to her mind to think she possesed the skill to ride with us. She will not again. She was nearly killed and she put my men in peril."

"The villagers of Dunloc swarmed us. Silversmith took an arrow, and he panicked," she said softly.

Gareth nodded and reined his horse around. As they approached the long road up to Draceadon, churls stood silent in the fields, watching them pass. Tarian smiled, hoping to allay their fears, but was rewarded with stony gazes. A cold realization filled her. Despite Malcor's deviance, he had been the lord here, as had been his father before him and his father before him, all the way back to Alfred the

Great, and these people resented not only the Normans but her as well, both strangers.

As they entered the bailey, more Draceadon churls stood and stared. There were no smiles, no welcoming cheers, only sullen resignation and distrust. She was the devil's handmaiden, cavorting with the demon Normans. Her audacious behavior was coming around to bite her in the tail. These people did not want a warrior princess who set out with the invaders; they wanted a levelheaded leader who looked and acted the part.

Tarian wrestled with who she was and what she needed to be. Her hoyden life was all she knew. And while she might have lost much by being shunned, the silver lining to her life was that she had unprecedented freedom. Nothing was expected of her except to behave shamelessly. The realization stunned her. Fighting was all she knew. Fighting for her place in the world, fighting for respect, and now? Fighting to survive. But if she conformed, she would lose her freedom.

To be lady here she would still have to fight, but if she were to win the war she would need to reassess her tactics. Her mind raced, and she wondered how prudent it would be for her to search out a Norman noble to husband. The people here did not trust her as it was: to bring in a Norman, a man who would have no sympathy for anything Saxon, would only serve to widen the gap. She sighed heavily. *Was* Rangor the answer? She shivered uncontrollably despite the heat she felt under her mail. Rangor was loathsome, and she did not believe she had it in her to lie with him. But more than that, she would lose her freedom, for he would be a demanding husband.

As they ascended the well-worn road to Draceadon,

Tarian had no option but to grab Wulfson's waist to keep from sliding off the rump of the great horse. If Wulfson had been rigid before, now he was as stiff as hewn steel. She smiled. He might desire her, this Norman knight, but he did not care for her overmuch. 'Twas unfortunate, because she found she liked him quite well.

When they came to halt at the stable, Tarian did not wait for assistance to dismount. She slid off the left side of the destrier and hurried to Silversmith, who stood tied to a post blowing hotly, his haunches and withers wet and quivering. Thankfully the arrow was not imbedded in the meaty part of his neck but clean through up near his mane. Shucking her one gauntlet, Tarian broke the arrow off at the crest near the feather fletching, and with a reassuring hand on his neck she spoke softly to him as she grasped the arrowhead toward her and pulled the shaft through.

She inspected the wound, and though it could take a stitch or two, she knew the stallion would not stand for it.

Wulfson angrily approached, yanking off his helm and tossing it to Rolf. "As you well know, an ill-trained horse can cause his master's death."

She looked up into his stormy green eyes and nodded. "Once he is healed, I wish you to teach us both your moves. I have never seen anything so beautiful."

Wulfson's brows rose almost into his hairline. "My horses and men have trained for years. It does not come overnight."

"I am a patient student and willing to work hard."

He stood for a long moment unspeaking, and she held her breath, praying he would not deny her. Instead he asked, "Are you hurt?"

She blinked. "What?"

"From your fall and attack. Are you harmed?"

"Nay, I managed to keep them at bay with my sword."

"'Twas foolish my allowance of you traveling with us this day."

"Nay, 'twas a lesson I needed to learn, Sir Wulfson."

He quirked a brow.

"The people of this shire. I had no idea how deep their hatred for me ran. I know where I stand with them and know what I must do to gain their trust."

"Tarian—"

She shook her head and pressed her fingers to his lips. He stiffened. "Do not say it, Wulfson. I am Tarian of Dunloc. As you said before you took me, your king is not a fool. He has more to gain with me alive than dead. He will see it."

He grabbed her hand and pulled her closer to him. "He is not here. He does not fully understand the situation."

"Then, as the captain of his guard, see that he is fully apprised."

She stepped back and drew her sword, placing it across her chest. "Sir Wulfson, I put my life squarely in your hands. See to it you do not fail me."

She turned then and led her horse away.

"She has a way of getting under a man's skin, eh, Wulfson?" Rorick said from behind him.

He would not deny it. "I know in my gut what she says is true. But will William see it?"

Rorick slapped him on the back of his shoulder. "As the lass said, bring him around."

Wulfson looked at his friend and shook his head. "You know as well as I that once William has his mind set there is no changing it."

"I would not give a king's ransom to be in your boots, my friend. You have lust in your eye for the lady, and I cannot blame you, but I caution you. Do not drink too often from the well. You must limit it, or you may find yourself afloat in it."

Wulfson could not argue the wisdom. "Aye, I will heed your advice."

Wulfson handed Turold over to Rolf to cool him down, and proceeded to the stable, where he knew the lady tended her own horse. She was on the other side of the structure, cooling the beast down. Wulfson stood back and watched the way she softly spoke to the stallion, and the way the horse's ears twitched back and forth, as if he understood her words. His body warmed beneath his mail, and he felt his cock stir. She infuriated him. He had nearly leapt off Turold when she went down in the mob. Foolish woman! She frustrated him. The way she thrust and parried with his lust had him constantly on edge. He had never met a woman who invaded his waking moments as well as his dreams. But mostly she amazed him. She was intelligent, beautiful, fiery, and passionate; and as he, she had learned to survive in a world that shunned them. That she had survived *and* thrived was an amazing feat.

At the end of the long aisle of the stable, she brought the cooled horse in and cross-tied him, then began to rub him down. Disappearing into the nearest stall, which was vacant, several long moments later she emerged sans her mail.

An invisible hand on his back pushed Wulfson toward her. He did not resist it. As he approached, the gray threw his head over his left wither, and Tarian soothed him. She stood on a stool, and appeared to be dressing the wound.

"He sees you as a threat, sir, please stand back," Tarian softly commanded.

Wulfson slowed his gait, then came to a stop several paces from them. "The first and most important lesson a proper warhorse must learn is to trust his master," he said quietly.

He could not help but drink in the vision before him. The late-afternoon sun broke through the slatted roof, its golden rays surrounding her, illuminating her long hair that hung around her shoulders and her back in thick luxuriant swirls. He had never seen hair so rich and thick, or so black. The Norman women were fairer of skin and tall. This girl was petite and lithe as a reed, but with womanly curves.

"He does trust me," she said as softly.

Wulfson began to remove his mail. He did it slowly and quietly so as not to agitate the horse. Rolf would see to the cleaning. When he stood in his linen chauses, boots and gambeson he moved slowly toward them. "Horses will react one of two ways when threatened. Flight or fight. Most fly. A true warrior steed will stand and fight, but only if he has confidence in his master."

Tarian looked over Silversmith's withers to Wulfson. "Are you implying my horse had no confidence in me?"

"He would not have resorted to hysterics if he did."

Her brows creased together, and she seemed to ponder his words. "How then do I gain my horse's confidence?"

"By being firm, consistent, and not sending mixed signals. You must also regularly train him in situations where he would have the natural urge to bolt, then stay him with your expertise, and show him there is no danger, until it becomes second nature for you both. He must feel your confidence and strength. If he does not, then he will fly."

Wulfson stood across from Tarian, the horse separating them. He slid a hand down the gray's thick neck, lightly touching the spot where the arrow struck. "'Tis not a bad wound. What balm do you use?"

"A concoction of Abner's. He swears by it."

"Stefan is our horsemaster. He has more vials and pouches of balms and salves than a midwife. I would have you take a look. His father has a great stud outside of Rouen, and he is well versed in all things equine."

"His father?"

"Foster. The comte d'Everaux, Stefan's birth father, has made no claim."

"How is he so sure then?"

"He looks a mirror image. There is no denying who his sire is."

"What of *your* sire? Do you resemble him?"

Wulfson's jaw tightened. "I have seen him only a handful of times in my life, the last time upon my return to Normandy after the conquest. He seeks favor with William through me."

"Has your king rewarded him?"

"*Our* king sent him packing just before I returned to England."

"What of your mother, Wulfson? What did she do that was so heartless you cannot forgive her?"

At the question his entire body stiffened. Long-suppressed anger surfaced. He had never discussed his mother with anyone, not even the Blood Swords. No one dared ask. But when he looked into Tarian's ocean-blue eyes he did not see scorn or contempt: he saw only a woman quietly questioning his feelings. *Feelings!* Bah! He bit back a sharp retort. Instead, because he did not want to set her running from him, he answered her honestly. "She took her life shortly after my birth. It was better than living with the blight of a half-Saxon bastard."

"I am sorry, Wulfson."

"Do not pity me."

"I do not. I only regret you did not have the love of a mother to nurture you." She smiled softly and ministered to her horse. "My mother, even if she had wished to die, would never have taken her own life. 'Tis a mortal sin against God. She feared hell more than the humiliation of me."

"Do you visit her?'

Tarian shook her head and bent over the gray's neck, giving the wound her complete attention. "Nay. I traveled to Powys, several years ago, to meet with her. She refused to see me. And as you are aware, my sire is dead."

"Aye, I know." And Wulfson wondered at the man who had sired such a woman. Sweyn Godwinson had never given the laws of man any respect. "Is there any truth to the rumor he is Canute's son?"

Tarian's head snapped back, and her eyes narrowed. "Nay! Just another lie of his! He was born a rebel and he died as he lived, in shame!"

She shook her head so violently her hair spilled across Silversmith's neck. Wulfson could not resist reaching out and touching the thick shiny strands. He moved closer and gently pulled her toward him. "Your sire was a fool, madame, your dam too proud, and your dead husband the biggest fool of all."

She nearly hung over the gray's neck, and as he brought her closer she resisted. " 'Tis true, all of it, but if the stars had not aligned as they had, I would not have the freedom I have and relish this day."

He nodded, understanding completely. "Aye, when an outcast, the rules of polite society do not apply."

She licked her lips and Wulfson's blood quickened at the sight. "Aye, society expects us to break with tradition and decorum." She smiled and leaned across the horse and pressed her lips just a breath away from his. "And because of it, we have greater freedom than our most esteemed legitimate peers."

"Is that why you agreed to wed with Malcor?"

She stiffened, and tried to pull away, but he held her captive.

Grudgingly she answered. "Aye, he was the key to the marriage cage. He in his perverse way was as much an outcast as myself. His deviance was expected. And because of it, people shied away from him." She smiled grimly. "Because he had no use for women, my freedom was guaranteed. 'Tis why I will never marry Rangor, or a man like him. He would insist on asserting himself as my husband true, and that I could not abide."

"What of William? He is a feudal lord, Tarian. He demands homage, loyalty, and the acceptance from all of his subjects that his word is the final word."

She smiled and leaned closer to him, her impish dimples teasing him. "I would pay homage to my king, so long as he pledged his loyalty to me."

Wulfson shook his head at the audacity of her demands. For one who was at William's mercy, she demanded from him what he demanded from all of his subjects. And despite it, Wulfson realized it was the same for him. If his king did not respect him and remain loyal to those who served him with their lives, Wulfson would wander off in search of a more worthy king.

He searched her clear eyes, and found righteous truth there. Once again he thought how foolish his king would be if he were to destroy this woman on the grounds of her bloodline. And he knew in his gut that Warner would bring word to move forward. And just as certainly, Wulfson knew he would have to go to Normandy and plead the lady's case in person. That notion settled his mind, but not his heart.

"What art thou thinking, sir knight?" she asked softly, pressing toward him.

"How much I would like to kiss you."

Her smile widened and she coyly batted her long black lashes. "You have my permission."

He could not resist what she offered even had he wanted to. Sliding his hand along her neck, he trailed his fingers into her thick hair, and cupping the back of her head he brought her to him. The contact sent a hard jolt of lightning to his groin. Her soft lips parted beneath his, as sweet and tender as a fresh bloom. He pressed closer, wanting more of her. Silversmith neighed and nipped at Wulfson's side, but not enough to deter him.

Tarian didn't know what it was about the Norman knight that made her feel like a twittering girl. Maybe that was part of it. Despite everything, he was attracted to her for *her*, not all that came or didn't come with her. She had never been courted or wooed; indeed, she had grown up faster than most, and, slight as she was, most men feared her.

His kiss stunned her in its gentleness. She did not think the killer knight had it in him to be gentle. Yet his lips were slow and thorough, and still left her breathless. Her young body warmed, her breasts swelled, and that oh so familiar ache associated with him spread through her. It could only be quelled in one way, and as much as she desired him, she would not also have it said she was leman to a Norman.

"Milord," she whispered against his lips, "you make me forget my horse."

"You make me forget more than that," he said softly, releasing her.

She turned her attention back to Silversmith, and said, "I would have Ednoth come to Draceadon. He is key to my success here."

"He is bastard half brother to your husband. Do you think you can find his support?"

She nodded, and began to braid the mane draping over the wound. "He has nothing. I would raise him up by giving him a position."

"There will be time for that later, Tarian, when things are settled."

She shot him a glare, her mood changing from soft and contemplative to angry. "You mean once I am either dead or permitted to remain alive?"

His dark face clouded and he stepped away from her. "Do not make this more difficult than it has to be."

She stepped down from the stool and came around to fully face him. "Difficult? We are speaking of my life! How much more difficult can it be?"

He stood silent and scowled down at her. She could almost see his mind at work. "Mayhap, milady, you should consider a trip to Normandy."

"Nay! I will never leave here!"

"You would be alive."

"I would rather die than spend my life a prisoner of William."

"There may be no other way, Tarian. Think on it." He turned and walked away, leaving her with much to contemplate.

She would not go as hostage to William. Once in his lair she would be nothing more than a prisoner; or as she had heard, she would not even be afforded the luxury of court but locked away and forgotten. The dungeons in Rouen were filled with rebel Saxons. Nay, she would fight for her right to live here in her homeland, and would rather die for the effort. That settled, she retuned to the chore of tending her horse, and once done, she led him to his stall and fed him.

As Tarian wrestled her mail into an orderly package that she could carry back to her chamber, Gareth approached. He took it from her, and she gladly handed it over.

"Where is your helm?"

"In the dirt at Dunloc, along with a gauntlet," she admitted, disgust lacing her words. He scowled, and she was grateful he did not query her further on the subject. Instead, as they walked back to the fortress, Tarian softly said, "He speaks of taking me to Normandy."

"'Tis what the Viking suggested to me as well."

Keeping her calm, Tarian evenly said, "I will fight him, Gareth. I will not go."

"Aye, to go would mean certain captivity or death."

"There has been no word of his man Warner returning from Normandy. My guess is the tides were not in his favor but ours."

Gareth smiled grimly. "A small blessing. Our men continue to wait for his return."

Tarian was comforted by that. Time was her ally; or it could prove to be the angel of certain death. Each morning when she awoke she lay quiet in her bed and listened to her body for any of the telltale signs of pregnancy. Edie laughed at her, telling her that more time was required for the signs. But emotionally she was near the end of her rope. Desperately she wished for a child. Another thought struck her. What if she *were* with child and the king demanded the babe as hostage? Despite the warmth of the fading day, the thought of giving up her babe chilled Tarian to the bone. *Never!*

When they entered the hall they found it alive with music, men, and flowing wine and ale. She had to smile when several of the villagers stopped and gawked at her attire. She was dressed as a knight. Chauses, undertunic, and quilted gambeson.

When her eyes clashed with the Normans gathered round a table playing what looked to be dice, they laughed uproariously. Her temper caught.

"*En garde*, men!" Thorin chortled. "England's most fearsome knight approaches!"

Not only did the Normans laugh in uproarious humor, but several Saxons joined in as well. She noticed that while Wulfson, who stood by the hearth, did not laugh, he seemed to be forcing back a smile. Her eyes narrowed to slits.

Stiffening, Tarian refused to be dragged into their rude humor and be the butt of their jokes. Gareth made to move toward them, but Tarian stayed him. "Do not engage with them, Gareth, you will only feed them."

Without further comment she made it to her chamber, where she nearly collapsed on the bed.

"Tarian?" Brighid said, flying to her side. "Are you injured?"

"Nay, just fatigued," she said, yawning. "Let me rest for

a candle notch and I will join you and the buffoons from Normandy after I bathe."

Brighid unlaced her chauses and removed them. "Tarian, do you think it wise to ride ahorse as you do?"

Tarian opened one eye. "Why would I not?"

"What if you are with child?"

"What if I am?"

"Harm could come to you or the babe."

Tarian closed her eyes and relaxed back into the soft linens. "Edith says 'tis not until the second half of a pregnancy that a woman should retire. I am healthy, and the babe would be protected."

"I would stay with you, Tarian."

"I would welcome that," she said, forcing back a yawn. "Now, allow me to sleep."

The last thing she remembered was Brighid tugging off her gambeson, before dreams swept her away. She dreamt of a golden lion, stalking an equally golden dragon, and of a great black wolf watching from the forest. The dragon's fire scorched the lion, but eventually the lion outmaneuvered the dragon and dug his deep claws into the dragon's back.

As the wolf entered the fray to save the dragon, at the last minute the wolf turned on the dragon, and together the lion and the wolf tore it apart, tossing its limbs to the four corners of the island—message to all that even the golden dragon could not overcome the might of the lion and the wolf combined.

Tarian woke with a start. The room was dim, only a lone candle across the room offered light. "Your bath is ready, milady," Edie said from her chair in the corner. Tarian stretched and nodded.

"The day's grime clings to me." But she made no effort to move from the bed. Edith came to her and helped her from her clothes, and when Tarian sank into the warm soapy water she sighed and relaxed.

"Do you wish to eat here or go below? I am afraid the Normans have turned the hall into a den of debauchery and celebration."

Tarian sat up in the tub. "Oh?"

Edith pinned up the mass of Tarian's hair, and nodded. "Your men did not take kindly to the insult of the Viking Norman. There was a challenge of dice and then arm wrestling."

"And?"

Edith smiled. "Gareth lightened their purses considerably, but the Normans took it back after the arm wrestling."

Tarian scowled.

"Gareth was no match for your Wulfson."

"Bite your tongue. He is not mine! He would pair up with his king and slay me in a heartbeat."

"Mayhap."

Tarian soaked in the tub, contemplating her position. If she stayed in her chamber it would look as if she hid from the Normans. If she descended into the hall she would no doubt be the butt of more ribbing. She shrugged it off. She had weathered far worse.

"And what did Alewith and Brighid do during the contests?"

"It appears the knight Rhys has an eye for your foster sister, and her father thinks to encourage it."

"Does he now?"

"Methinks he sees the gain in a Norman son-in-law."

Tarian sat up in the tub. "What of her betrothal to David?"

Edith shook her head. "The boy has flown with his parents to Scotland."

"He breaks the contract? When did this happen? Why did I not know?"

"They received word the day they traveled here. Methinks Brighid is not overly upset."

"But she is innocent; the knight will take advantage of her. Then she will have no chance of a suitable marriage. Dress me, Edie, so that I may go intercede on her behalf."

Tarian quietly descended into a wild frenzy of music, laughter, and, some would say, debauchery. The Normans as well as her own men made merry with the ladies of the manor. Amidst it all, Alewith sat across from Wulfson, engrossed in a game of chess. Trays of food littered the tables and several hounds helped themselves. Her eyes traveled the perimeter of the long hall for her sister and caught a glimpse of her blue kirtle as she slipped through the great doors. Tarian hurried to follow, but was stopped by Thorin. "Let them be. Rhys is an honorable young man."

Her eyes narrowed. "Your version of honor, sir knight, and mine have different meaning." She moved past him and he did not try to stop her. As she broke free from the hall, Tarian looked wildly about the bailey, and to her concern did not see her sister or the knight in the dusky light.

"Brighid?" she called and continued into the bailey. The night had approached and the usual hustle and bustle of the bailey was eerily quiet. Panic rose. What if he had his way with her? She would be ruined for a noble husband.

She hurried to the stable, hoping to find them there. As she came to a breathless stop at the open entrance, she heard the undeniable giggle of a maid, followed by a deep, manly voice. Silently Tarian stepped deeper into the shadowy structure. Two silhouettes at the far end stood outside of Silversmith's stall. The stallion neighed, and Tarian held her breath when Brighid scratched the gray's forehead.

"Tarian raised him from a colt."

"He has much to learn," Rhys said, and extended his hand to give the horse a scratch. Silversmith nipped at him. Brighid laughed.

"He does not like men overmuch."

Tarian watched the knight slip his hands around Brighid's waist and pull her away from the gray, only to press her against the near wall. "What of you, sweet Brighid? Do you also find men distasteful?"

Tarian strode toward them, making no effort to conceal herself.

"Some men I prefer more than others."

His head dropped to hers, and Tarian was certain he said, "Do you prefer me?"

"She does not!" Tarian said, coming upon them. Brighid gasped, but the Norman stood his ground, his hands resting too familiarly around the slender waist of her sister. "Unhand her."

Fifteen

Rhys nodded and stood back. Tarian knew it was not from any fear of her, but that the knight did not want to appear a complete knave in front of Brighid, whose face had turned the color of an autumn apple.

"T-Tarian," the girl stuttered, stepping away from the Norman. "We but came to see how your horse fared."

Tarian stood with her hands on her hips and glowered at them both. Rhys, though the youngest of the knights, was still years older than Brighid, and, she knew, well experienced. "He fares just fine. Does Lord Alewith know what you are about?"

Rhys laughed low and asked, "What *are* we about, Lady Tarian?"

Tarian quirked a brow. "'Tis obvious by your sweet words and actions toward my sister. She is not some wench you can weaken with your poetic words. She is innocent and will remain that way for her husband."

Rhys nodded again and stepped further from the girl. Brighid looked to him, then back to Tarian, this time with a set jaw. "I am no longer betrothed to that coward David. And, sweet sister, should I not remind you I am nearly sixteen? Why, I am practically an old maid!"

Tarian understood the girl's dreams of romance and took her hand and pulled her to her. "And a virgin. Do not forget it. It takes just one time, Brighid, and you could find yourself spilling a bastard's bastard. Our lot is hard enough; do not add more of us to England when you can prevent it."

She dragged her sister behind her, and as they were coming out of the stable Alewith and Wulfson nearly collided with them. Alewith took one kook at Brighid, then Tarian, and looked beyond to Rhys, who walked toward them with the cocksureness of a man who had just brought down an eight-point buck with a single arrow to the heart.

Alewith scowled. "What happened here?"

"Nothing, Papa! I swear it!" Brighid cried, throwing herself into her father's arms. " 'Twas I who suggested we come to the stables."

Wulfson looked angrily past them to his man who strode into the torchlight just outside the structure. " 'Twas I who made the suggestion," Rhys said gallantly. Tarian's eyes narrowed more. Why did he lie? But the answer was simple: he would not have Brighid look the coquette before her father. Their eyes met, and she nodded. In that moment he all but redeemed himself. But not enough.

"My orders were clear, Sir Rhys."

Rhys clicked his heels together and gave Wulfson a short bow. "My pardon." Then he strode past them all back to the hall.

Alewith looked pointedly at Tarian. "Your word that you did not witness any trespass on her."

Tarian nodded. "My oath. They were merely having a conversation outside Silversmith's stall. Nothing more."

Relief flooded Brighid's face, and she smiled. "See, Papa?"

He cast Wulfson a glance. "On the morrow after the evening meal, I will see you back at the chess table. Be prepared this time to lose your horse!"

Alewith whisked his daughter away, leaving Wulfson and Tarian quite alone.

"Are you not terrified?" Tarian sarcastically asked.

Wulfson quirked a dark brow. "Of what?"

"Of England's most fearsome knight!"

He smiled and chuckled good-naturedly. "Thorin only sported with you. He has quite a wit inside that one-eyed head of his."

"And you, sir, are a knave for allowing it."

He smiled again. "Come now, you have been the brunt of worse."

"That does not mean I like it." She grabbed one of the torches and walked back into the darkened stable. Wulfson followed.

"I will caution my men, then, to keep their humor to themselves if it upsets you."

She stopped and whirled around, nearly slamming the torch in his chest. He stepped back. "I appreciate your offer, but will pass. Should you ask that of your men it will make us both look weak. Is that what you wish?"

He stood for a moment and contemplated her response, then finally nodded. "You are wise for one so young, Tarian."

"'Tis how I have survived." She turned and made her way to the far end of the stable to her horse. She set the torch down in an outside ground sconce, then entered the stall, speaking softly to him. The light was dim, but she did not want to take a chance by bringing the torch close to a wounded animal. One false move and the stable would go up in flames.

Instead, she squinted, and with what light she had, she poked and prodded, glad to feel there was no heat coming from the site. She would clean it again in the morn and dress it with fresh balm. She turned to Wulfson and asked, "How fare your wounds?"

"The one on my thigh pains me greatly."

Her concern piqued, she said, "I noted your gait was slower. Is there much heat in it?"

He nodded.

Tarian sighed and moved from the stall, confident her horse was on the mend. She grabbed the torch from the sconce and beckoned the knight to follow her.

As they entered the hall, while there were still people about, the noise had subsided. She approached Stefan, who sat with his man Ioan over the chessboard. He glanced up to her and stood, as did the other men who noticed her presence. She nodded and said, "Would you send Rolf for the balm you use on your horses? The one used for open wounds."

Stefan looked from her to Wulfson, who stood silent but with a noticeable gleam in his eye. Stefan slowly smiled and nodded. "Of course, madame. Where should he bring it?"

"To my chamber." She walked past him and was halfway up the stairwell when she turned to find Wulfson standing with his men, all of them smiling, including Rhys, who sported a more twisted smile. She did not need a herald to explain to her what they all thought would happen in her chamber. And she was just as sure it would not. Her dream from her nap still weighed heavy on her mind, and each time she thought back to it, a coldness encompassed her. It settled in her that there was a very good chance that not only could her days at Draceadon be numbered but her time on earth as well.

"No need to fear for your knight. I give you my oath as England's most fearsome knight, I will not harm him this night." She turned and strode up to her chamber, only to find it atwitter with Brighid, Edith, and Noelth, her sister's maid.

"Tarian!" Brighid cried, flinging herself into her arms. "Forgive me!"

Tarian soothed the girl and walked with her into the room. "There is nothing to forgive, Brighid. I understand all too well the lure of the Normans. Do not think for one moment I have not felt the pull myself. But we must resist! They have come to slay me!"

"Sir Rhys would never do such a thing!" the girl defended.

"Aye, he would, and do not forget, their loyalty is not to England, but their king."

She extracted the girl from her arms and moved past her for the tray of linens and needle and thread. Brighid coughed back a sob, and turned to her maid for comfort. Tarian set her jaw and turned, tray in hand, to see the hulking Norman filling the doorway. She beckoned him in.

He shook his head. "I think not."

Exasperated, she said, "'Tis not as if they have never seen a man in braies. Come in and strip so that I can see the wound."

"Nay."

She remained as steadfast. She turned and set the tray down on a nearby table and faced him. "Then suffer with it."

He bowed slightly and stepped from the threshold, moving down the hall to his chamber.

"Stubborn man!" But she would not follow him. Nay, she would not be alone with him. She had given too much of herself already, she would give him no more.

Edith picked up the tray and said, "I will tend to him. Where is his wound?"

"On the outside of his right thigh. I stitched him several days ago. I would have thought it would be neatly knitting by now, but he says it causes him great discomfort. I fear infection."

As Edith left the room, Rolf appeared with a jar of balm. "Take it then to your master's chamber; he awaits it," Tarian said.

Rolf's brows drew together in confusion, but did as she bade. She closed the door after him and realized she was famished. "Noelth, would you fetch me a tray, please?"

The maid bobbed her head and hurried from the room. Brighid came to her from the bed. "You look weary, Tarian."

Tarian sank into Malcor's great chair, pulling her feet up beneath her. "I am. The worry is beginning to take its toll. I fear every waking moment William will arrive on his great steed and slay me with his sword. And after this morn, I fear the people of Dunloc would fight for the right to as well."

"I heard what happened. Who is this Ednoth, anyway?"

"He is Malcor's half brother. The resemblance is undeniable. I just don't know if Earl Llewellyn acknowledged him."

"Would it change things if he had?"

Tarian shrugged. "Mayhap. As the next son, he could stand to inherit Briarhurst at least. But I have Malcor's will."

"Briarhurst is the gem of the holdings. I do not understand your fascination with this dreary old fortress. I would tear it down and construct a castle worthy of a queen!" She looked pointedly at Tarian and pressed her hand to her flat belly, and smiled. "But if you carry the heir, then Ednoth has no claim to anything."

Tarian swallowed hard, not liking the position into which she had backed herself. It was one thing to smite that horrible uncle Rangor, but she'd had no knowledge of a brother. If Malcor had just left her Draceadon, there would be no strife for anyone. She sighed. If Malcor had just been a man and done his duty, none of them would be worrying whether she would live to see another English sunset.

"I fear a child may complicate things for me, Brighid."

Brighid dipped to her knees and clasped her hands together in a pleading gesture before her. "Flee from here! We will go to Turnsly, and from there you can hide in any number of Father's holdings. Or go north to Scotland, where there is no fear of William."

Tarian inhaled deeply and rolled back onto the thick cushion, closing her eyes. "I cannot, Brighid. 'Twould be the cowardly thing to do."

"Better to be a coward and live than brave and die. I could not bear the thought of life without you! Please! Think of others if you will not think of yourself."

Tarian's hand slid to her flat belly, her eyes rising to the clear blue ones of her foster sister. "What of the child I may carry? This place is his by right of blood. If I should run away from it?" As the lie left her lips, Tarian felt another twinge of guilt. While she was rightful heir by Malcor's will, the child was not by blood. But did it matter? For should she wed again, would not that child inherit all that was hers? She sucked in a deep breath. The right thing to do was to concede Briarhurst to Rangor, for it was the seat of the earldom; but if she did so, people would question her motives—if there was a child, then he would be, in the eyes of the world, rightful heir to all.

She closed her eyes. "Brighid, leave me alone. I tire of talk. Let me sleep."

It seemed only moments later that she was being gently shaken awake. "Milady," Edith called softly, "come and sup; there is food here for you."

Slowly Tarian roused, and there was indeed food, and hungrily she ate. "Was the wound infected?" she asked Edith as she sipped a cup of wine.

"He would not allow me to see it."

Tarian shook her head. "Foolish knight. He courts a stump for a leg."

"He asked once you had eaten that you go to him."

Tarian nearly choked on the piece of meat she chewed. "I will not!"

"He refused the assistance of his squire as well."

"I will not be prodded by guilt to tend him. If he is not man enough to strip and sit still in my chamber, then he must not be in too much pain. He will come to me on my terms when the ache is too much to bear."

She finished her meal, undressed, and sank into the cool soft linens of her bed. But dreams once more plagued her. This time they were of Wulfson, naked and stretched out beside her in the great bed, his rough hands sliding down her body and resting on her swollen belly. He kissed her there and their child moved vigorously beneath his hand. He looked up into her eyes, love burning bright in them. As he lowered his lips to kiss her belly again, he moved his other hand from behind his back, and the glint of a blade flashed in the morning sunlight. He brought it down.

Tarian woke screaming. Terrorized and breathing so heavily she nearly suffocated, she could not get enough air. Brighid, Edith, and Noelth all sought to calm her, but she could not be calmed. She rocked back and forth in the bed clutching her belly as hot tears rushed down her cheeks.

A sharp knock on the door followed soon after. Edith hurried to it, and Tarian heard Wulfson's deep voice. She cried out and moved against the headboard. "Nay, do not let him in!"

Wulfson did not heed the command. He pushed past the nurse and strode into the chamber. The women gasped at his state of undress. He wore only his braies. He pulled back the heavy drapery surrounding the bed and stopped in his tracks. Tarian's wild hair swirled around her and her wide blue eyes were red and glittered with tears. She clutched a pillow to her belly and slowly shook her head. She had the look of a madwoman. But deeper than that was a profound sense of fear. Like a wounded animal. His heart melted a little then. She wore her pride as she did her honor, as a protective barrier against the world. He understood it, he lived it himself, but she played the game in a man's world, and he could not blame her for her fear and breakdown. He set his jaw. And he only added to her misery. He would send another messenger to hurry Warner along. And he would plead a different case to his king.

He moved closer to her and she cried out, moving harder against the headboard. "I will not hurt you, Tarian," he soothed.

She shook her head, but slowly he saw the fear recede from her eyes.

"She fears for the babe," Brighid offered.

Wulfson stiffened, and he did not like the tightness in his gut at the thought of Tarian carrying another man's child. "*Is* she? With child?" he demanded, looking to the nurse for answer.

The old woman shrugged. "Mayhap. Another few weeks and we will know for sure."

Wulfson growled and turned back to Tarian, who, though she still clutched the pillow to her, had relaxed enough not to appear as part of the carved wood headboard.

He turned to the three women who hovered like barn flies around the bed. "Go to the hall; I wish a private word with the lady." All three jaws dropped. "I intend her no harm. Now go, and close the door behind you!"

They jumped at his tone, and when he heard the door thunk closed, he turned back to Tarian. She had moved to the other side of the bed. "Why were you screaming?"

She closed her eyes, then slowly opened them. "A nightmare."

He exhaled a long breath. He fought with wanting to comfort her but knowing he could offer her no promises. William's word would be final, and unless Wulfson was to defy his king and have a price upon his own head he could do naught but obey. The thought of it made him sick. He was not a murderer. He was a soldier; he met his foes face to face on the field of battle. He did not sneak about and hide in shadows only to plunge a dagger into a noblewoman's heart. 'Twas a coward's way, not his.

He swiped his hand across his mouth and chin. "Tarian—"

She shook her head. "Nay, do not make promises you cannot keep. Leave me."

He nodded and withdrew from her. When he opened the chamber door all three women tumbled in upon him. Brighid squeaked as her hand brushed his hard belly, and the two maids twittered like schoolgirls. He ignored them and walked slowly down the hall to his own chamber. And with each step his anger grew. His frustration, and his sense of right and wrong: in his gut he knew what his king asked of him was wrong.

He spent the next several days away from Draceadon. He and his men, with a handful of Gareth's, patrolled the outlying lands. He had not lied when he told Tarian the landscape pleased him. The weather had become much more agreeable, and he found that he enjoyed the sunny, mild weather infused with occasional rain. The hills were lush and green, the resources abundant; and though the people were sullen and on occasion adversarial, they were quickly handled.

When they returned on the fourth day, Wulfson was surprised to see Tarian working the gray, and Thorin, whom he had left in charge, schooling her in the ancient art of Greek cavalry maneuvers. He frowned, feeling a short stab of jealousy that his friend should be the one to teach the lady what she had asked of him. He watched her, still amazed at her audacious dress. She wore leather boots, woolen chauses, an undertunic, and a soft leather gambeson. When she drew her sword and, with her legs, commanded the gray to stop, she parried and thrust first to one side, then another.

The stallion worried at his bit and pranced crabwise, side to side. Thorin called to her, "Nay, nay, nay! You cannot instruct him to halt with your hands then with your gyrations of the sword give him another command with your legs."

"I did not!"

"Aye, you did. Your bottom was up and back in the saddle while your legs pressed and your spurs dug into him. You confused him. He must trust your commands, Tarian, or he will bolt time after time when you need his calmness the most."

Wulfson scowled at the familiarity with which Thorin spoke to her. He urged the black forward, and Tarian looked up from Thorin, who had placed her legs in the proper position to halt and stay a horse.

Thorin turned and followed her gaze. "Aye, you return!" He called to all the men. "Did you find any Welsh lurking about in the bushes?"

Wulfson dismounted. Rolf quickly took the reins, along with Wulfson's helm and gauntlets. Wulfson pushed back his cowl and ran his hands through his damp hair. "A few, but they ran like the cowards they are." He looked past Thorin to Tarian, who sat silent upon her horse. "Are you well?"

She nodded.

Wulfson could think of no pithy remark, so instead he asked Thorin, "Has Warner returned?"

"Nay, but the bastard Ednoth has come here twice to seek a word with you."

He could see Tarian's body stiffen. She dismounted and

walked toward Wulfson, leading her horse with her. "He claims the earldom. I would not produce the will until such time as you returned. I assure you it is valid. Not only did Edith and that cur Ruin witness it with their marks, but Father Dudley as well. They can all be brought forth as witnesses in person."

"First you must produce the document."

"I have it here, and will gladly present it to you, but if you do not mind I would have the matter done in private."

Wulfson nodded. "I can see no harm in that. I have a need for a good soak in the tub first." He grinned wide and winked at Thorin. "As the lady of the manor, 'tis it not your chore to see to the baths of all guests?"

He watched the color flood her cheeks. He grinned wider. She bent her head just enough to acknowledge him. "I will see to my horse, then to your bath." She turned on her heels and strode to the stable, her back as rigid as his sword.

Thorin laughed and slapped him on the back. "You are a better man than I, Wulf, to tangle with that wildcat. I swear she is a most intense student, but a most distracting one as well."

Wulfson could only nod in agreement, for he was not sure, if he spoke, that his words would not be construed as a challenge to his friend. And one thing the men had never done was quarrel over a woman. Share? Aplenty, but never quarrel over one, and Wulfson found he most definitely would quarrel over this one. He'd spent the last four days in the saddle, with nothing but thoughts of a different kind of ride altogether, and the only face that came to him in his daydreams and dreams late at night was that of the blue-eyed witch Tarian Godwinson.

Sixteen

As he lowered his aching body into the wooden tub of hot, soapy water, Wulfson could not help a deep sigh. "Ah, 'tis heaven." For long moments he reclined in the large tub, eyes closed, his head against the backrest, allowing the heat of the water to seep into his tired muscles. His wounds were healing, and he would have Tarian snip the stitches from his back and leg. He smiled. If he were slow and careful, he just might cajole the lady into shedding her clothes and joining him in the tub. When he opened his eyes and found her frowning down at him, his hopes were dashed.

"Sir, I have many chores that need my attention. So please sit forward so that I can bathe you and be done with it."

He did the opposite: he continued to recline, and scathed her with his gaze. "You look well."

She approached and dunked a thick sponge into the water near his feet, then put a bar of soap to it and vigorously rubbed up a lather. "I am quite well."

"Well enough, I see, to take lessons from Thorin."

"He has the patience of a saint." She cocked a dark brow at him. " 'Tis more than I can say for some other Normans I know."

He was not put aside by her quip. "You have not given me a chance. I am a tutor of considerable skill."

"I *have* given you a chance. You have proven you have only a single focus, and that is for your king. I accept that. Now accept that I want no further dalliances with you."

He grabbed her hand and pulled her toward him as he sat up in the tub. "Do you dally with Thorin, then?"

Her eyes widened in genuine surprise. She yanked her arm from his grasp and sat back on her heels. " 'Tis what you think of me? A camp whore who will lie with any man for a trinket or a morsel?"

Wulfson could feel the thump of his heart against his chest wall. Jealousy knotted up in his gut. He could not get out of his head the vision of Tarian arching beneath Thorin. He stared at her unblinking, wanting to believe her, but he knew women too well.

"That you classify me as of the same ilk as your other women only solidifies my decision." She lathered up the sponge some more and moved around to his back. He felt her touch the wound she had tended. "The threads have done their job. I will cut these out before they grow into your skin."

"There are shears in the chest there," he said softly, pointing toward it. He flinched when she ran her fingertips over the scar again; not from pain, but from her touch. He was a fool, he told himself, a fool to classify her among any other women. 'Twas impossible to do, for she was unlike any he had met or would ever meet.

"The stitches are brittle; I will dampen them so they will be easier to cut."

Wulfson set his jaw, knowing all hope of a tender moment between them was gone. She had abandoned him, and while he understood her reasons for doing so, it did not cut any less deep. Once the bath was complete, she told him to stand, and reluctantly he did. He could not help his engorged member, for while she might not want him, his yearning for her had not quelled. He heard her soft gasp, and had his mood not soured so much he would have made light of it.

"You are safe from me, Tarian, ignore it."

She hurried to pat him dry, and once done, she pointed to the chair nearest them. He wrapped the linen around his waist and sat.

When she approached him with the shears he locked gazes with her, and he saw fear in her eyes. His gut twisted as if he had some illness. He cursed softly and stood. "I will not harm you this night! *Jesu!* Do not look at me that way!"

She nodded, and motioned for him to sit. Grudgingly, he did so. Her hand was gentle with the shears; he did not feel even a prick as she snipped and removed the threads from his shoulder. He watched her face pinken as she pulled a stool up and pressed open his thighs. His hardness had subsided, but with her touch on his thigh so close to what made him a man, it thickened. "Ignore it," he said.

She looked up into his face, and he was relieved to see a twinkle in her eye. "'Twill be difficult—it is so intrusive." But she settled between his thighs as she had done nearly a fortnight ago, and as he'd done then, he now rose against her side. Wulfson gritted his teeth and endured the living hell of having her so close but being unable to touch her.

She pushed back the linen and looked at the neat scar, then turned her face up to him. "'Tis healed."

He nodded. "Aye."

"But—?" Her eyes narrowed and he watched his ruse dawn on her face. "It never festered!"

He grinned in embarrassment. "So you found me out. 'Twas a ploy to get you alone."

"You have no honor!"

"I never claimed any."

She shook her head and quickly saw to the threads. Once she was done she made to move away from him, but Wulfson stayed her with a gentle hand. When she turned, wide-eyed, he shook his head. "I will not harm you, nor will I attempt to seduce you." His cock flexed as he said the words, and they both caught their breaths. "My pardon, I cannot seem to control that whilst you are near."

She trembled in his arms, and he wanted to believe it was because he made her feel the same heat she made him feel. "I have a query of you," he softly said.

Nodding slowly, Tarian said, "Ask me."

"When last we were thus, did I displeasure you?"

Color flooded her cheeks and she looked down, then away. She shook her head, not looking at him.

"You pleased me greatly," he whispered, pushing her hair from her face and turning her to face him. "As no other before you. So do not think I compare you to other women. You are above them all."

Her eyes moistened. "Why do you say these things to me?"

"Because they are true."

"Nay, how can you say them when one night I will find you standing over my bed with your dagger in hand?"

He stiffened, and very carefully he spoke. "I told you once that my king was not a fool. I trust him to make the correct decision based on all the information presented to him."

"But how could you? Your man left here a month ago!"

"I sent another messenger, Tarian."

Her body stiffened, but he saw a softening in her eyes. "You did? Why?"

Her long hair had come forward; he brushed it away. "Because I believe to destroy you would be an injustice to us all."

Her bright eyes glittered in the candlelight. "You truly believe that?" she softly queried.

He nodded, set her from his lap, and stood. "Aye, I do. Now, get thee gone from here before I prove how violent a man I can be."

She did not hesitate to remove herself from the room. And he was glad of it. His mettle was once more pushed to the brink of no return. He did not know how much longer he could tolerate her so close at hand and him unable to lose himself in her.

Tarian was almost done with her change of clothes when there was a knock on her door. Edith opened it, and Gareth stood at the threshold. The minute she saw his face she knew that Warner had been detained and that the news was not in her favor. "Come in, Gareth. Close the door and bolt it behind you."

He did so, and as he approached she said the words. "The order stands." It was not a question but a statement of truth. Her guard paled and nodded. "What have you done with the Norman?"

"Our men have detained him just beyond Wycliffe. He has not been harmed, which is not what I can say for your guard. Two men were lost, one severely wounded, and three left to subdue the knight and his squire. They have a few lumps but will survive."

"Wulfson has sent another messenger to William. With more information as well as a stronger plea. I fear his king will be angered he did not carry out his order in the first place and Wulfson will lose favor, and in so doing I have no chance."

"Milady," Edith pleaded, "you must flee to Wales where you will be welcomed, or north to Scotland where no Normans abide."

Tarian nodded, and it was not an easy decision she made. Though she must, to survive. God willing, she would return. Her heart longed to stay here. A tight lump formed in her belly. Slowly and painfully it rose to her throat. "Gareth, prepare to leave this place. We begin tonight. Have the men leave quietly two by two so that no suspicions are raised. Edie, see that they are provisioned but not enough to draw question. It will take a few days and then we will muster who is left and flee under the cloak of night." She chewed her bottom lip. "My lord Alewith should be appraised of the situation. He will announce this eve that he and Brighid will return to Turnsly the day after the morrow. I will ask him for men to meet us just beyond the crossroads to Shrewsbury. From there we will move west, and hope we have enough of a lead on the Normans."

"Where will we go?" Edith asked wringing her hands.

"To Wales; but Edie, you must stay here. The journey is too dangerous for you, and the Normans will follow. Once I am settled I will send for you."

"Nay, I go with you!"

Tarian took her by the shoulders and shook her. "You

will stay here! I will not have your death on my hands." Tarian hugged the old woman to her, emotion running high. "Please, Edie, do not make this more difficult for me."

The old woman sobbed in her arms, but nodded her head. "And not a word to anyone, most especially Brighid or Noelth."

When Wulfson descended to the hall he found it to be boisterous and hot. Many people crowded inside, most looking for the evening meal. The lady of the manor was too generous with the stores, but after the display in Dunloc several days previous, he could not blame her. The quickest way to buy a man's loyalty was to fill his belly.

When the lookout shouted that riders approached, Wulfson's gut dropped to his feet and dread filled him. 'Twas Warner, and he knew the word would not be good. His men filed out behind him. A smile cracked Wulfson's face. "Rohan!" he shouted and started for the knight, who, when he spied Wulfson and the other Blood Swords, urged his mount into a canter. The hulking African, Manhku, was at his side.

When Rohan and Manhku dismounted, the knights laughed and slapped each other on the back. For the first time since December they were as they had been for years together—a most formidable force to be reckoned with.

"I have a son!" Rohan shouted. "A healthy, lusty son!"

The men cheered, and more backslapping and congratulating followed. As one they moved into the great hall. "Break open the wine barrels, for tonight we celebrate!" Wulfson called to the servants.

"How does your lady fare?" Thorin asked, his face nearly split in half with his grin.

"She is well. The babe came early, but he gave her no trouble. He is a fighter."

Stefan slapped him on the back and chortled, "Like his mother!"

"I have no doubt this time next year you will have another!" Wulfson chuckled, "What did you name the lad?"

"Geoffrey William Stephen du Luc."

"'Tis a most worthy name, my friend," Wulfson said, more than happy for his comrade.

Rohan grinned and took off his helm, and tossed it to his redheaded squire.

Wulfson's eyes widened. "Russell, you are nearly a man."

The lad grinned. "In two years' time I will have my spurs."

"I think not, boy," Manhku said in his thickly accented French.

"Manhku, the leg works?" Rorick asked, thrusting goblets of wine into their hands.

With their goblets full and one in each man's hand, Wulfson raised his high over his head. "To Rohan du Luc, his new son, and his lady, Isabel!"

The men cheered and drank.

Once they were seated together and calmed a bit, Wulfson asked, "What keeps Warner?"

Rohan scowled. "He is not here? He rode out two days ahead of us."

The men looked at each other, perplexed. Then Wulfson spoke, "'Tis not like him to dally, most especially with the message he bears from William."

"Aye, he seemed in a hurry to return to you. He lost much time waiting for the tides in Normandy to turn in his favor. He said he had a most urgent message for you."

"Did he say what it was?" Rhys asked.

Rohan shook his head and finished his wine. A servant quickly replenished it. "Nay, he did not, but he did not seem pleased."

Rhys caught Wulfson's scowl. Rohan looked at the men, then back to Wulfson. "What have I ridden into, Wulf?"

"Drink and eat; then we will apprise you of what is afoot here."

Rohan looked to the men, and they all shook their heads.

"I brought a half score of men with me. All knights, plus four squires, who, while they think they are ready for battle, I would use only as a last resort. What foes do we face?"

"The Welsh, to name one; the lady of the manor's uncle, to name another." Rorick looked about the hall. Several of Lady Tarian's men looked on, none to happy with the new arrivals. "And the lady's guard, to name three."

"*Jesu!* You are surrounded by the enemy, and yet you all seem to move comfortably about."

" 'Tis an uncomfortable truce."

"Come tell me of the intrigue of this interesting place. I have been lax these last months. I thirst for a good fight."

Wulfson shooed away the servants, and the men drew into a tight circle. "The lady of Dunloc is none other than Sweyn Godwinson's byblow by a Welsh abbess."

"How is that?" Rohan asked, shocked.

"Some twenty-one years ago, the savage abducted the abbess from her abbey and for a year kept her hostage. Lady Tarian is the result."

Rohan shook his head. " 'Tis unfortunate."

"Aye, so she is the niece of Harold; her dead husband, Earl Malcor, is connected to every damn Welsh king there is; and she may be with child, and that child will be as related to the Welsh as the sire was."

Rohan nodded. And as he did, his face stiffened. "William?"

"Wants all traces of all Godwinsons eliminated."

"*Jesu*! Murder a noblewoman?"

All the men nodded. "Is she with child?" Rohan asked.

"Time will tell. But things have become more complicated, and I think William acted in haste. I sent Warner with a message asking for reconsideration when I learned of her Welsh connections. Rhiwallon of Powys has already sent a train for her. She refused to go."

"Does she know why you are here?"

Wulfson slowly nodded. "When we arrived, she was at death's door in the dungeon; I was bent then and there to see the deed done, but—"

"When you meet the lady, you will understand," Thorin offered.

Wulfson shook his head. "Nay, it was more than that. Her uncle by marriage, Rangor of Lerwick, extolled her pedigree. He made it sound as if she were with child, and if we harmed it, we would feel the wrath of the Welsh upon us."

"Do you believe it?"

"Aye, I believed it then. I believe it more now. I have every reason to suspect the Welsh are mustering a force to take her from here. They have allied themselves with that devil Edric. They want her for all the reasons William does not. And while we all thirst to war, I did not think it prudent to throw William into an all-out war with the Welsh at this time."

"Where is she now?" Rohan asked, obviously intrigued.

Wulfson inclined his head over his shoulder toward the

stairway. "Up there, no doubt plotting the easiest way to separate my head from my shoulders."

"So Warner carried William's response?"

They all nodded. Rohan whistled and shook his head. Then he looked up and his jaw dropped. They all turned as one as Tarian descended into the hall in all her glory, the broadsword strapped to her leather belt.

Ioan nudged Rohan. "She wields the sword like a man."

"And shoots an arrow with more accuracy than all of us combined," Rhys said.

"She fought beside Harold at Stamford Bridge and Sen-lac Hill," Stefan added.

"Wulfson," Rohan said solemnly, "you have my deepest sympathy."

Seventeen

Tarian nearly lost her balance when she descended into the hall and saw the new influx of knights. Could the nightmare her life had become darken even more? She continued into the hot, humid area, and forced a smile when Wulfson and his men, along with the new faces, stood for her.

Wulfson made to step forward, as if he were to offer his arm, but he hesitated. Instead, Thorin did the honor. Placing her hand upon his brawny forearm, Tarian smiled gracefully up into his handsome face. His long blond hair was as glorious as any woman's, and his one deep hazel eye saw more than the two eyes of most men. Like his brothers-in-arms, he sported the same crescent-shaped scar on his chin, and as they approached a most handsome knight and a huge ebony giant, she noticed immediately that they too sported the same scar on their chins. More Blood Swords? What bound these men so tightly?

"Lady Tarian, I present Lord Rohan of Alethorpe, Dunleavy, and Wilshire, and his man, Sir Manhku," Thorin introduced.

Tarian extended her hand, and Rohan took it in his. His strength and warmth flooded her senses. He was as enigmatic as the others: there was something different, something special, something dark and unearthly about them all. Collectively they reminded her of demons on horseback. He pressed his lips to her hand as he made a short bow. "I am honored to meet you, Lady Tarian."

She returned his gesture with a brief curtsy. "As I you."

Manhku cleared his throat and looked to her as if he expected her to rend her hair and run away screaming. Instead she smiled and extended her hand to him, "Sir Manhku? An interesting name." Awkwardly, he took her hand and pressed his lips to her skin, then dropped her hand and hastily stepped back.

He nodded and rumbled, "My lady."

Tarian laughed, amused by his skittish behavior. "I assure you, sir knight, I do not bite, though I have been known to chop off a head or two."

She turned to Wulfson. "Are you such a bore you cannot make the proper introductions?" Before she would allow him to answer, Tarian turned back to Thorin. "Sir Thorin, your noble breeding shows. Would you escort me to the table? I am famished."

Her glib flirting was rewarded with a heavy scowl from Wulfson. But she would play the game, so as not to bring any undue attention to herself or her men.

When Lord Alewith approached with his daughter, Wulfson stood and made the round of introductions. Brighid stared, fascinated by the markings on the African's face. "'Tis rude to stare, Brighid," Tarian whispered.

Brighid shook herself and hastened to beg his pardon. She sat across from him next to her father. The platters were set, and when Wulfson called for a blessing, Alewith spoke up, "Father Dudley was called away to Silsby."

"Silsby? But that is a border town, a day and a half ride away. I need him here," Tarian complained. Of all the witnesses to the will, he was the most important.

Alewith shook his head. "There was an outbreak; he was called to bless the graves."

Tarian looked to Wulfson, who had insisted she keep her seat to his left. "Father Dudley was witness to Malcor's will. He is not here to give testimony."

"There is Edith and the other you mentioned?"

Tarian's eyes narrowed as she caught the glare of Ruin as he placed a platter of mutton on one of the lesser tables. She did not trust him. But he would not lie. Not with Father Dudley as witness. "Ruin, Malcor's manservant, whom I do not trust. He is thick with Rangor. I should have sent him off with him. 'Twas always my intention."

"After the meal we will see to the document."

Tarian nodded and bent her head to sustenance. She was famished, and worried and fearful her flight would be found out. She caught Gareth's gaze several times throughout the meal. She ignored the revelry of the knights. She was not interested in their past conquests. She was bent on survival. She wanted the meal over, the will validated, and to return to her chamber to prepare for her escape. But that was not to be.

The lookout called that someone approached.

Tarian pushed the trencher from her, surprised at the late visitor. She stood; the men did as well, and they waited.

A thick thatch of red hair gave the visitor away. At first she thought Rangor had returned, but the shabby clothing said otherwise. 'Twas Malcor's bastard half brother,

Ednoth. For a man who had nothing, he strode into the manor as if he were the rightful lord. On most days his arrogance would not have bothered her, but today, when she felt more vulnerable the she ever had, he got to her. Her hand moved to the hilt of Thyra. Wulfson's big warm hand covered hers.

"Easy, my lady, do not show your hand so quickly," Wulfson softly cautioned.

She looked up at him, surprised, and found his eyes bright and full of mischief. He nodded his head, so subtly she was not sure that he had. He presented his arm and led her to the lord's great chair and sat her upon it, then stood to her right and awaited the man who, once he spied her seated in the lord's chair surrounded by Norman knights, slowed his gait considerably.

Ednoth stopped before Tarian and made the proper bow to her. "Lady Tarian."

For someone whose stomach was a churning mill full of tension, Tarian smiled serenely and nodded her head. "Ednoth. What brings you to Draceadon?"

He glanced up at Wulfson, who stood casually beside her; then his gaze traveled around the circle of knights behind them. "I have come to stake my claim as rightful heir to all that was Earl Malcor's."

Tarian's heart pounded against her chest, but in a slow, even voice she asked, "What gives you the right to make the claim?"

"I am the son of Earl Llewellyn. His sole surviving male heir. All that was his is now mine, by our laws."

Tarian nodded. "I hear you, Ednoth, but you forget three vital facts. First and foremost, with some inquiry it has been established that Llewellyn never officially recognized you." He opened his mouth to argue, but she held her hand up, palm open toward him. "Allow me to finish."

He stepped back and nodded, but his pale skin had reddened considerably. "Secondly, it has yet to be confirmed that I carry the heir. But should I not, I have a valid will, signed by Earl Malcor, Father Dudley, my woman Edith, and Earl Malcor's manservant, Ruin. The document states that all that belonged to Earl Malcor would revert to me, his lawful wife, upon his death."

"But you murdered him!" Ednoth shouted.

The hall gasped as one, and Wulfson stepped forward. "It has been established, Ednoth, that the lady's life was in peril. She did as any person would do. She defended herself. I will hear no more accusations of murder!"

Ednoth blanched. "I insist the witnesses be brought forward and speak, and as blood brother to Malcor, I demand to see the document!"

"Ednoth," Tarian said patiently, "you do not understand. I am under no obligation by law to bring forth any witness or present the document. You have no claim."

" 'Tis a forgery!" Ruin shouted from the crowd.

Tarian gasped, and Wulfson inclined his head to Rhys to nab the upstart.

He dragged Ruin kicking and screeching toward them. Tarian stood. "What lies do you spew now?"

Ruin's eyes narrowed dangerously. He looked from Tarian to Gareth, who stood to her left. "She did not murder milord." He pointed a long bony finger at Gareth. " 'Twas him, her guard. He was jealous and could not stand my lord touching her!"

Gareth stood silent, furious at the outrageous accusation, but Tarian whirled around and stepped down to face

Ruin. "You are a liar of the highest order, Ruin. Malcor was as twisted as you, and when he could not rise to the occasion he beat me for it. When he took my own sword and laid it across my throat, I drew his dagger from his belt and slit *his* throat. Do not put the blame where it does not belong."

Tarian turned to Wulfson, then back to the crowd. "Hear the truth. Malcor was perverted, he was twisted to his soul. He gained pleasure by inflicting pain. 'Twas Ruin who made promises to the village boys that if they came to the hall and sat with the earl, they would be handsomely rewarded."

She looked up to Wulfson. "Edith will bear witness that Malcor was for once of sound mind when he had the monks draw up the document. Father Dudley will back the claim." She turned to Gareth. "Take him to the place he enjoyed so well with his master. And let him rethink the truth."

Gareth seized Ruin, who shrieked like a woman as he was led away. Tarian turned her attention back to Ednoth. "You have no claim. If you persist, I will take my claim to the king. Do not darken my doorstep again, unless you are willing to accept your lot here."

His fury was visible, but for the sake of his life, Ednoth gave her a shallow bow and retreated.

Tarian turned to Wulfson. "If you please, come to my chamber, and I will produce the document." She looked past him to his men. "Bring them with you."

The great chamber was greatly reduced in size, so full of hulking knights. Tarian went to her great chest and lifted the lid, then slid a secret panel to the side. There, rolled up with the earl's seal unbroken, was a scroll, and she handed it to Wulfson. He took it and moved to a small table where a candelabrum lit the room.

He glanced to her. "Break the seal and see for yourself," she said.

He did so, and as he read, his men gathered round. It was there in Latin, witnessed and marked by Father Dudley, Edith, and Ruin.

"Where is your maid?" Wulfson asked.

"I am here, milord," Edie said, bobbing her head and coming forward. Wulfson pointed to the document and asked, "Which mark is yours?"

She pointed to the one with a crudely written E. "I learned as a girl the letter my name began with. I have used it only a handful of times in my life. But that is my mark. Father Dudley drew up the document and Father Michael read it to us." She looked up to Wulfson and continued, "'Twas Earl Malcor's wish that my lady have it all."

"Why? When he was forced to marry her at swordpoint?"

Edith smiled a sly smile. "Milady reminded him that he would burn in hell for his sins on this earth. He was not all black of heart. He saw the righteousness in doing right by her when he had done so much wrong in such a short time. He begged her for her promise to pay for alms should he die before her."

Wulfson raised a brow. "And did she?"

Edith cackled. "Nay, she never promised him, and none were bought. He was the devil's spawn, that one. The fires of hell are too good for the damage he's done."

Wulfson turned and looked hard at Tarian. "Why would his manservant lie?"

She scoffed. " 'Tis what he does. He resented me the day I came here. He no longer had control over Malcor. I would not allow the boys to be brought here. Ruin is as twisted as my dead husband."

"Are you sure Ednoth was never recognized by Llewellyn?"

"Malcor never mentioned Ednoth to me. All of the documents pertaining to the earldom are at Briarhurst. 'Tis two days' hard ride from here." And as she mentioned the earldom's seat she formulated her plans. They would go there first and seize the documents, then head west to Wales.

She looked up to Wulfson. "With your permission, I would dispatch a handful of my men immediately to secure the manor. I fear Rangor may have his own designs on the documents. I should have seen to this earlier."

She watched Wulfson contemplate the request. He nodded. "I will send several of my men along for support."

Tarian did not dare argue. Not only would this be the perfect excuse to rid Draceadon of her men and have them build up, but it would put several of Wulfson's men out of the way. She would instruct her men that as soon as the opportunity presented itself, they should disarm the knights and consider them hostages. And the fewer men Wulfson had here, the fewer he would have to come after her.

"Thank you."

Wulfson rolled the parchment up and handed it back to her. "Reseal this."

She took it from him. "I shall, but there are two other copies should this one mysteriously disappear."

He quirked a brow, not sure if she meant that as a barb. She gifted him with a smile.

And so the next day as the sun broke the eastern horizon, ten of Tarian's men rode off with two of the knights Sir Rohan had brought with him. Her men had been instructed to disarm and unseat them, then hold them until she met up with them. By the time she let them go and they returned to Draceadon, she would be long gone.

Lord Alewith also left Draceadon, much to Brighid's and, she could tell, Rhys's unhappiness. But it was for the girl's best interest. Alewith would meet them in four days' time at Briarhurst.

Tarian was as jumpy as a mouse, and found difficulty in acting as if all was normal. Wulfson's eyes always seemed to be upon her, but when she turned to confront him he was otherwise occupied. She found his patient tutelage in horsemanship disturbing. Too many times when he touched her to show her the proper leg movement or the proper way to rein, his skin touched hers and burned.

Each time he helped her mount Silversmith, his hands lingered too long on her waist. On the last day before her flight, as she rubbed down the stallion, Wulfson came into the stall and pressed her back into the thick mounds of fresh straw, and begged her.

"You make me think of nothing but your skin against mine, Tarian. I cannot sleep because you haunt my dreams. Ease this ache I have for you."

Her body ached for him as much, but she would not give into her passion for this man. She fought the thing that was between them as viciously as she did her foe on the battlefield. Because she knew that if she gave in to it, it would destroy her.

He was relentless. On what was to be her last night at Draceadon, Tarian called for a hot bath. As she slid into the velvety water and leaned her head back, closing her eyes, there was a commotion at the door.

"My lord, my lady is indisposed at the moment!" Edith said sharply.

"Leave us," Wulfson said. Tarian gasped, and turned with her arms crossed over her chest to see Wulfson's predatory eyes piercing her from the threshold. He stepped in, and despite Edith's cries for him to leave, he pushed her out the door, closed it, then threw the bolt.

When he turned back to Tarian, he leaned against the thick door, a tight smile twisting his handsome lips. "The torment is beyond my endurance, Tarian. Give me what I seek."

She settled back into the tub, and smiled like the vixen she felt herself. "If I do not, will you rape me?" Slowly he shook his head. "Then leave me."

He shook his head again and pushed off the door and strode slowly toward her as if he were stalking a wary game bird. She ignored him and went about bathing herself. In a slow seductive motion, she lathered the sponge, and extending her right leg she set her toes to the edge of the tub. Leaning forward, in slow swirls she rubbed in the lather. When she was done with that leg, she washed the other in the same fashion.

She watched him watch her, and despite her need to torture him, her skin had warmed from more than the water. She sat up and arched her back, raising her arm and lathering it.

A sharp hiss of air from the knight made her skin flush warmer. She caught his brilliant eyes in the candlelight and smiled. "How does it feel, sir knight, to be so desperate for something you cannot have that it eats away at your innards?"

"Torturous," he said thickly.

She smiled again and slowly stood. His eyes widened to the size of fists. As if she were alone, she lathered her breasts, and hissed in a breath as she ran the soft linen across her nipples. They were full, sensitive, and tight. Wulfson's eyes narrowed. Slowly she shook her head, then lowered her hands to her belly and then to her thighs.

"Stop, Tarian," he whispered hoarsely. "Stop, or I will not be held accountable for my actions."

She smiled and reached for the pitcher of clean water, and in a slow pour she let it sluice down her body, washing away the thick, creamy lather. Wulfson stood as still as the walls that surrounded them. She stepped from the tub, only a hand's-breadth from him, and reached for the folded linen just past him. Her bottom brushed against his thigh, and that was the spark that set him afire. He grabbed her by the hips and brought her naked against him, his hands not moving from where he touched her. Tarian gasped, but did not move. She felt the hot length of him against her back. He was as rigid as steel, and she knew he fought a tremendous battle.

And he was not the only one. Her passion for the man who held her against him equaled his. She leaned back into him, arching her back, and bit her lip to keep from crying out. Her thighs quivered, and she had never wanted anything as much as she did this man at that moment. But she could not. He would keep her abed all through the night, filling her time and time again.

At the thought a moan did escape her throat.

"Yield to me, Tarian," he hoarsely whispered against her ear.

His warm breath stirred her more.

"I—I cannot," she breathed.

He turned her in his arms and grabbed a hank of her hair, pulling it back and forcing her to make eye contact with him. "Cannot or will not?"

His other hand slid down her back to her bottom, where his fingers dug into her tender skin, pressing her harder against him. She squeezed her eyes shut and forced away the vision of him taking her, as he had that night almost a month ago, and replaced it with the dream of him plunging his dagger deep into her belly. She stiffened, and felt the hot onslaught of tears in her eyes. She shook her head and choked back a sob.

"Please, Wulfson, do not make this thing between us more than it can be."

His face twisted in anger and passion, but she saw in his eyes that he understood. And that fact realized—knowing he knew as well as she that he could and would be the one to take her life should William insist on it—gave her the strength to move away from him. He let her go, and she wrapped the linen around her damp body.

"Please go," she said softly.

He did without hesitation. When the door thudded closed behind him, Tarian sank to the floor, despair filling every part of her, her heart most especially. It grew so heavy with grief that breathing became difficult. Edith was there now beside her, and moved her into the great bed.

"'Twill all work out, Tarian," she soothed stroking her cheek. "He will not kill the mother of his child." She pressed her thin hand to Tarian's belly. "In two months' time you will feel the babe move."

Tarian looked up to her nurse with watery eyes. "How do you know I am with child?"

" 'Tis early, I admit, but you are showing the signs."

Tarian sat up in bed and shook her head. "I feel no different."

Edith smiled. "Don't you?"

She shook her head. "Nay, I do not."

"Is your fatigue normal? Are your breasts tender to the touch? And for the last two days you have pushed your morning trencher away." She smiled. "But chiefly, your courses have not come this month."

And while the thought of the child should have pleased Tarian, it did not. He had been conceived under the falsest of pretenses, and he would never know the love of his true sire. A heavy fatigue overcame her at that moment, and Tarian gave in to it. "Wake me in four candle notches, Edie. Then we will fly."

Wulfson could not sleep. Every sound, every creak, every call of the owl had him on edge. He paced his room, and each time he turned it became smaller and smaller. Each time he looked to the tapestry he longed to slide past it and into Tarian's chamber. To take her in his arms and make love to her. But she would not have him, and he could not blame her.

He cursed, he drank more wine than he should have, and when the skin was empty he found himself candle in hand standing behind the secret door to her chamber. He paced back and forth, his lust waging a colossal battle with his better judgment. Finally, he retreated.

He was up before sunrise, stewing in the hall, pacing amongst his snoring men.

As he stood staring at the hearth, he suddenly stiffened. He looked about and saw none of Tarian's men. Gareth had not been asleep across her door. His hackles rose. He flew up the stairway to the lady's chamber and pushed open the door. "Tarian?" he called. Silence met him. He strode into the room, and her scent infiltrated his senses, but her mail and sword were gone!

A deep sense of dread filled Wulfson so completely he could scarcely breathe. And it had nothing to do with disappointing his king.

He turned and fled the room and hurried down the stairway, shouting, "Arise! Arise! To arms! The lady has flown!"

Tarian rode, literally, for her life. With her men behind her and Gareth at her side, she felt invincible should they run into anyone except Wulfson and his knights. As the sun broke over the eastern horizon, a hard chill bit her deep in her bones. Fear of what he would do to her should he catch up to them before they crossed the Welsh border terrified her. But even knowing what he was capable of did not ease the pain in her heart. Somewhere along the way, despite all that had transpired, she had grown more than fond of the surly knight.

Her belly churned in a way that made her want to retch. It was not from the babe, but from nerves, and sorrow and regrets. When they broke through the narrow pass that would lead to Briarhurst, the urge to retch overcame her. Not having the stomach to break the fast, Tarian bent over to the right of her saddle and allowed the dry heaves to rack her body.

"My lady," Gareth called in the dusk of dawn, "do you ail?"

Tarian waved him off and shook her head. She spurred Silversmith to move faster. She could feel her captain's eyes upon her, and shame at her deed encompassed her. He would put the pieces together, and she did not know if she could face him. But she convinced herself the babe was her guarantee that she would retain what Malcor promised her. But most of all, the babe offered her best chance of surviving William's wrath.

Stopping only once, they pushed their horses to the limit. By nightfall the beasts were blowing hard, and Tarian knew if they did not get rest soon they would be worthless on the morrow.

"There is the old Druid monastery several leagues ahead. A stream flows nearby; we will camp there for the night," Tarian told Gareth.

When they approached the place, night had long since fallen. Since the monastery was rumored to be haunted by the Druids who were slain there centuries ago, there were rumblings amongst the men. But Tarian ignored them. Though centuries had passed since its abandonment, it was still intact. Some said the forest Druids saw it as a shrine of sorts, and during the dark time ventured from the wood and tended it.

A large Celtic cross rose ahead, a foreboding sentinel signaling to all who traveled close by that this was sacred ground. Instead of fear, a deep sense of serenity filled Tarian, and she knew she would be safe here.

The horses were tended to, the men fed, and the lookouts posted. They would be ahorse again long before the first rays of the sun announced the new day. But, tired as she was, Tarian could not find sleep. She tossed and turned on the ground, finding no position comfortable. Strapping on her sword belt, she lit a torch from the low embers of the fire and quietly moved toward the structure. She felt the spirit of the place encompass her and carry her forward, in invitation to explore.

She pushed open the heavy wooden portal, the hinges creaking under its weight.

"My lady?" Gareth said from behind her.

She turned to him and smiled. Worry etched his face. He had aged ten years since their arrival at Draceadon. It felt like a lifetime ago. "Go back to sleep, Gareth, I am only slaking my curiosity. No harm will befall me inside."

His lips pursed as if to argue, but he only nodded, and instead of going back to his bedroll he found a seat on a nearby old stone bench. She continued into the building, and that sense of serenity filled her again. She touched the torch to an ancient sconce on the wall and was relieved to see it ignite. She walked further into the place, and could just make out a stone altar at the far end of the room. Several stone benches, like pews, dotted the interior. High windows allowed the soft moonlight in. And though she did not have a relationship with God, she set the torch in an old metal floor sconce and sat down on the bench nearest it. She folded her hands and looked up and closed her eyes, and for the first time since she was a girl, she prayed.

Her tranquility was disrupted by the hoarse call to arms from Gareth. The thunder of hooves shook the ground beneath her. She sat perfectly still, and dread filled every part of her body. Gooseflesh erupted across her arms and down her back. Her belly quivered with nervous excitement, and even though she had stood and fought at York and Hastings, for the first time in her life Tarian felt the windy chill of death swirl about her.

'Twas Wulfson, and he was not there to complain that she had not said her good-bye.

Panic grabbed her with sharp claws, shredding at her insides. Fear, anguish, anger, and despair wrestled for dominance. She drew her sword and ran for the door.

She flung it open to find Gareth blocking her way and a furious Wulfson upon his black steed, his double swords pointed at Gareth's heart. A quick scan of the camp revealed her men still on the ground where they lay, surrounded by armed knights.

"You will have to go through me, sir, to get to the lady," Gareth said, his voice harsh and unwavering.

Wulfson's face hardened to stone. "Do not be a fool, captain; we will reduce you and your men to scraps not fit for the hounds. Step aside."

"You will have to slay us all! I will not return with you!" Tarian said, trying to step around Gareth, who refused to allow her passage.

"Lady Tarian, are you willing to sacrifice the lives of your men for what will in the end be a futile battle?"

"Do you think, Sir Wulfson, we are so cloddish that several of your sacred Blood Swords will not find their end here as well? Is that *your* wish?"

He shrugged nonchalantly. " 'Tis always a possibility. Now hand over your sword, and you will all live."

"Will we? Do you include me? Can you guarantee me my life will be spared?"

Turold threw his head as if answering for his master. "I can guarantee your life this eve," Wulfson solemnly answered.

"But not tomorrow?"

He sat back in the saddle and eyed her cagily, then looked to Gareth. "I seek a private word with your lady, captain."

"Nay!" Gareth cried.

Wulfson sheathed his double swords and dismounted, but he kept his hand on the hilt of his broadsword. "I give you my oath no harm will come to her by my hand or by any of my men." He looked past Gareth to her, and Tarian felt her knees weaken. "A word." He pointed behind her. "In private."

Tarian wrestled with the request. He had given his oath he would not harm her, but more than that, her men would be spared, and she knew Wulfson de Trevelyn well enough to know that his oath was as good as done. She placed her hand on Gareth's shoulder. "I will speak to him. I will shout for you if I need you."

She backed away into the monastery. Wulfson followed and slammed the heavy door behind him and threw the bolt. When he turned to face her, she could see the furious glitter of his green eyes, and she knew a bone-chilling fear.

She raised her sword. "Do not proceed. Say what you must, then be gone."

His lips twisted into a deadly smile and he moved toward her with the stealth of a wolf.

She took a defensive position and raised her sword. "I will kill you," she whispered. And she thought she meant it.

He continued his path to her, not hesitating once in his step. He tossed his helm to the ground and pulled off his gauntlets, throwing them to land beside it. He unbuckled his double scabbards and continued toward her. He dropped them to the floor. Tarian backed up until a bench cut into the back of her legs. "I will not give you another warning. Halt!"

As Wulfson drew his broadsword, Tarian struck. With both hands she grasped the hilt of her sword and slammed it against his hand, almost but not quite enough to knock the sword from his hand. He cursed, and although she had used the flat side of the blade it still cut him. He looked up at her and his eyes narrowed.

Tarian turned and hopped from one bench to another, running across them as Wulfson chased her. She turned to bring her sword down upon his when he swiped at her. She hopped high, the blade narrowly missing her ankle. Fury was in every inch of her. She swung a backwards glance as she hopped to the next bench.

For his size and the mail he carried Wulfson was nimble, but she was more so; her mail lay beside her saddle and she wore only woolen chauses, braies, an undertunic and gambeson. She maneuvered around to gain an angle from which she could thrust at his side. He parried the strike with his sword, the steel slamming against hers, numbing her hands.

"You are skilled, my lady," Wulfson said, and he moved in on her. "But not skilled enough." He lunged for a thrust and she turned like a whirlwind, bringing her blade down to catch his before it ran through her leg.

She bolted away from him, putting several benches between them. Her chest heaved with exertion and her hands were numb, and when she looked up at him and saw the amusement in his eyes she realized he only toyed with her this entire time. Had he wanted her dead she would have been spitted like a boar. Fury soared. "Do it now, save me from this torture! Run me through!" As she screamed the words at him she charged him. He brought his sword down on hers with such a force she thought it would break in half. She stumbled past him to the stone floor. She rolled as he came toward her. She grabbed her sword from the floor, and, turning, hopped up, crouched, ready to fight for her life.

She saw only blood in his eyes. Humiliation and anger clouded her judgment. She lunged at him again and once again he parried her. This time he grabbed her by the back of her gambeson and spun her around, grabbing her sword hand.

He yanked her up hard against his chest. Now they both breathed heavily. "You sorely test my patience, Tarian of Dunloc. You will cease this play of yours and return to Draceadon with me!"

Vehemently she shook her head. "Nay! I will not!"

He squeezed her hand until she cried out and dropped the sword. He pulled her hair back so that her back arched and her chest thrust into his. "Aye, you will." His face was only inches from hers, and she knew that not only was his fury soaring but his passion as well. She could feel him against her. She struggled against him, knowing what was to come, and as determined for it not to happen. For if he bent her to his passion she would lose all to him.

"Finish me, then, for I will not return willingly with you."

"I will not let you go!"

"You cannot hold me!"

He dropped his sword to the floor. "You will come with me, Tarian. I will not let you die." And his lips crushed hers in a furious kiss that took everything coherent from her.

Tarian clawed at him. He growled and pushed her up against the wall, his lips never leaving hers. She could not breathe, nor could she stop him. For in her heart and soul she did not want to. At that precise moment in her life she gave up her rigid control, and in so doing laid herself open, exposed, more vulnerable than she had ever allowed herself to be before. She broke and gave into her passion for this man, just as he had broken and demanded from her what they both desired. With the surrender came a sweeping urgency to possess and be possessed that she had never experienced on any plane. It was all or nothing with this man, and she wanted to give all, even if it meant losing all in the end.

He yanked at her woolen chauses and her braies. When they would not give, frustrated, he ripped them from her. Cool air swirled across her hot skin. Her fingers worked at his mail chauses; when those loosened, she worked on his linen ones. She unhooked the ties, then tore at his braies, and felt him hot and thick against her thigh, "*Jesu*," he hissed.

He brought her up in his arms and pressed her tighter against the wall. In one swift stroke he entered her and they both cried out in shocked pleasure. She hung there in his arms for what seemed like eternity. His dark eyes bore into hers and she felt the earth move at that moment. He smoothed the hair from her cheek with gentle fingers. His lips hovered above hers. "I leave in three days' time for Normandy. I will not allow my king to destroy you, Tarian. We will find a way."

Hot tears welled in her eyes. "Thank you," she breathed. He took her then. He took her on a wild, wicked ride from which she was not sure she would ever recover.

Their passion was as potent and as violent as the battle at Hastings. Saxon against Norman. Man against woman, warrior against warrior, they came together as one, united as God meant man and woman to be. A wild rush of sensation curled inside her womb; like lightning it struck and unfurled inside her. Tarian cried out as the wild waves crashed through her. Her skin flushed and her limbs quaked. Wide-eyed, she stared at Wulfson. His eyes bore hotly into her, and she watched his face as he too found that sublime release. He jerked against her, thrusting high and forcefully. "Tarian!" he called hoarsely, burying his lips against her throat as the spasms wracked his body. She accepted him, her waves subsiding with his.

For long moments they stayed connected as one, their heavy breaths and sweaty bodies attempting to recover from the violence of the encounter. He pressed his forehead to hers and softly said, "I cannot move."

She pressed her lips to his, and as softly said against them, "Nor can I."

He turned with her, still inside her, dropped to his knees, and rolled with her in his arms onto his back. Tarian moaned. He was still inside her and still full. Her body was raw and receptive. He pressed her hips tighter to him. "You are not sated?"

She leaned up on her elbows and smiled and shook her head. "Nay, Wulfson, I will never have my fill of you."

He cupped the back of her head with his big hand and brought her lips to his. "Nor I of you."

Eighteen

Loud pounding on the door, followed by Gareth's shouts, drew them apart. Wulfson rose, bringing her with him.

"We must go," he said gently.

Quickly, they both dressed and armed themselves to a semblance of propriety. The damage to her clothing was repairable. Tarian, dressing, stopped and looked up at Wulfson. She would have the truth from him. She desperately wanted to believe what he had told her before he took her. To know he planned no ruse, no sleight of words or hand. For she could not help but wonder. She had been alone all her life and always relied on her own oath to herself for survival.

"Did you speak true about your travel to your king on my behalf?"

He halted as she adjusted his chauses and stared at her, perplexed. He had to see the worry in her eyes. His lips gentled with a smile, and he took her chin in his hand. "Look at me." He brushed his thumb across her bottom lip.

"You are most valuable, Tarian. To the Welsh, to the Saxons and to that cur Rangor. I am going to William to explain to him how valuable you are to him. Alive."

Tarian forced back a shiver at his words. Would he think her so valuable when he got wind of her detainment of his knight Warner? Anger spiked her mood. What would he have her do? Stand by and allow him to trot up with her death warrant in his hand, when she could prevent it? Any person would do as much. She did not wish to die!

"Tarian!" Gareth shouted. "Come out now or I will break down this door!"

"Hold, Gareth!" Wulfson called. "I bring your lady!"

Tarian looked up to Wulfson, unsure whether she walked into the wolf's mouth or if he did indeed mean to plead for her life. She finished dressing and looked up at him expectantly.

He grinned and extended his arm to her. "Come, *chérie*, let us see this through."

As they hurried to the door that looked as if it would come apart at any moment, Tarian asked Wulfson, "What do I tell them?"

He smiled and bent to kiss her. His lips were warm, and she wanted nothing more than to melt into him and allow him to take over. She was so tired of always being on her toes looking behind and ahead, always a step ahead. He smiled against her lips and whispered, "The truth."

She nodded, but her own guilt assailed her. She would have to tell Wulfson of her treachery, and the thought made her sick to her stomach. Not now. She slowly exhaled. But soon.

Wulfson unbolted the door, and Gareth nearly fell in. Tarian smiled, and felt her cheeks heat.

"I am well, Sir Gareth. We will spend the night here and return to Draceadon in the morn."

His eyes widened. She hurried to curtail more questions. "I want you to take a handful of men to Briarhurst and inform Alewith of the change in plans. I also entrust the documents there to you. Bring them to me at Draceadon."

He opened his mouth to argue, but she stayed him with her hand. "Nay, things have changed. Come now so that I may tell you where the documents can be found."

Once the Normans were settled and the camp back to a semblance of order, Tarian took Gareth aside. "The documents can be found in the chapel. There is a false bottom beneath the first pew on the right. Do not give yourself away to anyone, including Alewith. Those documents are worth more than the entire Danegold. I must have them, Gareth; much is at stake."

He nodded and looked past her to where she knew Wulfson stood. "What did the Norman promise you, should you return to Draceadon?"

She took in a deep breath and slowly exhaled. "My life."

Gareth scowled, but looked hard at her, then at the Norman. "I will kill him if he lies."

"He returns to Normandy to plead my case before the king. I could not ask for more."

"What if William refuses?"

Tarian closed her eyes and felt a wave of nausea crash through her. For a minute she wavered on her feet, and Gareth grabbed her as she tilted to one side. "Milady, what ails you?"

She leaned against him, suddenly feeling dizzy and fatigued. She had not eaten and she had been running for her life, and now it all caught up to her. Pressing her hand to her throat, she shook her head. "Too much, Gareth, too much." Her knees went out from under her and had he not held her she would have crumpled to the ground.

Wulfson watched the tender exchange between Tarian and her guard, and jealousy ripped through him. It was a new emotion for him, and one he did not care for in the least. As a man who had rigid self-control, he had found that when it came to Tarian Godwinson he was sorely at a loss. Though he knew there was nothing romantic between her and her captain, he wanted to be the man she turned to for succor. He frowned, wondering what that meant in the realm of them, together. There was no future, there was only the here and the now, and once William was convinced to spare her he would move on. A sudden thought occurred to him. And it did not sit well with him. In his gut, he knew that if he could convince William she was worth more alive than dead, his king would insist she come to Normandy and reside there as a hostage. He still held her uncle Wulfnoth, Godwine's youngest son, these many years past. William had no intention of releasing him. He would die in Normandy. Wulfson knew Tarian would do the same, and it saddened him greatly.

She did not belong in an obscure castle in Normandy where her life force could not thrive. She would wither and die, like a flower without sunshine. He continued to watch her speak with her captain and accepted that sentence, for at least she would be alive.

He bolted toward them when he saw her crumple. Gareth caught her limp body to his, just as Wulfson reached for her. The guard hiked her small form up into his arms and glared at Wulfson. "My lady ails; leave her to my care." He turned then and stalked with her into the old ruin. Wulfson stared at his retreating back.

"What is this about, Wulf?" Rohan asked from beside him.

Wulfson sucked in a long breath and let it out. He looked directly at his friend and knew that if any man could understand what he felt, it would be Rohan. "When did Lady Isabel become the one thing on this earth you must possess at all cost?"

Rohan threw his head back and laughed. He slapped Wulfson on the back, and while Wulfson did not think the question amusing, Rohan sobered. "I knew the minute I saw her standing alone in that empty hall clutching that dagger to her chest as if she would single-handedly defeat William and his army that she was my destiny. It took my pride and common sense much longer to realize it."

Wulfson nodded. "I knew it when I saw Tarian in the dungeon. She has haunted me ever since. I cannot make the feeling go away. It is worse then the torture in Jubb, that hell of a prison."

Rohan nodded, but a heavy frown worried his brow. "What of William?"

Wulfson cursed and punched the air. "I cannot defy my king! But I want her." He began to pace a small ditch in front of Rohan. "I fear if I can convince him she is worth more alive than dead, he will insist she come to him in Normandy, and there she will remain."

Rohan nodded and clasped Wulfson's shoulder. "At least she will be alive."

"'Tis not a worthy existence for one such as she. I fear what she would do." Wulfson raked his fingers through his long hair. "I fear there is no solution agreeable to both sides."

"Mayhap a Norman husband is in order," Rohan suggested. "If she is with child, she will need a father for the babe."

The thought of Tarian lying with another man, Norman or not, made Wulfson feel as if he had been kicked in the gut by Turold. He looked hard at his friend. Rohan remained silent, and Wulfson let the truth settle in. So be it. Life over freedom, with or without a Norman husband: so it would be for Tarian Godwinson. For freedom meant a live threat to William. And that was not an option.

Wulfson refused to give thought to her carrying Malcor's child. The thought of it sickened him. What if the child came out pale-skinned and flame-headed, and grew into one as perverse as his sire? His stomach did a slow nauseous roll at the vision of Tarian under the likes of Malcor, or worse, that eel Rangor. For her sake he prayed she was not with child. If William allowed her to live, so then the child would be a hostage, and if a son, more of a threat than his mother. Children had a way of disappearing, or becoming sickly and dying mysteriously. As much as he did not wish she was with child, for his own selfish reasons, he wished for her own good that she was not pregnant. Despite what had been a terrible upbringing for her, Tarian would be a fierce mother, protecting her babe with her life.

A sudden well of emotion rose in him. He had no knowledge of any bastards he'd left behind, but he had always vowed he would never ignore his own blood. He was not father material, but he would make sure the child was seen to, and he would do what he could, as a sire should.

And so he resolved Tarian Godwinson's fate in his heart. She would live her life out in Normandy, hopefully with a husband whom she could respect, and not alone in a dungeon as a hostage. And though he should rejoice in that small comfort, he did not.

Long after the men had bedded down and snores filled the cool air of the night, Wulfson lay awake, his hands behind his head and stared at the stars. His eyes focused on one star in particular. 'Twas the only one in the sky with an orange glow. His eyes wandered past it across the sky, but they always came back to that one star, and sitting up he realized that it was the beacon of the constellation Draco. He smiled. The dragon force dominated the sky.

He turned and stared at the open door to the monastery, where Gareth had bedded down. He toyed with demanding Gareth stand back, but he shook it off. He'd already stared down more than a few knowing looks from his men—as well as angry glares from Tarian's. He would not give them more to chew on. He would not disturb her.

Before they embarked on the return journey to Draceadon, Tarian watched Gareth and a handful of her men, along with Ioan and Stefan, mount up and ride for Briarhurst. Sheepishly she'd told Wulfson of her orders to unhorse the men he had sent with her contingent to Briarhurst. He only scowled and informed Rohan, who smiled at her from across camp. He later thanked her for not harming his men.

As the day drew on and the ride became more arduous at the slower pace, Tarian tried on several occasions to explain to Wulfson why she had detained Warner, assuring him he was unharmed, and that she was most surely with child. More than anything, she wanted to tell him the child was his, but she feared not only his wrath but the wrath of William, the wrath of her Welsh kin, and the wrath of her own people. A Norman bastard conceived under the guise of passing him off as the heir to an English earldom would not endear her to anyone. Despite her subterfuge, she could not help but feel a little happy that the child was Wulfson's. His seed was as virile as he, and the child would be as strong. And, she realized, she had tender feelings for the child's sire.

She let out a long, pensive sigh. 'Twas true. Her heart ached for him.

"What prickles your mind, Tarian?" Wulfson asked, reining the black to slow to her pace. Silversmith tossed his head, not caring for the other stallion being so close. He nipped at Turold, who ignored the assault. Tarian reined the gray back. "Smith! Mind your manners!" He shook his head again, as if saying that manners did not count with Norman horses, but he quieted, though she could feel his muscles tight beneath her.

"Your king will not change his mind."

Wulfson scowled. "He will listen to me."

"He will throw me in the dungeon with my uncle."

"I will beseech him to find you a noble Norman husband, Tarian. 'Twill not be so terrible."

She flashed him an angry glare. Just like that, he could pass her off to another man? "I'm tired of you making decisions on my behalf."

"I but think of your well-being, woman! Every noble on both sides of the Welsh border makes a case for you."

"Aye, they do, because they see my value. 'Tis no doubt why your king wants me dead."

"You have an army, Tarian! Of course he sees you as a threat. He is not blind. Add to it your sire's line and that of your dead husband's, and you are of great value to William's foes!"

She shook her head, not wanting to see the totality of it. "I was never of value to anyone until I married Malcor and may carry his child. Now I have too many suitors!"

"You will have more. Take a Norman husband as father to the child you may carry."

"Nay! I will never wed with a Norman. Normans have slain my entire paternal line! How could you expect such a thing from me?"

Wulfson's face turned to granite. Looking straight ahead, he said, "When Gareth returns, I will depart for Normandy. In two months' time at the most, you will have your answer."

And what if William continued to insist she die? Would she stay here, a hapless victim to his wiles? She glanced at Wulfson's stony face, and her heart softened toward him. He too was up against a wall. And she knew in her heart he would plead for her life. That he begged her to take a Norman husband told her he did care what happened to her. But the female part of her took umbrage. That he could hand her off to another man rankled her deep.

But, if she were honest with herself, what choice did she have in the matter? 'Twas the best solution in his mind, should William extinguish his kill order. But she would never go to Normandy, under any circumstances. When she married again, *she* would choose her husband. Not her king, not her overlord, and not Wulfson; no one but she would make the choice. And with her resolution forged, she felt better equipped to deal with her precarious position.

When they crested the hill into the bailey it was long past nightfall, but Tarian had pushed. The roads were well marked and the torches bright. She did not want to spend another night on the hard ground. Exhaustion nearly overcame her, and she was glad for Wulfson's strong arms assisting her dismount.

Rolf took the horses. As they walked into the hall, all was quiet, except for Edie, who waited with open arms for her. "Dear child. Come, come, you must be exhausted." She pressed her hand to Tarian's belly and softly asked, "How fares the babe?"

Wulfson stiffened beside her. She looked up into his stony face, and her heart stopped beating for one long moment. "I—I was not sure, but Edie seems to think—" She did not complete her sentence. The storm that mounted on his face was too much for her to stomach. Guilt assailed her, and she felt foolish, and ashamed.

He made a short bow. "I suppose congratulations are in order." He bowed again and strode past her calling for food.

The thought of any food in her belly made it swell and ebb. "I wish to soak in a hot bath, Edie."

And so she returned to her room and stripped naked, and waited until the tub was filled, and there she sat until her skin was cold and pruned. Emotions swirled in her heart with the force of a maelstrom. She longed for the knight down the hall; she longed to be lady here; to finally have a place she could call home, a place where she belonged, where no one could question her right to exist; she longed for her babe. And she did not know how to manage it so that she might have it all.

She looked to Edie and said quietly, "My path was so clear a month ago. Now I feel like a ship with no sail in a turbulent sea. I know not what to do."

Edie rinsed her and patted her dry with a warm linen. "It will all shake out, child. Have trust in yourself and in yonder knight."

As Tarian curled up in the big bed, her only thought was of Wulfson's strong arms around her. She wanted his warmth to lull her to sleep and she wanted to awake in his arms as he kissed her and stroked her body to those hot thrilling heights again. As she closed her eyes, her last thought was of his scent, as his lips suckled her tender breasts and his hands boldly stroked her.

Wulfson lay staring at the ceiling, rage, frustration, and longing driving him mad. He longed for Tarian, but the thought of her carrying another man's child tore him up inside. How could he touch her? How had he? He rolled over and pummeled his pillow. Did it matter?

Since he'd first laid eyes on her that had been a possibility. Why now did it disturb him so greatly? He rolled from the bed, and, as he had done two nights before, he paced the small confines. His gaze fell upon the tapestry each time he passed it, and each step brought him closer to it, and to her.

Why had she not told him? Did she think to spare him? Did she not know how his body ached for her? *That he defied his king for her!*

"God's blood!" he swore. "I cannot bear this agony!" He grabbed up a candle from the table, strode to the tapestry, and pulled it from the wall. There would be no more barriers. He wanted Tarian Godwinson, and he would have her for as long as he could.

He found the latch and sprang the door. He took a deep breath and strode through. He would have his way! He stepped halfway to her chamber. But was she of like mind? He moved on to find out.

When Wulfson pushed the tapestry aside, he heard a female cry. He looked up to see Edith sit up on her pallet. He put his fingers to his lips, and she quieted. "I am not here to hurt her," he said gruffly. But he would take her from the bed where she slumbered. For he would not lie with her in the same bed where she had once lain with Malcor. The maid did not question him, but sat silent.

For a long moment Wulfson did not approach the bed. When he did, he pushed aside the drapery and stood and stared at the slumbering beauty. Her long black hair lay in a thick mass around her, her pink lips were parted in sleep, and long black lashes swept the creamy smoothness of her face. Her full breasts rose and fell beneath the smooth linen chemise. His eyes traveled lower to her belly. 'Twas flat, and he knew it would be months before she began to show her pregnancy. The thought of Malcor's child growing inside her displeased him greatly. But, he had to concede, it might be the one trump she had.

He could not, in his wildest dreams, think William would murder a noblewoman with child. In fact, Wulfson knew he would not. Once the hue and cry went out across the land there would be a high price to pay. 'Twould mark William as an evil warlord, and that was the last thing his king wished. Wulfson knelt beside her on the bed and pressed his big hand to her belly, his fingers splayed across it, covering her. When her hands pressed against his and her hips moved, he looked down into soft blue eyes.

She smiled, and he could not help himself. "You have bewitched me," he said softly, as he slid against her and took her into his arms and kissed her as if he had never kissed her before. She melted into him and he lifted her up into his arms. He moved to the door he had just come through and down the dark passageway where the light from his chamber guided him.

Brief moments later they lay naked upon his bed, skin to skin, heart to heart, and he could not get enough of her. Like a starved man he ravished her. Her breasts were full, and when he pressed his lips to them she hissed in a breath. He withdrew, thinking he had hurt her, but she pressed her hands to his head and moved her hips beneath him. "Nay," she whispered. "Take all of me, Wulfson, all of me now."

"If I take you tonight, Tarian, I take you for as long as we have together."

" 'Twill have to be enough."

His lips descended to hers and hungrily she accepted him. Her body swelled beneath his. His entire being heated to rival a smith's forge. His fingers sank deep into her hair and her young body arched beneath his and he could not consume her fast enough. His kiss deepened, her thighs parted. Her hands traveled down his back, pressing him harder against her body. When her fingers dug into his backside, he nearly spilled his seed on her. He groaned, catching his breath when her hand stroked the length of him.

"I cannot wait, *chérie*, I want you now," he said huskily against her lips.

"Then do not wait," she breathed.

He swept his hand down the length of her to her thigh, and when he pressed his palm to her mound 'twas her turn to moan in pleasure. She was hot and moist. He slid a finger across the hard nub there and she cried out. He slid his finger back and forth against the silken spot. Her body tensed in passion, her chest filled. "More," she pleaded.

And more he gave her. He slid a finger into her silky wetness. "Wulfson," she moaned, his name floating from her lips in a slow sensual cadence. He touched his lips to a turgid nipple and as his finger moved slowly in and out of her, he suckled her in the same slow tortuous rhythm. He felt her skin warm, followed by a sultry flush. Her hand wrapped tightly around him, and in the same slow sensual glide she pumped him.

It was too much for him. He released her only to grab her hands by the wrists and push her arms over her head where he held them in his, and then he slowly filled her. It was pure unadulterated Paradise. He clenched his jaw and closed his eyes, savoring the hot, tight moistness of her. Her honey and violet scent swirled around him and was more intoxicating than five skins of wine. He lost a piece of himself to her at that moment, and knew so long as he lived he would never find another woman who moved him as she did.

He sank deeper into her, and she met him, thrust for thrust, stroke for stroke; and, as in the monastery, he felt the same storm build inside her, that hard rush of pleasure he knew would consume her.

"Wulfson," she cried, her body twisting and undulating wildly beneath his. He still held her hands, but when she sank her teeth into his shoulder he released inside her in a hard, violent burst, and she followed, crying out his name again and again. Each time she cried it, she took another piece of his heart.

Hot, sweaty, and panting, they lay entwined as one, the waves of passion going from crashing to a slow ebb-and-flow tide. Thus they fell into a deep, exhausted sleep.

Nineteen

When the lark began his morning serenade, Tarian woke, knowing they would have to face the world. And she desperately did not want to.

She pressed a kiss to her knight's lips, and he stirred against her. "Wulfson, let us ride north, far from England."

His strong arms wrapped around her and his hands pressed into her bottom. She reveled in the warmth of his skin against hers. His scars did not bother her; indeed, they made him the manliest of men in her eyes. She'd traced each one of them with her fingertips. Her cheeks flushed when she thought of the carnal knowledge they had had of one another.

Long, thick fingers smoothed a tendril of hair from her cheek, and she felt the heavy surge of him against her. She looked up into two brilliant green eyes. They creased at the edges with his smile. Her heart thumped wildly against her chest and her belly did a slow roll. His smile changed everything about him. Whereas normally he had the look of a dark, petulant angel, a smile transformed him into the most handsome of men.

"We cannot flee our duty, *chérie*. We will meet it and triumph over it. I give you my oath."

She rose up on her elbows and kissed him, then looked deeply into his eyes. "You know your king will not change his mind."

Wulfson rolled over onto her. His eyes searched her face, and he said slowly, "What if you are right? What if, knowing this, we fled to Scotland? What do we do then? I cannot marry you. I have nothing to offer."

"I do not want a husband. I want to live."

"And what happens when I fill your belly with brats, and my Blood Swords, the men I have sworn an oath to, come looking now for me as well as you?" He shook his head. "Nay, Tarian, I will not live that life. Nor will you. I give you my promise: we will see this through to our advantage."

"Promise?"

His arms tightened around her and he bent to kiss her. "My promise is my oath."

And she knew he believed in his heart that he spoke the truth. And for that, for the first time other than to Gareth and Edith, she gave her trust to another.

She hurried from his bed before Rolf made noises to come in. While she was not ashamed of her union with Wulfson, she did not want there to be any more gossip amongst the servants and villagers than there already was. She had learned from her escapade in Dunloc that she must show a certain propriety to gain the trust of her people, and nightly trysts with the resident Norman lord would not endear her to any of them. So, carefully, she slid from the bed amidst his calls for her return, and made her way down the dark passageway to her chamber, where Edie anxiously waited.

When she finally descended, Tarian was surprised to see Wulfson and his men lingering in the hall. He hurried to assist her and set her at the table. She noted his men watched them with blank expressions. "We awaited you to break the fast, Tarian."

She smiled up at him and thought how considerate he was, but when the aromas of the platters wafted her way she was suddenly no longer hungry. And though she had not eaten more than a few bites the previous day, Tarian could not stomach the pottage. Her belly made uncomfortable sounds, and she felt as if it rose up into her throat. She looked up to Wulfson, whose eyes widened. He hurried to assist her to a more private area in the hall. Pressing her hand to her throat, Tarian shook her head. "'Twill pass."

He frowned and his gaze dropped to her belly, and she knew he was not pleased, thinking it was Malcor's child. "I—Wulfson, if you would not mind, I would like for Edie to fix me an elixir to settle my stomach."

He nodded and presented his arm, and escorted her to her chamber.

When he strode back to the hall he found every set of Norman eyes upon him. He scowled heavily and told them what they all suspected. "It appears the lady is with child."

"Will you send word to William?" Thorin asked, handing Wulfson a flagon of mead.

Wulfson shook his head. "When Gareth returns, I go to William myself to plead the lady's case."

His men gathered close, shutting out any others, and,

as they always had when a situation arose, they put their heads together for the best solution. "I will take only Rolf and two of you with me to Normandy," Wulfson explained. "I fear that leaving this place unguarded will bring out the vultures. Too much has been gained to lose it." He looked to Thorin. "I leave the lady's health and the welfare of this fortress in your hands, my brother."

The Viking nodded. Wulfson looked to his men. "It will not seem right riding so light. I miss Warner's jests and his able sword."

Rhys looked to his friends. "Some mayhem must have befallen him."

For long moments the knights sat silent, and each dealt with his sorrow over the loss of one of their own.

Rorick shook his head, and said, "There is hope yet that the rascal survives. He has a way with the ladies, and that smooth tongue of his has gotten us out of many an unsavory situation. Let us not give up on him yet!"

"And to be sure, his message was not what you would have liked to hear. But your second messenger has not returned, Wulf. Let us hope William sees the error of murdering a noblewoman with child," Thorin mused aloud.

Rohan nodded and took a full draught of his mead. "I agree. Wulf, once you present all to William he will relent."

Wulfson drained his flagon. "Aye, he will relent only on the condition she comes to Normandy as his hostage."

They all looked at each other, knowing full well what that spelled.

"I would take my dagger to her myself before she rots in a Norman dungeon," Wulfson softly said. And with his words a dark pall settled over the hall.

"Marry her off to a Norman count," Ioan suggested.

Wulfson shook his head. "She does not want a Norman husband."

Rohan slapped him on the back and said, "Not even you, Wulf?"

Wulfson's head jerked back. "Indeed! I am a bachelor for life. I will never marry!"

Rorick tsk-tsked him. "Not even for love?"

"Love? What is the meaning of the word? I have no concept of it. Lust and passion, aye, a fine pair they are, and I can well relate to them, but is it enough to cement a union for life? Nay, I think not. And I do not want to be tied down to a wench I will grow tired of. The misery of the yoke of marriage would drive me mad."

Rohan thumped him on the back. "You will know love when it hits you."

"I respect Lady Tarian as a warrior and a survivor, nothing more."

Rohan slapped him again. "If you say so."

Wulfson scowled and turned from his men. "Aye, I do. No more talk of love and marriage; it makes my stomach churn." He stood then and said, "Come, let us spread the word that there is gold for any man or woman who has word of our brother-in-arms!"

Some time later, Wulfson and his men set out to Dunloc. As when they entered the town previously, they were met with surly stares and taunts, but this time no attack. The churls were subdued but wary. Wulfson understood their resentment. But he did not coddle them. He believed with his heart and soul that William was the rightful king, and he would to his last breath defend the throne.

He stopped in the square, and from atop his horse he

called to the townsfolk, "I am Wulfson de Trevelyn, knight of William. I come in search of my knight Warner de Conde. I offer gold for information of his whereabouts."

He stared down the group that had gathered. "I also offer death to anyone here who has done him wrong."

The crowd mumbled and grumbled. They would not meet his stare, but stood quietly milling about, not sure how to respond. He continued, "Understand that any attack on any of my men is an attack on William. Neither he nor I will stand back. Come to Draceadon with your information and I guarantee your safety and the gold. I seek only my man."

He spurred Turold, and his men followed. They spent the day alerting each hamlet to the offer for word on Warner and the reward of gold. Upon their return to Draceadon, Wulfson sent forth messengers to villages and hamlets along what would have been Warner's return route from Alethorpe. He was confident that, if there was information to be had, gold would change more than a few loyalties.

Tired and disheartened, the men infused the great hall with a dark mood. The sun had long since sunk beyond the western horizon and few people were about. Despite his worry over Warner, Wulfson felt a different tension fill him. His loins were heavy, and the ride had done nothing to quell his hunger for the woman who had come to torment his every waking moment. He took a long draught of wine and demolished a platter of roasted venison, but his hunger was not sated. His gaze swept up toward the stairway and his blood quickened.

"She is like a fever you cannot shake," Rohan said, coming to sit beside him.

Wulfson nodded, then shook his head. "She is in my blood, Rohan, I cannot shake her."

Rohan nudged him with his elbow. "Go to her and savor the time you have. I will keep the men occupied and remind them that even our mighty king has his weakness in his Mathilda."

Wulfson raised his gaze to Rohan's. "Aye, Tarian is *my* weakness, and I fear she will be my demise."

Rohan smiled, his lips twisting in sour humor. "Your duty is to your king first. I know you will make the right decision should the time come."

Wulfson threw back another goblet of wine. "Aye, and it will kill me to do so." With heavy heart and dragging feet, Wulfson left his men to their dark mood and strode up the stairway as if he were meeting the gallows. His heart and gut and mind twisted in a wild frantic battle over duty and propriety. He no more knew what to do then than he had that morn.

He scowled when he found his bath prepared but no Rolf waiting by. A small movement from the bed caught his eye, and his blood heated.

"Good eve, milord," Tarian said, sauntering slowly toward him. "I have missed you these last hours. Why have you dallied?"

His body quickened, and he could not wait to shuck his clothes and press her into the sheets. But when he broke toward her she stayed him with a raised hand.

"Nay, you will bathe first, as I know you and your men do not care for the day's grime to stay with you. Come and let me assist you."

He tried to catch her to him, but she was nimble and moved away.

As he settled into the hot soapy water, he asked, "How dost thou fare?"

She took up the sponge and lathered it. She smiled softly and caught his intense gaze. "Better. Edie made a soothing balm. It seems to have some effect. She says in time the sickness will pass."

Wulfson could offer no response: In his heart of hearts it tore him up that she carried Malcor's child.

She pressed cool fingers to his brow and smoothed away his frown. "What troubles you?" she asked softly.

He grabbed her fingers and brought them to his lips. "I fear for your health. 'Tis all."

She smiled gently, and the gesture tugged at his heart-strings. He wondered, if things were different, if he could raise another man's child. When he thought of Malcor and the perverseness of him, his gut twisted that such an insidious seed as his would have struck fertile ground in such an amazing woman. 'Twas not right. And in his gut he knew each time he looked at the child he would see the father, and in so doing not give the child what it needed. And shame filled him. He had thought he was a better man than that.

"Edie says women who have the sickness tend to have stronger babes. If that is true, my son will be conqueror of the world."

Wulfson scowled, and she caught it. "The child displeases you?" she asked.

He could not tell a lie. "The thought of Malcor's brat growing inside you displeases me. Yes."

She sat on the bench next to him and began to lather the scar on his chest. "Would that it was yours, would you be likewise displeased?"

His head shot back and he looked at her with narrowed eyes. "'Twould be bastard, and a bastard would not please me. I have nothing to offer a child, Tarian. I have no land, no place to call home except where I find my pallet each night. I have no parental skills. I have my horse and my swords. 'Tis not enough to rear a child." He smiled then, and took her hand and brushed his lips across her fingertips. "But should I ever wish for a child, I would have none other than you as his mother."

He watched tears form and spill down her cheeks. He reached for her, but she shook her head and moved away from him. He rose from the tub and went to her. Taking her into his arms, he pressed his lips to the top of her head. "My pardon if my honesty has offended you."

She shook her head against his chest and looked up to him. He could barely detect the color of her eyes, her tears were so thick. "Nay, Wulfson, no offense. Your confidence in me as the mother of your child was not expected."

"How could you not see it?"

She breathed back a sigh and smiled through her tears. "No one has thought me worthy of anything, and yet you stand here and say only I would be worthy enough to bear your child. I am honored."

He lowered his lips to hers and kissed her. When he moved back, he had the urge to take her up on her suggestion they fly to Scotland. There, unharassed, he could keep her belly full of sons. But he knew he could not. He released her and stepped back. "Come see to my bath so that we can"—he grinned—"sport."

He was not even dry when he swooped her up into his arms and tossed her onto his bed. He ripped her chemise from her body, and the sight of her full rosy breasts sent him into a sexual spiral. Sliding his hand up to her slender waist, he pulled her to him, her back arching and her breasts spearing the cool evening air. He gorged himself on the supple mounds. Her short gasps and the way her hands clawed at his back told him that he pleasured her well. As always with her, he could not get inside her fast enough. He never wanted to linger and savor her body, not until after that first desperate thrust where he came undone.

In one hot fell swoop he entered her. Their bodies rose and hung suspended as they each savored the feel, the sensation, the exquisite union they would never find in another.

And then the sweet wild undulation as nature intended. The give-and-take of making love.

"Wulfson!" Tarian cried, and hot tears stained her cheeks. Wulfson gathered her tightly into his arms and whispered, "Never fear, *ma chère*, I will always protect you."

He found his release then, and knew that he would die for her.

Tarian lay for a long time in Wulfson's arms. His soft snores and steady heartbeat told her he slept. The maelstrom of emotions wreaked havoc inside her heart once more. She was so torn she did not know how to even begin to think her way out of her situation. Her first thought was to protect the child she carried, at all costs. Her wishes and Wulfson's were second and third. After them, no one and nothing else mattered.

She played a deadly game of chess with a king who had no compunction about erasing his foes. And William saw her bloodline as a foe. A most real threat against his reign, should she choose to exploit it. She could not blame him.

He had killed her beloved uncle. The golden king whom all of England had loved and adored. Gone. Never to return.

She would never come to love or adore William. But she could respect him as her sovereign, and had pledged her loyalty to him. She was not a fool. He was king now, and he would remain so.

Tarian rolled over and pressed her cheek to the man who, in more ways than William, held her life in his hands. Emotion once again stirred so deeply in her that she could barely breathe. And she wondered at the onslaught of it all. She had always kept her feelings buried deep, and as much as she wanted to trust this man, she feared his oath to his king would ultimately trump anything between them.

Mayhap her emotional upheaval was because of the babe. She slid her hand down to her taut belly. Sighing heavily, she looked up to see sleepy green eyes watching her. She rose to him and kissed him, knowing in her gut that their time together was drawing to an end. And that tugged at her heartstrings almost unbearably. But, she decided, she would confess her part in Warner's absence. At the very least to ease his mind, and at the most to ease hers. And she would make him understand.

When the cock crowed, Tarian slid from the bed and made her way back to her chamber and called for Edie. "Prepare a basket. I wish to take milord knight to the pond for the day. See that Rolf prepares our horses."

As she came back into his chamber, she smiled and said to Wulfson, who grinned naked from the bed, "Get thee dressed. I have a special place I wish to share with you this day."

As they rode from Draceadon, the day could not have

been more perfect. Blue skies, puffy white clouds, and the air most temperate. The place she had in mind she had found quite by accident, her second day at Draceadon. She had fled to it several times to get away from Malcor and the stink of perversion that clung to him.

She smiled at Wulfson, who was for once not clad in his mail, but looked most handsome in dark woolen chauses, a smooth green linen undertunic beneath a studded soft leather gambeson. Only his broadsword accompanied him, as did hers. But the pond was secluded and not far, and Edie knew of its location.

"'Tis not much further, milord." As they rounded the narrow path, a thick copse of trees appeared to block the way, but Silversmith moved easily through it, and there on the other side, just down a velvety green slope, a crystal-clear pond—the recipient of the cool water tumbling from a mountain spring—greeted them. It was private, yet there was just enough of a break in the heavy copse of trees surrounding it to give way to the sunlight.

She smiled back at Wulfson and her blood warmed. She would coax him naked into the water, and encourage him to make love to her on the velvety bank. They would eat and nap and make love. And then she would confess all.

They tied the horses to a nearby tree, and Tarian spread out a thick fur throw. She looked up to find Wulfson watching her with a huge grin splitting his face. "Come here, wench."

She shook her head, playing the coquette. Stepping backward, she hastily undressed. She laughed as his eyes widened, and when he lunged for her she screamed and ran from him and dove into the cold clear water. When she surfaced, she scanned the bank for him, expecting him to be there, but there was no sign of him.

Strong arms grabbed her from behind and she screamed again, but this time he silenced her with his lips. Tarian could do naught but wrap her arms around his neck and sink with him into the water. He scooped her up in his arms, strode with her to the bank, and dropped her to the furs, and in the quiet morning sun he made love to her. And she had never felt more cherished.

As they lingered naked on the bank, she fed Wulfson pieces of meat and cheese. They drank wine, and they napped under the warm sun.

Little was said, for no words were necessary. Their bodies spoke for them.

As she lay with her cheek pressed to his chest and traced a lazy finger down his scar, Wulfson cleared his throat, and she immediately stilled.

"Tarian," he said softly, "I expect Gareth to have returned when we leave here. As you know, I go to Normandy immediately when he is back."

She nodded, not wanting to look into his eyes, afraid of what she might see. "I ask you to consider going with me."

She stiffened. She looked up at him then and saw quiet desperation in his eyes. "I—I would never return," she breathed. He nodded, and she moved away from him. "Nay, Wulfson, I would rather die than be hostage to William. My uncle has been hostage for years."

He sat up. "It may be the only way."

She was adamant. "I will never leave England!"

He nodded and drew her into his arms. But she did not want his comfort. She wanted her life back, she wanted her freedom, she wanted to live in peace with her child and his father. And with crashing realization she knew it was all but a dream.

Wulfson pressed his hand to her belly. It shocked her. He did not care for the child, she knew. "Think of your child, Tarian, if you will not think of yourself."

She flung his hand away and stood. She pulled her chemise over her head and then her kirtle. "I *do* think of my child! Could you allow your son to be raised in a prison with no hope of freedom? Or worse, that because of his Godwinson blood his life would be in constant jeopardy? Nay! I will never go to Normandy. *Never!*"

Wulfson rose and stepped toward her. "I value your life above mine, Tarian! I will not see you dead!"

She whirled around, her fists tight. "Then turn your back."

He shook his head. "'Tis too late for that."

They stood several strides apart, each desperate for the other but neither having the answer. She vacillated about whether to tell him the child was his. But she despaired he would force her to Normandy. She desperately wanted to ease his mind about his man Warner, but she feared he would lash out at her. And that she could not bear. He set her above all other women, but her lies would tumble her into the dirt in his eyes. She could not bear it if he thought her *nithing*. Yet she knew she could not keep her secrets from him. Never him.

Slowly he dressed. As he picked up his sword belt, he said to her in a low, meaningful tone, "Tarian, I want you as I have wanted no other woman. But I cannot marry you. I have nothing to give. William will see the advantage of a marriage between you and a Norman noble. Take it, and live. Take it and give your child a father. Take it, Tarian, for I could not bear to see you live out your days alone as William's hostage."

"Wulfson," she softly said. "I—I have to tell you—"

He pulled her to him and smoothed back her damp hair. "No more words, *chérie*. I ask you once again to put your trust in me. I will find a solution." He drew her to him then and kissed her. She stopped fighting, for there was no point. It was what it was and she would do what she had to do. And while the doom that loomed ahead of her should have overshadowed her, she did not allow it to. She would take her time with Wulfson while she had it and make the best of it.

She threw her head back and laughed, clasping his neck. "Kind sir, you hold my life in your hands. Take great care with it, for it is the only one I posses."

He smiled. " 'Tis in good hands, milady."

As they folded the throw and packed the basket, Tarian glanced over to Wulfson to find him warmly watching her. "Stop looking at me thusly, or we may linger here more than we should."

He grinned and dropped the basket he held, and strode toward her. "I could not get enough of you, Tarian, not in a thousand years."

Her heart stopped beating as the forest shook like thunder about them. Her eyes widened and she looked to Wulfson, whose face blanched. She started for him when six mounted men, cloaked in black from head to toe, broke through the glade, swords raised, going straight for Wulfson. He saw them when she did. "Run, Tarian, run to the forest!" he shouted, then dropped to the ground. He rolled to his sword and was up and prepared to fight in the blink of an eye.

She stood transfixed, horrified, unwilling to leave him to stand against this unknown enemy. Tarian broke toward him to grab her own sword and stand with him and fight. But she was grabbed up from behind and slung harshly against the rider's horse's neck. She screamed frantically, reaching out for Wulfson, who ran toward her shouting for her, and suddenly her sight went black.

Twenty

W ulfson watched, horrified, as, just as suddenly as the horsemen had erupted into the clearing, so now they disappeared. Hastily he strapped on his sword, vaulted onto Turold's back, and gave chase.

Desperation clawed at his innards, his mind's eye replaying over and over the brutal blow to Tarian's head and then her body going limp. Each man's face was shrouded by a dark hood, only eye slits giving them away as human. He spurred the black on to a faster pace, crashing through bramble and brush. Limbs tore at his face and stung his arms, ripping his skin. He felt nothing. His heart beat so fast and so furious in his chest that he feared it might burst from him. The tracks turned north away from Draceadon, and he followed as if the demons of hell nipped at his heels. He saw them up ahead; only two riders. The one with Tarian, and another. They did not race from him; instead they looked back, almost as if waiting for him. Turold screamed out in pain as an arrow struck his right wither. Wulfson roared his battle cry, drawing his sword, and the steed lunged forward, faster.

From the forest more riders erupted, coming straight at him, and when he turned to look over his shoulder more followed. Turold slammed into the lesser horses, but the contact was enough to slow his pace. And like a swarm of bees attacking a wasp, they encompassed him, taking him down.

Tarian woke to the stink of vinegar beneath her nose. Her head jerked back and she made to move but found she could not. She was tied to a chair! Wildly she searched the dim room, and her memory came flooding back. "Wulfson!"

Deep, familiar laughter from behind her wafted over her like a plague. "How tender that you think of that arrogant Norman before yourself," Rangor said, stepping in front of her. His pale blue eyes glittered in the low light of the candles on a nearby table.

"What have you done?!" Tarian screamed, immediately regretting the outburst. Sharp shards of pain spiked ruthlessly at her head where she had been struck. She closed her eyes and sucked in a long breath, then slowly exhaled and opened her eyes. The unadorned room tilted right, then left, before righting itself. Rangor as usual was overdressed and bejeweled. His arrogance was nauseating.

"You did not think I would give up so easily, Tarian, did you?"

"Where am I? What have you done with Wulfson?"

Rangor pulled up a rough-hewn chair and placed it a safe distance from her, then sat and faced her. "You are where no one will find you. All traces of our horses have been erased. 'Tis only you, me, and that arrogant bastard you are leman to!"

Tarian flinched at his harsh words. She had been called

worse all her life and had shrugged it off. But when the words spewed from Rangor's mouth, he made what she shared with Wulfson sound dirty.

She fought against the tight ropes that bound her, her fury nearly overcoming her. "Let me go! You have no right!"

Rangor smiled and crossed his legs and peered at his nails as if they were not up to his meticulous standards. He looked over at her, a nasty smile twisting his thin lips. "Oh, I will release you, my sweet, but not until you give your oath to marry me."

"Never!"

He shrugged and bit at a nail. He spat it to the floor and stood. "'Tis too bad for your lover then. For each day you refuse me, he feels another score of lash stripes on his back."

"Nay! Do not take your anger at me out on him! He does not deserve it!"

Rangor only shrugged again, and as the door closed behind him Tarian lost all vestiges of control. "Rangor!" she screamed. "Release him!" She pulled and twisted at the ropes, so much so that the chair tipped with her in it. She hit the dirt floor with a hard thud, the breath forced from her chest. She was undeterred. On her side, she scooted with her legs across the room, and then with her feet kicked at the door. "Rangor, I will see you in hell before I marry you!" She kicked the door again and again, screaming at him, until finally her voice was too raw to speak. Her strength gone, she collapsed against the dirt floor, and exhaustion overtook her.

Hot shards of pain speared his arms, his legs, and his chest. He was bound and stretched on his back. After he fought through the white-hot pain, Wulfson's first thought was of Tarian. He tried to open his eyes but they were swollen shut. He roared his anger and his pain, but only a harsh rasp came forth.

He could not speak, he could not see, and his body felt afire. Then he remembered. The fists to his face, the lash to his back, the blade crisscrossing his chest. He had screamed in agony for so long that his voice was lost.

He tried to swallow but could not; he tried to move his head, but the pain was too excruciating. "Tarian," he said, but no sound came forth.

A deep chuckle reverberated in the room. "She cannot help you now, Norman," a male voice he did not recognize said from his left. "She is lost to you forever."

The words hurt more than the gaping wounds. Wulfson tried once more to force his eyes to open, but like mortar, dried blood caked them shut. He turned his head to face the voice and the movement cost him; angry jolts of pain speared his neck and shoulders. "You will ride my sword to hell," he hoarsely croaked.

He screamed in silent agony when his torturer struck his bad thigh with a club. White-hot agony tore into him, and then, thankfully, blackness.

Wulfson drifted in and out of consciousness, and each time his mind awoke, his first thoughts were of Tarian. The thought of her enduring what he did was more painful than his actual wounds. Would they rip the babe from her? Would they violate her tender body? Would she pray for death as he did?'

Nay, she would not. She was a warrior, as was he. His resolve galvanized, but he knew he was without food or water, and unless he was somehow freed from the bindings, he would die in this hellhole, blinded by his own blood. From out of nowhere he was struck again, this time on the side of the face. Though he could not see, bright stars burst inside his brain and once more darkness took him away.

Tarian was kicked awake. "Wake up!" Rangor hissed, and he pushed his way past her. He righted the chair, and if Tarian had had the strength she would have torn off his ear. As it was, she was depleted. He pressed a cup to her lips and forced her to drink the watered wine. She coughed and choked but took all she could; she would need her strength.

She shook her head and turned away when she had had enough.

As he had previously, Rangor sat across from her. "Have you had sufficient time to change your mind?"

She shook her head. "I will never marry you."

He threw his head back and laughed. "Oh, but I think you *will* change your mind." He rose and pulled his dagger from his belt, and she hissed in a breath and shrank back. But all he did was cut the ropes across her lap and legs. Then he cut those keeping her chest and back secured. But her hands were still tied. He yanked her up with the blade to her belly. "Give me the slightest cause, and I will slice the babe from your belly."

She hissed in a surprised breath. How did he know? "I have spies everywhere, Tarian. You underestimate me." He shoved her forward to the door. "Now, I have taken pity on you and your whoreson. Would you like to see him?"

Dread filled her at what she might behold, but she nodded vigorously. He smiled. "Good, I think you will be—surprised."

He yanked open the door and roughly pushed her through into a dark passageway. It ran long, and, try as she might, she had no clue to her whereabouts. At the end of the long hall was a large studded door. Rangor knocked on it and it opened, and the sight that greeted her nearly killed her.

Wulfson lay naked, save for, his braies, on a rough-hewn trestle table. His arms were pulled high over his head and tied to spikes, as were his legs. But what tormented her the most was the slick blood that covered nearly every inch of him. Lash marks glittered in macabre symmetry across his chest and thighs. The right side of his face was so swollen she could not detect an eye. Emotion flooded her with such a harsh current at the moment that she fell to her knees. Hot tears sprang forth like a spring flood, and her heart twisted so tightly she could not breathe. Her entire body shook at the thought of Wulfson's death. She could not bear it. He was her one true love on the earth, and if he was gone she had no wish to remain here without him. The revelation made her pain all the more tormenting. She was the cause of his wounds, she would be the cause of his death. She looked up at Rangor. Hate seethed from every inch of her. Despite her bound hands, she managed to stand. She stepped toward him.

"What have you done to him?" she screamed. She turned and made to fly to Wulfson's side, but was yanked back by Rangor.

"Look closely, Tarian. He hangs to life by a thread." Rangor nodded to the hooded man standing beside Wulfson. He brought up a club and hit Wulfson's right thigh. "Nay!" she screamed, pulling hard from Rangor. But he held her fast.

In silent horror she watched Wulfson's body stiffen. He opened his mouth to scream in pain, but no sound came forth. His pain was her pain, and she could scarce breathe. She retched up the wine she had just drunk, and she felt as if she would die. If she could take some of the pain away she would. The hooded man brought the club down again on Wulfson, and this time his scream was heard.

"Stop this! Stop this now!" Tarian screamed at Rangor. She turned to him, and if she could have, she would have grasped his hands and dropped to her knees and begged him. But her hands were tied behind her back.

"Your oath for marriage," Rangor softly said,

"I give it! Anything, but spare him his life"

"Do you swear on the life of the child you carry?"

"Aye! I swear it! Now release him to me!"

Rangor's eyes glittered in triumph. "I knew you would see the value to our union." He turned to the hooded man. "Cut the ropes that bind him; he will not be going anywhere."

Rangor cut the ropes from Tarian and she rushed to Wulfson. "Dear God, please do not let him die," she begged. She smoothed trembling fingers across his face and pressed her lips to his. "You will live, Wulfson, as my oath to God I will see you live!"

Rangor grabbed her away. "Come and sign the contract."

Tarian was given a horse and she flew, pushing the steed to his last breath just as they broke into the meadow below Draceadon. Her heart pounded like a hammer in her chest. The horse dropped beneath her, so hard had she pushed. She jumped clear of him and raced up the hill, screaming for assistance.

Several of Wulfson's men were mounted and thundered toward her. "Thorin! Rohan! Hurry, Wulfson lies dying!"

Thorin ground to a halt before her and with one arm snatched her up from the ground. So winded was she that she could barely speak. "He is dying! Thorin, we must get to him!"

"Where, Tarian?" he demanded, shaking her. Her head rattled and she nearly fainted.

"Almost a half day's ride north. Gather linens and balms, get me a fresh horse, and I will take you to him," she gasped.

Thorin reined his horse and swung him around toward the fortress. Rohan, Ioan, and Rhys joined them, all demanding to know what had happened.

"Wulfson lies gravely wounded. Saddle the horses and gather the men!" Thorin called.

Tarian jumped from the destrier as soon as Thorin slowed at the doors. "Edie!" Tarian screamed, breaking into the hall. "Fetch me linens and balms!"

Out of nowhere the nurse appeared, and hurried to bring her the items. Tarian turned to run back into the courtyard, but was abruptly stopped by a gauntlet of Wulfson's men. They stood scowling down at her, distrust clearly lining their faces.

"Why do you tarry? Let us fly!"

Thorin shook his head. "First tell us what happened."

Incredulous, her jaw dropped. "He—we—I—was kidnapped! Wulfson came for me, and they tortured him!" She grabbed Thorin's hand and pulled him toward the door. "Come, there is no time to waste!"

Edie ran toward her with a full satchel. Tarian grabbed it. "Do not believe me, then! But I am going to back to him. He needs me!" Tears erupted in a shameless flood. "He needs *you!*"

She rushed from the hall and knew by the pounding of feet that the men followed. Silversmith was already tacked, and for the first time in her life Tarian did not need assistance mounting him. She leapt up to the gray's back, and before she had the satchel fully wrapped around the pommel and the reins in her hands, she kicked him and they galloped off.

She could not push the gray hard enough. But unlike the horse she had ridden in, Silversmith had great strength and endurance. Anxiety tore through her as she realized she did not remember exactly whence she had come, so intent had she been on reaching the Blood Swords for help. But some instinct inside her guided her back to the small ramshackle structure from which she had fled.

She reined Silversmith to an abrupt halt, and, not waiting for the men to follow, she leaped down and gathered the satchel from the pommel. Pushing open the thick doors, she ran through the small vestibule and down the dark hall to the studded door. She heaved it open and her heart flew high into her throat, terrified she would find her beloved dead.

He was as she had last seen him, bloodied and barely alive upon the trestle. She hurried to him, and as gently as she could, she pressed her ear to his bloody chest. Her heartbeat pounded so loudly in her ears she could not detect his own. *Dear God, dear God! Please do not take him from me!*

A strong hand grasped her shoulders and gently pulled her away. She looked up through hot tears to see Thorin's face twisted in anger, and something else. Fear? His men gathered around him, and she watched as Rohan pressed his hand to Wulfson's mouth. A small smile cracked his lips, and he nodded and looked up. "He breathes."

Tarian's knees gave way, and had Thorin not been so close she would have crumpled in relief to the ground.

"Water!" Thorin boomed. Quickly Ioan ran from the room. Rhys threw the ropes that lay on the table aside and pressed his hand to Wulfson's brow. "He burns with fever."

Ioan returned with water skins and wineskins. Tarian stood back and watched in humble silence as the Blood Swords tended to their fallen brother. They washed the blood from his body. And she cringed at the wounds. While they were not deep, they were many. Stefan pulled a bag of balm from his belt and carefully applied it to the raw flesh. Gently the men rolled Wulfson over and did the same to his back, which thankfully did not appear to have sustained the same severity of damage.

Not once did Wulfson make a sound. And that worried her overmuch. He was in a deep sleep from which nothing but time could wake him.

When his body had been cleaned and the wounds dressed, the men wrapped him in sheets of linen. "Manhku!" Rohan called to the giant. "Help me lift him."

The African stepped forward, and as if Wulfson were but a babe, the giant lifted him up into his arms, as tenderly as a mother would her child. He turned dark angry eyes on Tarian, and she knew they all blamed her. And they were right. 'Twas Rangor's greed for her that had driven him to this. She nodded, taking their anger in stride. She would feel no differently.

Manhku carried Wulfson from the room out into the waning sunlight. Thorin mounted his great steed, and between Rohan and Manhku they lifted Wulfson's damaged body to him. Once secure in the saddle, Thorin slowly turned his horse for Draceadon.

Her strength exhausted, Tarian dragged her feet to Silversmith, and realized she did not have the energy to attempt to mount him. The Blood Swords had all turned away from her, paying her no notice.

Tears welled up again, and she felt as if her life force was gone. She did not care that she had promised her soul to Rangor. Her freedom was a small price to pay for Wulfson's life. Nay, that his men had turned their backs on her was as much of a blow to her as if Wulfson had done it himself.

She took Silversmith's reins, and instead of finding something to stand upon, she began to walk behind the knights, feeling as if she truly were *nithing*.

'Twas some time later when she felt several sets of eyes on her. She looked up to find Rohan and Rorick stopped and staring at her. She tried to smile but could not. Rorick dismounted and without a word hoisted her up onto Silversmith's back. "*Merci*," she said softly.

Flanked by the two knights, Rorick demanded, "Tell me from the beginning what happened."

The other knights slowed to hear her tale. And a tale it would be, for she could not tell the truth. Taking a deep breath, Tarian looked at each man, not wavering in her stare. " 'Twas the day Wulfson and I took a trip to the pond in the glade. We were packing to return to Draceadon when from the forest came a group of hooded, mounted men." She swallowed as she relived the shock and horror of being taken from Wulfson. She looked pointedly at Rorick. " 'Twas me they were after. One grabbed me as Wulfson went for his sword. I know not what happened to him after that, for I was hit on the head and all went black."

She pressed her fingertips to the back of her head where the wound still smarted. "How did you escape?" Rorick asked, emphasizing the word *escape*, as if she had walked away as carefree as a maid in May.

She shook her head. "I did not escape. I was released."

"Why?" Rhys asked.

She looked at the young knight and forced a smile. "They showed me what they did to Wulfson." She swallowed again as emotion clogged her chest. "I told them I would give them whatever they wanted for his life."

"And the price?" Ioan demanded.

"My dowry. I told them where to find it at Briarhurst. The leader sent a man and when he returned with it, they gave me a nag of a horse and disappeared. I came to Draceadon as fast as I could."

"How many were there? Were they Saxon?" Rohan asked.

"Only two that I saw at the structure, but almost a half score who abducted me. The leader spoke English."

Rohan scowled. "Why would they release you once they had the gold? Why not finish you off?"

Tarian's heart smacked hard against her chest walls. She shook her head and lied again, and it did not sit well with her, but what else was she to do? She had given her oath, had signed a document that she would marry Rangor. She could not go back on her word. She accepted the price she must pay for Wulfson's life. "I told the leader that if they did not allow me to return to Draceadon and the Norman died, there would not be a rock they could climb under to hide in all of England, for *les morts* would hunt them all down and kill them inch by inch." She looked around to each of the men, and knew her words resonated with them. Rorick and Rohan nodded, and then Rhys and Ioan; but Stefan watched her as if he did not believe a word she said. She stared at him, not giving him more cause to doubt her by looking away. After a long moment, he too nodded.

Twenty-one

It took two days of constant battle with the Blood Swords before they relented and allowed her entry to Wulfson's chamber. She understood their guarded behavior with her, but even they realized the urgency of Wulfson's coming out of his sleep, and if he would not for them, then he might for her.

She cast them all to the threshold of the room, and instead of Stefan's horse balms, Tarian insisted on Edie's balms and poultices. And in just two days' time, they worked miracles. His skin healed; but his fever did not break, despite the tepid baths she gave him four times a day. Tarian began to be concerned in earnest. 'Twas not natural that he slept so soundly for so long. He had not had any sustenance save the wine she could sponge into his mouth. His body was slowly losing bulk.

With the help of his men who constantly lingered in shifts at the threshold, they rolled him over so that she could tend the wounds on his back. Each time she gently rubbed the healing balm into his raw skin and he moaned in pain, she moaned with him. How he had survived such torture she did not know, but she thanked God every day that he had.

His men were silent, and she saw the worry and the anger on their faces.

"With Gareth's help, and the offer of gold to anyone with information on the scourge, we have covered every hide of land from the Welsh border, north to Hereford, and have not seen any persons fitting your description, Lady Tarian," Rorick said, coming from another hard day's ride. And she knew they would not.

Feeling uncomfortable with her lies, she broke the tension. "Help me roll him over, Rorick, I need to change the soiled linens."

The great warrior was as gentle with his friend as she would be with her babe. Their devotion to one another moved her beyond tears. The bond these men shared was truly profound. That they allowed her to tend their leader bespoke their trust in her, and once again shame and guilt assailed her. She pushed it away; her only goal now was to see Wulfson's health restored. For he was at death's door because of her.

Tarian bathed him where he lay, and noted that despite Wulfson's deep sleep and fever his wounds were healing. But once night had fallen, her fears for his life came back with a vengeance. She could not lose him once found! Not now, not like this.

She slid into the bed, gently pressing her cheek to his chest, and took his hand and laid it to her belly. "Your child grows inside me, Wulfson. He will need his father. *I* need his father." With her head to his chest, she lay silently hoping for a shift in his heartbeat. Though strong, it was dull, and she thought too much time passed between each beat. "I love you, Wulfson, more than my own life. I will go to Normandy with you. I will follow you to the ends of the earth." She pressed her lips to his chest. "But you must wake up, Wulfson, you must fight. Your child needs you. I need you. Please wake up and live."

Throughout the night and into the next day, she made him promises she knew in her heart she could not keep, but she knew of no other way to give him the will to survive: if not for himself, then for his child. She pressed the damp sponge to his lips; she rubbed balm into his cracked lips and knitting wounds. She sang to him, she spun wild tales of the two of them fighting side by side, conquering the world. She spoke earnestly of her love for him, and asked his forgiveness.

His fever broke that night, and his swollen eyes opened. "Dear God, Wulfson, do you see me?" She prayed they had not taken his sight.

She watched him focus and squint. He closed his eyes again, only to slowly open them. His calloused, scarred hand moved to hers, and she let spill the hot tears that had been building for nearly a week. "Wulfson," she breathed, "you live."

He nodded and swallowed. She brought the cool damp sponge to his lips and pressed it to his cracked lips. He sucked the wine from it. "You must eat. I have porridge for you."

His dull eyes looked up at her, and her heart broke all over again. She smoothed his hair from his face and pressed her lips to his forehead. "Wulfson, do not leave me again. You are alive. You will heal."

He closed his eyes again, and she let him sleep.

She spent the rest of the night watching over him,

smoothing away the vestiges of the fever from his skin. She fell alseep, then, came slowly awake, and realized his breaths were strong and even, his skin cool against her fingertips. She rose up to find his eyelids slowly opening, and her heart sang at the fierceness of his gaze. She smiled and pressed her lips to his. "Welcome back, milord. I have missed you."

"What happened?" he asked hoarsely.

"I will tell you all just as soon as you sip some broth."

She helped him sit up in the bed, putting several pillows behind his back, careful not to chafe his tender skin. He winced, but did not show any other sign of discomfort. As she spoon-fed him, she asked, "Do you remember the day at the pond?"

He nodded.

" 'Twas as simple as a kidnap. I was the target."

He stopped her hand and took it in his own. "Were you harmed?" he asked, his voice a low rasp.

"Nay, I told them they would not get a copper should they touch me. I gave them the same threat regarding you." Her eyes filled with tears. "Oh, Wulfson, I nearly died when I saw what they had done to you!"

"How, did you escape?"

She looked down at the bowl in her hand. "I gave them my dowry money. For your life and mine."

He sat silent for long moments, and she prayed he would not ask more questions. "How? How did you get it to them?"

Her hand shook as she raised the spoon. "There was a casket at Briarhurst. I but gave them the location. Once they returned with it they abandoned us."

He shook his head and squeezed her hand. "I failed to protect you."

"Wulfson, there were too many of them, and they had planned well. No man could have fought them off and survived."

"What of my horse and sword?"

"That black devil returned here, as did Silversmith. He gave your men and mine much cause for alarm. Your sword is secure by the hearth; it awaits only your hand." She pressed another spoonful of broth to his lips. When the bowl was empty, she said, "Let the broth settle and I will get you something heartier. Now I must tell your men you have come out of the fog. They have been like worried nursemaids, the lot of them."

When she made to move from the bed, he grabbed her hand and tugged her back. He did not have the strength to pull her all the way down. His eyes rose to hers. "Did I dream it or did you tell me that the child you carry is mine?"

Emotion rose up in her belly. She desperately wanted to tell him the truth. But she could not. He would force her to go to Normandy, and that she would never do. "If it pleases you to think it so, then I do not mind."

He scowled, and she smiled. "Ah, there it is, the infamous scowl."

When she moved again, again he stayed her. "Did you tell me you love me?"

Heat flushed her cheeks but that she could not deny. "Aye, Wulfson, with all my heart I love you. Would that it could change things."

His brow wrinkled in confusion. "Where does that put me?"

She smiled sadly, and touched her fingertips to his lips. "Where you have always been: you will kill me if your king commands it."

He shook his head. "Nay! It will never be so."

She shushed him and hurried from the room.

From that moment, Wulfson recovered at a miraculous rate. He was out of the bed and walking slowly around the chamber the next morning, though with a noticeable limp. "They made my bad leg worse," he told her. But he soldiered through the pain. He ate with the gusto of ten men, and on the second day after he awoke he insisted on dressing and going down to the hall. He was welcomed with wild cheers, not only from his own men but hers as well, and several of the villagers who milled about. That night there was a great feast, and Wulfson called his men to him.

"I leave for Normandy in three days' time."

"Nay, Wulfson!" Tarian gasped. "'Tis too early. You must heal completely."

He scowled. "I appreciate your nursing, Tarian, but I am not a milksop of a boy who needs more coddling. I will be well enough to ride and defend myself in three days. Do not nag me to stay."

She nodded and bowed her head just slightly, then turned and hurried to her chamber. She knew he would be well enough to ride in three days, but then she would have to pay for his life. So be it. He was alive, and that was all that mattered.

Wulfson fought the urge to give chase to Tarian but he resisted it. His heart weighed heavy with emotion for her, but he would not show weakness for a woman, even one as spectacular as she, in front of his men. Instead, he turned to them with a tight, bitter smile. "I want the bastards who did this to me, and I want them alive. I will ride to the corners of this miserable place until I hunt each of them down and split their bellies open with my own sword."

Manhku growled low, and said in his broken French, "'Tis too gentle. Burn their eyes out and cut their fingers off one at a time, then their toes, then their hands, then their feet." He grinned at them all, his sharp teeth glittering. "Hack them to death piece by piece."

Wulfson smiled and raised his cup, "Manhku, you devil!"

His men drank and they plotted and they planned, but more than that, they celebrated Wulfson's survival. Long after the torches had been put out, Wulfson made his way up to his chamber. He would apologize to Tarian for his gruffness, but he would also make her understand he was not a child. For the first time since he awoke, he felt the hot surge in his blood for her. But he doubted he had the strength necessary to make love to her.

Wulfson was surprised to see his squire and not Tarian at the threshold of his chamber. The lad smiled and bowed. "Sir Wulfson, I am most happy to see you up and about. You gave us all a great scare."

Wulfson stopped and gazed at the boy, who was struggling to keep the moisture in his eyes from rolling down his cheeks. He cuffed the boy lightly, and gruffly said, "I too am happy to be up and about." He looked past him into the empty room. "Where is Lady Tarian?"

"Her chamber, sir. I will fetch her for you. But before I do, I have prepared a bath for you."

Wulfson shook his head. "Nay, lad, I do not have the stomach to sit in warm water. Mayhap tomorrow. Go fetch the lady, then see to your own needs."

As the door shut behind the boy, Wulfson slowly moved about the chamber, undressing himself. His body, while it did not flare with fire, still stung. His leg pained him greatly. The heat where the club had struck him would not subside, though the cool cloths Tarian had pressed to the area had soothed him. He would ask her to do so again when she came to him. Carefully, he sat on the edge of the bed and rubbed his thigh.

He heard the creak as the door opened, then closed. "Tarian," he whispered.

"I am here, milord."

He looked up into her bright eyes and saw no vestige of hurt. Indeed, she looked about to fight. He smiled. He raised his hand to her and she moved closer to him, but not close enough for contact. "Do not fear for my health, *chérie*. In a few days, the fever will be gone from my leg and the weight of my mail will not cause me any discomfort. I have survived worse."

She shook her head, her eyes still bright. "How could you survive worse than this? You were at death's door!"

"Trust me, I survived a year in a Saracen hellhole. I can survive anything a cowardly Saxon metes out." He patted the bed beside him. "My blood is on fire for you, Tarian, but I fear I have used my strength for the day."

Instead of sitting beside him, she brought a full pitcher of cool water to the nightstand and dipped linens into it. "Lie back so I can lay the compresses on your thigh."

Clad only in his braies, he lay back and they both smiled at the rise in his braies. "The day I can no longer rise to you, Tarian, is the day you can bury me."

She laughed softly and pressed the linens to his skin. "Aye, I fear your heart would long have stopped beating but your cock would still salute. 'Tis a most voracious limb you have there."

"Aye, when it comes to you, he has a mind of his own."

Tarian sat down beside him and pressed the palm of her hand to him. Wulfson hissed in a sharp breath. "Thank God they did not touch you there."

He wrapped his hand around hers and he squeezed. "You make me forget I have no strength."

She shook her head, her long hair cascading around her shoulders and waist, and pulled her hand from his. "Nay, not this night." She hovered over him and pressed him back into the pillows. "I do not want to hurt you."

His arm slid around her waist and he pulled her against him. She did not resist, nor did she engage. "You could never hurt me," he said softly, kissing her.

She kissed him back and he tasted the wet saltiness of her tears. He pulled back. "Why the tears, Tarian?"

She only shook her head, unanswering. Frustrated by her behavior, Wulfson demanded, "What is wrong, Tarian? I cannot abide your tears!"

She sniffed back a sob and shook her head. "I—I have not recovered from seeing you so tortured. I feared for your life, Wulfson. I was terrified. I would have done anything to save you."

He pulled her into his arms, and the only pain he felt was the swelling of his heart. He kissed the top of her head and quieted her with soft words. But he did not admit that he too was terrified, for in his gut he knew that William would not relent.

Twenty-two

The next two days passed in a whirlwind of activity. The energy in Draceadon was palpable as Wulfson made arrangements for his trip to Normandy. His men as well as hers had a sense of hope that Tarian could not share.

On the third night, the night before Wulfson was to depart, Gareth took her aside. "My lady, word has come. The knight Warner has escaped." Dread took hold of her so tightly she thought she would faint from lack of breath. From his continued scowl, she knew there was more.

"William's royal messenger was sighted. He comes with a large contingent of knights. It does not bode well for you. We must flee tonight."

Tarian's worst nightmare was realized. William was bent on her destruction. She nodded. "Gather the documents and wrap them in a skin, then put them in a leather cask and keep them with you, Gareth. I have sent word to Rangor to meet us just past Dunloc. We will fly west to Powys, where Rhiwallon awaits with men."

Gareth's scowl turned ugly. He was solidly opposed to

her marriage to Rangor. "Keep your sharp words to yourself, Gareth. 'Twas either marriage to that ruffian or Wulfson's death. I would rather live as Lady Lerwick than see Wulfson dead because of my fickleness."

"When the Norman learns 'twas Rangor who kidnapped you and ordered his torture, there will not be a rock on this island for him to hide beneath."

Tarian nodded. "He will not come to Wales."

"Do not be so sure of it."

Her captain stalked off, and Tarian turned to find Wulfson's eyes on her across the hall. She smiled and made her way toward him. "Come and sup, milord."

He did not move when she took his hand and tugged him toward the trestle. "Is all well with your captain?"

She smiled up at him and said, "He worries overmuch. Come, the food is ready."

As they were seated, and the prayer said, Tarian forced herself to make merry as the others. Hope and anticipation rode the men hard, for in the days since Wulfson's torture the Blood Swords had slowly allowed her into their inner circle, acknowledging her dedication to their brother, and they had hopes also that if anyone could change William's mind 'twould be his captain. But try as she might, Tarian could not follow along. Because it mattered not. By then she would be long wed to Rangor, and all would be for naught. Wulfson sensed her mood, and she was grateful when he retired early with her. But once the door was closed behind them, she saw the hot glitter in his eyes.

"Come to me, Tarian, as God created you. Give me all that you have this night, for it may be months before I set eyes on you again."

She smiled, her blood warming despite her fear of what

the morrow would bring. Slowly she undressed before him, only the low glow of the candlelight exposing her. When she pulled the shift over her head and dropped it to her feet, she heard a sharp hiss of breath from Wulfson. She stared at him, knowing that the passion in his eyes was reflected in hers. He slowly walked toward her, his limp barely noticeable. He pulled off his tunic, then his under-tunic. His chest rose and fell with anticipation, and she noted he had regained most of his lost weight. He looked the picture of health—except for the scars that crisscrossed him. He quickly divested himself of the rest of his clothing, letting it fall where it would.

He stopped a hand's-breadth from her, and stared at her. Her skin warmed and her full breasts quivered beneath his gaze. He reached out a hand to her left breast and laid it upon the high swell of it. She felt her heart lurch against his touch. Her nipples tightened painfully. She closed her eyes, willing his lips there. Hot shards of desire pierced her womb when his hot lips took a nipple into his mouth and he gently suckled her. She leaned against him, her knees not having the strength to support her. His strong arm wrapped around her waist, holding her to him. In complete surren-der she offered herself up to him. He hoisted her in his arms and strode to the bed, where he gently laid her down. He was hot and hard for her. She reached up to touch him, and it was his turn to hiss in a harsh breath.

He knelt beside her on the floor and pressed his lips once more to her breasts, then trailed them down to her belly. He splayed his hand across her there and looked up into her eyes and she nearly confessed all to him at that moment. His lips traveled lower to her mons. Her hips rose to him. He pressed his lips to her and she cried out. Digging her fingers into his thick hair, she pressed him more firmly against her. In a wild undulation, her hips rocked to his suckling of her there. She could not forestall the harsh wave of desire that hit her instantaneously, nor the subsequent one when he slid a finger deeply into her. "Wulfson!" she gasped, squeezing her eyes shut as the sublimity of him overwhelmed her.

His lips and hand rode out another shattering climax. Her body undulated wildly beneath him and she knew if he did not fill her soon she would die of want.

He rose above her on the bed, and spread her thighs with his knee. He gathered her up into his arms and watched her as he slowly entered her, inch by sensuous inch. She watched his face harden in passion, his brilliant eyes never wavering from hers. "You are mine, Tarian Godwinson. No man but I will ever have you."

Emotion welled up with the force of a summer storm. He thrust high into her. "Say you are mine."

Barely able to speak, so wrought with emotion, she gasped out the words, "I belong only to you." And it was the truth.

He thrust into her again and again, and she thought she would come apart at the seams. His lips descended on hers in a violent kiss. His arms tightened around her, nearly squeezing the life from her. His hips drove into her with the force of a thunderstorm. His breaths became hoarse and ragged, as if emotion clogged his chest. They hung suspended, their eyes wide in awe, then together they climaxed, and the entire world shifted around them.

For long moments, they held each other as if to let go would mean the end of their world. For Tarian, 'twas reality.

"*Chérie*," he said softly against her breast, "do not give up hope. Believe in me."

Her heart swelled so swiftly and so fully she could not breathe. Not trusting her voice, she nodded against his chest, where his heart beat solid and strong. But her resolve held firm despite the crumbling of her heart. For she did not flee because of Warner. Nor did she flee because of her oath to Rangor. She must fly because in her heart of hearts she knew his king wanted her dead and she could not put Wulfson in the position of seeing his oath to his king carried out. 'Twould kill him as he killed her.

She left him soon after. He lay spread-eagled and naked on the bed, his deep, even breaths of hard slumber giving way to her escape. For that was what she did. Escaped. She escaped the pain of his rage when he found her out, and the wrath he would bring down upon her when he learned of her marriage to Rangor. She slipped through the secret door to her chamber where Edie awaited. Together they flew down the other end of the passageway and out to the courtyard, and then beyond to the meadow where Gareth and her men awaited.

"The Normans?" she asked him.

"They sleep like babes." He smiled grimly and looked past her to Edith. "The entire manor sleeps. Edith's herbs are strong."

Tarian nodded. "Then let us fly."

Wulfson woke to pounding on his door. "Wulfson!" Rorick called. "Warner has returned!"

Wulfson sprang up in the bed and immediately realized that Tarian was gone. He looked to the secret passage and saw the door ajar. Her early departure from their bed could not override his elation that his friend lived. He hurried to dress, and when he passed Tarian's door he scowled, seeing Gareth's empty pallet. Mayhap she was already up and about? When he came down the stairs he found his men groggy but in good spirits. And Warner no worse for the wear.

They clasped hands and gave each other hearty slaps on the back. And before Wulfson could ask, Warner gave him the dour news. "I have been held captive these last weeks. I escaped just three days ago."

Fury mingled with dread in his gut. "Who?" he asked, already knowing the answer.

"They wore Dunloc's colors. Lady Tarian's men."

Rage simmered in his belly. "Give me William's message."

Warner shook his head. "They destroyed the document, Wulfson, but William anticipated that. He told me his order."

The men gathered around. "What does he say?"

"He cautioned you to keep yourself clear of the lady's black magic, and to see the deed done with most haste. He will not forgive her her murder of Malcor."

Wulfson sank to the bench beside him. "I sent another missive after you when more details were brought to light. I will await his word."

Warner sat beside his friend. "He was most adamant, Wulfson. He cared not for her plight. He said he would gladly deal with the Welsh if they were so bold as to cross the border."

The lookout shouted that riders approached. The men hastened to see a score of knights, and flying above them the red and gold lion standard of William. Dread filled

Wulfson. He could not blame the lady for sidetracking a single man. But she could not stop William's knights.

The messenger dismounted and walked directly to Wulfson. "Sir Wulfson, a missive from the king."

Wulfson reached out for it, and he felt as if he would empty his spleen in the dirt. He broke the seal and read Tarian's death sentence. He screamed out in rage. "*Nay!* This cannot be!" He was not ready to give her up! A deadly silence ensconced the air, and he looked up at his men and read their own pain in their eyes. But they would never know the pain he felt. He turned and stumbled back into the hall, ignoring the commotion behind him.

He kicked a wooden bench, the first thing in his path. He shoved the trestle table next to it out of his way. He hurled several chairs and drew his swords, and in a wild, feral display he reduced several more chairs to splitters.

"Wulfson!" Thorin shouted, coming toward him. Wildly, Wulfson turned on his man. "Nay! Do not come near me!"

He strode to the tapestry adorning the walls and ripped it down. His rage was so complete he could see naught but red. He strode back to where the parchment lay on the floor. He read it again, sure he had misread it the first time. When the same words leapt at him, he screamed his rage again, then sank to the nearest upright bench. He dropped his swords, then the parchment, to the floor, and hung his head in his hands.

"Sir Wulfson!" Rolf gasped, bursting into the hall. "The lady flees to Wales where she has an army awaiting her!"

Wulfson's head snapped back and his eyes narrowed. "What say you?"

The lad gasped for breath, and pressed his hand to a

large knot on his head. "I overheard her captain Gareth last night. She meets with Rangor: they are to wed."

"Nay!" Wulfson shouted. "She will not!"

Rolf nodded, his eyes full of sorrow for his master. "Methinks they return with Welsh reinforcements."

Thorin stepped forward. "It makes sense, the alliance, Wulf. The Welsh are powerful and see the benefit of her bloodline. Wedding with Rangor, she keeps what is hers, gains what is his, and, with the Welsh backing, William will be hard pressed to be rid of her."

Anger swiftly replaced his anguish, seething hot and deadly in his gut. Thorin shook his head. "She plays the game better than we. She fooled us all."

Wulfson stood and snarled at his men, "Could you blame her? Warner carried her death warrant!"

For a long moment, Wulfson stood. He could not see, his vision blank. He could not hear or smell; he could not feel anything but twisted fury at the situation and at Tarian. Had she lied to him all this time? Her oath last eve meant nothing, and in his heart of hearts he knew that if she truly loved him as she claimed she would not take up sword against him. He would find out for himself!

Finally, when he was able to see through his angry haze, he said coldly, "Mount up. We ride west to Wales." He swept past his men and hurried to his chamber, where he methodically donned his battle gear.

Tarian refused to ride beside Rangor. She also refused to see the priest until they were safely in Powys. "He watches you like a dog over a bone," Gareth grumbled as they broke upon a ridge overlooking the river they had just crossed. 'Twas only another half day's ride to the border. From behind her, Tarian watched a column of Welsh make their way up to them. Rhiwallon had come through with men. She looked across Rangor's garrison, which included Ednoth. Rangor had no doubt promised him the moon should he side with him against the Normans. Then there were Rhiwallon's men, and her own. Combined, more than one hundred and fifty strong. Most of them foot soldiers. But. She glanced over to her own garrison. Some fifty strong and all ahorse. Seasoned warriors, all of them. But in her gut she knew they were no match for the Normans. Still, combined with Rangor's men and those of the Welsh king, they had a chance should they not make it to the border.

"He can drool all he wants, Gareth. But he will not have me until we are safely behind the Welsh curtain."

She looked east, where Draceadon was but a distant memory, then up to the high rise of the sun and beyond. The hair on the back of her neck rose. There, not too far off, a low dust cloud rose on the horizon. Her heart stuttered in her chest. "Wulfson," she whispered.

Gareth turned in his saddle, and she watched the color drain from his face. "He comes for you."

She swallowed hard. "Aye, he comes to do me in." Reining Silversmith around, she rode hard up the hill.

The scene reminded her of that fateful day almost a year ago at Senlac Hill. The Normans would have to come up at them, thus giving Tarian and her army the advantage. But even more to their advantage was the swift-moving river that separated them. Once the enemy made it through the water, they would then have only a narrow strait on which to regroup before the mound rose at a rolling slope. Despite their advantage, a dark foreboding overcame her. She did not want to die this day; and she could not, despite the bad blood between them, wish that Wulfson or any of his men, whom she had come to know and respect, should go down either. For the first time since she fled that morn, Tarian questioned her own motives. But as she sat upon her horse and watched the cloud of dust come closer, with terrifying speed, she knew there was no other way.

They would stand and fight here, and not be caught on the run.

She reined Silversmith and rode back to the men. "The Normans come!" Tarian called to Rangor and Ednoth.

The two men—so much alike—smiled. "Let them!" Rangor called. He maneuvered his horse to face his men. "The Normans approach. We will stand here and fight and rid our land of them once and for all! Bring the archers forward."

Tarian sat upon the hill and watched in quiet awe what unfolded before her. Wulfson had at least thirty more knights than she had anticipated. She swallowed hard, her heart tightening as she watched him lead the cavalry to the edge of the water. He urged his mount halfway across, and looked up. She nudged Silversmith down the hill, despite Rangor's shouts for her to stop. She ignored him.

She stopped just at the edge of the water. She raised her sword and called to Wulfson, "Return to Normandy!"

He laughed, the sound caustic and deadly, and urged his mount forward. " 'Tis impossible. I am of *les morts*."

She nudged Silversmith forward to the edge of the water. She could see Wulfson clearly. Tarian shook her head at the dense man. How could she make him understand Rangor would kill him this day? And there was nothing left for her to bargain for his life with. "I have done everything to protect you!" she cried out to him.

"I do not need your protection!"

"Nor do I need yours! Leave me. Tell your king I will not go to Normandy. I will not marry a Norman, I will not raise up an army against him! But I will protect my child at all costs! Now go!"

"Nay, Tarian. I asked you to trust me. You gave me your oath that you did. Is this how you honor it?"

Pain like a band of steel clamped around her chest. "You expect me to stand by whilst you separate my head from my shoulders?"

"Tarian—"

"Nay! Do not lie to me! Your man Warner brought word and"—she pointed with her sword to the new contingent of William's knights behind him—"and by this show of force I know the answer from the second messenger is the same! Do not play me false!" She shook her head, and hot tears blurred her vision. "William wants me dead, Wulfson, and he is the vilest of men to ask you to do the deed." She straightened in her saddle and set her mind to the matter. "And I love you too much to let you do it, for you would not be able to live with yourself." She reined Silversmith back, but quietly said, "Let me fall today by any other sword than yours."

"Tarian!" Wulfson shouted.

But she continued to back away. As she did, Rangor drew up beside her. He glared menacingly at Wulfson. "She gave her freedom to save you," he laughed, and turned to Tarian, "Now he will see you slain for the effort!" He sneered and looked back to Wulfson and spat. "Was he worth it?"

Tarian gasped, and turned to see Wulfson's eyes narrow behind his helm. " 'Tis a lie! He taunts you! Return to Normandy!" she cried, then spurred Silversmith past Rangor, cringing at his last taunt to Wulfson.

"Tonight will find her in my bed as my wife, Norman," Rangor crowed. "We will celebrate your death!"

Tarian cast a glance over her shoulder to see Wulfson unmoving in the water. He raised his eyes to her for the truth. She could not turn back. There was no future for them. As she crested the hill, a hailstorm of arrows rained down. She spurred Silversmith faster. Rangor raced up behind her.

"Prepare to engage!" she called. The men came forward, and she turned to watch as Wulfson charged through the river, his men behind him, his battle cry reverberating against the hill.

The archers would soften the knights before the horses and foot soldiers engaged. But Tarian watched in awed fascination as the knights all formed the tight quadrant, their shields raised in such a fashion that the arrows were hard-pressed to slip through.

"Foot soldiers!" Tarian yelled, and the Welsh flew down the hill, followed by Ednoth's men. As they came closer in the water, the archers had a more difficult angle from which to hit true. The clash below was brutal, and she watched in horror and awe as Wulfson and his men hacked their way through the water.

Rangor took several of his men and moved down along the bank before entering the water to come around on the Norman's flanks. But the Normans were prepared.

Tarian could not tear her eyes from Wulfson. Ednoth and several other men on horseback swarmed him. She caught her breath when a blade slammed across his back. He turned with his double swords in hand and hacked off the arm of his closest assailant. But three more replaced him. Her heart pounded high in her throat. She raised her hand and brought it down: the signal for her men to engage. With Gareth by her side, they plunged down the hill and into the fray, her eyes never leaving Wulfson, who literally battled for his life. Ednoth and his men were all over him, and though Wulfson made mincemeat of many, he was outnumbered, and his men were equally engaged.

As her horse thundered down the hill, a hard rush of emotions tangled dangerously in Tarian's heart. Her life for Wulfson's. He had asked her to trust him and she had failed him!

"Gareth!" she called to her captain. "Pull the men back! All of them!"

And in that instant she gave herself over to William. Her oath to Rangor meant nothing. For he would see Wulfson dead this day. She would, in exchange for Wulfson's life, live out her days in Normandy if William would allow her to, for nothing meant more to her than Wulfson's life. Not even the child she carried.

As she came charging down the last of the hill and into the water, she saw Wulfson look up. Their gazes caught and held. Her eyes widened as Ednoth's blade came down on his back. "Noooooooo!" she screamed. "Noooo!"

Wulfson took the brunt of the blow, and as she spurred Silversmith toward him, Rangor turned, and she realized he knew he had lost her. As she plunged into the water downstream from Wulfson, Rangor turned his horse and charged toward her. "You gave your oath, Tarian!" he shrieked. "His life for your hand!"

Tarian set her jaw and raised her sword. She would see to Rangor once and for all. Abruptly she reined Silversmith around, and he came full turn. Using her legs and one of the maneuvers Wulfson had taught her, she gave the horse a sharp command and drew up on the reins. The gray reared and came down on Rangor's horse.

She twisted in her saddle and raised her sword to plunge it deep into Rangor's chest, but his horse broke free. Rangor snarled, and with both hands he took up his sword. As his horse turned he used the velocity to bring his sword around.

"Wulfson!" she cried, and watched in horror as Rangor, both hands grasping the hilt of his sword, struck her in the belly, unseating her. Pain shot throughout her entire body. She heard Wulfson's enraged snarl, and then cool water encompassed her.

Twenty-three

Rage and anguish tore through him like a thousand swords to his gut. Wulfson roared in pain, fury, and desperation. He died the instant Rangor's blade struck Tarian. But when the water swallowed her up, claiming her for all time, he knew he would rather die than live a day without her. He spurred the black forward through the throng of men trying desperately to take his life. Seeing the bloodlust in his eyes, Rangor turned tail and fled. But Wulfson had eyes only for Tarian.

Flinging his helm and swords from him, he leapt from his horse, diving into the chest-high river where she had fallen. Desperately he felt for her in the murky water. Each time he surfaced without her, another piece of his heart broke off. He dove again, his eyes searching desperately for her. His chest swelled with no air, but he would not give up until he found her.

He surfaced, gasping great gulps of air, then dove again. And again, and again.

Just as he had no more breath, he touched something

hard. His finger grasped it and he pulled it up with him. He cried out, triumphant. Her arm. He pulled her limp form from the water into his arms. Choking on the water, he coughed and spewed the liquid from his lungs. His legs felt like stones. He pulled her up to him, his arm clasped around her waist keeping her face free of the churning water. She hung limp in his arms, her dark hair plastered across her face. He pushed it away, wanting desperately to see her beautiful blue eyes sparkling in mischief at him. Instead, her eyes were closed, her skin white as paste, and her lips blue. He shook her limp body. "Tarian! Open your eyes!" he shouted.

When she did not respond, he looked to the bank where most of his men had gathered, and trudged through the deep water, her cold limp body hanging in his arms. His chest felt as if it were going to rip open from the excruciating pressure of his emotions. He pressed his lips to her cold ones and breathed his breath into her. He shook her again when she did not respond. He pushed harder for the bank, continuing to breathe his own life breath into her.

He stumbled, and nearly fell with her in his arms into the cold swirling current. With strength born of desperation, he kept his balance, and when he looked down he nearly dropped her. Blood swirled around her hips. "Nay!" he screamed. He threw his head back and like a wild wounded animal he howled his sorrow to the heavens. He felt hands grasp him and pull him toward the bank. He dropped to his knees with Tarian still in his arms and laid her down on the soft mud.

"Breathe!" he shouted at her. He shook her and pressed against her chest. Her lips turned darker blue before his eyes. He pulled he to him again and threw his head back and cried out, "God! Save her!" He was oblivious to all that happened around him.

He tore her mail from her small, cold body. Blood stained her chauses. He pressed a shaking hand to her belly, and knew that the child died with her. Like a wolf whose mate had succumbed to hunters, Wulfson screamed his pain and heartbreak. His hands furiously moved across her face and chest as great sobs racked his body. He pulled her face to his and pressed his lips to hers, again and again blowing his life into hers. Still she lay limp. He rolled her over on her side and pushed against her back. Slowly he realized shadows surrounded him. He looked up to find his men surrounding him, their faces drawn and haggard.

Rohan knelt down beside him and put his hand to his shoulder. "She is gone, Wulfson."

"Nay!" he roared and pushed on her back again and again. He pulled her limp form up into his arms and rocked her, pushing the wet hair from her face. "She but sleeps," he whispered, and pressed his lips again to her cold blue ones.

He moved his hand to her chest, desperate to feel the beat of her heart.

"Set her again on her side and thump her back!" Gareth commanded running up to him. He slid down into the mud beside Wulfson. "Rid her chest of the water so that she will breathe!"

Wulfson rolled her onto her side, and this time he pounded with his fists. When she did not respond, he pounded her back again. Her chest heaved in a sudden convulsion, then she coughed and gagged as water spewed from her. But she did not open her eyes. He pressed his ear to her chest. And there, he felt, barely a whisper of a heartbeat. Hope swelled.

He shucked his mail and scabbards, then hauled her up to him and stood with her still and limp in his arms. "My horse! Bring me my horse! And find her nurse. Bring her to Draceadon!"

With Tarian in his arms, he rode like a demon to hell for Draceadon. He refused to think of her not surviving. He would bargain with the devil if he would give her life. When he entered the hall with her in his arms, he strode directly up to his chamber, and there, lovingly, he placed her on his bed. His heart stopped when he saw the fresh blood between her thighs. His gut tightened as if a fist twisted it. Gently he pulled her wet muddy clothes from her body, and just as gently he cleaned her, but the blood did not stop. He wrung his hands, pacing the room, unable to help her.

When Gareth broke into the room, Wulfson turned snarling at him. "How could you allow her to battle?"

"She's a warrior! She was fighting for her life and that of her child! Would you have her do anything different?"

Wulfson swiped his hand across his face, wanting to lay violent hands on the captain. "She almost died! The child is gone!"

"Through no fault of yours! At every turn you let her know her life was but William's whim and you his henchman!"

Wulfson could not take the truth. "She lied to me!"

Gareth shook his head in disgust. "Aye, she did, but once again she had no one to defend her."

"She had you."

Gareth's head snapped back, and Wulfson saw the pain in the Viking's blue eyes. He felt the same pain. They had both failed her.

"I have failed her miserably," Gareth said slowly. "I indulged her every whim. She is most hard to resist once she has her mind set."

"Was her heart set on Rangor?" Wulfson sneered, thinking of the Saxon he would love to finish off.

Gareth snapped then. Wulfson saw it in his eyes and his face. He strode right up to Wulfson's face and snarled, "She sacrificed all for you, can you not see it? 'Twas Rangor who held the power over your life. To save it, she agreed to marriage. Today she forsook her life to come to your aid, and in doing so she nearly lost it." He looked at the small pale form in the bed. "She lost the babe, and may still lose her life." Gareth stepped to the bed and sat down on the edge, taking her limp hand into his. "There is too much blood," he choked.

As the words left Gareth's mouth, Edith burst into the chamber and flew to her lady's side. "Move aside and let me tend her!"

Gareth and Wulfson stood back and watched the nurse poke and prod Tarian. She turned grave eyes to them. "Her brain is asleep. But that is not my concern. The babe is lost, and I fear she will bleed to death."

Wulfson knelt down beside Tarian and pressed his hand to her heart. "Tell me what to do."

"Her womb is full of blood. Get me linens and straw to soak it up from the bed."

He hurried to the task and for long hours he watched Edie tend Tarian. Relief overcame him when he noticed the blood begin to lessen. But still he worried: for such a mite, she had lost so much.

Wulfson looked down at the small naked form in his bed. He knelt beside her and took her cold hand into his much bigger, much warmer one. If he could give her his own blood he would. "Will she live?" he asked the nurse.

Edith did not look up from where she sat close by. "If there is no more blood she will. Many women survive miscarriages."

"Will she be able to bear other children?"

Edith looked at him sharply. "Mayhap. Time will tell." She stood and kneaded Tarian's belly once more, and both watched for the linens to darken. When they did not, both Edith and Wulfson let out a long sigh. The nurse looked up at him. "Are you angry with her?"

Wulfson shook his head. "Nay. How could I be? She sacrificed everything for me."

"What of your king?"

Wulfson sighed heavily and stood. "Once he understands she has no desire to take up arms against him and that she does not bear a child of Royal Welsh blood, he will listen."

"He will keep her in Normandy."

Wulfson nodded. "There is no other way."

"I go where she goes."

Wulfson nodded, and thought the same thing.

Twenty-four

The pain in her womb was gone. The pain in her chest subsided, but the pain in her heart, in her soul still gaped, raw and bloody. She knew the minute she awoke to see Wulfson sitting beside her that their child was lost. She had relived the blow to her belly over and over in her nightmares. She would kill Rangor for that.

For a long time she watched the Norman knight who had become her heart and soul, her sight and her breath. He looked haggard, as if he had aged a decade. She tried to move her hand to his, but she was too weak.

"Wulfson . . ." she croaked, and swallowed, her throat raw.

He was instantly beside her. Taking her hands, he pressed them to his lips, and she watched in stunned shock as tears filled his eyes. "*Chérie*, you gave me the scare of my life."

She smiled slowly, for it too took strength she did not have. "Wulfson—" She had so much to tell him. So much to ask forgiveness for.

He pressed his fingers to her lips. "Shhh, there is time to talk later. You need to eat."

"Thirsty."

He turned to pour her a goblet of watered wine, and helped her sit up to drink it. The liquid worked its warm way down her throat. She lay back in the bed, and it was her turn for tears. "Wulfson, I am so sorry. For everything."

He moved to the side of the bed and drew her up into his arms. "Nay, Tarian, you have nothing to be sorry for. The situation was impossible, and you did what you had to survive. I do not fault you that."

"Not even my oath to marry Rangor?" He smiled down at her, and she choked back a sob. "He was bent on your death, Wulfson, 'twas my last resort."

He kissed her forehead. "Thank you."

She moved his hand to her belly. "The child I carried was not Malcor's, Wulfson."

He was still then, and she watched emotions play across his face as her words sank in. "What are you saying?" he softly asked.

Hot tears welled up in her eyes. "I drugged you, and came to you in the night. I took from you what Malcor could not give me."

He shook his head. "I—I do not understand."

She inhaled a deep breath and slowly exhaled. He brushed the tears from her cheek and waited patiently for her to speak. "Malcor could not perform his husbandly duties. 'Twas because of it he went into a fit of rage and nearly killed me. You know what happened to him and why. But when you pulled me from the hole, and there was talk of the possibility of a child and that the child could save my life, I came to you." Fresh tears erupted, and she grasped his hands to her chest. "Wulfson, your child made me very happy. I mourn for his loss."

After long-drawn-out moments, when he finally turned his green eyes to her she saw sadness but no anger. "Rangor will pay with his life for forcing the child from you."

She set her jaw. "You will have to stand behind me. I get him first." She threw her arms around his neck and drew him to her. "Do you forgive me, Wulfson?"

He drew slightly from her and pressed his lips to her wet cheek. "There is nothing to forgive. I love you, Tarian, and come what may, I will stand by you."

His words were more potent then any balm, and finally peace settled over her and she closed her eyes. He loved her.

He pressed her back into the pillows. "Rest, *chérie*. I will call for your nurse. She has paced a hole in the hallway."

Tarian's recovery was slow and steady. Her strength came back with each day, and Wulfson watched for the day she smiled and blushed up at him, her impish dimples teasing him.

His spies told him that Rangor had gathered an army in Wales and was now on the move south. He wanted to wait until Tarian was stronger before they left for Normandy, but time was running out. He had yet to broach the subject with her, but after the evening meal he took his men aside and told them to be prepared to leave the next morn. He also informed Gareth, but asked him not to speak to Tarian on the matter. He would do so himself later that eve.

He had grown fond of the old Viking and gave credit to him for saving his beloved's life. For had Gareth not instructed him to pound on her back as he did, he doubted the water would have worked its way up.

He came upon her as she soaked in the tub. He grinned and motioned to her nurse to be gone from the room. His heart pounded in his chest and his blood quickened. He knew it was too soon for her, but that did not change how he felt.

"Good eve, milord," she said softly.

"Good eve, milady," he returned. He pulled up a stool and sat beside her. Taking up the sponge, he lathered it and said, " 'Twould appear you need assist with your bath."

She settled back into the tub and arched her back toward him. His cock filled at the sight of her full, rosy breasts bobbing in the soapy water. "*Chérie*, you play with fire."

"I have longed for you, Wulfson."

He bent down and kissed her but when her arms slipped around his neck and drew him more tightly to her, he pulled away. "Nay, Tarian. 'Tis too soon."

She sat back into the tub and pouted. He smiled. "I must speak with you on a very important matter."

"Normandy?"

He nodded. "I know of no other way. I—"

She held up her hand. "You do not need to explain, Wulfson. When I turned on Rangor, I knew that should I survive, the very most I could hope for was that your king would accept me as his hostage. I am prepared to live out the rest of my life in a Norman dungeon."

"Nay! You will not reside in a dungeon. 'Twill not be that way!"

He rose and began to pace the room. But he wondered whom he was trying to convince more, her or him. "Rangor has amassed an army, and he travels south toward us. We leave for Normandy at first light."

"I will be ready."

*   *   *

As the coast of Normandy broke the horizon, trepidation filled Tarian with the force of a summer storm. Strong arms wrapped around her and brought her up against a hard body. Warm lips pressed to her ear. "Draw on my love for you, Tarian, as your strength, and place your trust in my hands."

She smiled and warmed to his touch and his words. "I do trust you, Wulfson. I have from that night in the ruin. 'Tis your king I do not trust."

He turned her around to face him. His eyes searched her face. "Then why did you flee me?"

"I knew what word Warner carried, and I knew of the contingent of knights to come with the second messenger. I would not put you in the position of taking my life." She smiled and kissed him. "Besides, I have always looked after myself. 'Tis my nature to take matters into my own hands."

He grinned and kissed the tip of her nose. "Well, 'tis a habit you will have to break. I am here now."

Once they had landed, much to Wulfson's fury he learned that Rangor of Lerwick had arrived several days before them.

"The fool," he said to Thorin. "What does he think to achieve by walking into the lion's den?"

He kept the news from Tarian. The travel had taken its toll on her. She did not do well on the water and the roses had gone from her cheeks. He was given some hope when William did not meet them with an armed escort. Indeed, he sent his son Geoffrey to welcome them. The boy was a man now, and would one day inherit Normandy from his father.

When they entered the castle at Rouen, excitement stirred in Wulfson's belly. Here was familiar ground. Here William held court, and the most powerful men on the continent came to pay him homage. He was powerful and ruthless, but he was fair. And 'twas that fairness in the man he respected above all others that Wulfson counted on.

Tarian and Edith were shown to a private solar. William was wily, Tarian thought. He did not want any of the women to make a friendship with her. Out of sight and out of mind. She found the bed comfortable, and the food edible. Almost immediately she called for a bath and as she languished in the hot sudsy water, she forced the tension from her body. Closing her eyes, she let Edie wash her hair with aromatic violet-scented soap. And when she was dried and sitting before a large table with an oval-shaped mirror, she watched Edie methodically brush her long dark hair to dry. She closed her eyes and wished with all her heart that Wulfson would appear and tell her there was no need to see William, but when there was a knock on the chamber door she knew 'twas but wishful thinking.

Edie took the message: the king requested an audience with her in two candle notches. And so Tarian would do as she had done all her life: rely on herself to see the next day, and to achieve that she would painstakingly prepare. It was her life and a life with Wulfson she fought for, and the Conqueror would find her a most worthy opponent.

She smiled, despite the nervous tremors in her belly. "Come, Edie, we have work to do!"

A little more than one candle notch later, she stood before the mirror, resplendent in her finery. A formfitting, deep-sapphire velvet-and-silk kirtle with wide, long sleeves embroidered with rich crimson, gold, and silver threads set off her dark coloring and blue eyes. A golden circlet of a dragon head adorned her head, her hair hung free and wavy down to her waist. She smiled as she slid her broadsword into her ceremonial scabbard of gem-encrusted gold, hammered to a burnished glow and hanging from a gold and leather embroidered girdle. She wore a simple gold necklace with the dragon medallion of Draceadon hanging heavy between her breasts. Thick gold and silver bracelets adorned her arms, and the final touch was her soft leather and silk golden shoes.

She looked the warrior princess she felt herself to be. She nodded to Edie, who stood back in silent awe. Tears filled the old woman's eyes. Tarian felt a rush of emotion for her, and shook her head, blinking back her own tears. "Do not, Edie. I cannot take more pressure."

The nurse bobbed her head and smiled, smoothing a curl from her cheek. "You are worthy of a king, Tarian. William would be a fool to set you aside."

Tarian smiled. "'Tis not a king I fancy, Edie, but a dark knight with a surly disposition."

The old woman smiled knowingly.

It was not much time later when the page arrived. Tarian cast a glance to the candle. 'Twas still shy of two notches. So, William was impatient to see her, was he? She smiled. No more than she was to meet him.

Edie opened the door to find an attendant standing to attention. "Lady Tarian, His Highness King William requires your presence in the great hall." He bowed, and Tarian looked to Edie. The maid grasped her hand and squeezed it.

"Let us go."

The servant shook his head. "Only Lady Tarian."

Tarian shook her head and stepped toward the young man. "My nurse comes with me or I do not go."

Color blanched from his face. Hastily he bobbed his head and stood back. Both women followed.

When the door to the great hall opened, Tarian could not help the nervous skitter in her belly. She nodded to Edie, and took a deep breath; then she swept into the richly appointed hall as if she were Queen. She suppressed a smile as a collective gasp went up as she made her entrance.

She looked directly ahead to William, who sat upon a high dais at the head of the great room, his regal robes signifying who he was to all. To his left was a woman so tiny Tarian thought it must be a child. But on closer inspection she knew it to be his duchess. To William's right were his knights. Wulfson, whose eyes she could see burned bright for her, Thorin, Rohan, Rorick, Warner, Stefan, Rhys, and Ioan. The only one missing was Manhku. Farther down from the knights stood Gareth. She nodded to the Blood Swords, then to her captain, as she continued to make her way forward. Tarian stiffened as her gaze swept to the left. 'Twas Rangor! And Alewith? Why did *he* stand with Rangor?

Tarian stopped at the end of the long aisle to the steps that led to William and peered daringly up at him.

Twenty-five

Wulfson's heart beat like a smith's hammer against his chest. He could not tear his eyes from Tarian. She looked more regal than any woman, queen or otherwise, that ever he had set eyes on. Her color was high, her back straight and confident, her clothes fit for an empress, and her sword hung proudly from her slender waist. Her pride and confidence made his chest tighten with love for her. He wanted to break a smile and lay claim to her in front of every person in the room! How could William destroy such a woman?

He watched her stare confidently up at William, and just when he thought she would show insolence by not sinking to her knees in a deep curtsy, she did.

But her eyes never wavered from the king's. Wulfson held his breath; men had died for the same thing. Trepidation played with his pride. If she were not careful—

William stood and stared down at her. He took a step toward her. "So you are the one who has been giving me all this trouble."

Tarian rose, and answered his challenge clearly. "Aye, I am Tarian Godwinson, daughter of Sweyn, granddaughter of Godwine. Niece to the late King Harold the Second, and widow of Earl Malcor." She smiled, and added, "And the trouble you accuse me of has come through no fault of my own, sire."

Wulfson held his breath and looked to William, who cocked a brow at her and took another step closer. Tarian stood proud and calm, but he could see the short, rapid rise and fall of her breasts.

"Do you have an army, Lady Tarian?" William asked, as if an accusation.

Tarian nodded her head. "I do, sire."

"What are your plans for it?"

"My men are at your disposal, if you but ask."

"Did you slay your husband in cold blood?"

Tarian smiled. "Aye, I slew him, but in cold blood? 'Twould depend on your definition."

"I would define it as a slaying without cause to gain something which is not yours to take."

Tarian's smile widened. She inclined her head toward William. "Then, sire, I would most defiantly have to answer nay to your question."

William stood with his hands behind his back and stared at her. "Then what was the cause of Earl Malcor's death?"

"He became most frustrated when he could not rise to his husbandly duties. He took his frustration out first by beating me. But after he tired of that, he took my own sword and pressed it to my throat. I but returned the favor by taking his dagger from his belt, and slit his throat."

Another collective gasp went up in the room, most notably, Wulfson saw, from the duchess. 'Twas not a good sign.

William nodded. "I find your candor refreshing, Lady Tarian." He cocked his head and asked, "Did you sign a contract to wed Rangor of Lerwick and then break it?"

Tarian looked to Rangor, and Wulfson could feel her hate for the man across the room. She turned back to her king and nodded. "Aye, I signed a document. But 'twas the only way I could save your man Wulfson's life—by promising marriage to that rat!"

"So, are you claiming you were coerced?"

Tarian threw Rangor another glare and turned back to William. "What would you call it, sire, when someone kidnaps your beloved, tortures him, then before your eyes tortures him further, until you are forced to agree to a most disagreeable union?" William glowered Rangor's way, and Tarian was pleased to see the lord pale a few shades. " 'Twas a means to save your man. I would do it again."

William stood for a long, contemplative moment, then turned to Rangor. "It appears we have more to discuss, Lord Rangor. I do not take kindly the torture of my men. Do not leave the hall until we have spoken." William narrowed his eyes and added, "In private, of course."

Rangor swallowed hard, but gave his king a short bow.

William turned back to Tarian, and drew his broadsword from his sheath. Wulfson made to move toward her, but Rohan and Thorin held him back. He watched her sink to her knees. She folded her hands and bowed her head, prepared to meet her fate. Wulfson could not bear it. He tore free from his men, and as he made to stop his liege,

he watched in amazement as William placed the flat side
of his sword on Tarian's right shoulder, then on her left.
"Tarian Godwinson, do you pledge your fealty to me, King
William of England and Duke of Normandy, forfeiting all
others and serving me in any capacity I may ask?"

Wulfson's knees nearly gave when Tarian looked up to
his king. From where she knelt, he could see the glitter of
tears in her eyes. "I do," she whispered hoarsely.

William raised his sword, "Then I dub thee, Lady Tarian
of Dunloc, a knight of the realm. Arise and pay homage to
your king!"

The room was deathly quiet, and slowly Tarian stood.
She cast a gaze to Wulfson, and he smiled so broadly he
thought his face would split in two. She stepped to William, took his hand, and kissed his signet ring. "I, Tarian
Godwinson of Dunloc, pledge my loyalty to you, William,
my only sovereign."

He nodded, and then clasped her hand. "Now, Lady Tarian, I will make my first request of you."

She cocked her head and nodded. "I am at your command, sire."

"I wish you to *parle* with your Welsh in-laws, who I fear
are bent on breaching my borders, and entreat them to stay
west of it. I do not want to clash with your kin, but if
pushed I will strike."

Tarian smiled and curtsyed. "Aye, my liege, I can oblige,
but I have a request of you in return."

Wulfson rolled his eyes. She knew not what she did!

William's eyes narrowed. " 'Tis not protocol to ask your
king for a favor when given a royal order."

"I understand, but bear with me, sire, I am new to this
protocol."

William stood rigid, and Wulfson knew he would put her in her place. But he did not. "What do you wish in return for negotiating with the Welsh?"

"I want your man, Sir Wulfson of Trevelyn, as my husband."

Wulfson nearly fainted. But William threw his head back and laughed so loudly the rafters shook. "Lady Tarian, you are a bold wench!" He looked to Wulfson, who had the grace to blush. His men ribbed him, but he stood still, his gaze locked with Tarian's. "Are you up to the task? Those Blood Swords are not wont to stay put for long."

Tarian smiled, and gazed at Wulfson. "Aye, sire, I am up to the task, for no other man will do."

As if on a cloud, Wulfson floated down the steps to his lady, and clasped her in his arms, twirling her around amidst her happy cries and his men's cheers.

William called for silence, and turned smiling to the couple. "I have but one request before I hand my man over to you, Lady Tarian, and this is but a simple request, from a man who admires and respects your husband-to-be, not a royal order."

Arm in arm, Tarian and Wulfson turned to their king. "Sire?" Wulfson asked.

"I wish to be godfather to your firstborn."

Tarian smiled. "We are most honored."

The hall erupted with more cheers and congratulations. William called for the tables to be set and a feast to celebrate the nuptials.

Tarian was ecstatic, and Wulfson could not stop beaming. William stood to the side, as if he were a proud new father. After Tarian had been swung up into the arms of each of the Blood Swords in turn, and twirled around until she could not see straight, she landed in Gareth's arms. He beamed down at her and she saw tears in his eyes.

She smiled up to him and hugged him close. "Gareth, be happy for me," she whispered against his chest. He pulled back and looked at her, his lips trembling in a wide smile.

"Tarian, you are more precious than a daughter to me. I am most happy for you."

She smiled back, her heart so full she could barely contain her love. "Give me away."

His blue eyes blurred with tears. "Aye, 'twould be my honor."

Wulfson swept her from his arms, and as he threw her across his shoulders as if to carry her off to someplace private, William called out to him. "There will be none of that, Trevelyn! There are enough of us bastards running around. Show some respect and wait until your wedding night."

"Then I will marry her here and now!"

The room erupted in laughter, but Tarian pulled at his sleeve. "Nay, Wulfson, I would be married in England. At Draceadon."

He pulled her off his shoulders, and she slid down the front of him, grinning when she felt his hardness against her belly. "You will have to wait, milord. For there will be no play before I am your lawful wife."

His eyes searched her face, and he asked, "Why Draceadon? We both suffered so much misery there."

Tears seemed to come to her easy that day, and once again they burned her eyes. "Aye, but it was also a place where we made a child and fell in love. I would like to build a strong castle there and raise our children."

He smoothed the tears from her cheeks, and took her

face between his hands and kissed her. When he drew away, she saw that his eyes had misted as well. "You are a most amazing woman, Tarian Godwinson."

"And thou art a most amazing man, Wulfson Trevelyn," she returned, smiling up at him.

Wulfson's heart swelled more, and he wondered how he had managed to live and breathe these six-and-twenty years past without her. The urge to keep her close and protect her from the world, so that he would never lose her, nearly toppled him. Any thought of leaving her sent his stomach to somersaults. And leave her he would have to. As a knight of William it would be years before England was settled. He, as had Rohan, would leave his family behind to serve and protect the realm. A calmness settled within him then. 'Twould make him all the more diligent in his dealings with the enemy to come home to her. For she would be like that bright burning star Draco in the sky, the constant beacon home. And home would be wherever this incredible woman was.

He pulled her back into the circle of his arms and guided her from the hall to a private alcove of which he knew. His blood ran hot and thick in his veins and when he pressed his lips to hers, he swelled against her. He groaned. He could not marry her fast enough!

"You are as bad as a rutting stag, milord," Tarian whispered against his lips.

"Aye, I am worse when you are near."

Tarian laughed and threw her arms around his neck. His heart thumped with the force of a hammer against his chest. He smiled down into her laughing ocean-blue eyes. As he bent to kiss her again, he saw them widen in surprise, then alarm. She pushed off him and drew her sword.

Wulfson turned on his heel, thrusting Tarian behind him, drawing his own sword.

"For Malcor!" Rangor screamed, lunging toward him, his sword poised at Wulfson's gut.

In unison, Tarian thrust her sword past Wulfson as he thrust his own. Both blades, that of Norman and Saxon, combined to tear into Rangor's gut, leaving him hanging like a skewered pig.

Wide-eyed, Rangor looked up from the impaling blades, first to Wulfson, then to Tarian. Red, frothy bubbles oozed from his mouth. "I will see you in hell, witch, and there you will scream for eternity," he hoarsely said before his body went limp.

Wulfson took Tarian's sword and, with both hilts in hand, he kicked Rangor's body from the blades. Several servants and bystanders had stopped at the commotion. Gareth, Alewith, and Ioan hurried to them. All stopped to watch the circle of Rangor's blood spread across the stone floor.

Alewith looked to Wulfson, then Tarian, who calmly watched her guardian, still curious as to his presence there.

"I will see him returned to Lerwick and buried," Alewith quietly said, then turned on his heels and walked away.

Tarian stood and stared down at the dead man, and try as she might, she could not shed a tear for Rangor. His twisted love for her, then his demonic need for revenge, had nearly killed the man she loved, not once but twice. He had taken the most precious life of her child from her. That, she would never forgive. Aye, she might see him in hell yet, but 'twould be he, along with Malcor, not she, who would burn for eternity.

The feel of Wulfson's big, warm hand as he took hers settled her more than any soothing balm Edie could concoct. He pulled her out of the door to a small, open courtyard. The sun was high, the skies blue, and the soft fragrant scent of violet wafted through the air. He gathered her into his arms and said softly, "You hold my heart and soul in your hands. Be gentle with me, Tarian, for I could not bear to lose you again."

Emotion clogged her chest, and she could only nod before she could speak. She raised her lips to his, and said against them, "Have no fear, sir knight. England's most fearsome knight is here to protect you."

Epilogue

August 1067
Draceadon

The sound of tankards pounding the trestle tops, combined with the joyous voices and the succulent scents of a great feast, clogged the air in the great hall.

"To Lady Tarian and Lord Wulfson!" Rorick shouted above the din to the gathered throng of Saxon and Norman alike. He raised his cup high and scores followed. "May they have lusty sons and beautiful daughters, and may my brother Wulfson always return from battle with *all* his swords intact!"

The double meaning was not lost on the merrymakers. Tarian's smile was so wide it pained her cheeks. She laughed when her husband hoisted her up over his shoulder and twirled with her in the air. Catching her breath, she peered out at the happy crowd from her high perch and bawdily said, "To be sure, so long as the sword between his legs survives, we will remain a happy couple!"

The Blood Swords laughed heartily, as did Tarian, and she was most happy to see many of the sullen villeins who had ventured forth from Dunloc smiling and, for the most part, content. Since their arrival home and immediate nuptials Tarian had sensed a calm resignation to her as lady and Wulfson as lord here. For William had insisted the charters be signed and affixed with the royal seal, giving legal rights of the earldom to his trusted man and his wife.

But despite the happy occasion for this day, there were dark undercurrents blowing in from the West. Alewith had disappeared, and she knew in her gut he plotted with the Welsh. And that fact saddened her. Having spent some time with William in Rouen, Tarian knew him to be a most determined man. He would not give over a hide of the land he had conquered and held in a choke hold without a fight. And fight he was prepared to do.

Aye, there would be bloodshed on both sides, but in her gut Tarian knew William was here to stay.

"Give her over to me, Wulfson," Lady Isabel, Rohan's lady, softly commanded of Tarian's husband.

Tarian grinned and shook her head, still slung over her husband's shoulders. He would not give her up so easily. His patience was at its end. He had taken great pains these last weeks not to break his oath to her and his king to keep her chaste until they were wed. He would take her there on the trestle if it were not such an impropriety.

Wulfson scowled but gently brought Tarian down to stand beside him. He bowed shortly to Lady Isabel but said, "I give you precious few minutes before I claim my wife, milady. Make all haste with whatever it is you women do, or you will be witness to what I have dreamed of doing every waking moment these last weeks."

Isabel blushed but she stood up to him. In her own way, the beautiful lady was as much a warrior as Tarian. And on that front alone they had become instant friends. "Nothing you could do, milord, would shock me!" Isabel took Tarian's hand, and as she led her away Tarian looked for Brighid, whom Alewith had sent to her only days before. There was no missive, just her sister, her maid, and a handful of men. Her gaze caught the girl across the hall, hanging spellbound upon Sir Rhys's every word and gesture. Tarian scowled and Isabel followed her gaze. "Leave them be, Tarian. I have watched them these last few days; Rhys is an honorable young man. He will not breach your sister."

Tarian was not so sure. The girl had become too bold. Her infatuation with the handsome knight had grown since they had least seen each other. And it appeared the young knight was as infatuated with the maid. "'Tis not Brighid who should be worried!" Tarian laughed, but did not in truth feel so light of heart. Rhys would break Brighid's tender heart, for there was much trouble brewing, and Alewith would not sanction a union between the two. Why then had he sent her here? For protection, mayhap? But from who?

A commotion stalled the ladies' ascent to the lord's chamber. Tarian and Isabel turned to see a royal messenger elbow his way through the throng.

"Lord Wulfson!" he called. "An urgent missive from the king!"

And just as suddenly, the merriment halted. Wulfson inclined his head to the Blood Swords and to Tarian and Isabel, and as one large group they moved to a more private place in the crowded hall.

"I have dour news," the messenger began. "Our spies tell us that Earl Edric, along with several Mercer lords, has formed an alliance with Rhiwallon and Bleddyn."

Tarian gasped, unable to believe it. Strategic negotiations were in motion. "But I only just sent a message to both kings for a meeting and they agreed with great haste!" Tarian cried, unable to believe they would renege on their word. 'Twas not only an insult to her, the wife of a powerful earl, but to William, as well.

The messenger slowly shook his head. "The alliance has been forged. 'Twill bode ill for England and Normandy."

Wulfson nodded. "Edric has been a thorn in William fitz Osborn's side for months; he has his eyes set on Hereford." He looked to his Blood Swords, who Tarian could see were champing to stand and deliver. Her own blood had warmed at the thought of battle, but trepidation diluted it. She could not bear to lose Wulfson. Her gaze caressed his tall, handsome form and her chest tightened. Nay, she would stand beside him and fight if only to make sure he came home safe.

"I will muster my men to arms," Wulfson said. He looked pointedly at his wife. "Call your men to arms, milady; our combined strengths will soon be tested." He stepped to her and slid an arm around her waist and drew her to him. "And I expect with Dunloc allied with Normandy, we will seize the day!" His lips crushed down on hers, taking the breath from her chest; then he hoisted her up into his arms. As he swept her up the stairway, he called to the throng over his shoulder, "Do not disturb me this night, any of you! For you will pay with your life!"

When Wulfson tossed her onto his bed, in what was now the new lord's chamber, his gaze did not leave her. In a frenzy, he divested himself of his clothing and watched under the soft glow of candlelight the color rise in his wife's cheeks. It occurred to him that she might be shy, with so much time since the last time they'd met as one.

Disappointment flooded him. "If you are not comfortable, Tarian—"

She rose from the bed like a silvery shadow and floated toward him. His body thrummed and his cock rose so swiftly it hurt. "I will not be comfortable, milord, until you fill me to capacity."

She pressed her softness against his hardness and on her tiptoes she reached up and snaked her arms around his neck, bringing his lips down to hers. "Make love to me now, Wulfson. Make love to me all night long and into the morning. I have waited all my life for you."

He gathered her up into his arms and gently he laid her upon the big bed. His heart burned so full and so hot with emotion that he did not trust his voice. When he spoke, his words were low and throaty. "Tarian Godwinson, you are the very air that I breathe. Promise me you will never cast me aside."

She smiled and unhooked her girdle and cast it away, then untied and removed her deep-sapphire-and-white silk kirtle trimmed with ermine. When she removed the soft linen undertunic and her creamy, smooth skin and rose-tipped nipples popped into view, Wulfson could not contain his passion for her. He pulled her up to him and sank his teeth into the tender flesh. Her lithe body arched into his and he could not wait. In one swift motion he entered her and nearly died of pleasure.

"Wulfson," she purred, "my heart is yours to possess, and with it I give you my oath: I am yours for eternity."

And together they became one; and on that night the beginning of a legacy forged in the bowels of a Saracen prison was unleashed.

Delve into a *passion* from the *past* with a *romance* from Pocket Books!

LIZ CARLYLE
Never Romance a Rake
Love is always a gamble....But never romance a rake!

JULIA LONDON
The Book of Scandal
Will royal gossip reignite her husband's passion for her?

KARIN TABKE
Master of Surrender
The Blood Sword Legacy
A mercenary knight is bound by a blood oath to reclaim his legacy—and the body of the one woman he desires.

KATHLEEN GIVENS
Rivals for the Crown
The fierce struggle for Scotland's throne leads two women to courageous new destinies...

**Available wherever books are sold
or at www.simonsayslove.com.**